SPEAK NO EVIL

Also by Philip Caveney

The Sins of Rachel Ellis
Tiger, Tiger
The Tarantula Stone

SPEAK NO EVIL

Philip Caveney

HEADLINE

First published in 1993
by HEADLINE BOOK PUBLISHING PLC

10 9 8 7 6 5 4 3 2 1

British Library Cataloguing in Publication Data

Caveney, Philip
Speak No Evil
I. Title
823.914 [F]

ISBN 0-7472-0728-3

Phototypeset by Intype, London
Printed and bound in Great Britain by
Clays Ltd, St Ives PLC

HEADLINE BOOK PUBLISHING PLC
Headline House
79 Great Titchfield Street
London W1P 7FN

This one is for Clare,
who heard it first

'An evil man is set only on disobedience but a messenger without mercy will be sent against him.'

Proverbs 17, 11.

'Then I saw an angel coming down from heaven with the key to the abyss and a great chain in his hands.

He seized the dragon, that serpent of old, The Devil or Satan, and chained him up for a thousand years; he threw him into the abyss, shutting and sealing it over him, so that he might seduce the nations no more till the thousand years were over. After that he must be let loose for a short while.'

Revelation 20, 2 and 3.

Diary Extract

4th October

There was a fly in my room this morning. The buzzing woke me a little after one a.m. and I spent some time looking for it, but it wasn't there. Still, it struck me as significant. You don't get many flies in October. They crawl away into little crevices in the wall and wait for warmer weather, but this one – it was buzzing around my head and it wanted to wake me. I'm sure of that.

Still not used to this climate. I have to wear so many clothes, even in bed at night, layer upon layer. Then I wake up sweating and have to throw them all off again. I couldn't get to sleep after the thing with the fly, so I switched on the radio and listened to him again. He was talking to one of his handmaidens – some pathetic quiz. You could tell from her voice how she worships him, and yet she has not the first idea about who he is. I don't think he knows, not yet. But he will, in time. I lay there listening to them and then the sexy feeling came over me and I had to masturbate. I seem to be doing it more and more these days, but I know it's not me that wants to do it. He's in me now and He makes me do these things. I listened to the woman's voice and my cock swelled, grew harder. She kept making mistakes and then she would giggle like a child, a totally false image of herself because I know she does the things that women do, opening her legs to the world and taking the pain into herself. Women are bad. I know that now.

I decided she could be first. I have her name and I know the area she lives, so it would be simple to find her. Tracking her down would be fun, like being a detective; but doing it to her, that's just a formality. He wants it to be her. He told me when I was coming. But He says I must tell everything. This must not be

1

covert in any way. She doesn't interest me, not in the least, but He keeps saying she will be fuel. I don't really understand this.

Afterwards I felt calmer and I switched off the light and tried to sleep. The fly came back after a little while, so I switched on the light again, but I couldn't see him. So I got up and started to move all the furniture away from the walls, because I knew he'd be there somewhere, hiding from me, waiting to disturb me again when the lights were out. I found him behind my bedside table, a big, fat bluebottle. The cold weather had made him slow and stupid, and it was easy enough to catch him.

I ate him, crunching him between my teeth, chewing very slowly. He tasted sweet and slightly nutty.

After that, I went back to bed. I slept better than I have in ages.

Chapter One

I was late leaving for work that night.

This was nothing unusual, as in fact I made a point of always being late leaving for work.

I'd been hosting the after-midnight phone-in slot for *Metrosound* for something like nine months, and I was already pretty bored with it. So I'd invented this little game with myself of not leaving the house until the last possible moment, knowing that I'd have to drive like a madman to make it to my post in time. It seems infantile, I know, but it gave me a buzz doing that, as it got my adrenalin flowing, and I suppose it pysched me up for talking to all the peculiar types who would be phoning me later on. When I was buzzing, I could deal with them better.

How did I end up as a DJ? It's a question I was often asked in those days, and one that I am only able to answer with hindsight. I suppose it goes back as far as *Scam* magazine. You may remember it? Maybe you loved it, bought it by the skip-load. Crass, nasty, absolutely the most self-opinionated rock magazine in all existence. And I was their lead writer. It had taken me some years to get where I was: years of scraping around for no-hope publications, of sending off pieces to *Melody Maker*, *Sounds*, *New Musical Express*, only to have them returned with ill-disguised contempt. And then, suddenly, there I was, in what was considered a major position at *Scam*, my every word hung upon by adolescent music fans who thought their lives were immeasurably enriched by my opinions. Oh, yes, I was bringing home the bacon for a while. Somewhere in the thick of all this I met a girl, fell in love, got married and fathered a son, all without really thinking about it. The bricks just fell into place and I suppose I should have been happy with my lot – but I wasn't. I soon got tired of the poseurs I was obliged to work with in London, and started to think longingly about moving back North to my roots. The decision was made for me when *Scam* went suddenly and spectacularly bankrupt. So I packed up my spare shirts, my toothbrush and my family, and came back to Manchester. For a long time I didn't do much of anything other than write reviews for an insignificant what's-on magazine which paid peanuts to its contributors. Our savings began to evaporate and I found myself faced with the awful prospect of having to get myself a serious job. To cap it all, my marriage, foundering on the reef of my own disatisfaction with life, began to break up.

Then one night, at a party, I met this DJ from the local radio station. By all accounts, Des Connolly was doing very well for himself, despite his limited intellect. He drove a BMW, holidayed twice a year in Marbella, and went out with a page-three girl. In those days, God help me, I was impressed by that kind of thing. I'd been drinking heavily at the party and consequently I started mouthing off about how lousy his station was; how I'd handle it if I was doing his job. All credit to him, he didn't punch me in the face, which he probably should have done. Instead, he suggested I make a demo tape of what I had in mind, and he'd personally see that it was handed on to the programme controller – which is basically what happened. The programme controller, at the time, invited me to contribute reviews and interviews on a freelance basis. After just a few weeks of that, I was offered a contract.

It was the beginning of a long and varied career in radio, and for the first time in my life I seemed to have discovered something I had a genuine flair for. But of course at the time I didn't visualise myself, five years later, stuck on the graveyard shift, talking to a bunch of misfits who had trouble constructing an audible sentence. No, I saw myself zipping about in a Porsche and fending off the advances of sycophantic teenage girls. Radio isn't like that, but I didn't know it then. I guess you could say I've learned the hard way.

So there I was, eleven-fifty Wednesday night, driving into Manchester at about seventy-five miles per hour. It was raining heavily and the windscreen wipers were having to work overtime to ensure some kind of visibility. I reached out a hand and hit the preset on the radio, which was always tuned to *Metrosound*. Sure enough, I got the suave, well-modulated sound of Ray Wood, signing off for the night. Smooth sod, Ray. To hear him talking, you'd visualise a slim, handsome, debonair man in a sharp suit. He actually resembled something the cat sicked up. But, then, the beauty of radio is that you can't see who's talking. The day they invent a televisual equivalent, a lot of lucrative careers are going to bite the dust.

'. . . well, boys and girls, that's about it for this evening,' announced Ray. 'We're going to play out with our Golden 60s classic, a little thing called 'Whiter Shade of Pale'. After the news headlines at midnight, Tom Prince will be here to welcome you aboard his Nightboat programme, and he'll keep you talking and dancing until four a.m. so don't touch that dial! For now, this is Ray Wood wishing you goodnight and God bless.'

Boys and girls indeed! Ray was a kind of throwback to earlier, more gracious times, when the DJ was a kind of ever-cheerful Butlin's redcoat on amphetamines. But he'd survived over ten years at the station, so he must have been doing something right. I was the radical, ground-breaking innovator at *Metrosound* and I was also the one whose career was slipping inexorably down the lavatory.

As usual, Ray was right on time; there were exactly three minutes of airplay left before the following five-minute news bulletin. Which left me exactly eight minutes to get to work. I changed down to second and eased the Renault around a right-hand bend and along a side-street, saving myself valuable seconds.

With four minutes left, I cruised into the town square. To my right, I could see the large, squat plaza that housed *Metrosound*. From a series of plateglass windows up on the first floor, the faces of several DJs grinned down at me, twenty times larger than life and twice as ugly. My own face featured amongst them, and I found myself staring disbelievingly up at it as I went by. I saw a thin, dour-looking man in his late twenties, with cold blue eyes. This version of me sported an unruly mop of fair hair, though it had since been trimmed to a more fashionable length. There was, I thought, a vacant look about the eyes, as though the camera had somehow sensed my own discontentment with life. It was unmistakably me and yet, for all that, it was not a good likeness. There was something forced and unconvincing about the photographic smile I'd been persuaded to adopt for the purposes of publicity. I rarely smiled like that in real life.

I turned right into the entrance to the multi-storey car park and accelerated up the concrete ramp. One minute later, I pulled into my regular parking space on the first floor. I grabbed the stack of LP records on the passenger seat, switched off the engine and got out, then used up another thirty seconds in walking briskly from the car to the *Metrosound* reception area. I pushed open the swing doors and stepped into a room that was probably typical of radio stations all over the world: a small box-shaped area, the walls covered with khaki-coloured Hessian. Here and there, more framed photographs of the resident DJs greeted me with insincere smiles, and a black plastic notice-board paid welcome to the various celebrities who had called in earlier that day with records to sell or axes to grind. I noticed that this particular morning the airwaves had been graced by an elderly female novelist, a historian, a clutch of pimply pop stars and a recently defrocked bishop.

In passing, I nodded briefly to Julie, the large indolent girl who always manned the desk at this hour. She was eating a doughnut and reading a Jackie Collins novel, her pasty face expressionless as she munched. She did not so much as glance up, but simply pressed a button that released the lock on the door leading through into the inner sanctum. From the hidden speakers mounted in the ceiling, I could hear newsreader Dave Hibbert, going morosely through the more sensational items currently on offer.

'A man was turned into a horrific blazing fireball in a pub in Stockport today. Horrified customers looked an as twenty-three-year-old Steven Kendall was literally burned alive.'

Where did they get these stories from? Last month the favourite subject had been Rottweiler attacks. This month, it was all about spontaneous human combustion. To hear Hibbert talk, you'd believe that it had reached epidemic proportions in the pubs and clubs of Manchester. This was the fifth case this week.

Without slowing my pace, I stepped through the door and

passed into the corridor beyond. I paused in an alcove on the left, where a large coffee machine was housed and I punched the button that served me with a paper cup full of tepid drinking chocolate. Snatching it up, I swung back out of the alcove, turned right into the main reception and headed for the double doors that led into Studio One. On the way I nearly collided with the squat heap that was Ray Wood. Having finished his stint for the night, Ray was on his way home; or rather, he was on his way *out*. Ray rarely made it home to the wife without passing through a succession of night clubs en route. This man was fond of the bottle and fond of jailbait, though not necessarily in that order. 'Cutting it fine, as ever,' he observed in passing.

'We must stop meeting like this,' I called back over my shoulder. I was aware that Hibbert was now on the weather forecast.

'. . . a low depression leading to fog in inland areas and occasional bouts of heavy rain. Temperatures below average for October . . .'

I swept silently into the studio and flicked a casual 'V' sign at Hibbert, who was ensconced in a tiny, soundproof glass box on my left. Hibbert returned the favour without dropping a word and began to wind up the bulletin as I slid into my familiar seat, snatched a theme-music cartridge from the rack on top of the console and slotted it into position in the deck. Glancing through the glass screen ahead of me, I nodded at the hulking, pot-bellied figure of my regular Technical Officer Steve Acton, who was looking listlessly at a well-thumbed copy of *Penthouse* and eating a Mars Bar.

'. . . temperatures no lower than two degrees Celsius, thirty-five degrees Fahrenheit. *Metrosound* News, it's now five minutes past twelve.'

I punched in the cartridge and a doo-wop harmony group bleated out an irritating jingle while I slipped my opening record on to a turn-table.

'*Metrosound* Radio, the greatest sound around!'

I cued the first record, slid the microphone fader to the 'up' position and launched into my opening monologue over the music. 'Five minutes into the midnight hour here on *Metrosound*. This is Captain Tom Prince welcoming you aboard the *Nightboat* for another four hours of music, madness and mayhem. We'll be taking our first caller right after this mighty groove from Marvin Gaye; the number is 226 1234, the lines are open and our starter subject tonight is immigration. Should the laws be tightened up? Should they be relaxed? In light of recent racial attacks on the streets of Manchester, can we really hold our heads up with true Northern pride? The ball is in your court, phone now and air your views. Back in a mo!'

I slid the fader down and acknowledged the sign from Steve, which told me that the switchboard was already lighting up on the other side of the glass. My ever-eager fans, ready to chew the fat. As usual, my spirit sagged. These were not the world's most stimulating conversationalists. Most of them still needed help with tying their shoelaces. I removed my leather jacket and flung it over the back of the chair, then sipped at my drink which tasted reassuringly disgusting. I closed my eyes for a moment and listened to the back-beat of the song, remembering earlier days when I was new at this game and it had all been a little more exciting. Keeping the excitement alive, that was the problem. Some of the jocks at *Metrosound* had that trick, but I, unfortunately, did not. A few moments later, Steve was chasing through with a handful of scribbled notes, names and locations, his bare belly hanging out of a woefully inadequate *Metrosound* T-shirt.

'I see the *Jane Fonda Workout* tape hasn't helped,' I said.

In reply, Steve simply belched the smell of undigested chocolate into my face, dumped the scraps of paper on my desk and scuttled back to his lair on the other side of the glass. That was the great thing about Steve. He never surprised you by being good-mannered or jovial or even halfway pleasant. You always knew exactly where you stood with him. He was a total pig.

I sifted half-heartedly through the notes, finding names I recognised and others I didn't. I relegated some to the bottom of the pile, only to be used in an emergency. These were people I'd crossed swords with before and I knew that, in radio terms, they were guilty of the greatest sin of all: they were deadly dull. Live radio thrived on controversy, stupidity and just occasionally the odd dash of wit. Polite sensible individuals with monotone voices and decent values did not tend to come over well when filtered

8

through a transistor radio. But of course, with a new name, you had to give the caller the benefit of the doubt the first time around. I fixed on a name I didn't recognise and as the record faded down, I slipped on my headphones and came in over the top of it.

'All right, a bona-fide classic to kick the show off with; and now let's see if we can get some classic comments from Mike, over there in Gorton. All right Mike, you're through to Captain Tom, what's your point?'

Some hesitation. Then; 'Er . . .'ello Tom, nice to be on the show. Well er . . . it's just like ummm . . . you know . . .'

Just what I needed. Another moron. There were plenty of them around and they all seemed to have my number. 'Come on Mike, spit it out. It might be a gold nugget.'

'Pardon? Er . . . oh yeah, well like, don't get me wrong, I'm not a racist or anything but it's hardly fair is it, all these darkies coming over here and gettin' our jobs and that . . . and committing all this crime and such.'

'Crime, Mike? You're an expert on crime statistics, are you?'

'Er . . . no . . . but I was reading in this newspaper like, that eighty per cent of crime in the North-west is committed by blacks.'

'Which newspaper was this Mike?'

'Er . . . it was the *Sun* actually.'

'Oh, I'm sorry, I thought you said a newspaper. Not a comic. And naturally, you believe everything that's printed in the *Sun*, don't you?'

'Well I wouldn't say everything.'

'Oh, then you admit that occasionally it prints lies.'

'No, I wouldn't say that either.'

'Oh, so sometimes you don't believe the truth, is that what you're saying?'

'Er . . . no, look I'm talkin' about this article. It reckoned as how ninety per cent of crime was done by blacks.'

'*Ninety* per cent, already! Does this reflect the rising crime rate, folks? It's risen ten per cent in the last thirty seconds. Mike, would it be fair to say that you're a raving bigot?'

'A what?'

'A bigot, Mike. Do you know what a bigot is?'

9

'Er . . . no I—'

'Well, I tell you what you should do. Just leave your phone there and go straight to your bathroom. Have a look in the shaving mirror. I guarantee you'll see one.'

I cut off Mike's line before any reply could be offered and proceeded to my next caller, Kathy, a regular on the show.

'OK, now it's time for a few words of wisdom from our very own housewife and sex-siren, Kathy, from the depths of darkest Harpurhey. Hello Kathy, how's it going?'

Kathy's offering was prefaced by her habitual trademark, a long, lascivious sigh. It was supposed to seem sexy, but down a telephone line it had an unfortunate tendency to sound like sinusitis. Kathy's husband was a truck-driver who spent most of his nights away from home. She was lonely and worked it out of her system with rampant innuendo.

'Hello Tom. I was just lying here, drinking a glass of gin and feeling lonely . . . so I thought I'd phone the sexiest man on the radio.'

'But Derek Jameson was having a night off, so you tried me instead?'

A deep, throaty chuckle. 'Oh, Tom, you are *awful!*'

'Hmm. Albert's away again, I take it. Where is he this time?'

'Oh, Southampton I think. Anyway, let's not talk about him. Let's talk about us. You know, I was thinking, I can't possibly drink this whole bottle all by my little self. Why not, when you've finished tonight, pop over and help me. We could play some games.'

'Uh huh. Would this be Ludo or Trivial Pursuit? I'm very good at Trivial Pursuit.'

'Oh, I thought we might make our own entertainment, Tom.'

'Yes, but Kathy. By four in the morning, all I really want to do is crawl into bed.'

'Uh huh? Sounds interesting.'

I rolled my eyes towards the ceiling. Kathy was harmless but she could be very trying. Sometimes she was worth milking for a few cheap laughs but tonight I wasn't in the mood. 'Kathy, I hate to be a party pooper, but perhaps you'd like to give me your views on immigration. That is, after all, the subject of this phone-in.'

'Immigration?' Kathy sounded disappointed, but made an effort to compromise. 'Well, they do say these black men are very well endowed, don't they? And what I say is, if they want to come in, I'm just the sort of person to say yes to them . . .'

I cut her off before the discussion got even more lurid. You could always count on Kathy to bring the conversation down to the level of a snake's belly.

'Yes, well, we'll let Kathy take a cold shower I think, and we'll head over to Droylsden for a chat with William.'

William was another old friend, the programme's resident religious-nut. I had this pet theory that he was possessed by some kind of demon, because he seemed to experience violent mood-swings. Sometimes he was as meek and mild as the proverbial lamb; other times, he came on like Rasputin the Mad Monk. It seemed to be the latter incarnation that was phoning in tonight.

'You're damned, Tom Prince. Totally beyond redemption!'

'Oh, thanks William, it's nice to have a little reassurance from my fans. What particular commandment have I transgressed this time?'

'Don't make mock of me! I've been listening to this programme very carefully. Over the last few weeks the moral tone has plunged deplorably. Women like the one who was just speaking are to be pitied, but you encourage . . . yes, *encourage* them to speak their wanton thoughts aloud, where they can be heard by honest, god-fearing people. When I think of the potential harm to young children, listening to this programme . . .'

'Young children? Willy, it's twelve fifteen a.m. I hardly think that there will be many youngsters turning in to *Nightboat*. And if they are, it's surely their parents who are remiss.'

'Just listen to this, Tom Prince. Proverbs 24, Verse 8. "A man who is bent on mischief gets a name for intrigue; the intrigues of foolish men misfire and the insolent man is odious to his fellows." '

I wasn't going to let him get away with that one. I'd long ago learned to have a copy of the bible standing by, with a few prime passages underlined in pencil. I snatched it up and found a section I'd marked for just such an occasion.

'Since you're so keen on proverbs, William, here's one for you. Chapter 18, Verse 4. "The words of a man's mouth are a gushing torrent, but deep is the water in the well of wisdom." '

William paused for a moment as though searching his mind for an appropriate retort. Then he came back with Chapter 17, Verse 11. "An evil man is set only on disobedience, but a messenger without mercy will be sent against him." '

'All right! How about this? Chapter 16, Verse 13. "Honest speech is the desire of kings, they love a man who speaks the truth." '

'The truth? The truth as *you* perceive it, you mean! And you can quote back at me as much as you like, those listeners who have ears will know that you are bending the words of good men to suit your own purposes.'

I sighed. William was best suffered in small doses. 'Since we seem to have strayed off the subject, William, I'll leave you with one last quotation. Suffer not the babbling speech of the self-righteous, for surely they talk a load of cobblers. That's Tom Prince, Chapter 1, Verse 1. Bye Willy!'

I cut off the angry tirade that must have followed and went directly to a Ralph in Bolton, who made a very rude sound down the line; there are some childish fuckers in the world, aren't there? So I moved over to Dianne in Swinton, who wanted to know if I thought arranged marriages were a good idea. Since Dianne clearly had a bigger quota of brain cells than most of my regular callers, I spent some time on this one, winding her up, getting her to contradict herself, deliberately misunderstanding what she was getting at. At first she matched me quite well but as the argument wore on, her resolve broke down and she started to get angry. As her rage increased, so the construction of her arguments crumbled and by the end of the call she was screaming abuse at me. I was almost sorry to have to cut her off but she was edging dangerously close to the forbidden 'F' word and, naturally, I couldn't fucking allow it.

After this, I took a record break and allowed things to cool down a little. Steve ferried through another selection of names. The look of contempt he gave me suggested that he thought Dianne had been unfairly treated, but I'd trashed her quite deliberately, knowing that a score of people would phone in her defence. I sifted through the names, placed somebody called

John at the top of the pile and waited for the record to wind down.

As soon as I got John on the line, I suspected that I might have made a mistake. At first there was a long pause, as though whoever was there had bottled out of speaking. But then, a voice did come through the headphones, a strange course whisper. 'Hello Tom. How's it going?'

'Well, it's going just fine, John. What would you like to talk about?'

'Err . . . murder, Tom. I'd like to talk about murder.'

'Murder. I see . . .' I glanced warily through at Steve and made a universal gesture, drilling an index finger into the side of my head and crossing my eyes. We got more than our fair share of headbangers on the show, but sometimes they could be a damn sight more entertaining than their more rational counterparts. 'And what particular aspect of murder would you like to discuss, John. The reintroduction of capital punishment, perhaps?'

Another pause. Then a low, husky laugh that inexplicably sent a shiver of doubt through me. 'Oh no, I should say not! I'd be letting myself in for big trouble if I did that, now wouldn't I? You see, Tom, I'm speaking from a very special point of view here. I actually am a murderer.'

In the short silence that followed, I considered my options. If I simply cut the silly sod off now, it would be an obvious cop-out on my part, a moral victory for him. Better by far to ridicule the man, show him up for the childish prankster he undoubtedly was.

'Ah . . . so you're the man we've all been looking for. A murderer, eh? But I thought the butler always did it. Unless of course, you *are* a butler?'

'No, I'm not a butler. Just a murderer. And to be honest with you, I've not been one for long. Only half an hour or so. You see, I just killed this woman.'

I froze, my hand on the panic button. My professional instincts warned me to cut the caller off immediately, but I did not move a muscle; for in that same instant I had realised with a dreadful sense of conviction that John was telling the simple, naked truth, a commodity that very rarely finds its way on to the airwaves. The strange matter-of-fact quality in his voice could not have been faked and I was momentarily mesmerised by it. John continued to talk and his voice was simultaneously relayed to around ten thousand radio sets all over the North-west.

'I murdered her, see . . . and I got an urge to tell somebody about it. Well, I always listen to your programme. Wouldn't miss it. And I thought, I know, I'll phone Captain Tom! So here I am. And there she is. All sort of crumpled up on the kitchen floor. I done her with a knife. It was weird. It kind of twisted in my hand and she just made this little sound . . . like a gasp, you know? And that was it. I'm standing by her right now as I phone you.'

I took a deep breath. I could see Steve staring at me through the glass screen, his eyes bulging, his mouth hanging open like a stranded fish. 'John,' I said quietly. 'I know that many other people will be hoping, as I am right now, that you're pulling my leg. Own up and I'll pop an Academy award in the post.'

'Oh no Tom, this is straight up. She's dead all right. Send somebody to check it out if you like. The address is 9, Manor Drive, Levenshulme. Of course, I won't be there when they arrive but I've enjoyed our little talk. In fact, I've enjoyed tonight tremendously. I think I might do this again soon. When I do, I'll call you. Bye!'

His line went dead. I sat there, stunned. For the first time in my career, I was at a loss for words. I glanced back towards the glass partition and saw Steve Acton frantically dialling a number on the external phone. Acting on automatic pilot, I managed to cue my next record. I sat there wondering vaguely what I was going to talk about for the rest of the show.

Detective Inspector Drayton was waiting to speak to me when I finally stepped out of the studio. By that time I was pretty wound up, having hosted the remainder of the programme that was inevitably devoted to the same subject. Was this John character on the level? I mean, had he really done what he claimed? Or was it just an elaborate practical joke?

One glance at Drayton's face was enough to convince me that this wasn't funny. Not at all. He was an odd-looking character, who might have stepped right out of the pages of a pulp detective-novel. He was a thin, dowdy-looking individual, dressed in a shapeless grey mackintosh and a battered trilby. He had the kind of mousey little toothbrush moustache that few people still favoured unless they happened to be going to a fancy-dress party as a famous German dictator. He stood in one corner of the main reception, his hands in his pockets and a facial expression that suggested somebody was holding a dog turd a couple of inches under his nose. He clearly didn't like what he saw at *Metrosound* and as I slouched wearily towards him, his grey eyes seemed to appraise me, taking in my casual clothing, the stub of the cigarette that drooped from my mouth. Disapproval was written large across his face.

'Mr . . . Prince?' Even the name seemed to cause him distress. 'I've just come from the address that your caller gave.'

I dropped into one of the seats opposite the inspector. 'And?' I inquired hopefully.

'It all checked out, I'm afraid. Exactly as he described it.'

The news hit me like a clenched fist. I think up to this point I'd been holding out a hope that it was some kind of wind-up. Now I found it difficult to catch my breath. 'Christ!' I gasped. 'What a mess.'

'The woman lived alone. As far as we can tell, she must have just opened the door to the killer. Her name was Margaret Donavan. Mean anything to you?'

I stared at Drayton. It was somehow familiar and yet for the life of me, I couldn't place it. 'It . . . it rings a bell,' I admitted.

'It ought to. Her next-door neighbour told me she was featured on your programme about two weeks ago. Apparently, she answered questions in some kind of competition and won a T-shirt.'

'My God, yes! *Maggie* Donavan she called herself. I remember her now. Quite a clever girl . . . well, clever for my show, anyway. She got a full score in the pop-trivia quiz. Christ, what an awful coincidence.'

'Coincidence? Oh, I doubt it, Mr Prince. I doubt it very much.' He paused as though waiting for this observation to sink in, while he watched me with his cold grey eyes. 'Now, this fellow who

15

phoned tonight. Your Mr Acton is sorting out a tape of the incident for me . . . but I'd just like to ask a few questions if I may.'

'Sure, why don't you sit down? I'll get some coffee from the machine . . .'

'If you don't mind, I'd prefer to stand. And I'll skip the coffee. I never drink—'

'While you're on duty? Listen, it was just coffee I was offering, we don't keep anything stronger here.'

Drayton's expression showed no trace of amusement. 'I'm sure you don't,' he said. 'I was going to say that I never drink hot liquids. They give me heartburn.' He glanced briefly around the reception area, evidently bothered by the sounds of pop music pumping from the unseen sound system. 'Is there any way that racket can be turned down?' he inquired irritably.

I reached obligingly up to a control switch on the wall beside him and turned the background music to its lowest setting. 'It never goes off completely,' I told him.

Drayton nodded irritably. 'Now, about this character that called you up.'

'John.'

Drayton's eyebrows lifted. 'You know him?'

'No, of course not. That was the name he gave us, that's all.'

'Why, *of course not*? You know some of the people that ring, don't you? I mean, you have regular contacts.'

I agreed wearily. 'Yes, I have regulars, but this guy wasn't one of them.'

'You're sure?'

I glared at him for a moment. 'Yes, I'm sure. A first-timer. And a last-timer, I hope. My show thrives on controversy, but this kind I can do without.'

'But it doesn't sound like it will be the last time, does it Mr Prince? From what your Mr Acton told me, this John suggested he would call you back . . . next time.'

'He did say words to that effect, yes.'

'Odd, don't you think?'

'Odd? I'd say that's a bit of an understatement. Fucking weird is the expression I would use.'

Drayton winced, narrowed his eyes down to disapproving slits.

16

A prude, I decided. The kind of guy who takes a cold shower whenever a lusty thought crosses his mind.

'Quite. But it does suggest a certain intimacy between the two of you; and yet, you claim that you don't know this man.'

'Hey listen, don't read things into this that aren't there. I get all kinds of arseholes ringing me up night after night. Some of them would maybe like to *think* they know me, but believe me they don't. I'm just a public service. Between midnight and four every morning I go on the air and I'm available to any crackpot who has an opinion. After that, I go home, take a shower and get on with my life. There's really no mystery.'

Drayton looked unconvinced. 'There are some people who would question the wisdom of a programme like yours Mr Prince. There are some who would say that it's an open invitation for every deviant in the city to find access to the airwaves.'

I nodded. 'There are those who have already said just that,' I replied. 'Me, I think it's usually a healthy enough hobby . . . speaking your mind, I mean. This time we just got unlucky, that's all.'

'I'm told you have a cut-off facility incorporated into the system. Apparently you chose to disregard it.'

I shook my head. 'Not at all. The fact is I was stunned; by the time I'd recovered, the cat was already out of the bag. It certainly wasn't intentional.'

'Think you'd be able to recognise the voice if you heard it again?'

'I doubt it.'

Drayton glared at me. 'Are you deliberately being unhelpful?' he demanded.

'No, not at all. It's just that this character was whispering – you'll understand what I mean when you hear the tape.'

'You think he was disguising his voice? A handkerchief or something?'

'No, not exactly, he was just . . . whispering . . .' I glanced edgily at my watch. 'Look, it's four in the morning, I've had a lousy night and I'd very much like to go home and get some sleep now. Do you think that would be possible or do you have any more questions?'

'Well, we'll need to get a statement from you sometime; but

I suppose that could wait until tomorrow. If you'd come into the station, say around three?'

'Sure. Anything you say.' Gratefully I rose to my feet and began to move towards the exit doors; but Drayton could not resist throwing a parting shot after me.

'Another strange thing, Mr Prince . . .'

I paused, my hand on the door. 'Oh, what's that?'

'Miss Donavan's neighbour told me she was very proud of the T-shirt she won. She'd been showing it off to her just a couple of days earlier.'

'So?'

'We searched her flat from top to bottom. No sign of the T-shirt.'

I shrugged. 'Maybe she gave it to somebody else,' I suggested.

'Maybe. Or maybe the killer took it with him. A little memento, perhaps. From what I've heard, this man is a big fan of yours.'

'Could be. That's not a crime, is it?'

'No. That's about the only thing we can't put him away for.'

'What are you getting at?'

Drayton spread his hands. 'I'm not getting at anything,' he said. 'It's just . . . odd, don't you think? Tell me, do you enjoy your work, Mr Prince?'

'Not much. But it pays the bills.' I glanced briefly back at Drayton. 'What's your excuse?' I asked; and I went out, letting the door swing shut behind me.

Chapter Two

It was Jamie's absence that woke me; the warm empty space beneath my arm, that an instant earlier had been reassuringly filled. I opened my eyes, blinked, then raised myself on one arm to gaze at her. She was sitting at the end of the bed, dressed only in underwear and stockings, examining her reflection in a small hand-mirror as she carefully applied mascara to her lashes. I watched her for a moment in silent fascination, telling myself that one of these days I would succeed in convincing her that she should marry me. I studied her profile for a moment, my gaze moving slowly from her long, curly chestnut-coloured hair and down the graceful curve of her back to the cute little cleft of her buttocks, peeking from the top of her panties. We'd been living together now for close on six months and she still aroused in me the hot, sticky passions that had marked our brief court-ship. I extended one arm and traced an index finger slowly along the fleshy highway of her spine.

She turned her head, surprised. 'Good morning,' she said. 'I'm sorry if I woke you . . .'

'Don't mention it.' I opened my arms to her and she put down the mirror with a wry smile and dropped into my embrace, tracing her lips gently across my neck and cheek. I felt desire coiling like a snake in the pit of my stomach.

'You were sleeping so soundly, I thought I'd let you rest,' she whispered.

'I can sleep later,' I assured her; and I lifted one hand to pull hopefully at the clasp of her bra. Realising my intentions, her body stiffened and she pushed herself safely out of my grasp.

'Oh no you don't! A cuddle is one thing, but that's strictly off the menu. I'll be late for work.'

'Oh Jamie, come on, it's been weeks!'

'Days,' she corrected me. 'And didn't your mother tell you that good things are worth waiting for?'

'Leave my mother out of this,' I told her. 'I've never had sex with my mother and anyone who says different is a liar.'

She picked up the mirror and resumed the meticulous application of her make-up. I flopped back on to the mattress with a groan.

'Jesus Christ!' I exclaimed. 'We've got to do something about our hours.'

'Fine. I'll have a word with Sister McAuliffe about it.' She turned to face an imaginary supervisor. 'Excuse me, but I was wondering if I could go back on nights for a while; only my old man is a horny sod and he's not getting enough lately.' She laughed at the idea. 'Don't hold out too much hope,' she advised me. 'The old bat's got it in for me.' Jamie got up off the bed and went over to the wardrobe to get her uniform. I watched in silent frustration as she slipped the white cotton garment over her head and did up the poppers. She noticed me watching her and she slipped into a saucy pose, lifting the hem of her uniform to reveal the tops of her stockings.

'Don't,' I groaned. I grabbed a pillow and crammed it down over my head.

'A cup of tea?' inquired Jamie, ignoring my protests. 'Or would a bucket of cold water be more appropriate?'

'Prick-teaser,' I growled.

'Thank you for your comments. We aim to please. And this is the last call for passengers requiring a hot cuppa.' She strolled towards the bedroom door. 'How was work?' she asked.

Until that moment I had actually forgotten. Remembering was quite a shock. It must have been my silence that stopped her; and the odd look on my face as I pulled the pillow aside. She had always been well tuned to my changing moods, sometimes her abilities bordered on the telepathic. 'Something wrong?' she asked, pausing by the door.

I nodded. 'Somebody got murdered on the show,' I said.

'What? On the air? I know *Metrosound* like to break new ground but that's going a bit too far.' I didn't react to the joke and she began to realise that I was being serious. She moved back to the bed and sat beside me, ran a hand tenderly through my hair. 'Need to talk?' she asked.

'Thought you were late for work.'

'If I skip breakfast, I can let you have five minutes,' she assured me.

I told her what had happened. She listened intently, saying nothing until I'd finished. When I finally asked for her opinion, she said simply; 'I think you should get out of that job.' This was hardly a surprise. She'd been telling me the same thing for months. Jamie had this unswerving faith in my abilities and I think she was more indignant than I was when I got shunted into the late-night slot.

'I might not have the option to stay after what's happened.' I told her. 'I've had no official reaction from upstairs yet but any way you look at it, it's a mess. Trouble is, what else can I do? Being a jock is all I know . . .'

'Don't be silly. You can do anything you put your mind to. I keep telling you, you're throwing away genuine talent on that sleaze-bag show. You belong in television, Tom, I'm sure you could have a big career there. And you've got plenty of contacts, you know you have! It's just laziness with you, there's no other excuse. Why don't you go in there tonight and tell them to stuff their contract? Tell them you don't want to be associated with something like this.'

I grunted. 'Sure. And live on what for the next year? A staff nurse's wages and a weekly dole cheque?'

'We'd manage,' she said. 'Until you sorted something out for yourself.'

I shook my head. 'It probably won't come to that. And let's face it, this was a one-off event. It's not likely to become a fixture.'

'That's hardly the point, Tom. A woman was killed, for Christ's sake! It's not just something you can pass off, like mispronouncing a name. Of course, you weren't to blame . . . well, you know how narrow-minded people are. Shit always sticks, whether it's your fault or not.' She glanced helplessly at her watch. 'And speaking of shit, if I don't shift myself, I'll be up to my neck in it.' She leaned forward and gave me a brief farewell kiss. 'Tell them tonight, Tom,' she urged me again. 'I've never liked that show. It's not worthy of you.'

I took one of her hands and squeezed it. 'Funny, I've always thought it was me that wasn't worthy. Of you.' I masked this genuine observation with a quip, something I invariably did when I was in danger of being sincere. 'Anyway, I've enjoyed our little talk. We must make an appointment to have another one, very soon.'

Jamie grinned ruefully. 'I'll pencil you in for tonight,' she assured me. 'Who knows, if somebody takes the trouble to lay on a romantic meal for two and a bottle of wine, there might just be time to take care of your more carnal needs before you go in to work.' She gave me an outrageous wink. 'Bye love. See you tonight. You get some more sleep.' She went out of the room, closing the door behind her.

I managed to drift off again but I was troubled by disturbing dreams in which I was hosting the show and scores of voices were coming across the phone lines simultaneously. They were all asking me about the same thing but my mouth was horribly dry and I found myself unable to construct a single coherent sentence . . .

I woke around midday, my breath tasting stale, my eyelids gummed together. I slid reluctantly out of bed, put on a bath robe and clumped downstairs to the kitchen to make a cup of strong coffee. Sipping at it, I went into the study to sort through the mail and listen to the calls stored on my answerphone. The first one was from Karen, my ex-wife, and I experienced the usual sinking feeling I got whenever she contacted me. We'd been separated for nearly a year now, but she still got in touch on a regular basis, as though reluctant to release her hold. I didn't much care for her persistence. I knew for a fact that Jamie sometimes felt threatened by it and also by my need to keep in regular contact with my seven-year-old son, Daniel. Danny was a great kid, the one good thing that had come out of my relationship with Karen. I didn't really see enough of him and I suppose I felt guilty about that. I also lost sleep worrying how the break-up might have affected him. It was hard to tell, he didn't really give much away. In that respect, he was very like his old man. Karen, on the other hand, was an open book.

'Hello, stranger.' I had to shake my head at her greeting. I'd last seen her four days ago, when she'd insisted that I go over to help bleed her central-heating system. 'I need to talk to you urgently,' she said. 'It's about Daniel, he's having trouble at school. Call round this afternoon; I'll be working at home all day.' Naturally, she'd made no allowance for whether the visit would be convenient for me; but a summons from Karen was rather like one from Buckingham Palace. One simply didn't dare refuse it. I sighed.

The next call was from my mother, halting and indecisive, because she'd never really come to terms with talking to a machine. 'Hello, Thomas?'

I cringed involuntarily. My parents were the only people in the world who ever called me that.

'Your father and I . . . were wondering when we'd be seeing you again? I know you're very busy, but . . . it's *months* now and if you could find time in your schedule to pop over for a while, we'd love to see you . . . and Jamie, of course. Anyway, uh . . . well, I'm sure there's no news at the moment. Do at least ring us and er . . . let us know how you're going on . . .'

I sighed at the end of this message, too. I had been putting off seeing them, it was true. And there was another source of guilt that was much harder to pin down. If it had been simply that I didn't get on with them, it would have been easier to accept. The fact was, that my parents idolised me. Whenever I went up to the little Cheshire community that was now their home, they all but put out the red carpet for me. 'Our son the radio star,' was how they invariably introduced me to bemused friends and acquaintances. I found that profoundly embarrassing. Worse still, was our mutual inability to communicate. They got on famously with Jamie, chattering happily away about this and that, while I crouched sullenly in the corner watching the television. We all knew there was a problem but none of us had the first idea about how to rectify it. And so it went on and I put off visiting them until the passing of time shamed me into making the effort. The irony of it did not escape me. I could talk my head off, night after night, to thousands of strangers. To the two people who sired me, I could find nothing to say. I put a large question mark in my diary, which I suppose said it all.

There was only one other call logged and this one was inevitable.

'Hello Tom, it's Simon. Look mate, sorry to bother you so early but I think we need to talk about last night. Can you get in here this afternoon, around one-thirty? If there's a problem, ring me at the office, we'll reschedule.'

Simon Radcliffe was programme controller at *Metrosound*. Clearly the shit had already hit the fan. This was a call I couldn't afford to ignore. It occurred to me that it was time for the midday news-bulletin. Curious, I reached out and flicked on the miniature radio that sat on my desk, just in time to hear the impassive voice of the female newscaster who read the day-time headlines.

'. . . twenty-five-year-old woman was brutally murdered in her Levenshulme home in the early hours of this morning. A bizarre twist was added to the story, when the murderer made a telephone call to *Metrosound*'s own Tom Prince on his *Nightboat* show, in order to make a confession. The man, who identified himself only as "John", left the following chilling message.' There was a brief pause before the extract from the master-tape that had been recorded the night before. It had been professionally cut and edited back together but there was no mistaking that strange, whispering voice.

'She's dead all right. Send somebody to check it out if you like. I won't be there when they arrive but I've enjoyed our little talk. In fact, I've enjoyed tonight tremendously. I think I might do this again soon. When I do, I'll call you. Bye!'

The newsreader's voice cut in again. 'Police are appealing for anybody who thinks they recognise that voice to call them on a special hot-line. The number is . . .' But with a curse, I was out of the study and heading for the bathroom to shower myself awake. 'What the fuck's going on?' I asked myself aloud, as I stood beneath the rush of hot water.

Fifteen minutes later, I was driving downtown at a far from cautious speed; twenty-five minutes later, I stalked unannounced into Simon Radcliffe's palatial office.

Simon glanced up from his desk in mild surprise. He was a

slim, well-groomed twenty-three-year-old who had risen to the dizzy heights in only two years. There were many at *Metrosound* who hated him for this very fact and who were quick to label him a ruthless bastard of the lowest order; but it was interesting to note that there were few who would not have admitted that he was singularly good at his job. I probably had more cause to hate him than most. After all, it was Simon who had got me into my current predicament, who had taken me from a prime-time investigative-journalism programme and sweet-talked me about his plans for a 'late-night cult chat-show'. He had managed to make it all sound incredibly subversive and exciting, whilst down-playing the anti-social hours, the meagre listening figures and the rampant stupidity of the participants. I'd fallen for it hook, line and sinker; and it was too late now to hope for a reprieve. Simon had stitched me up, good and proper.

He sat there now, a slightly quizzical expression on his face; then slowly, he raised one elegantly tailored sleeve and pulled it back to look at his Piaget wristwatch.

'Tom, this is an unexpected pleasure. I wasn't expecting you till—'

'Never mind about that Simon, just what the fuck are they playing at?'

He ushered me to the vacant seat opposite his desk. 'Well, that rather depends on which particular "they" and which particular "fuck" you're referring to,' he replied. A southerner, Simon had the kind of refined, slightly camp voice that did strange things to any four-letter word, making it sound somehow quaint, even charming. He seemed mildly amused by my evident distress. 'I'm afraid you'll have to be more specific,' he concluded.

'You know bloody well what I'm on about! I just listened to the *Metrosound* news bulletin . . .'

Simon rolled his eyes ceilingwards. 'My God, devotion above and beyond the call of duty! We expect you to do the shows, Tom, but you don't have to feel obliged to *listen* to them as well!'

Simon was a past-master at defusing anger in this way, but I refused to let myself be sidetracked. 'Whose idea was it to feature that tape of the murderer?' I asked him.

'Mine, of course! And a little gem it was, too. The voice of the killer, right there on the airwaves! A *Metrosound* exclusive.

Listen, it's a shame we don't get more things like that dropped into our lap. I might add the police were rather keen on the idea as well.'

I sneered. 'Oh yes? The squeaky clean Inspector Drayton? I thought he didn't like the idea of . . . what was it? Oh yes, deviants on the airwaves!'

'Are you kidding? If that rule applied, half of our resident jocks would be out of a job. But really Tom, I don't see your problem. It happened. We reported it. Simple as that. Why get so het up over it?'

'Because . . . well, because I think you could have shown more restraint, that's all. Plastering his voice all over the bulletin like that, it's sick.'

Simon smiled. 'Oh, I don't doubt it. But it's also bloody good radio. And if we don't make the most of what we've got, there are others who will, quite happily.' He picked up a folded copy of the *Evening News* from his desk and threw it down in front of me. 'Seen the early edition?' he inquired with mock innocence. I glanced at him uneasily for a moment, then picked up the paper. My own photograph, a smaller copy of the image that decorated the side of the *Metrosound* building, stared back at me from the front cover. PRINCE OF DARKNESS blared a headline at the top of the page and then in slightly smaller letters; '*Metrosound* DJ in whispering-killer horror.'

I stared at the article for several long moments, stunned. I opened my mouth to speak but nothing came out. Eventually Simon spoke for me.

'It's a nice likeness, isn't it?' he chirped.

I finally managed to put enough words together to construct a short sentence. 'Oh, shit.' I ran a hand through my hair. 'How did they get this . . . so quick?'

'Well, a good question. It must have taken some pretty frantic rejigging of the presses to crank that out in time. Would have needed a hot tip-off too. But as I said, that's a genuine scoop. I should think they'd have been very grateful to get their hands on an item like that, even round midnight. Grateful as in, *generous*.'

I did a quick mental back-flip; came up with an image of a fat, chocolate guzzling Technical Officer with access to an outside line. 'Acton!' I growled. 'That slimy bastard. When I get my hands on him—'

'Oh, take it easy! You can't really blame him, Tom. After all, he's got several kids to feed. Even if he doesn't happen to be living with any of the mothers. Anyway, you may as well accept the inevitable. This is just the start. By tomorrow morning, all the nationals will have hold of it. Some of the tabloids will make what you've got there look positively restrained by comparison.'

'Oh no . . .' I dropped the paper and buried my face in my hands. 'Well, I suppose that's it,' I murmured. 'I'm screwed. I may as well hand in my notice now.'

'*Quit?*' Simon seemed positively horrified by the idea. 'You arsehole, you'll do nothing of the kind!' He got up from his desk and walked around to sit on the edge of it. He adopted a conspiratorial air. 'Let's not lose sight of something,' he said. 'This is the biggest thing that's happened here since the air disaster. You remember the mileage we got out of that? Oh sure, it was sick, over the top, melodramatic exploitation. Wouldn't argue the point. But our ratings were never higher than over those few weeks. And here's an even bigger irony. The advertisers were virtually killing themselves to get their products on the air. Nothing sells a product like disaster, Tom. If you can cut straight from an interview with a grieving relative to an advert for supersoft toilet tissue, you can be sure that you've got the collective ear of the North-west. Now, let's look at The Whisperer.'

I stared at him. 'Who?'

'Our John. The *Evening News* has already dubbed him "The Whisperer"; take it from me, that name is going to stick. Now, with this story, we have one element that the air disaster didn't have. Know what that is?'

I shook my head. 'I don't think I want to,' I replied.

Simon told me just the same. 'A couple of hundred people fry in an airplane. What happens? Great news item, but short-lived. Over, if you'll excuse an awful pun, in a flash. Oh sure, a few opportunities to get interviews with sobbing parents and distraught fiancés, but then it's all down to small beer. Inquiries into why it happened, whether it can be prevented. Worthy stuff but not the kind of item that grabs an audience.'

I listened, numbed, as Simon came to his chilling conclusion.

'Your killer now, that's a different proposition. There we've got longevity. People are going to listen in to see if he keeps his promise. Will he phone you again? More importantly, will he *do* it again? The call suggests he will. Tantalising stuff, right? And nothing new of course, the public's been creaming its collective jeans over stuff like this since Jack the Ripper. And meanwhile, the police are trying to track him down. Suspense! Will they get to him before he gets to somebody else? You see what I'm saying, Tom? It's too good an opportunity to miss.'

He was positively drooling. I had to struggle to keep my reply rational.

'Have you gone mad or something? I mean, do you realise what we're talking about here? We're talking about murder. A woman was killed. She was carved up with a knife, Simon. Others could be killed; and you want to turn that into some kind of fucking sideshow?'

Simon shrugged. 'Unfortunate turn of phrase,' he observed.

'Maybe, but that's exactly what it would be. Didn't you know they banned freak shows years ago? Anyway, don't count on me to play ball. I don't want to have anything to do with this, it stinks.'

'Only the sweet smell of success, dear boy. Your being moralistic at the moment and, I suspect, a good deal more naïve than you ought to be. But when you've had a chance to consider . . .'

'Oh no, Simon, I really don't think so.'

'And naturally, I couldn't dream of letting you go at this time. As you know, your contract isn't up for renewal until next September.'

I stared at him in disbelief. 'But if I choose to go now, there's nothing you can do to stop me.'

'True; but there's also nothing to stop me from suing the balls off you for breach of contract. I don't know if your finances are stable enough to take something like that.'

'You'd try that? Under these circumstances?'

Simon nodded. 'If I have to.'

'Then you're an even lower bastard than I had you down for.'

Simon shook his head and smiled benevolently, as though he

was a schoolteacher dealing with a particularly petulant child. 'That's how you see it *now* Tom, but you're angry, irrational. Let me explain it to you this way. I'm not treating you badly. I'm simply looking to put *Metrosound* up at the top of the heap and I'm offering to take you up there with it. Think about it! Do you like what you're doing for us now? I mean, *Nightboat* is an amusing little show but it's hardly putting you in the tax-exile bracket, is it?'

'Listen, you bastard, you got me into this mess in the first place!'

'No, you listen! This thing is going to put your face on every newspaper, every television set, every chat show that's going. Fame is fame, Tom, it doesn't particularly matter how you come by it. Look on this as a convenient stepping-stone. I've always told you that you are not achieving your full potential in this business. You've got the talent but you haven't had the breaks. Not until now. Come next September, when Cliff Monroe leaves to take up his stint for Auntie Beeb, there's going to be a seat vacant for our breakfast show. Suddenly we're not talking cult programme any more; and we're not talking the kind of cat-farting salary you've been used to. We're talking one and a half million listeners, we're talking high-profile media personality and mostly we're talking about unlocking a whole series of doors that have previously been closed to you. You've always had a desire to get into television, haven't you? Well kid, you're twenty-eight years old, you aren't going to get any more opportunities like this one.' He paused to extract a menthol cigarette from a box on his desk. He lit it with a gold lighter and blew out a cloud of smoke. 'It's your last chance, Tom. Don't be a fool. Take it. Grab it with both hands and hang on tight. And stuff the goody two-shoes routine. Frankly, it's not your style.'

I sat there feeling a cold hatred fill me. I wanted to tell him what to do with his filthy plans and his lousy radio station; but in the self-same instant, an awful truth dawned on me. I knew with a terrible conviction that I would go along with it. Despite the disgust and guilt that would inevitably claim me, I would do it. Why? Because I had always wanted a shot at stardom. Because I had always been ambitious and believed that fate had conspired to cheat me of success. And mostly because I was unhappy with my lot and this sorry affair might conceivably offer me a way out, an opportunity to fry bigger fish.

Simon was smiling confidently now. He had me and he knew it. He got up from his seat and walked over to his well-stocked cocktail cabinet. He took out a bottle of Scotch and two tumblers. 'A little drinkie-poo,' he purred. 'Just to unofficially seal the bargain. Then we'll sit down and discuss how you'll handle the press conference.'

'The . . . press conference?'

'Sure. I've invited the whole media circus over. They'll arrive in a couple of hours. You're going to meet them and tell them exactly what they want to hear; and you'll make damn sure that you mention the name of the station at regular five-minute intervals.'

I studied my fingernails shamefully. I felt like a regular Judas. 'You went ahead and organised it,' I muttered. 'You must have been pretty confident that I'd play ball.'

Simon smiled graciously and poured out two generous measures of whisky. He handed one to me and raised his own glass in a mocking toast.

'To John,' he said. 'And to success.'

The whisky tasted bitter going down; but I drank it. God help me, I drank it just the same.

Chapter Three

I pulled the car to a halt outside Karen's apartment building and sat there for a while, enjoying the silence. The day had not been a good one and I was left feeling like I needed a hot shower.

The press conference had been hellish; I'd found myself besieged by a veritable army of rumpled journalists exuding a collective fog of cigarette smoke and sour whisky fumes, all of them seemingly intent on extracting the sleaziest possible story from me. After that, I'd thought that making a statement to the police would prove a comparatively simple matter, but I was wrong. When I got to the station, I was taken to an incident room they'd set up. It was chaos in there, people running around, phones ringing, computer equipment being installed. Drayton took me into a separate office and set about giving me the third degree, going over the facts again and again, even making me look at photographs of the murdered woman. If he had seemed stand-offish the night before, he was now downright unpleasant. Several times, I had to remind myself that I wasn't one of the suspects. Drayton managed to make me feel as though I was and I was grateful that, if nothing else, I had a cast-iron alibi.

I glanced at my watch. It was just after three o'clock and the grey, drizzly day was already succumbing to darkness. I hoped that Karen wouldn't give me a hard time, something she was pretty adept at. That would be the last straw. I got out of the car, locked it and crossed the road to her building. As I approached the communal entrance, the front door opened and a thin bearded fellow wearing a leather biker's jacket stepped out, almost colliding with me. He stood for a moment, smiling oddly, as though he had recognised me and was about to ask for an autograph or something. But then he stepped aside, holding the swinging door open before it could lock itself, allowing me to enter without using the intercom. I nodded my thanks and went through, relieved. I have always hated being recognised and I was not in the best mood to deal with the sycophantic drivel of one of my listeners. Then it occurred to me that maybe he was actually one of Karen's young men, she had more than she cared to admit to. I toyed with the idea of confronting her, but thought better of it. She would only deny it anyway. Despite everything that had happened since we broke up, she was always defensive about her conquests, as though she wanted to give the impression that she'd been wearing sackcloth and ashes since the divorce.

I went straight up the staircase, halted at the familiar stripped-pine door and rang the bell. The sound of sustained, synthesised chords from within told me that Karen was working and I was obliged to wait for a lull in the music, before ringing again. The noise came to an abrupt halt and a few moments later Karen opened the door. Her thin, androgynous figure was draped in a garishly striped jumpsuit and she'd had her blonde hair cropped even shorter than usual. The result made her look as though she was on day-release from Aushwitz, but I decided not to comment on it. She stood there a moment, eyeing me critically.

'You made it then,' she announced flatly, which struck me as a pretty obvious remark. 'I was hoping you'd be here earlier. Danny will be home from school soon.'

I shrugged an apology. 'It's been a bit of a day,' I told her.

'Hmm.' She was clearly unconvinced by the excuse. I followed her into the spacious and meticulously tidy front-room of the flat. 'Help yourself to a drink,' she said over her shoulder. 'I just want to get this bit sorted out.' She moved over to a bank of electronic keyboards, set against one wall of the room. A television and video stood alongside and she hit the 'play' button, resuming the slow, vaguely oriental theme she had been working on earlier. I watched the screen dutifully for a moment. The camera panned slowly across a desert landscape, towards the distant ruins of what looked like an Egyptian temple. In the bottom of the screen, a digital display ticked away the seconds. Karen seemed intent on her work but I knew that she was only posing, wanting to demonstrate how bloody successful she was.

32

I'd always found this 'Look Mum, no hands!' tendency irritating. I moved to the other side of the room and helped myself to a large gin and tonic from the drinks cabinet.

'Want anything?' I called over my shoulder.

She shook her head disdainfully. To Karen, the idea of a drink before six p.m. was unthinkable. For all her desperately urban chic, she was in many ways a real prude. I busied myself with an ice-cube tray, reflecting that I had been married to this woman for nine years. Now the idea seemed faintly surreal. We were little more than kids when we got married. I have no idea at what point I stopped loving her, but I suspect that my feelings for her declined in direct proportion to the way her career took off. When I first met Karen, she was an energetic young music-graduate who played in bar bands for pin money; these days, she was considered hot stuff, one of the most eagerly sought-after musicians in the business. She was writing scores for cinema and television, making a disgusting amount of money and was on first-name terms with famous actors and film directors. With my own career in permanent stagnation, it had become surprisingly easy to resent her every move.

It was only after we split up that I learned from various friends about her occasional affairs over the years; 'flings' is the word she liked to use. I'd had no inkling of them while I was actually living with her and in retrospect I was only angry that she had never told me the truth to my face. I knew now that whatever was left of my feelings for her would always be coloured by the fact that I trusted her just about as far as I could throw her.

Jamie was quite a different creature. After only a comparatively short time together, I would have trusted her with my life. It sometimes worried me that I had given myself so readily to her. In all the time I'd spent with Karen, I'd never let her in under my defences. That was half the problem. But Jamie had arrived so suddenly in my life, perhaps I'd not had time to put up the barriers. She was the complete antithesis to Karen: considerate, easy-going and slovenly. She had no more than a clutch of O'levels to her name and probably thought Antonioni was something she might order in an Italian restaurant. Naturally, Karen had never forgiven me for throwing her over for somebody like that. The two women had never met. A pity. It would have been quite an occasion, provided you were standing at a safe distance.

Karen seemed satisfied. She switched off the video and stepped back from the keyboards with a slight nod of self-congratulation. She turned to look at me. 'What do you think?' she asked.

'Not bad. A horror film, is it?'

'A documentary!' she retorted scornfully. 'I finished the horror weeks ago. This is the series for Beeb Two. *Lap of the Gods.* Remember, I told you about it?' Then she added casually. 'I just heard we've got Geilgud to narrate.'

'Oh, that's nice. Who?'

'Sir John Geilgud.' She spoke slowly as though to a difficult child. I continued to feign ignorance. There was no way I was going to give her the satisfaction of being visibly impressed. 'I'm having drinks with him on Friday,' she added.

'How absolutely spiffing. You said something about Danny?'

Karen put her hands on her hips and shook her head in a pitying sort of way. Then she motioned me to the sofa. She came and sat beside me. 'I got a phone call from the headmistress at his school. A Miss Ward.' She lowered her voice as though confiding an awful secret. 'She said Danny's been involved in a fight.'

'Has he been injured or something?'

'No, nothing like that. Apparently it happened some days ago, I didn't even know about it . . .'

I shrugged. 'All kids get into fights,' I said dismissively. 'We used to thump the shit out of each other at school. Did she say if he won?'

Karen glared at me. 'That's hardly an issue, now is it? Besides, it's not just that, he's been very moody lately. Miss Ward said that he's been inattentive in class. And lately he's been very uncommunicative with me.'

'Oh dear. Well, it's probably just a phase.'

'There's more. He . . . he swore at me the other day.'

'Swore at you? That doesn't sound like Danny. What did he say?'

Karen frowned. 'I told him he couldn't stay up to watch a film and he said I was a . . . well, if you must know, he called me a silly twat.'

I tried not to smile. 'Well Karen, that's not too dreadful, is it? He's probably been tuning in to his old man's radio show on the quiet.'

'He'd better not have been.' Karen made no secret of her contempt for *Nightboat*. In her book, it rated on a level with *Mein Kampf* and extracts from the Klu Klux Klan's bumper fun-book for boys. 'Anyway, I'm not having him talk to me like that. The next thing you know, he'll be using the "F" word.'

'Hmm. Well, I'll have a chat with him when he gets in, shall I? He's probably just heard somebody at school saying it. I wouldn't worry.'

'But I *do* worry! It's no picnic raising the boy on my own, you know. And, frankly, I'd appreciate a little more help from you. It's obvious why he's upset, he just doesn't see enough of you. If you'd make the effort to get over and see him more often . . .'

I sighed. Here ten minutes and she was already on to her favourite subject. It was a wonder she hadn't arranged a violin accompaniment.

'Yes Karen, I know, I know. But it's difficult to find the time. Especially lately, with Jamie and I working different shifts.'

Karen pursed her lips and looked disapproving, something she habitually did when Jamie's name was introduced into a conversation. 'I don't see that it's anything to do with her,' she griped. 'Daniel is your son and you have responsibilities to him. Just because she resents it every time you come round here . . .'

'*She* has a name, Karen. And Jamie doesn't resent Daniel, not one bit. But you have to appreciate that Jamie and I need time to be together.'

'Oh, spare me the great love story, purrrlease! How is the lady with the lamp, still giving your erogenous zones a decent work-out? Or has that worn off a little?'

I sipped at my drink. 'I hardly think you're the one to talk about erogenous zones, dear. Who are you knocking off at the moment? The French director with the Camembert complexion? Or is it that lisping toyboy who carries a spear in *Hamlet*?'

'You know perfectly well neither of those were serious relationships.' She looked suitably soulful. 'There was only one real relationship in my life and you chose to put an end to it.'

'Oh really. How inconsiderate of me! I bet that thought never crossed your mind when you were shagging your way through the phone directory.'

She glared at me. 'You're a born exaggerator, do you know that? So, I made a few mistakes, I'd be the first to admit it. But let's face it, if you'd paid a bit more attention to my needs, when I . . .'

I raised a hand to silence her. I needed this, like I needed AIDS. 'Listen Karen, I didn't come here to argue with you. I've had a bellyful today and I was hoping for a few hours of peace and quiet before I go into that madhouse tonight, so . . . just back off a little, all right?'

She must have caught the edge of desperation in my voice. Suddenly, she was all sympathy, wide-eyed and approachable. 'What is it, love? Something to do with work?'

I nodded. 'You'll hear about it soon enough,' I assured her. 'It'll be all over the papers tomorrow.'

'The papers?' That line really rattled her. 'My God, Tom, what's happened?'

I was getting fed up with recounting the previous night's misadventures but I could see there was nothing for it. I told her all about John. She listened, her face becoming graver by the second.

'But that's awful!' she said, when I'd finished. This had to be the understatement of the year. 'That bloody programme. You need to get out of there, fast.'

I grinned ruefully. 'Well, at least that's one thing you and Jamie are in full agreement over. But it's like I said to her, I'm stuck. I'm tied to a contract there and I'm qualified for nothing else.'

'Bollocks! I've already told you what you should be doing. Writing.'

'Oh God, where do you women get your ideas from? Jamie thinks I'm a potential Terry Wogan and now you've got me down for the Pulitzer Prize. I wish I had that kind of confidence in myself.'

Karen shrugged dismissively. 'You've worked as a writer before,' she reminded me.

'Karen, I wrote reviews for a music paper. That doesn't make me Salman bloody Rushdie, now does it? And how the hell would I survive while I was writing the great novel?'

The question remained unanswered as the door opened and a hyperactive bundle of energy burst unexpectedly into the room.

'Dad!' Daniel dropped the painting he was carrying and ran to throw his arms around my neck. I found myself looking into a grinning, excited face, saw my own face mirrored in his too-large blue eyes. I ran a hand fondly through my son's unruly mop of blond hair.

'Hiya buster, how's it going?'

'Great Dad, I did a painting today, the teacher said it was really good.'

'Well, let's have a look at it, shall we?'

The picture was retrieved by Inga, the young au pair who had entered the room several steps behind Daniel. She moved over to hand it to me, smiling in undisguised invitation. She was an attractive, big-boned Norwegian girl, with the kind of body that most women would kill for. She never made any secret of the fact that she worshipped the ground I walked on.

'Hello Mr Prince. I listen to your show, is very funny.'

I stared at her. 'Last night?' I asked her incredulously.

She looked puzzled. 'No, last night I go to the pictures with my friend. Night before, is very funny. I laugh and laugh.'

'Inga, I think perhaps it's time to get Daniel's dinner ready,' interrupted Karen, testily. Inga's interest in me was a constant source of irritation to her.

'Yes, Mrs Prince.' She flashed me another dazzling smile and prowled in the direction of the kitchen. I stared after her thoughtfully. On more than one occasion I had entertained certain fantasies about Inga, but I knew that anything more than fantasies would cause all kinds of problems I could well do without. She didn't live in and for all I knew she probably had some possessive Norwegian boyfriend lurking in the background.

'Look at my picture, Dad! Look at my picture!'

I made a mental effort to get my thoughts back to the present. I found myself looking at a garish powder-paint image of what appeared to be a huge, screaming head covered with splashes of blood. The effect was quite disturbing.

'Oh, that's . . . that's very good,' I said lamely. I passed it to Karen, saw the look of concern that crossed her face.

'It's a monster,' explained Daniel. 'A great big boogie-man monster and he's going to eat you up!'

'Yes, he looks kind of hungry,' I admitted.

Karen got up from the sofa. 'I'll leave you two to have a chat,' she said, glancing meaningfully at me. 'Will you be staying to dinner?'

I shook my head. 'Can't tonight. Jamie's expecting me home.'

Karen scowled, but said nothing. She went into the kitchen. Daniel slipped an arm around me and sat there, looking sheepishly down at his scuffed trainers, aware that he was in some kind of trouble.

'Danny, your mum tells me you've been fighting,' I said quietly.

Daniel nodded.

'Want to tell me what happened?'

He shrugged. 'Just a fight,' he said evasively.

'Hmm. Did you start it?'

Daniel shook his head, then grinned. 'I finished it,' he said. 'These two lads, they started pushing me around. Well, I had to punch them, didn't I? Sometimes, you just have to.'

I tried to look stern. 'Well, your mum doesn't like it, so take it easy, all right?'

Daniel nodded. 'OK,' he said.

'And what's this about you calling your mother a bad name?'

Daniel scowled at his feet, his face colouring a little. 'She wouldn't let me watch *Time Blasters*. It was only eight o'clock.'

'You could have asked her to video it for you.'

'I did. She said it was . . .' He struggled to repeat the half-remembered phrase. 'Reactional 'Merican violence and it wasn't no good for me.'

'I see.' I looked at him for a moment and then added quietly. 'Jesus. What a twat!'

Daniel glanced up at me and his face broke into a grin. We laughed together conspiratorially and I slipped an arm around his narrow shoulders. It was at rare moments like this that I missed Daniel terribly and wished there was some way we could always be together. But the thought was irrational. Karen was a good mother and if it ever came to a fight for custody, she'd win hands down, no contest.

'She won't let me listen to your programme, neither,' complained Daniel. 'She keeps sayin' "when I'm older". How old do I have to be to listen to you, Dad?'

I stopped laughing. It was a damned good question. 'Just . . . older,' I replied. 'Don't worry. I'm keeping it all on tape for you. One day the two of us will sit down together and listen to it. Maybe you'll be able to explain it to me.'

'How d'you mean.'

'Oh, nothing.' I cast around for a suitable way of changing the subject. 'Hey, it's coming on Christmas. What would you like Santa to bring you? I take it you still believe in Santa?'

'Course I do. I saw him in a film once. And you took me to see him in town, last year, remember? You gonna take me this year?'

'Sure I am. Wouldn't miss it for the world.'

Daniel smiled excitedly. 'Great,' he said. 'And Dad, d'you think he might bring me a *Time Blasters* laser gun, the one with the back pack that makes all those weird noises?'

I smiled. 'I should think there's a very good chance,' I said. 'If you play your cards right. That means no more fighting and no more swearing. Think you can handle that?'

'Sure.' He paused for a moment and then an expression came over him, a distinctly sneaky one. 'Dad, I wish you'd come and live here again. Like you used to. Mum's always saying she wishes you would and I—'

I glanced at my watch, interrupted the flow of emotional blackmail that I knew would inevitably follow. Sooner or later it always came back to this. Karen had been working on the kid, she had him well trained. 'Gotta go now, Danny,' I said. 'Things to do. Say goodbye to your mum for me.'

'But Dad . . .'

I gave Daniel a swift peck on the cheek. 'I'll give you a ring about Santa, OK?'

Danny sniffed and nodded, went back to the scrutiny of his feet. He looked small and somehow pathetic sitting there alone, but I steeled myself to move away. I let myself out and went quickly down the stairs, hating myself but knowing it was the only sane course of action. Karen was easy to cope with, but the kid really got to me sometimes. I had to keep myself distanced from that. Otherwise it hurt bad and I'd never been much good at coping with emotional pain.

Coward, I thought. *Always running away. You can run but you can't hide.*

Outside it was dark and a light drizzle was falling. I got into the car and drove away, not glancing up at the lit windows of the flat, knowing that Daniel would almost certainly be watching me, his nose pushed up against the glass. I swore bitterly beneath my breath and flicked the switch of the radio, letting the music envelope me as I drove home.

When I stepped through the *Metrosound* entrance that night, everything seemed different. It was as though I was seeing the place for the first time. Outwardly nothing had changed: the same hessian-covered walls, the same inane photographs of grinning DJs. Dave Hibbert's toneless voice droned through the usual series of sensational reports freshly made up by the people in the newsroom. Tonight, it was teenage terror-gangs, high on crack and armed with Uzi machine-pistols, apparently raping anyone or anything that got in their way. But no matter how predictable the news was, something was different, the air seemed to tingle with an electric charge of apprehension the moment the glass door swung shut behind me. For once, Julie transferred her attention from the paperback she was reading and appraised me from behind the barrier of the reception desk, her brown, cow-like eyes seeming to stare straight through me for an instant. Then she favoured me with a forced smile and handed me a pile of notes with one pudgy hand. 'Requests,' she said brightly. 'They've been coming in all day.'

I took the considerable pile from her and glanced at the top sheet.

'Why don't you go fuck yourself?' it read. There was no name to go with the message. I tried not to let the shock register on my face.

'They're not all like that,' Julie assured me hastily. 'Some of them are genuine.'

'Uh huh.' I pushed the notes into the pocket of my jacket and headed for the studio doors. I was aware of Julie's eyes burning into the back of my neck as I went through and I couldn't help feeling that she'd enjoyed watching my reaction, that it had probably made her night worthwhile. I couldn't imagine why she might have cause to enjoy my predicament. As far as I was aware, I had always treated her well enough. I felt edgy already. The planned romantic supper with Jamie had not gone well. People at the hospital had been talking about last night's show and Jamie didn't really know what to say to me. The atmosphere between us had been strained to say the least and the hoped-for horizontal refreshment simply hadn't materialised. I get particularly wound up when I haven't had sex for a while. I suppose it's the one time when I really open up, reveal the poor sorry creature that lurks behind the façade.

As I helped myself to my usual beverage from the machine, Ray Wood stopped in the doorway of the alcove and cleared his throat. 'Hell of a business, last night,' he said. 'You must feel like shit.'

'I've felt better,' I admitted.

'Yeah well . . . anything I can do to help mate, just ask.'

I turned and studied Ray for a moment. He was a chubby, big-jowled man, his head prematurely balding. I noticed that his shirt-collar was frayed around the edges and that he had a large, red boil on his chin. It occurred to me that I had never really looked at him closely before. We'd never been anything more than passing acquaintances. Then another more troubling thought struck me. I wasn't close to anyone at *Metrosound*. There ought to be somebody there I could talk to, confide in. Always the loner, that was my trouble.

'Thanks,' I muttered awkwardly. 'Appreciate it.'

Ray smiled sadly, seemed to be on the point of saying something else. But he simply nodded and moved on along the corridor.

I headed for Studio One and went inside. From behind his glass screen, Dave Hibbert raised his eyebrows in greeting and went on with his news report.

'An Asian family were forced to leave their Moss Side home after a vicious fire-bomb attack left it totally gutted last night. Mr and Mrs Mumtaz complained of victimisation by neighbours, some of whom are active members of the National Front. A police spokesman said . . .'

Steve Acton stood by the mixing desk, adjusting a loose fader with a screwdriver. He made an effort not to look up at me as I slipped into my seat and began preparing for the show. I let the bastard sweat it out for a few moments before I spoke to him.

'How much did they pay you?' I asked him, matter of factly.

Steve glanced up, feigning puzzlement. 'Sorry?' he muttered.

'Don't come the innocent with me, you fat bastard. How much did you get for shopping me to the papers last night?'

Steve's corpulent face presented a picture of outraged innocence.

'I don't know what you're on about,' he protested.

'Yes you do,' I assured him. 'You're the only one who could have got the news to them in time. And don't try and tell me you did it out of the goodness of your heart.'

'Look, all I did was report some facts. I figured it was my duty—'

'Your duty! Do me a favour!' I dropped an album on to the turntable and cued the first track. In the glass booth, Dave was already moving on to the weather forecast. I glared at Steve. 'Listen,' I said, 'I have to work with you and that's my bad luck. But you put one flabby foot wrong from here on and I'll take the greatest pleasure in punching your teeth down your throat.'

'You can try,' snarled Steve. 'I don't know who the fuck you think you are, anyway. At least I can go home after this show and sleep soundly. At least I'm not responsible for some poor tart lying there with her throat cut.'

I felt a surge of anger pulse through me. I began to rise out of my chair, with every intention of punching the bastard clear out of the studio; but then I heard my cue from Dave. My hand moved automatically to slip in a cart.

'*Metrosound* Radio! The greatest sound around!'

I dropped back into my seat, hit the start-up button on the nearest deck and swamped the airwaves with the introduction to a Steely Dan track. 'You really are a piece of shit, Acton,' I observed. Then slid up the fader, leaned closer to the mike and spoke into it. 'Ahoy landlubbers! This is Captain Tom Prince welcoming you aboard the *Nightboat* for another four hours of mirth, myth and musical mayhem. The lines are open and tonight's theme is luuuurve! Is there enough of it in the world? Brotherly love, sisterly love, love thy neighbour! And where does love end and lust begin? Are they one and the same thing? The number is 226 1234! Phone in now and air your views. But first, a classic plank-spanker from the Dan. 'Rikki Don't Lose That Number'! And don't lose our number either. I'll give it you again, 226 1234. Let's groooooove!'

I slid the fader down and turned my attention back to Steve Acton, who was still standing there, his face grim, his huge fists clenched.

'Well?' I said.

'Well, what?'

'Get your fat arse next door and answer the phones.'

Steve scowled, took a halting step nearer to the desk; but then, typically, thought better of it. He sneered, turned and waddled obediently through the connecting door. A moment later, I saw him donning his headphones and taking the first call. I took the notes from my pocket and spread them out on the desk, sifting through them for the genuine requests. There were just three of them. The rest were abusive, all of them lacking a name. *Cowards*, I thought. *Cowardly scum*. Well, it didn't matter. Sticks and stones. I could handle that . . . I honestly thought I could. I would learn in time. I crumpled the notes into a ball and threw them in the direction of the litter bin.

And then I was waiting. Waiting for a call I dreaded receiving. But, though the murder was the only subject anybody wanted to talk about, John didn't phone. Not that night, anyway.

Chapter Four

Kevin was a prize jerk. I knew that the moment he came on the air, the way he ignored the official topic for discussion that evening and went, instead, straight for the proverbial jugular.

'It's a publicity stunt, isn't it?' he said. 'This John character. It's something you've cooked up to improve the ratings.'

I sighed, lit another cigarette. It was on nights like this one that the real retards came slithering out of the woodwork. 'What makes you say that, Kevin?' I asked.

'Because it's the sort of thing a radio station would do.' Kevin had an annoying accent that I placed somewhere to the North of the city limits, an exaggerated yobbish tone that fairly smacked of the streets. It was strange, but I had a good idea of what he would look like. He'd have that weird Mancunian haircut, all spiky on top, the back and sides razored to a stubble. A thin face with eyes that carried a constant 'I am hard' message. And almost certainly, the ultimate accessory, A T-shirt which bore the message 'And on the eighth day, God created Manchester.'

'An expert on radio are you, Kevin?'

'Not really. But I know what goes on, like. And you're not telling me that all the publicity you're getting won't be good for the programme.'

'You could be right about that,' I admitted. 'But tell me, Kevin, if it is just a stunt, how do you explain the coverage in the newspapers and on the television? More importantly, how do you account for the existence of a new corpse in the city morgue? Do you really think I'd go that far to get some publicity?'

'How do I know there's a corpse? I mean, I haven't *seen* it, have I?'

'You haven't seen *air* but it's there. You're breathing it, unfortunately.'

'And as for the news and all that . . . well, you could all be in it together, couldn't you? Helping each other out, like.'

'Oh, right . . . well, of course, Kevin, you're absolutely on the ball there. What you've uncovered is a major conspiracy. And naturally, everyone is in on it. Everyone from the Director General at the BBC right on down to Captain Birdseye. Your local councillor is in on it. The police force are in on it. Even your milkman is in on it. Everyone in fact, except you. And do you know why? Because, Kevin, you are terminally stupid. We had a meeting before we started all this and we said we'd let everyone in that had an IQ above three. You were the only one who didn't meet the basic requirement.'

'All right, all right, there's no need to be sarky! I just phoned in to give you an opinion . . .'

'That's not an opinion, Kevin. That's the oral equivalent of a wet fart.' I cut him off and glanced at the next name on the list. 'Let's go over to Sally in Middleton. Hello Sally, you're through to the Captain. Your views on love, please.'

'I feel sorry for him, actually.'

'For who, Sally?' As if I didn't know . . .

'For John. To do what he's done, he must be so lonely, so frightened.'

'We all get frightened and lonely, Sally. Most of us don't go out and murder someone, do we?'

'No . . .' A pause while Sally got her liberal brain-cells into gear. I sketched a mental picture of her while I waited: a thin, awkward girl in her late twenties, with unfashionably long hair and sensible clothes. She probably attended a lot of meetings at the town hall and still lived with her parents. She almost certainly had never been laid. I pictured her sitting on a bed in a little room that was decorated in a tacky pink-gingham wallpaper. On the bed was a selection of cuddly toys, all in that same lurid pink. The telephone receiver she was holding was pink. On the wall above her was one of those 'Love Is . . .' cartoons in a pink plastic frame.

'I'm . . . I'm not trying to condone what he's done, Tom. The taking of a human life is a mortal sin. But you see, I work for the Social Services. And I can tell you that it's the society we live in that creates people like John. He probably had a terrible childhood.'

'My childhood wasn't exactly Disneyland,' I argued. 'Despite that, I grew up amazingly psychosis-free. Apart from a rampant desire to use my cut-off button from time to time, I'd say I'm a fairly well-adjusted human being.'

'Not everyone's as strong as you, Tom! Some people are fragile, like flowers. Easily crushed. I see John as a victim of society.'

'Oh really. So if he comes knocking at your door one of these nights, I suppose you'll be offering him a course in basketwork while he's attempting to take your head off with a chainsaw?'

'That's disgusting! You shouldn't make jokes about things like that.'

'It wasn't meant as a joke, Sally. It just seems to me that it's very easy to forgive from a safe distance. If Margaret Donavan was in any position to speak on her own behalf, I doubt if forgiveness would be the first thing on her mind.' I cut Sally off before she could reply and went on to another caller. 'OK, come in Eddie from Edgeley. And perhaps we could make an effort to change the —'

'They should fry the bastard for what he's done!' Eddie's voice sounded like it was reverberating through a body that weighed in excess of twenty stone.

'I'm sorry, Sally, I thought I'd cut you off . . .'

Eddie sounded genuinely puzzled. 'No Tom, this is Eddie,' he protested.

'Oh, I'm sorry. Your tone was so similar to our last caller, I got confused. Well, for your information Eddie, we don't fry people in this country. Neither do we grill them, poach them, or make them into a fricassee. We don't even hang them any more. And most rational people would argue that life imprisonment is a very effective deterrent.'

'Bollocks,' said Eddie, who clearly wasn't a man to mince words. 'That's bullshit. See, Tom, I've spent a lot of time working in Saudi. Over there, they know how to handle this kind of thing. They let the punishment fit the crime. Like, for instance, if you steal something they cut off your hand. And if you rape somebody . . .'

'They cut off your electricity supply. Yes, yes, Eddie, most effective I'm sure. And doubtless if you were the Prime Minister of this country . . .'

'. . . I'd introduce the electric chair, no problem. They still use it in the States, don't they?'

'In parts of it, yes. Where violent crime is much more prevalent than here and rising all the time. So it's not really a deterrent, is it?'

'Well, it . . .'

'Is it, Eddie?'

'I reckon . . .'

'Eddie, answer the question! It's not really a deterrent, *is it*?'

'You can't compare them, can you? It's a more violent society anyway.'

'You brought up the subject, not me.'

'All right, but look, all I'm saying is this. If you have a cancer, right, what do the doctors do?'

'They put you on a five-year waiting list.'

'No, they cut it right out, don't they? And if you have a mad dog, if you've got any sense, you have it put down. That's what I'd do with this John character. Then he wouldn't bother anybody ever again, would he? I'm just sick to death of listening to bleeding-heart lefties like the woman who was just on, who let psychos like him get away with murder. If I had my way, I'd put his ass in the chair and fry it till it was medium rare.'

'Right. And no doubt you'd volunteer to throw the switch, wouldn't you?'

'I'd be the first in the queue. And it would be a long queue, believe me!'

'Oh, I don't doubt that, Eddie. And I don't suppose you'd be interested in comparisons between your behaviour and John's. You wouldn't be very pleased if I pointed out that you would simply be performing institutionalised murder.'

'The bible says, "An eye for an eye, a tooth for a tooth." '

'Ah, that old chestnut. So you're a religious person, are you? Go to church every Sunday, do you?'

'No, I'm not religious. I just think the bible makes good sense, that's all.'

'Well, you've dug your own grave there, haven't you? The bible also says, "Thou shalt not kill." I don't recall there being anything like, "Thou canst fry someone's ass in the chair if they are clearly psychopathic." '

That stumped him. I could imagine his underused brain creaking and grinding as he searched frantically for an appropriate retort.

'People like you always have a smartarse answer, don't they?' he complained bitterly. 'But you're just playing with words, that's all. You don't have any real answers.'

'I know the answer I'd like to give you, Eddie. Unfortunately, my contract forbids me from using language like that on the air. So let's simply part company.'

I punched the cut-off button, patched in the next caller. 'All right, Jack in Swinton. You're through to the Captain.'

A long pause. Then a familiar whispering voice.

'Hello, old son. It's not Jack. It's John. I used a false name. I just phoned to say that you're next on my list, Tom. I'm going to be waiting for you tonight . . .'

For a few seconds only, I was fooled. I felt a quickening of the heart, a crawling sensation beneath my scalp. But then I realised that the voice didn't have quite the same tone, the same edge of menace. It was a fair impersonation, but an impersonation all the same.

'I have just one thing to say to you,' I interrupted. 'Grow up!'

There was another pause; then the speaker attempted to continue, but was suddenly taken by a fit of hysterical laughter. His voice was instantly joined by that of an accomplice who contributed a loud raspberry to the proceedings. Then the phone was slammed down.

'An eloquent testimonial there to the benefits of lobotomy,' I said. 'No, but seriously, I laughed till I stopped. Time for a record-break, I think.' I cued a track, removed my headphones and leaned back in my chair with a sigh. The standard of repartee on the show was never very high, but tonight it seemed to have sunk to an all-time low.

The connecting door opened and Steve came through. The expression on his face suggested that he had not forgotten or forgiven our skirmish earlier that night. He dropped a bunch of notes on the desk and handed me a couple of advertising carts destined for the next slot. I glanced at the latter with interest, noting the names of two new advertisers, a building society and a theme park in Morecambe. I raised my eyebrows and glanced at Steve.

'Looks like we're going up in the world,' I observed.

'Makes a change from bleeding miracle spot-cream,' he muttered. He was referring to one of our longest running ads, a company who had taken a five-year contract to promote an anti-acne product. We had both heard the ads so often, we could have quoted them word for word. Perhaps Simon's forecast of an influx of new advertisers hadn't been so wide of the mark.

'By the way, Steve,' I said. 'That last call. You're supposed to weed out wankers like that before they ever get to me. It's part of your job, you know.'

Steve shrugged. 'Bloke sounded on the level,' he said. 'How was I supposed to know he was going to pull a stunt like that?'

'I don't know how, Steve. Just use your head in future, OK?'

Steve grinned maliciously. 'What's the problem? Starting to get to you, is it?' He traced one stubby finger across the top of the mixing desk. 'What you going to do when he phones back?'

'*If* he phones back,' I corrected him.

'Oh, he will. Just a matter of time, I reckon.'

I shrugged. 'I'll cross that bridge when I get to it,' I said. I studied him for a moment, never the most pleasant of pastimes. I noted a smudge of dried tomato-ketchup at the side of his mouth and felt another irrational desire to hit him, but with an effort I pushed it aside. 'When he first rang up . . . didn't you think he sounded odd? I mean, that weird voice and everything. Didn't you even think about passing him over?'

'It's no good crying over spilt milk. Anyway, you know the policy here, we can't discriminate against a caller just because he has a funny voice. You have to let them on even if they sound like Elmer Fudd.'

'And he didn't seem suspicious in any way?'

Steve glared at me. 'Well, he didn't say he wanted to talk about murder, now did he? Said he had a point to make about immigration. Anyway, it's your own fault. If you'd cut the bastard off the minute he started in on that killing stuff, you wouldn't be in this mess, would you?'

I thought about that. How one brief, simple action might have made a difference. It might have changed the course of my life as things turned out. I'd hesitated, just for a moment, and then somehow it had all been too late. I was to spend a lot more nights thinking about that over the next few months.

'Nothing would have changed really,' I argued. 'The girl would still be dead.'

'But not all over the airwaves, she wouldn't. Trouble is, people are always going to link the two things now. Murder . . . and *Nightboat*. And whenever somebody mentions your name . . .'

'Yes, all right, Steve, I get the general idea!' I indicated the record which was fast approaching its fade-out. 'Let's get back to it, shall we? And do me a favour. Try and find me one or two callers who have more than double figures in brain cells, OK?'

He sneered and made for the exit. The smug expression on his face suggested that he felt he'd scored a victory, ample revenge for the bollocking I'd given him earlier that evening. Once again I wondered how much he'd been paid for dishing the dirt on me. There was no such thing as professional integrity in this business. The dole queues were littered with former jocks who'd washed their dirty laundry in public, via the newspapers. I reminded myself that my own brush with the tabloids was due this very morning. It was not a comforting thought.

I put on my headphones, opened the mike channel and came in over the record's fade-out.

'The very excellent and wonderful New Order there with "Blue Monday". OK, back to the discussion, if we can dignify it with that title. And let me take the opportunity to remind you that, officially, we are talking about aspects of love. So I would appreciate it if tonight's callers would cooperate. Over to . . .' I glanced at my notes '. . . Marion in Hulme. Marion, you're through to the Captain. Your views on *love*, please.'

'I . . . I'm sorry, Tom, I have to talk about the murder, I'm afraid.'

I rolled my eyes towards the ceiling and held back an expletive. 'Look Marion, I think I've about exhausted my interest in that particular subject.'

'But you see, it's very important!'

'I'll give you just five seconds to come up with another one and then I'm afraid I'll have to cut you off.'

'Please don't do that, Tom. You see . . .'

'Five, four, three, come on Marion!'

'I just have to . . .'

'Two, one . . .'

'Pleeeeeease!'

I froze in my seat, struck rigid by the desperation in her voice. It had been a shriek of genuine despair.

'Marion?'

'My name's Marion Donavan, you see. Margaret is . . . was my daughter.'

The silence was so intense I could hear it hissing like steam from the big studio-speakers. I glanced up and saw Steve watching me intently through the glass screen. The expression of surprise on his face assured me that he had not known about this. Even he wouldn't have stooped this low. My mouth started working but nothing much came out, just a sort of brief groan.

'Tom? Mr Prince, are you still there?' I was struck by how refined she sounded. A nice, middle-class lady, I decided, who under normal circumstances wouldn't have come within a hundred miles of a show like mine. Just an indication of how desperate she must be.

'Yes, Marion,' I said glumly. 'I'm listening.'

'I hope you don't mind me calling. I know that Margaret was a big fan of your programme and I . . . I was sitting here alone, thinking about what happened and I wanted to talk to somebody. I'm a widow, you see.'

Oh no, please, not this, not this. I sat there listening to her voice at the other end of the line. I had the distinct impression that I was growing rapidly smaller, dwindling in my chair until the orb of the microphone hanging above me looked like some great metallic planet.

'They tell me you talked to Margaret a couple of weeks ago. I hadn't spoken to her in ages. Some silly little row we had. I regret it now that it's too late. But I thought you could tell me how she was. How she seemed.'

'Talked' to her! That was a hard one to take. I had ridiculed her, perhaps, made fun of some vocal affectation she'd had. I had patronised her certainly and had even made some innuendo-laden remarks when she had quite innocently said something that I had interpreted as suggestive. And finally, I had hosted her through a pathetic trivia-quiz and awarded her the dubious prize of a *Metrosound* T-shirt. Then I had pressed the button and promptly forgotten all about her. Poor Margaret Donovan, living her tiny life somewhere out there in the ether . . . until John had stepped into that life and ended it.

'She . . . she seemed in very good form, Marion,' I said. 'She struck me as a very intelligent, and very amusing girl.'

'Yes. Yes, she was intelligent. Oh and a good girl too! I feel I have to say that because . . . well, because in the evening paper, I thought there was a suggestion that she might somehow have deserved what she got. Something about her apparently opening the door to the killer. Inviting him in. It seemed that they were suggesting she might be rather less than she was . . .'

'Oh, no, Marion. I don't think there was any intention to . . .'

'It was there, Mr Prince!' Her voice suddenly hostile, rigid with baffled anger. Then softer. 'Oh, I'm sorry. I didn't mean to . . . I'm a little confused just now. Everything seems to be going so fast. I thought, Mr Prince . . . you could tell me, why . . . ?'

'Why, Marion?'

'Why . . . oh, why . . . ?' Her voice caught, snagged on some awful, rotten knowledge that lay just beneath the surface of her composure. It trembled at the very edge of total grief. 'Why did it happen to her, Mr Prince? Why her? A good girl like that? And all the truly wicked people in the world, getting away with terrible things every day of their miserable lives . . . ! Why her? Why?' Her voice dissolved into a helpless wail, a powerful heartrending display of sheer anguish. I sat there listening to the sobs exploding in my earphones and I had no answers to give her, nothing that could lessen the awful pain of her misery. I thought of what Eddie had said a few minutes earlier. 'You're just playing with words. You don't have any real answers.' He had been right about that much at least.

My hand moved to the panic button and hesitated, trembling slightly. What did I do now? Cut her off, like I would cut off some idiot who was winding me up? Should I put on a record perhaps? An uplifting jolly singalong, grindingly inappropriate to the situation? Or should I just slam in an advertising cart with its wacky endorsements for spot cream and building societies?

I sat there in an agony of indecision and then, luckily for me, the woman got control of herself.

'I'm sorry,' she gasped. 'I shouldn't have called. I'm very sorry.' She put the phone down. And suddenly, automatically, I went into a spiel, so false, so patronising, that I wanted to bite back the words even as they tumbled turd-like from my lips. And as I talked, my hands were thumbing through the record racks, looking for the right song: a heart-tugging, sensitive ballad to display to the world at large what an absolute *brick* I was. I heard my own voice delivering a creepy monologue and it was as though I were observing somebody else entirely, a man I didn't know and didn't like very much.

'I think everybody listening tonight will appreciate the very special kind of courage it took for Marion to make that call. I'm going to interrupt the flow for a moment and play a song now, which I'd like to dedicate to the memory of a very special girl, Margaret Donavan.'

I found the perfect record. 'The wind beneath my wings.' Nothing like a dose of glitzy, Hollywood sentimentality when your ass is on the line! I managed to get it cued up and running without missing so much as a beat. I considered what I had just done. It was a display of the kind of phoney, professional sentiment I had always despised and yet it had come naturally, without even thinking about it. Now all I had to do was to get to the end of the show without throwing up.

I saw Steve's face peering at me through the glass screen. He looked genuinely impressed and he was holding up one hand, the thumb and forefinger describing a circle. *Nice one*, his eyes seemed to say. *You handled that well.*

I began to feel a little bit afraid of what was happening to me. I didn't want to earn the admiration of people like Steve Acton. I didn't want to become adept at defusing genuine grief with phoney sentiment. But perhaps it was already too late to worry. I had the impression that I was setting out on a long journey across dark, forbidding waters. I didn't know my eventual destination. I just knew I would have been far happier to stay right where I was.

Chapter Five

'I thought you deserved breakfast in bed this morning,' announced Jamie. She placed the wicker tray down carefully in front of me. I lay there, red-eyed after a sleepless night, thinking that breakfast was about the last thing I wanted right now. Jamie was still wearing her pyjamas and glancing at the clock, I noted that she had got up half an hour earlier than usual. I stared at the tray, unable even to feign an interest in food. All my favourites were there. Two boiled eggs, marmite toasted soldiers, Greek yoghurt with honey, a cup of aromatic Earl Grey tea. She had even placed a single long-stemmed rose in a tall glass vase. But I knew she was just trying to soften a blow that I would have to face up to sooner or later. I took a piece of toast and chewed methodically at the corner of it, not even aware of its taste.

'The papers?' I asked her.

She gave me an evasive smile. 'You can look at them later,' she told me. 'Why not have your breakfast first?'

I shook my head. 'The papers,' I said again, a little more firmly this time. She shrugged, got up from the bed, padded dutifully downstairs to collect them.

Reading the papers was an occupational hazard. Since current affairs dictated a good deal of the topics for discussion on *Nightboat*, I always had a wide selection delivered. On this occasion Jamie bought them up and the two of us went grimly through them, one after the other. They ranged from the ill-informed to the downright offensive. In the case of the two tabloids I took, it became difficult to locate one sentence that was based on recognisable fact. Jamie read out a sample extract to me.

'Sexy DJ Tom Prince is known as a bit of a lady-killer in his home town of Manchester; and he's used to hearing anything and everything on his controversial radio programme . . . *Nightbite*.' We exchanged puzzled glances over this misnomer. 'But when he talked about his recent on-air run-in with a *real* lady-killer, the groovy radio Romeo sounded like he had learned his lesson. "I've had all sorts on the show," said Captain Tom, aged twenty-nine, speaking at the offices of *Metrosound* Radio. "But this sicko-psycho was the last straw!" Tom is no stranger to weirdos and headbangers, though. As he confessed to our reporter, "One woman proposed to me over the airwaves and then her husband phoned me up, offering to smash my teeth in. And female fans are always inviting me round for a bit of nookie." On other occasions, some of the Captain's naughty admirers have even sent him pairs of knickers in the post.'

Jamie glanced at me and raised her eyebrows quizzically.

'That's complete bullshit!' I protested. 'I never said any of that! As I recall, the man asked me if I'd ever received anything odd in the post; and I said, "Such as?" And he said, "Women's underwear, stuff like that . . ."'

I felt an abrupt anger course through me and snatching the paper from Jamie's grasp, I crumpled it into a ball and threw it against the nearest wall. 'Jesus, I don't know why the lying bastard bothered to talk to me in the first place! He'd already decided what he was going to say about me. *Nightbite*, for Christ's sake! And they didn't even get my age right!'

'Calm down,' Jamie advised me. 'Tom, you should be used to this kind of thing. You always tell me that *Metrosound* makes up half of its news items.'

'Sure! But this time it's happening to *me*!' I struck the breakfast tray emphatically with my fist, breaking some crockery in the process. 'Oh shit, that's all I needed,' I snarled.

Jamie rescued the tray and set it down out of harm's way. Then she turned back and studied me intently for a moment. 'This is just the start, you know. It's going to get much worse. Are you sure you can take it? Because if you can't, you should pack it in now.'

'I told you,' I said wearily. 'I went through all this with Radcliffe. If I step down, he'll hit me with a law-suit the size of the *Titanic*. That's the last thing we need.'

'I think he could be bluffing.'

'Possibly. . . . but . . .'

'But what?' She looked at me suspiciously, sensing the existence of an ulterior motive. I could never hide anything from her for very long. I started to explain myself, haltingly, but couldn't make it sound like anything other than a sell-out.

'Well, it's just that . . . from what he's saying, it's not all bad news. I mean I . . . I could come out of this well. It could give me that shot at television we were talking about.'

Jamie's eyes widened in surprise. She stood there staring at me as though she could scarcely credit what she had just heard. 'Excuse me?' she murmured. 'Did I get that right? This could be your big break? *This*?' She snatched up the crumpled newspaper from where it had fallen, waved it angrily in front of me. 'This piece of shit?'

I nodded, waved a hand to still her protests. I was finding it very difficult to look her in the eye. 'Yes all right, Jamie, I know it's not exactly *The Times Literary Supplement*. But listen, why not? Why shouldn't something good come out of this? The woman's dead and of course, it's awful, tragic. But there's nothing I can do about that, now is there? So maybe, just for once, I should start thinking about myself here. I'm on the front page of the nationals. It's an opportunity to do myself some good—'

But Jamie had turned away, shaking her head. She moved across to the wardrobe and began to dress for work. 'I don't believe I'm hearing this,' she told me. 'It's not you talking, it's that slime-bag Radcliffe. I don't know how the hell he's got at you, but he has.'

'Oh, don't be ridiculous!' I protested. 'It's *me* talking and perhaps it's high time I did. When all's said and done, Jamie, I'm a radio man; and there's not one other person at *Metrosound* who'd let a chance like this slip by.'

She rounded on me and I was shocked to see tears in her eyes.

'But you're not like *them*!' she cried. 'Don't you see, you've never been like them. You're basically a good person, a caring person.'

'Oh, yes,' I sneered. 'I'm Mother Theresa!'

'Don't mock me! You are a good person! Despite the image you project to the world, all that glib, "Don't-give-a-fuck" front you put on. It might fool your listeners, but it doesn't fool me. I've seen behind it once or twice. And this . . .' She crumpled the newspaper a second time. 'This is something that you would normally crawl a hundred miles to avoid. Think Tom, for God's sake. Is this really what you want?'

My only defence was cheap sarcasm. 'What's the matter?' I sneered. 'Afraid of being connected with it? It would have been all right if it was confined to the trendy leftie papers, I suppose. But the tabloids, now, that's very hard to slot in amongst the muesli and the pine shelving, isn't it?'

She glared at me, her eyes brimming. 'You fool,' she said. 'It's not me I'm worried about. I don't care what you do, so long as it makes you happy. But this will destroy you Tom, I know it will. You won't be able to live with yourself afterwards.'

'Oh, so now you know me better than I do!'

She sniffed, nodded, dabbed at her eyes with the sleeve of her uniform. 'I think so,' she said. Then she turned away, glanced at her watch. 'Late again,' she whispered. 'I'd better go.' She moved towards the door and I watched her from the bed, knowing that at this point I was supposed to call out to her, open my arms to offer an embrace. But some hard vein of pride, deep within me, prevented me from making the gesture. I said nothing and Jamie went out of the room, slamming the door. I heard the sound of her feet moving down the staircase, the soft scuffling in the hallway as she put on her coat.

'I'll be all right,' I said aloud; but in a voice that was not forceful enough to reach her down the hall. 'I know what I'm doing.' I was desperately trying to convince myself and doing a bad job of it. I was just beginning to sense the enormity of what I had done and it was a bad feeling, like standing on the edge of a crack in the pavement and watching as it slowly opened up into a yawning black pit.

The front door slammed and it was very quiet in the house, after she left.

To tell the truth, I hadn't expected John to phone back quite so soon. It was only two nights later when he next rang in; just before the police had finalised the installation of their tracing equipment. The instructions from Simon Radcliffe had been

60

quite precise. If John phoned, Steve was to pipe him straight through to me. I was then to get as much air-time out of the conversation as possible. 'Go right through the night if you can,' Simon had urged me. 'And forget about the rights and wrongs of the situation. Get into the nasty little fucker's head. Let the listeners know what makes him tick.'

Talking to him for a second time had seemed quite surreal. The only warning I'd got was the insect-buzz of Steve's voice in my headphones saying; 'Tom, he's on the line.' I promptly cut in over the record that was playing. 'All right, that's enough of that, we're now going straight over to talk to John in . . . well, somewhere out there. Hello, John? You're through to Captain Tom.'

A pause. Then that familiar whispering voice. 'Hello Tom, old mate! How you doing?' The tone was friendly, good-natured. I had to remind myself that this man was a killer; and I had to work very hard to keep my own voice under control.

'Well I'm fine, John. That was quite a surprise you gave us the other night.'

A brief laugh. 'Yeah, it was a bit, wasn't it? You didn't believe me at first, did you? You thought I was trying to pull some kind of stunt. But I thought I came over very well. Not my first time on radio, of course, but I was very pleased with the way it went.'

'You've phoned me before?'

'No, Tom. Not you. But I've set you thinking now, haven't I? By the way, I saw all the stuff in the papers. We got some nice coverage between us, didn't we? I must say I was surprised by your photograph. You don't look like your voice, know what I mean?'

'And do you look like your voice, John?'

'I dunno. Perhaps I should have sent a photograph of myself to the papers, eh? Except that would be a bit of a giveaway, wouldn't it?' A pause. Then; 'I suppose you've got tracing equipment on this call?'

'No.'

'Hmm. Well, I'll take your word for it, Tom. I trust you, you know. I think we're alike in many ways, you and me.'

'Alike? What do you mean?'

'We're both in show-business aren't we? You on the radio. Me on the streets. My act is a bit harder to catch, of course. Not as well publicised as yours. But the end result is a winner. If I was selling tickets, people would be falling over themselves to get hold of them.'

I felt my scalp crawl and, for the first time, I realised that I was afraid of this man. Afraid of what he had done – and what he might do. 'John, I hardly think you can describe what you did the other night as "an act". We're talking about murder; the destruction of another human being. And I really don't much care for the suggestion that I've got anything in common with that.'

'People rarely enjoy having the truth shoved in their face, Tom; and I'd love to go deeper into this subject with you another time. But I've got the stop-watch on this call and I don't want to go over two minutes. Just in case.'

'I thought you trusted me.'

'Only up to a point, old son. I know that if the cops insist on a trace, there's not much you can do to stop them. Anyway, the main reason I phoned tonight was to let you know that I'm planning to kill again, soon . . .'

'John, no! Just listen to me a moment.'

'No, you listen! And all you people sitting at home in your centrally heated, luxury-furnished houses, thinking you're safe and secure. You're *not*. I've been given a mission to perform in this town and I intend to carry it out, to the letter. The first sacrifice has been made, but there will be more. The gods demand it. Don't think this is a one-off. That was just the start.' A brief pause then. 'Well Tom, that's about it for now. Be talking to you!'

After the receiver was replaced, the ensuing silence seemed to scream until I automatically cued my next record: a bland string-driven instrumental that could do nothing to dispel the horror of the preceding message. A crushing weight had settled across my shoulders. I already knew enough about John to appreciate that he was a man of his word. 'That was just the start,' he had promised. It was a promise that he was not long in honouring.

Looking back, the next two months seem like a blur. I stumbled through them in a daze, gradually becoming aware of the fact that the ground beneath my feet was a treacherous morass into which I was slowly sinking. On one level, there were all kinds of exciting things happening for me. Within days of the Donovan killing, the media were phoning me up for interviews, asking me to appear on television. It was the kind of action I had longed for and here it was on a plate; and yet there was a hollowness to it, none of it was anything I could take pride in. This was compounded by the realisation that Jamie and I were gradually drifting apart. She didn't talk much about what was happening to us, but then she didn't need to. I sensed the division between us, an invisible wall that seemed to rear up inexorably, making everything strained and unsatisfying. I know now that I should have discussed it with her, I should have opened myself up a little. But I'd never been any good at voicing my feelings to anybody that mattered.

My parents were baffled by it all. My mother phoned soon after the news broke and talked around the subject. From her hurt tone, you'd have thought I'd arranged the whole thing just to punish them. For years they'd been foisting my so-called fame on friends and neighbours and suddenly I had acquired a notoriety that was much less attractive. They were horrified to find themselves besieged by newspaper reporters looking for an interesting angle and their only defence was to lock themselves up at home, out of harm's way. It seemed my father couldn't even go into his local pub without being pestered for an inside story. I felt desperately sorry for them but there was really very little I could do on their behalf. They were just innocent bystanders, caught up in a tragic accident.

Danny and Karen were affected too. Karen phoned several times to tell me that our son was being victimised at school by older kids who knew all about the killing; and Karen was outraged when an interview she was doing with an upmarket glossy suddenly turned into a grilling about her former relationship with me. Her remarks were typical of her and certainly not something any respectable magazine could publish. She was clearly worried that her own career might suffer.

My colleagues changed their attitudes completely. On the surface, they appeared sympathetic; but on more than one occasion I overheard people bad-mouthing me, saying how terrible it was that anybody should advance their career in such a ghoulish manner. *Fucking hypocrites.* I knew only too well that in a similar situation they'd be grabbing every opportunity to further their own numbers, but this knowledge did little for my own conscience. One day I found a Barbie Doll in my locker at work. It was wearing a tiny *Metrosound* T-shirt and it was hanging from a length of string, tied in a noose around its neck.

I kept telling myself that none of this mattered, that I could take the knocks, rise above them. But however much I rationalised, I was aware that it was affecting me more than I was admitting even to myself. Before all this began, I had managed to get my smoking down to a couple of cigarettes a week; now I found myself going through two packs a day. I began to lose weight and found that I was unable to sleep for more than an hour at a time. And at the heart of it all was *Nightboat*, the bed of nails to which I had to drag my aching carcass five nights a week. John phoned more often than I could have anticipated. The police had installed their equipment in the control room: the latest digital equipment. To trace a number all they had to do was press a button. But John only called from public phone boxes and by the time a car got there, he was gone, melted into the shadows. He never went over his precious two minutes. I never quite knew what to expect from him. Sometimes he was jokey, playful, a regular Jack the Lad. Other times his voice had a hard-edged, threatening tone that I found totally unnerving. And on two occasions over this period, there was a gloating quality in his voice that was absolutely unmistakeable.

'I've been a bad boy, Tom. I've been a bad, bad boy.'

I quickly came to learn that these words were the prelude to the announcement of another killing; and I found myself waiting for them, I'd be on a hair-trigger while John chatted happily on the end of the line, taunting me, mocking my inability to stop him. I felt like an accomplice to each crime. I felt I was in some way responsible. And for the first time, I began to ask myself why John had chosen to confide in me.

Diary extract

3rd December

I'm getting the hang of it now. I'm even beginning to enjoy it in a strange way. I killed the first one myself and I admit that was a chore. When I put that knife into her chest and twisted it, it was my hands that did the work. He was just an observer, cheering me on from the sidelines, enjoying it yes, but in a detached way. It was He who made me take the trophies afterwards. I didn't want to but He had some kind of use for them, He said. I found an empty yoghurt-carton in the litter bin and I washed it out before I put the things inside. I keep them in the icebox of the fridge. He says He wants them preserved.

But when I came to make the second sacrifice, He was inside me, it was His hands that locked around the woman's throat and squeezed until her face was purple and her tongue lolled from her mouth, black and bloated. It was I who observed that time, marvelling at the power in Him, the simple economy of His movement, the calm decisiveness of His actions. At one point, I glanced in a mirror and I saw His face looking back at me. It was a good moment. I knew I had started the transformation, that the sacrifices were already having an effect.

The third woman was a joy to kill. It was interesting to note that she looked just like her voice on the radio. She was cheap and sluttish and the perfume on her almost made me gag. Her eyes were already dead, long before He wound the stocking around her neck and pulled it tight. I was amazed by the power in His arms. The strand of nylon cut so deep into her throat that there was never any hope of removing it. It had become part of her flesh.

Afterwards, the sexy feelings came over me, but there was never any thought of touching her. She was probably rife with disease. I masturbated up in her toilet and was very careful to flush away all traces afterwards. I even treated the bowl with toilet cleanser, something that slut clearly hadn't done for years.

I talked to Tom again last night. He's changed these last weeks. All the cockiness has gone out of him and he's like an attentive pupil, hanging on the words of a master he fears. I feel sorry for him, but He assures me that Tom has wronged Him and that he does not deserve pity. When I weaken and begin to have doubts, He sends me visions. Visions of temples and sand dunes and people praying. He reminds me of what is to come and tells me that such things are not easily earned. I know I can't deny Him anything. He has only to crawl beneath my tongue and swell like a big black bubble and then I am speaking in His voice and I know I will kill a thousand people if He directs me to.

It's a shame about Tom though. I told him the other night, he should play more happy songs on his programme. Too many of his records are bleak and ugly, they do nothing for the spirit. Perhaps I shall send him some requests.

Chapter Six

I took another cigarette from the box on Simon's desk, lit it and inhaled deeply. I blew out a cloud of smoke. Simon watched me critically.

'You're chain-smoking,' he observed. 'I thought you'd given up.'

I shrugged, shook my head. 'I gave up giving up,' I told him.

'But they're menthol,' he persisted. You don't even like menthol.'

'Who gives a shit?' I snapped. 'You can afford it, you get them on expenses.' I turned in my seat and stared irritably at Inspector Drayton. He was pacing slowly around Simon's office despite the fact that there was a vacant chair set out for him. His hands were clasped behind his back and he appeared to be in a state of deep contemplation, like an actor preparing to tread the boards. These little meetings were, by now, a regular occurrence and I had come to know Drayton pretty well. Frankly, I was sick to the back teeth of him.

'Can we get on with it?' I asked bleakly.

'All in good time, Mr Prince. All in good time. I'm just gathering my thoughts.'

'That should take all of thirty seconds,' I muttered.

Simon slipped hastily into his Henry Kissinger mode, attempting to defuse the tense atmosphere with some small talk. 'Saw you on the box the other night, Tom. Thought you came over very well.'

'Oh, *brilliantly*! Like a cross between Eichmann and Machiavelli. The man evidently thought I was a piece of shit and he made me feel like one.' I adopted the voice of the smarmy chat-show host, who'd given me the third degree on Channel Four the previous night. 'Tell me, Mr Prince, what's it like to be responsible for three murders.'

'He never said that!'

'No, he just implied it.'

'Sounds distinctly like paranoia to me.'

'Does it? Does it, really?' I glared at Simon. His glib assurances got harder to stomach with each passing day. 'Well, the way I see it, I've got plenty to be paranoid about.' I indicated the large pile of letters on the desk beside me. 'Here's this week's selection of fan mail, Simon. Would you like to hear a few examples?'

'Tom, I don't really see—'

But I'd already snatched a letter off the top of the pile. 'Tom Prince. You're to blame for them girls. You better be careful when you go home at night. We'll be waiting for you.' I smiled coldly at him and flicked my cigarette in the general direction of the ashtray, scattering speckles of grey across the immaculate surface of his desk. 'I don't know who sent that, but I'll lay you even odds that it wasn't the Women's Institute!'

'Really, Tom, I—'

'Do you know what it's like to inspire that level of hatred, Simon?' I paused for a moment, then added, 'Yes, I suppose you do. You just don't get letters about it.'

He chose to ignore the remark. 'You can't take people like that seriously, Tom. You just have to ride it out.'

I laughed bitterly. 'Listen, last night some drunken arsehole stuffed a dog turd through my letter box. I took that pretty bloody seriously, I can tell you. So don't tell me I'm being paranoid, all right?'

Simon sighed, leaned back in his chair. 'I accept that this is no bed of roses for you. But on a personal level, you haven't done badly out of it have you? Television interviews, features in magazines . . . now I hear a publisher's offering you big money for your story when all this is over.'

'When it's over? God, Simon, are you stupid or something? It'll *never* be over. Not for me.' My voice was hoarse with anger. After two months of shit I had just about reached the end of my tether. I was ready to hit out at anyone or anything that crossed my path. I hated Simon for talking me into this mess, but worse, I hated myself for being so gullible, for not realising that John was a compulsive killer and that the whole affair would get horribly out of control.

Drayton cleared his throat. 'Gentlemen, if you've finished your little disagreement, I think we should begin. As usual, I'd like to start by refreshing our memories about what's happened so far. Much as I hate to admit it, we're no nearer to catching our killer than we were two months ago. In short, we have nothing on him. There's no doubt that we're dealing with a devious and methodical mind here.'

'You've had tracing equipment in the studio for at least six weeks now,' Simon reminded him. 'Surely you can . . .'

Drayton closed his eyes and rocked gently on his heels. 'If it was as simple as that, Mr Radcliffe, we'd have had some kind of results by now, I can assure you. But how do you trace a man who uses a public call box in a different location every time he calls, a man who never stays on the phone for more than two minutes? Even with the most sophisticated equipment, there's no way we can get to him in time. As I keep telling Mr Prince here, it's up to him to keep John on the line till a car can get there . . . yet time and again, he fails.'

'Would you like to suggest just how I should go about doing that?' I snapped. 'He won't be tricked, believe me I've tried.'

'Then *keep* trying, Mr Prince. If at first, you don't succeed . . .' Drayton left the sentence hanging and picked up a slim file from the desk. 'Now, this William Godfrey character, the one who made the threat against you.'

'It wasn't exactly a threat,' I corrected him. 'It was a biblical quotation.'

'Umm . . . yes . . .' He glanced at the file. 'A man who is bent on mischief gets a name for intrigue . . . but a messenger without mercy will be sent against him.'

I spread my hands helplessly. 'Maybe it means nothing. I just remembered that he said that to me, that's all.'

Drayton nodded. 'Well, we've had a word with your Mr Godfrey and we've ascertained that he couldn't have been responsible for any of the killings. We were interested in him for a while because he had previous form. Sexual offences mostly. Exposing himself to little girls, that kind of thing. But I've now conclusively eliminated him from our list of suspects.'

'List? I chided him. 'He was the only one on the list.'

'Yes, thank you Mr Prince, I am aware of that fact. Which puts us right back to Square One. Believe me, I don't find this any less frustrating than you do.' He paced up and down a moment, staring at the ceiling, as though seeking inspiration. 'It may appear to you that we're doing very little to find this man . . .'

'Now that you mention it.'

'. . . in fact, nothing could be further from the truth. We've launched a massive inquiry. Everything that can be done, *is* being done. We've created the biggest database ever assembled in the North-west. Every day, it's updated and examined. We're looking for any kind of link we can find. We've made exhaustive door-to-door inquiries, every possible lead is followed up in the smallest detail. We've got a Home Office pathologist on the case, we've got the best forensic team in the country, we've got . . .'

'Absolutely nothing,' I reminded him. 'Not a clue.'

Drayton scowled, chewed his bottom lip for a moment. He turned on his heel and started pacing again. 'Let's examine what little we do know. We know that the three victims are linked only by two discernible circumstances. All of them had at one time or another, been featured on the *Nightboat* programme. Margaret Donavan, Edith Walters and most recently, Kathy Squires.'

I shook my head. I still couldn't believe that Kathy was dead. Of all the regulars on the show, she had been the most harmless, the most pathetic. Drayton, however, had little sympathy for her.

'Foolish woman. Actually giving out her address over the air. And indulging in those smutty invitations. I suppose if one were uncharitable, one might say she got exactly what she was asking for.'

I glared at Drayton. 'Don't try saying it, Inspector. Not when I'm around. She was just a lonely woman looking for a few laughs.'

'Nobody's laughing, Mr Prince, I can assure you. And as somebody who encouraged her to be as reckless as she was, you've probably already said more than enough on the subject.'

'Oh no, I'm just the poor sod who has to cope with the threats made by her husband.'

'Yes . . . well, that was unfortunate. But given the circumstances, it's understandable that he should act in an irrational manner. He's been cautioned, Mr Prince, I don't think you need worry any more on that score.'

'Oh well, that's fine, I'll sleep better for that!'

Drayton ignored the sarcasm, continued to pace. 'The only assumption we can make is that our murderer has been using your programme as some kind of grotesque shopping catalogue. He's cottoned on to the fact that women who phone in at that time of night are likely to be lonely individuals who spend a good deal of their time on their own. Miss Donavan and Miss Walters were both single. Mrs Squires' husband was away from the house for long periods of time . . . once again, a fact that was widely advertised on your programme.'

'As you instructed, we've now made sure that no locations are mentioned,' said Simon hastily. 'Addresses are absolutely forbidden and Tom makes no mention of where the calls are coming from. Furthermore, we only identify callers by their Christian names.'

I tackled the inspector again, 'You said the murders were linked by two circumstances . . . but you've only mentioned one.'

Drayton nodded. 'The other thing concerns the murders themselves. A certain similarity.'

'But I thought the method was different. The first girl was stabbed, the other two were strangled.'

Drayton nodded. 'True . . . but it's something that was done to each of the bodies, after the death.'

Simon leaned across the desk, intrigued. 'What would that be?' he asked.

'Calm down,' I advised him. 'You'll be drooling in a minute.'

'Not at all,' protested Simon. 'It's just interesting, that's all.'

'If I tell you,' said Drayton, 'I would have to have an undertaking from both of you that the matter would not be divulged to anyone else. It certainly wouldn't be for inclusion in your news bulletins.'

'The thought never crossed my mind,' said Simon, unconvincingly.

'Very well.' Drayton lowered his voice as though afraid of being overheard. 'It's the eyes,' he said.

I stared at him. 'What's that supposed to mean?'

'Quite simply, none of the victims had any when we found them.'

Even Simon grimaced. 'Christ, you mean the killer gouged them out?'

Drayton nodded. 'And took them away with him. We found no trace of them at any of the murder scenes.'

There was a long stunned silence before Simon spoke again. 'But what . . . I mean, what possible reason could anyone have for . . . ?'

Drayton shrugged. 'I haven't the faintest idea. But then I'm not stark staring mad, am I?' He paused as though waiting for a reply, but none came. Perhaps neither of us was sure on that point. He continued. 'So you can appreciate the kind of sick animal we're dealing with here. He's clearly deranged, he's out there and he could kill again at any time. He's also bloody clever. We know that he wears surgical rubber gloves . . . we found clear prints of them at the scene of each crime. He takes care to erase every trace of his presence and kills very quickly, very efficiently. It's interesting to note that not one of his victims put up a fight. This suggests that they either knew the attacker or were overpowered so quickly, they had no time to struggle. Also interesting is that none of the victims were interfered with.'

I laughed out loud at that. Drayton's prudishness was often unintentionally hilarious.

'I'd say they were all seriously interfered with,' I told him.

He stared at me. 'You know exactly what I mean,' he snapped. 'Cases like this usually have some sexual motive. John appears to have no interest in . . .'

'Fucking them,' I finished. 'Why don't you just say it?'

Drayton winced. He closed his eyes for a moment and I noticed a muscle in his jaw twitching rhythmically. He took a long pause before he continued.

'As you know, we've debated long and hard about the wisdom of letting Mr Prince's show continue. In the end, we decided that taking it off the air would be the worst thing we could do. It's our only link with John. Lose that and we'd have absolutely nothing to go on.'

I sagged. I had been praying that someone else would take the initiative and pull the plug on *Nightboat*. When I'd first got into this, I had thought I could handle it; but now the lice were crawling out of the woodwork all over town and taking over. The hypocrisy of it was unbelievable. Most people, if asked, would have registered disgust at the whole affair, yet it was evident that thousands of them were eschewing their television sets, neglecting their usual bedtimes and tuning in to *Nightboat* for entertainment of a more salacious kind. It now had higher ratings than our breakfast show.

The advertisers had not been slow to recognise the potential of what was on offer. Companies were openly competing for what they saw as a newly created late-night, prime-time slot; and the powers that be at *Metrosound* saw little problem in allotting time to tasteless tie-ins, provided of course they were charged at the new 'special' rate for air play, an abrupt and unexplained increase of twenty per cent over the usual late-night fees. And so the manufacturer of an electric carving-knife was able to feature a grotesque commercial using the sound of serrated blades cutting through a Sunday roast; a famous brand of stockings were advertised by a woman babbling on about 'the great feel of nylon', only days after Kathy had been strangled to death with just such material.

I was all too aware that I was now the captain of a ship that was increasingly out of control. I felt as though I was tied to the helm, unable to jump clear. It could only end if and when John was apprehended. Until then I had to see it through.

Drayton cleared his throat again. 'Moving on to the subject of the letters you've received allegedly signed by the killer . . .' He pulled a plastic bag from the file which contained the latest batch, crudely written notes either signed 'John' or 'The Whisperer'. 'We feel that they are red herrings; most likely copy-cat notes from people with a sick sense of humour. Certainly, there's no consistency in them, they all have different handwriting, different ink, different postmarks. *One* of them could be genuine, of course, but we've examined them all without getting any further and forensic tests will continue as a matter of course.' He sighed, turned to approach a tape recorder set up on a desk. 'That brings me to the recording of his last call.'

'Do we have to listen to it?' I pleaded. 'It's got so I can't stand the sound of his voice.'

'I appreciate it must be difficult for you; but if you could bear with me? I'm hoping that from listening to these tapes, something might emerge. Some kind of pattern . . .' He hit the 'play' button and I heard my own voice, sounding edgy, nervous, all semblance of professionalism gone.

'Hello? Hello, John, is that you?'

'Hello old son! How's it going? Been listening to the show these last few nights. Not very exciting when I'm not on it, is it? And even then, it seems I'm the only interesting subject. I've heard you trying to lead callers on to other topics and all credit to you for that; but people's hearts aren't really in it, are they? So I've been listening to the adverts. Getting a lot of them now, aren't we? Used to be just one or two every break, now there's as many as six at a time. Lot of new products on offer. Seems to me they're using me to sell those products; and they're using you to sell me. Well, I'm a commodity in a way, aren't I? Just like a set of heated rollers or a DIY kitchen. There's a need for people like me in the world. Like I already said, I was chosen to do this work; but why me, Tom? Why me?'

'Please tell me.'

'Because, deep down, people *want* somebody like me. They look around the city streets and what do they see? Drunkenness, lechery, fornication . . . all those things their instincts tell them are wrong. And who causes it all?

'Who?'

'The women, Tom! The handmaidens. With their revealing skirts, and their painted faces. *Whores*. Oh yes, I've seen them! We've all seen them. They parade their disgusting bodies around trying to arouse good men like me and you. Decent people see that kind of thing every day, and they are disgusted. Afraid. Deep down they long for some force to come and remove those creatures from their sight. It's not murder Tom, it's a service I provide. I'm here to punish them. The gods know that and they applaud me for it.'

74

'No John, you're wrong! No compassionate god would condone what you're doing. He'd want you to give yourself up. He'd want you to stop this madness. *I* want you to stop. You claim to be a friend of mine, but despite all my appeals you go on with this senseless killing.'

'*Not* senseless, Tom! Not at all. Carefully planned, prepared, rehearsed. There's method to what I'm doing, you see. And I'll tell you something else. There's lots of people who'd love to do what I do. Oh yes, thousands! But they haven't got the guts. So instead they tune in and listen to me.'

'Wrong again, John. We have letters here every day, all of them from those decent people you're talking about; and all of them calling on you to stop it. Would you like me to read some of the letters to you?'

A short derisive laugh. 'Still trying to detain me eh, Tom? But it won't work. Clock's coming up to time now. Oh, one other thing. The music on the show lately. It's been very bleak, very doomy. You should play some happy songs. Something to lift the spirits, make people sing along, they don't want to be dwelling on bad things all the time, do they? Anyway, that's all for now. Be talking to you!'

The click of the receiver. I pictured the interior of the studio as it had been at that moment. The awful empty silence that briefly ensued before the stylus etched itself into the moving vinyl. As usual I had raised my eyes to see Steve Acton staring contemptuously at me through the glass partition; beside him, the two policemen manning the tracing equipment, slamming the headphones down with frustration as they failed once again to get a car to the scene of the crime. Now I relived the sensation that always swept over me at such times. Guilt. A powerful, all-pervading emotion that I carried home with me, that stayed with me all through the mornings and deep into the following nights; when, of course, it was time to start all over again.

I shuddered involuntarily, stubbed out my cigarette, helped myself to another one.

'That voice,' muttered Simon. 'Gives me the creeps.'

Drayton nodded, switched off the tape. 'We got in an expert on speech patterns. He analysed the recordings. His conclusion was that John isn't disguising his voice in any way, but that he might have sustained some damage to his larynx or vocal chords. If that's the case, he must speak like that in everyday life. It may be our best bet for recognising him. That's why I'm taking every opportunity to keep that voice on the airwaves. One day, a shopkeeper or a bus conductor is going to remember hearing it and he's going to phone us.' He frowned. 'Any thoughts, gentlemen?'

'There is something,' I said, lighting the cigarette. 'Gods.'

'I beg your pardon?'

'He says *gods*, plural; not God. I've noticed he always says it like that.' I shrugged. 'Maybe it's nothing, but . . . well, the first time he mentioned it, I figured he was a religious nut, like our William. But gods, plural . . . doesn't that suggest something . . . well, pagan? Along with all the talk about sacrifices, handmaidens.'

Drayton sneered. 'Pagan, Mr Prince? Who do you think is calling you, Atilla the Hun?'

I glowered at him. 'Listen, you asked for an idea, I gave you one.'

'Right. I'll make a note of it. I'm sure it will give the lads down the station a good laugh. Mr Radcliffe? Do you have anything to add?'

Simon chewed a fingernail thoughtfully. 'I do have one observation,' he replied. 'I get the impression that our John is familiar with radio. He seems to understand how it works. And I remember him saying on an earlier tape, that it wasn't the first time he'd been on the air. Remember that, Tom?'

I nodded. 'Yeah. He said . . . that he hadn't been on *my* show before.'

Drayton stroked his chin, his eyes narrowing down to slits. 'So you're suggesting that what we might have here is another DJ?'

'Not necessarily,' replied Simon. 'Unfortunately, there's all kinds of people featured on the radio. Writers, historians, pop stars, critics . . . you name it. All I'm saying is that I feel if we were to put John into a studio, he'd have a good idea of what he was doing. Maybe there's a connection there, somewhere back in the past.'

Drayton nodded, seemed pleased. 'Well, it's something to

consider,' he admitted. 'At this stage, I'm about ready to consider anything.' He glanced mockingly at me. 'Within reason.'

I felt my temper flaring. 'Get off my back, Drayton,' I snapped. 'You've been pushing me ever since this thing began and frankly, I can do without your sarcasm.'

Drayton smiled coldly. 'Luckily, Mr Prince, it's a free world. I'm obliged to work with you on this, but there's no law that says I have to like you. If you really want to know the truth, I think what you're doing is contemptible; and if I was the sort of person who wrote anonymous notes to radio stations, it would probably sound distinctly like the one you read earlier.'

'Then do me a favour,' I said quietly. 'Take the show off the air. Please.'

Drayton shook his head. 'It's too late for that, I'm afraid. You should have thought about it earlier. I want this bastard's head on a plate and unfortunately, you're the only one in a position to give it to me. So until I say differently, you'll carry on as usual.' He nodded to Simon. 'Good afternoon Mr Radcliffe. I'll be in touch.' He turned and went out of the office, letting the door swing shut behind him.

There was a long uncomfortable silence after he had gone. When I finally spoke, my voice was hoarse with anger. 'God, I hate that smug sonofabitch.'

'He's only doing his job, Tom.'

'Sure. Like you were only doing yours when you talked me into this.' I fixed Simon with a look of cold hatred.

'Tom, you're a mess,' he said. 'You've got to try and keep it together.' He looked guiltily at his own well-manicured fingernails. 'When all this started, I had no idea it would go on this long. I thought maybe, a couple of weeks, you know? And you have to admit, doors have opened for you because of it. Now, sooner or later, this man is going to make a mistake and when he does . . .'

I shook my head. 'He isn't going to make mistakes, Simon. He's too clever for that. I've got to know him over these past few weeks. Sometimes, I feel I've known him a lot longer.'

Simon looked puzzled. 'How do you mean?'

'I mean there's something familiar about him. The occasional

77

turn of phrase he uses, a reaction, a line. I think he's somebody from way back, a bad penny who's turned up after years. But I can't place him. Not yet.'

'Why didn't you say something to Drayton?'

I laughed. 'I wouldn't give that bastard the time of day. Besides, at the moment it's no more than a feeling.' I leaned across the desk. 'And I don't want to find out that you've told him anything about this, either. When I've got it straight in my own mind, then I'll decide what to do about it.'

Simon studied some notes on his desk, as though unable to meet my gaze. 'Just as you prefer, Tom. Now, I've got a planning meeting in a few minutes. If I were you, I'd go home and get some sleep.'

'Sleep?' I nodded. 'Sure, sleep . . . I remember that. It used to be what got me through.' I studied Simon for a moment. 'Do you sleep all right, Simon? And when you sleep, do you dream?'

Simon fiddled nervously with a gold-plated fountain pen.

'I really have to get to this meeting,' he said evasively. 'We . . . we're talking about the new schedules in September. The break-fast show. Remember, we talked about that?'

'Yeah, sure. Big plans for the future. My reward for going along with all this. So I'm supposed to feel that everything has been worthwhile, eh? Ever read *Doctor Faustus*?'

He still could not meet my gaze. 'Look Tom, I know what you're getting at . . . but success never comes easy. There's always a price to pay. And don't think you're the only one suffering over this. I've done my own share of soul-searching, believe me.'

'My heart bleeds for you,' I sneered. 'Still, you've got what you wanted, haven't you? Ratings, publicity, advertising . . . you've worked hard for it, Simon. I hope it was worth it.'

This time he didn't answer. He continued to stare at his desk as though it held the answer to some unfathomable riddle. I stubbed out my cigarette on his jotter, helped myself to another from his supplies, then left the office.

I drove home with the radio turned up loud.

At home, I tried to bury the pain beneath layers of normality. I decided I had fallen into a melancholic rut and it was time to climb out of it. I simply needed something to occupy myself.

A meal. I'd cook something and have it ready for Jamie when she got in from work. *Lasagne al forno.* My speciality. I made a trip to the local shops and bought all the ingredients. Then, in the brilliantly lit kitchen, I worked methodically, knife blade slicing effortlessly through onions, peppers, mushrooms. I liked the feel of the metal biting into the crisp vegetable matter and clunking rhythmically against the chopping board.

I wonder if John derives a similar pleasure from using a knife.

The thought had sprung unbidden into my mind and I made a mental effort to shake it. No John, not tonight. Cooking. I had always enjoyed cooking. I opened a particularly nice bottle of Muscadet I had been saving for a special occasion and poured myself a large glass, savoured the dry taste against my tongue.

I wonder if John likes to drink wine?

I shook my head, ground my teeth. I began to feel the longing for a cigarette. I had to get the bastard out of my mind somehow. Music! Loud music. That usually did the trick. I moved across to the radio and flicked it on. I got the impassive voice of a newsreader.

'. . . year-old man went on a homicidal rampage, gunning down fourteen fellow-students before turning the weapon on himself. The . . .'

I scowled, fiddled with the dial. Too close to home, that. I found another station.

'. . . nuclear cloud reported to be drifting over Cumbria. Thousands of sheep have been ordered to be destroyed and many local farmers are facing the worst – '

No, no, no! Music. It had to be music. My hands were shaking and I could feel beads of sweat breaking on my brow. Doggedly, I tried again, aware of black clouds massing at the edge of my mind.

I found a community reggae station pumping out a reassuringly laid-back groove and I managed to relax a little, began to arrange the layers of ingredients in a baking dish. I even hummed along to the music as I poured a rich sauce over the pasta.

I was just putting the finished dish into the oven when I heard the front door open and close. I smiled, topped up my own glass and poured a second one for Jamie. I waited for her to come into the kitchen, then realised that she was a long time in the hallway, hanging up her coat. I went out to her and found her standing there, her coat still around her shoulders. She was leaning against the wall and was crying.

'Jamie? For Christ's sake, what's the matter?'

'Nothing,' she said dismissively.

'You don't cry about nothing.' I walked over to her and put my arms around her. She was stiff and unyielding in my embrace. 'What is it, darling?'

She could not meet my eyes. 'It's just something somebody said to me. At work.'

'McAuliffe been laying into you again? That bitch, what is it this time?'

But Jamie was shaking her head. 'It wasn't Sister McAuliffe. It was . . . actually, if you really want to know, it was Bob Latimer.'

I recognised the name of a young consultant on Jamie's ward, an arrogant, upper-class twerp whom she usually had no time for, though the man had never made any secret of his interest in her.

'Latimer? Since when do you take any notice of what he says?'

Jamie sniffed, dabbed at her eyes with the back of her hand. 'Since he started talking about you,' she said.

'Oh, I see. Well, most people have got some opinion about me these days. Why should he be any different?'

'He told me he thought what you were doing was obscene. He accused you of using somebody's misfortune to further your own ambitions. He said you were little short of a vampire, a parasite that was living off the blood of the innocent. And what else? Oh yes, he said he thought that in a way, you were indirectly responsible for those other killings; that you were almost egging on the murderer, getting him to go one step further each time.'

I turned away from her, not wanting her to see the dismay on my face. I had had those same thoughts and had never really persuaded myself that I was innocent of the charges. But, of course, I couldn't admit it, not even to myself. 'Well, that's quite a list to be going on with,' I said tonelessly. 'But really Jamie, if you're going to let a snot-nosed little twat like Latimer upset you . . .'

'It's not what he said that upset me,' she said.

I stared at her. 'Then what . . . ?'

'What really upset me Tom, what absolutely slammed me to the bone, was the fact that deep down inside I couldn't help but agree with him.'

'Jamie!' I spun back round to glare at her but she was crying again, her shoulders shaking with the grief of it. 'You don't mean that,' I told her.

'Tom, I'm sorry but I do! I have to say this. I hate what's happened to you. I hate what's happening to *us*. For weeks now, I've been defending you, giving out the same lines. It's your career. You're just doing your job, helping the police to catch him. But I don't know if I believe it any more. I don't know if I ever believed it. And the worst thing, Tom, is you won't talk to me about it, about what you're feeling. I come home and it's like I'm talking to somebody who's been broken up and stuck back together again, badly. I can see the cracks, and they get bigger all the time.'

'Jamie, listen—' I stepped towards her but she shrank from me, as though I had raised my fists to strike her.

'I'm sorry,' she gasped. 'I can't talk to you now.' She turned and went running upstairs to the bedroom. She slammed the door behind her with a force that shook the entire house.

That night, before setting off to work, I dumped the burned remains of a *Lasagne al forno* and an empty wine bottle into the bin. I had looked in briefly on Jamie but the lights in the bedroom were out and her regular breathing suggested that she was asleep. I stood there in the doorway, feeling the emptiness spread through me. I thought about waking her but didn't have the first idea of what I would say. So I drove erratically to work, not caring that I was way over the limit. I needed to talk to somebody. I needed to talk to John.

Chapter Seven

As a rule, I never drank before a show, so I began this one feeling distinctly muzzy. When I made my introduction, my voice sounded thick and slurred in the headphones and I tripped up over several words; but I was past caring about that. I felt hurt and betrayed and I wanted to vent my anger on somebody. I chose the most accessible target, the thousands of unseen faces that constituted my regular audience.

'Ahoy scumbags! It's twelve o five here on *Metrosound* and this is the Captain . . . this is Captain Tom, welcoming you aboard the *Nightboat* for another four hours of music . . . and stuff. Tonight we're talking about . . . lemme see now, what are we going to talk about? Well, who gives a shit, you people will talk the usual old bollocks anyway. So get your nasty little one-track minds into gear and phone me on . . . ah, you know the number! Here's some Springsteen, to get us off to a nice clean start . . . he's going down to the river to get washed which sounds like bloody good advice to me.'

I lit a cigarette and inhaled deeply, causing a surge of dizziness to river through me. The stale air of the studio made me feel worse than I normally might have done and I felt oppressed by the three curious faces examining me from the other side of the glass. I was in no mood to suffer fools gladly and the first half-dozen callers were dealt with in most uncompromising fashion. When their ranting became boring, I simply cut them off in mid-conversation. One caller had a slight stutter and I took delight in mimicking the man, totally humiliating him. Then, just as I was settling into my stride and was beginning to derive some kind of perverse enjoyment from the punishment I was handling out, John called in.

'Hello Tom, my old mate. How's tricks?'

The familiar whispering voice was a goad tonight; and where I would normally have held back, the wine had blurred my ability to judge the best course of action. So I snapped back, my voice thick with hatred. 'Don't you "my old mate" me! You're no friend of mine!'

At the other end of the line, John registered genuine dismay. 'Not a friend Tom. But I thought—'

'You thought what? That I was your Father Confessor perhaps? Some kind of perverted agony aunt offering advice to the lovelorn and the psychotic? Listen to me, you maggot; and listen good. I'm sick to death of having to sit here politely while you spill your guts to me. All the pretty little details. Who, when, where! As though such filth could be of interest to anybody who wasn't sick in the head. Like you are, John. You hear me? You're sick. And the biggest tragedy of all is that you believe you're doing this for a reason. Well there is no justification for murder, John; you can rant and rave as much as you like, but I don't intend to listen to it any longer. I don't want you to ring me again.'

'Not ring you, Tom?' There was a brief pause; as though John were thinking, trying to understand this abrupt change of attitude. Then, 'Oh, I see. What you're saying is you don't *need* me any more. I've been useful to you for a time but now the engagement is off. Well, I can't say I'm too surprised. Naturally, I've been reading all about your success outside the station; and I've watched you on the chat shows on television. So I can understand that you've come up in the world of late . . .'

'What are you saying?' I cried. 'Are you trying to suggest that you've put me where I am? *You*? A yellow creep who gets his kicks from slaughtering innocent women. You're nothing! You hear that? Zero!' My voice was now so loud the microphone was beginning to distort, but John's reply was calm, precise.

'If I'm nothing Tom, what does that make you? Because you see, it's quite apparent that you couldn't have got where you are without me. I'm your meal ticket, son. And if you lose me now, how long will you stay there in the spotlight? A few weeks. A month maybe . . . and then?'

A succession of images and voices welled up in my head. I saw

Jamie's face, tear-streaked. I heard Simon Radcliffe's smug voice calling the shots. I saw Inspector Drayton's disapproving expression. I heard Steve Acton's snide remark about how *he* could sleep at night. And for the first time on air, I lost my temper.

'You arrogant bastard!' I screamed. 'Just who the hell do you think you are? Telling me what to do! Well, I'll tell you something. You're off this programme as of now. You hear that? I'm going to have your calls refused, and I'm going to have you banned.'

A dry, throaty little chuckle of amusement. 'Oh come on now Tom, they'll never let you do that.'

'Don't you believe it! This is *my* show, Goddamnit! And my word goes.'

'But you're wrong, Tom. It's not *yours* any more. It's mine. I'm the star of this show. I'm the one people tune in to hear, not you. And I will phone in again, you can bet on that. Because there's more work to be done. More sacrifices to be made. And you'd better—'

I hit the cut-off button. Saw the policemen in the adjoining room react with fury. Heard Steve Acton's voice over the intercom. 'Tom, you idiot! They nearly had him that time. He was going over the two minutes. He—'

I cued a heavy-metal record and cranked it up to top volume, drowning out Steve's voice, trying in vain to drown out the truth and knowing only too well that the truth spoke louder than any record. And then it finally hit me, what I had sold to be where I was at this moment. I felt a terrible queasiness rise in my stomach and, lurching out of my seat, I stumbled towards the studio door and made it to the staff toilets with only seconds to spare. Bent double over the cracked porcelain sink, I heaved and retched away the sickness in my belly and it seemed for a moment as though I would never stop puking. At least, straightening up, I tried to examine my reflection in the mirror. But my eyes were full of tears and all I saw looking back at me was a faceless blur, something grey, insubstantial and completely without an identity.

Simon listened in silence to what I had to say. Then he took a deep breath, shook his head. 'It's out of the question, Tom,' he said calmly. 'Totally out of the question. The police won't buy it and I won't either. Frankly, you had no right to say that to John.'

'No right?' I stared across the broad expanse of Simon's desk. I was doing my level best to keep my temper, having already learned the consequence of losing it. I surveyed the confines of Simon's office, seeking, perhaps, some means of escape. 'Simon, listen to me. The whole thing has gone too far. You must see that.' I had woken that morning with a splitting headache and an empty space in the bed beside me. Jamie had gone off to work without waking me, without talking to me. As I'd showered myself awake I'd come to the conclusion that I had been avoiding for too long: I had been railroaded long enough. I had to claw my way out of this self-made trap, whatever the cost. But if I had hoped for any kind of sympathy from Simon Radcliffe, I was clearly on to a loser.

'Tom, you have to see this from a programming point of view.'

'Fuck that! Did you hear what he said to me last night? Do you really think I'm going to sit there and take that kind of shit? I mean, that's *my* show, Simon. I created it, I built it up from nothing. Now that sick sonofabitch thinks he can take it away from me. Don't you see, you've got to back me up on this? If you don't, we'll be admitting that he's right. It *will* be his show.'

Simon studied his fingernails for a moment. 'Tom, don't you think you're taking this all a little personally?' he asked.

I laughed at that, a shrill, hysterical giggle of sheer disbelief.

'You are amazing, do you know that? Absolutely fucking amazing! Yes, I'm taking it personally. How would you deal with it if John phoned up and suggested he should be *Metrosound*'s programme controller? He'll be doing that next!'

Simon shrugged. 'Looking at it logically, I'd have to admit he'd be a damned good controller. He's managed to take a late-night show into the top ratings slot which is something neither you nor I have ever managed. Of course, his methods are a little unconventional . . . .'

I shook my head. 'You're as barking mad as he is,' I observed. 'That has to be the answer. Everybody here is crazy, except me.' I glared at Simon, seeking some glint of humanity in his impassive face. But I found myself looking at a mask. 'Well,' I said, 'since that's the case, there's only one sane thing I can do. I'm getting out, Simon. I'm handing in my notice.'

Simon smiled coldly. 'Hardly the sane thing, old chap. You recall we discussed that scenario several months ago?'

'Yes and I let you walk all over me. But not this time. I'm getting out, whether you like it or not. And you can sue me for every penny I've got if it makes you feel better. To paraphrase a famous movie, Frankly my dear, I don't give a fish's tit. Do whatever you like!'

Simon thought for a moment. 'Let's be rational about this, Tom.'

'Oh yes, let's be!' I leaned across the desk and fluttered my eyelids at Simon. 'By all means, let's keep our heads.'

Simon smiled sourly at me. 'I'm going to appeal to your better judgement. I'm going to ask you to put aside your own feelings for one moment and consider the public. After all, *Metrosound* has a responsibility to the community and your duty . . .'

'*Duty*?' I could barely keep from screaming. 'Simon, don't get into a subject you know nothing about. Talk to me about ratings, money, presentation, any other aspect of radio and I'll listen to you. But duty, for God's sake! From a man who'd sell his mother to white slavers if it would push up the ratings! Do me a favour!'

'I'm *trying* to do you a favour!' snapped Simon. 'Despite what you think of me, I wouldn't derive any pleasure from suing you for breach of contract. You may think me a grinding bastard . . .'

'In a nutshell, that's just about right.'

'. . . but I know enough to appreciate that *Nightboat* is the one thing that could lead to the police catching John. *They* aren't going to like you quitting the show; and I wouldn't like to be the man to incur Drayton's displeasure, not right now.'

'I'll take the risk,' I assured him.

'Yes, but listen a minute. OK, you want out . . . and it's just possible I could get another presenter for the show. Somebody that John would relate to, just as he's related to you. Believe me, I wouldn't be short of offers. There's plenty of people less squeamish than you. But I can't find the right man overnight. Now, as you know, the minimum notice required by the company is one month.'

I eyed him suspiciously. 'Are you by any chance trying to play for time?' I snarled.

'Not at all. But I won't be left in the lurch over this. Here's what I'm proposing. You work out your notice of one month and I give you my word that I'll release you from your contract with no fear of litigation.'

'Your word, Simon? Jesus, how much is that worth?'

'All right, I'll have a contract drawn up to that effect. You'll leave here on good terms, without a black mark on your record. You know that if I put out the word, you'd be *persona non grata* at every station in the country?'

'Oh, I don't doubt that.'

'Of course, you may want to consider what you'd be giving up. The breakfast-show slot has yet to be inked . . .'

I threw back my head and laughed. 'God, you must think I'm stupid! As if there's any likelihood of that happening, now! Oh, it'd go down very well with the toast and the rice crispies, wouldn't it? Tom Prince, the zany, wacky presenter who introduces a psychopath into every home! That's a non-starter and you know it.'

Simon looked sheepish. 'Well, yes, I can see your point. Your image isn't exactly Mr Clean these days, I'll grant you. Anyhow, my offer stands. You work the notice and you allow us to use the format of your show. It'll still be Nightboat but there'll be a new captain at the helm. You sign a contract to that effect and I'll be happy to let you go with no strings attached. You'll be able to start over. Now, does that sound fair?'

'From you, it sounds decidedly fishy. I keep thinking, where's the catch?'

'No catch, Tom! I understand you've been under phenomenal pressure and considering the circumstances, you've coped admirably. Now it's time to let somebody else take the strain. Just another four weeks, that's all I ask.'

I considered the proposition for a moment. Put in those terms it seemed easy enough. Another twenty shows to do, with a definite pool of light at the end of the tunnel. My instincts told me to quit now, throw the offer back in Simon's face; but my better judgement reminded me that it would be hard enough to pick up the pieces as it was. With a law suit on my back and the potential damage that Simon's bad-mouthing could do me, it would surely be impossible. I would have to accept the offer. It was a compromise; but one that I felt I could handle, just.

'OK,' I said. 'But I want to see it in writing.'

'I'll have it drawn up,' Simon told me.

'With effect from today,' I reminded him.

'As you wish. Oh, one other thing, Tom. Over this last month, I expect you to exercise the same degree of professionalism as always. Steve Acton told me that you were er . . . a little worse for wear last night. You know the rules about alcohol. See that you abide by them in future.'

'Yes boss.' I touched my forelock sarcastically. 'You know Simon, I'm going to miss our little chats when all this is over.'

Simon smiled coldly. 'Really? You'd better be running along now, Tom. I have things to do.'

'I'm sure you have.'

'And Tom, if John should phone again . . . be civil, all right?'

I nodded, got up and left the office. A month, I wondered. Could I really hope to last that long? But as I left the building and walked across the car park, I felt the weight beginning to lift from my shoulders. Yes, I decided, as I climbed into the car. I'd make it . . . now that I had something to work for.

That night, when Jamie came home, I greeted her at the door with a bouquet of roses and a kiss on the cheek. It was a hopelessly sentimental gesture but I was desperate. She stood there uncertainly, as though not knowing what to say to me, as though she had been accosted by a complete stranger. 'Tom,' she whispered. 'About last night . . .'

'Forget about last night,' I told her. 'Just congratulate me.'

'On what?'

'On handing in my notice at *Metrosound*.'

She stared at me, as though disbelieving. Then her anxious expression melted into a smile. 'You mean it? You really did?'

I nodded. 'Should have done it long ago. Should have listened to you when you tried to put me straight. Anyway, it's done now. One more lousy month of it and I'm a free man. Radcliffe even came up with a deal for me. He won't be suing.'

'Oh Tom, that's wonderful.' She dropped the bouquet and put

her arms around me, gave me a fierce, warm hug. 'Oh thank God,' she said. 'I was having such thoughts . . . such crazy thoughts.'

I stroked her hair. 'What thoughts?'

'I was thinking that it wasn't working with us any more, that I couldn't make it work. I was thinking that I was going to give up on it, or give you some kind of ridiculous ultimatum.'

'Then for once, I got my timing right,' I observed. Now came the tricky bit . . . except I was vaguely surprised to find that it wasn't as difficult as I'd envisaged. The weight was off my chest now, the words just seemed to tumble out. 'I'm sorry Jamie, sorry for everything that's happened. I'm sorry for dragging you through all this. But now it's going to be all right.'

She pulled away from me a little and gazed hopefully into my eyes.

'A month, no more. You promise?'

I nodded. 'It's all they could do to stop me walking out today. But Radcliffe came up with this deal and it was too good to pass up. But you see, it'll be OK. I don't quite know how we'll make ends meet but . . .'

She touched a finger to my lips. 'We'll manage,' she told me. Then she took my hand, led me towards the staircase. 'Come on,' she said. 'I want you to make love to me. Do you know, we've barely touched for a month now?'

A month? It hardly seemed possible. I pulled her to me and we kissed hungrily, our tongues exploring. It had always been as easy as this before the recent void between us, that had prevented us from even touching. I fumbled eagerly with the poppers on her uniform. By the time we reached the top of the stairs, we were half naked. We fell on to the reassuring softness of the bed, our bodies clinging together as though attempting to fuse into one. Our lovemaking was fast, furious, imbued with the hungry passion that had marked our first couplings. When I entered her it seemed to me that every part of my body was on fire with yearning; and when I came deep within her, I was not only relieving my lust, I was also confirming my new resolve as to the future. It was a cleansing experience for both of us.

Afterwards, we lay holding each other in the darkened room, smoking cigarettes, whispering together like teenagers in love.

More than anything I felt this all-pervading sense of relief. I realised how close I had come to losing Jamie. Eventually she fell asleep. I kissed her gently on the forehead, pulled the duvet over her and went into the bathroom to shower and shave. I examined my reflection in the mirror and saw a positive expression gazing back at me. The thin lips curved into a reassuring smile, the blue eyes gazed back at me steadfastly.

Down in the kitchen, I grabbed a sandwich and then selected some records from my collection. I would make these last shows the best I could manage and I'd make up tapes of the highlights to submit to other stations. I had a vague idea about offering a similar format to the television networks, I felt sure the idea could work, especially in a late-night slot. I'd make it work. I owed it to myself. And to Jamie.

I set off for work much earlier than usual. No sense in racing any more, I decided. I'd take the last lap at my own pace. Breaking the finishing tape would be so satisfying. I could hardly wait to get started.

Chapter Eight

I faded the music and came in with my voice-over. 'All right landlubbers, splice the mainbraces and batten down the hatches! This is Captain Tom and that was Lou Reed taking a "Walk on the Wild Side". We're getting into some wild discussions tonight and in case you've just tuned in, we're talking about the rights and wrongs of abortion. As ever, the number to ring is 226 1234, so if you've got a view, share it with me. Ring in now and we'll chew the fat, straight after this record.' I punched the 'start' button on the deck, faded the microphone and leaned back in my seat. In a perverse way I was actually enjoying the show tonight, and so far, I had managed to keep my callers reined in to the official topic for the evening. It was an emotive subject and, for once, I'd had some articulate speakers on the line. In the frank exchange of views that had occurred, I'd almost rediscovered the elements that had attracted me to this line of work in the first place; but I knew that what was keeping me going was the knowledge that the exit door had opened. My mind was made up. When the time came, I would leave *Metrosound* behind in a cloud of dust and I would not look back. I glanced up as Steve Acton waddled into the studio and I cheerfully reminded myself that in a few weeks time I wouldn't have to look at that ugly face ever again.

'Ah Steve, old chum! What have you got for me?'

Steve's piggy eyes narrowed suspiciously. 'How come you're being so bleedin' matey?' he growled, depositing a heap of notes on the mixing desk.

'Didn't you know, these days I'm everybody's pal?'

'Decided to lay off the sauce tonight, I see.'

'Yeah. New leaf. I'm keeping my act clean. You should try it

Steve, it'd do you a power of good.'

Steve sneered, turned back to the studio. I adopted the refined voice of a fashion-show announcer, holding my nose between thumb and forefinger. 'And here's Steve, modelling the *Metrosound* spring collection. Note the puce T-shirt with matching custard stains and the delightful bum-hugger jeans with that tantalising inch of white flesh peeking over the top. Wear this one to a cocktail party and make all your friends envious!'

Steve half turned and flicked a casual two-fingered sign in my direction; but he couldn't help smiling, despite himself. He went back into his control room and joined the two hulking policemen who were manning the tracing equipment. I glanced through the notes and spotted William's name amongst them. It occurred to me that I had consigned this character to a thankless ordeal at the hands of Drayton and his crew. It would have been easy to leave William out entirely, but tonight I was feeling magnanimous. I put the name up at the top of the pile, faded the record and punched in my mike.

'All right, hello William, you're through to the Captain; and I think I should begin by offering you an apology. In fact, under the circumstances, I'm surprised you're still talking to me.'

'I had to think long and hard about it. But I came to the conclusion that in your own confused mind, you thought you were acting for the best. I will pray for you, Tom Prince.'

'Well, that's jolly decent of you, William! Incidentally, dear listeners, I'm aware that all of this is rather puzzling to you, so let me just say that William and I are discussing a private matter between ourselves, which has no bearing on tonight's discussion. So, William . . . your views on abortion please.'

'All life is sacred, Tom. The good Lord alone should have the power to consign a young child to oblivion. The bible clearly states that . . .'

In the middle of William's ranting, Steve's voice hissed in my headphones. 'It's John.'

I acted instinctively, cutting off William in mid-sentence. 'Well, thanks Willy, fascinating stuff! We'll move on now, because we have an important message from John. John, you're through to the Captain. Say your piece.'

There was a pause before that hateful, smug whisper crackled in my earphones.

'Hello Tom. I bet you didn't expect me back on the air this soon.'

'Well, no. We had a bit of an altercation, last night, didn't we? To tell you the truth, I wasn't feeling quite myself. I got a little . . . heated. I said a few things without really thinking about them.'

'I see. And I said a few things, too. Do you remember how I told you that they'd never let you ban me from the programme?'

'Er . . . yes John, I seem to recall something to that effect.'

'I was right wasn't I?'

'Yes John, you were. I discussed the matter with people here at *Metrosound* and the decision was to let you continue.' I struggled to keep my voice toneless, impassive. It wasn't easy eating humble-pie, but I was determined not to get riled this time. I would just have to sit there calmly and listen to the honeyed vitriol dripping down the telephone line. I could not allow myself to get angry. Not this time.

'I was upset by what you said, Tom. Very upset. You see I thought we were kindred spirits, you and me. I thought you understood me. I thought you were my brother. But you said terrible things I couldn't come to terms with. It was a betrayal of trust, Tom, and it made me very angry. And when I get angry, things happen, don't they?'

I shifted uncomfortably in my seat, sensing the black cloud massing overhead. 'Well John, you shouldn't let my opinions get to you. It's like I said, I had a bad night, that's all.'

'And *I* had a bad night, Tom. Thinking about what you said. Turning it over and over in my mind. And then I knew what I had to do . . . I've been busy tonight. I've been a bad, bad boy.'

Oh God, no. No, not again.

I felt a coldness settle within me. The black clouds were gathering around me, shutting out the light. I could hardly control my breathing. 'John, listen to me . . .'

'Can't just now, Tom. I'm standing beside her right now. She put up a fight, but she went down in the end. Used my knife on this one. Did you think I was going to stop just because you were angry with me? I'm doing this for you. Because I love you. Even if you don't love me anymore, I know what's right for you.'

'Please.' My own voice, desperate now, drifting alone on the airways.

'Too late, old son. Done now. All done. You'll want the address I suppose. No need to write it down, Tom. You know this one. I'm at your house.'

The clunk of the receiver. The stunned silence after. The sound of dust settling in the air as I sat, rigid, my hand supporting the weight of a record stylus. Below it, the record spinning in anticipation, the mad spiral whirling around and around, lusting for the needle.

I said something. I don't remember what it was.

There was a long moment when the air seemed to turn into something solid. The strength seemed to flow out of my limbs, draining me. The record arm dropped from my nerveless fingers and went skittering across the surface of the disc, making an idiotic squawk. Through the glass on the other side of the studio, three pairs of eyes stared at me in horrified fascination. I remembered to draw breath and then, the air around me seemed to shatter. I stumbled from my seat and moved towards the exit like a man caught in the depths of some awful dream. I don't even remember getting out of the building.

And then I was driving like a madman through the rainy streets; and for reasons I didn't stop to analyse, I had the car radio tuned to *Metrosound* all the way home. Somebody'd had the bright idea of putting on Sinatra's 'New York, New York' which came thumping out of the speakers, bold, brassy, totally surreal. I let it play because silence would have been too much to bear. And turning into my own street, I told myself for the hundredth time, that this was a practical joke. My home was impregnable. Murders didn't happen at home, they happened in other people's houses, people you read about in the papers, stories you hear on the radio.

And then I saw the flashing light of the police cars; the scattering of uniformed men in the driveway. Without finding a parking spot, I slewed the car to a halt, scrambled out and raced towards the house, bumping and pushing my way through the crowd of strangers standing in my garden. People tried restraining me.

'I'm her husband,' I screamed desperately. It was not exactly a lie and it seemed to work. The crowd parted before me and I ran to the door, hardly able to control my own breathing.

And I was in the house. The suddenly unfamiliar house, that somehow smelled strange. In the sitting room everything looked the same but there was a perceptible aura of fear in the room, something almost tangible. I raced upstairs, aware of voices in the bedroom. A policeman was trailing after me, trying to pull me back, telling me I should wait. I swore at him viciously, pushed him away. I saw the bedroom door was open and I ran on inside, barely aware of the startled faces that turned to stare at me. Men, standing around something on the bed. Something broken, something spattered with blood. I think I screamed her name. I flung myself down beside her, elbowing the men aside in my frantic haste to touch her.

And then the miracle happened. She moved beneath my touch and her blue eyes stared up at me in uncomprehending shock. An ambulance man was fumbling with a hypodermic syringe, trying to jab it into her arm, but she sat up abruptly and looked me full in the face. 'Black dog!' she said frantically. Her hands clawed at my arms, the nails drawing blood. 'Black dog. Black dog. Black dog . . .' She kept repeating the two words over and over, her voice guttural with some unseen terror. I wasn't sure if she recognised me.

'Jamie,' I gasped. 'I'm sorry. I'm sorry!'

'Black dog!' She was tearing at my shirt now, shaking her head from side to side. I saw that there was blood spreading across the white sheet the men had thrown over her legs. The ambulanceman finally got the needle into her arm. She kept repeating the two words over and over until the drug suddenly took effect and she went limp in my arms.

I clung to her and the policemen had to prise my hands away. I was dimly aware of Drayton's voice, talking to me, trying to reassure me.

'She's all right Mr Prince, she's alive. She's alive, do you understand? She's going to be all right.'

And then, somehow, I was in the cold, rocking womb of the ambulance, sitting beside the ashen-faced girl who was so still and limp beneath the blankets. She looked too peaceful lying there and the ambulanceman had to keep reassuring me that she was alive, that she would be OK, that it really looked much worse than it was. The sound of the siren filled my head and it was only then that the tears came, flooding me, claiming me totally. I buried my face in my hands and wept like a frightened child. I knew in that instant, that it was not over, that it never could be over as long as John was still out there in the darkness somewhere, planning, scheming, plotting his next move.

Then I remembered what Jamie had said to me. 'Black dog,' I said quietly.

The ambulanceman stared at me. 'Come again?' he said.

I shook my head. I had no words left in me and I did not speak again until we had reached the clinical sanctuary of the hospital.

The young nurse examined the cup and saucer and shook her head admonishingly. 'You haven't even sipped your tea,' she observed. 'Shall I fetch you another one?'

I shook my head. I was slumped on an uncomfortable wooden bench, my head in my hands. I seemed to have been waiting for hours and I had spent that time turning the events over and over in my mind, in a kind of horrible slow-motion replay. I kept telling myself that if I had held back my anger the previous night, if I hadn't drunk the bottle of wine, if I hadn't argued with Jamie, then maybe everything would be the same as before. Alternatively I reminded myself that Jamie was alive, that we both had much to be thankful for; but still nobody had told me exactly what had happened to her. The hospital seemed deserted, the bleak fluorescent-lit corridors grim and cheerless, stinking of antiseptic. 'How much longer?' I asked the nurse.

She shrugged. She was a pretty girl with large hazel eyes and small, delicate features. 'Hard to say. Doctor Latimer's with her at the moment.'

'Latimer?' I groaned. 'Oh, perfect. Just perfect.'

She brightened. 'You know Bob then?'

'We've met,' I said.

The nurse stared at me intently for a moment. 'My name's Sharon,' she said. 'Sharon Wheeler?'

I looked up at her, baffled.

'You probably don't remember,' she said. 'I phoned you once. We talked for nearly fifteen minutes. About the Health Service?'

I shook my head. 'I'm sorry,' I said. 'I don't remember.'

'I love your programme. I listen whenever I can. When I'm not working nights.' She seemed on the point of saying something else. Then she shrugged, moved off down the corridor. I watched her walk away, noting how her hips swayed, how the white cotton of her uniform hugged the curve of her buttocks. Then I realised what I was thinking and was absolutely horrified, wondering how I could be interested in such things at a time like this. Maybe it was true what everyone said. Men were beasts. But there were harmless beasts and then there were beasts like John.

A sudden wave of terror swamped me and I felt pinpricks of sweat break out all over my body. I remembered what Drayton had told me about the eyes of the other victims and for a hideous instant, I pictured Jamie's lovely face staring up at me, marred by two empty sockets. John had spared her that at least . . . but what other terrors might he have inflicted on her? I remembered the blood on the sheet that had draped Jamie's legs and, not for the first time, I asked myself if she had been raped. God no, not that! I couldn't stand to think of it.

A door swung open and Latimer came out. He registered me sitting there and he did nothing to mask the expression of intense dislike that was etched into his chubby, squeaky-clean face. He strolled towards me, as though there was all the time in the world. He stopped a short distance away and rested his hands on his hips.

'Well,' he said. 'I hope you're pleased with yourself.'

I forced myself to ignore the taunt. Another time, another place, I would have punched the bastard's teeth down his throat, but the night's events had left me impotent, desperate. He had me by the balls and he knew it. 'How is she?' I asked quietly.

'She's heavily sedated. She'll sleep through till morning.'

'That's not what I mean and you know it. How . . . how bad is it?'

Latimer considered the question for a moment, as though it was somehow beneath his contempt to answer me. Then he shrugged. 'Physically, the wounds are fairly superficial. There'll be some scarring on her legs, of course, but in time, with proper treatment, we'll be able to take care of that. The emotional scars, however, are an entirely different matter. She's clearly been terrorised to the very edge of sanity.'

'Has she . . . I mean, was she . . . ?'

'Raped? No, I don't think so. She's had sex sometime in the last few hours.'

'That was me,' I said hastily. 'Around six o'clock, we . . .'

He peered at me beneath half-lowered eyelids, a look that seemed designed solely to make me feel dirty. It succeeded.

'Hmm. Well, she has no injuries consistent with rape. Your friend John evidently gets his kicks in a different way.'

'He's not my friend!' I snapped. 'Why does everybody insist on making that suggestion?'

'Calm down,' suggested Latimer. 'It's not going to help anyone if you lose your rag, now is it?'

'It might help me,' I told him. 'Listen, I've been sitting around here for ages and nobody's had the grace to come and tell me exactly what's happened to Jamie. You said something about scars, and there was a lot of blood back at the . . .'

Latimer raised a hand to stop me in mid-sentence. 'Like I said, the wounds are fairly superficial. He's . . . well if you really must know, he's used the point of a very sharp knife to carve words into the flesh of her thighs. Here, and here.' He demonstrated by stroking his index finger along the inside of his own stubby legs. 'Judging by the marks on Jamie's wrists and ankles, he must have tied her up in order to do it.'

I stared at him incredulously. 'What words?'

Latimer frowned. 'Well, nothing that makes any kind of sense. Some kind of magical mumbo-jumbo.'

'What exactly?' I persisted.

'I don't really know how much I should tell you. The police want to—'

'Stuff the police! Listen to me, that woman in there is my wife . . .'

'Your wife? But I didn't think you were married.'

'No, not officially. But we live together, to all intents and purposes she is my next of kin. So will you please tell me about these words? It may be important.'

Latimer frowned, shook his head as though he was about to

confide a state secret. 'Very well. Umm . . . let me see now, on the left leg, it says "Seth calls the tune". And on the right leg, I think, yes, "Chaos returns". Like I said, complete nonsense. Or does it perhaps mean something to you?'

Latimer had caught the look in my eye. I did recognise the words. At least, there was something familiar about them, though I couldn't think where I had heard them before. I was experiencing the same dull sense of recognition I had sometimes felt when talking to John. There was something in those words, something from years ago, something I couldn't place yet. But they struck a hazy chord.

'Why?' I whispered. 'Why did he do that? He could have killed her but instead . . .'

Latimer eyed me critically. 'Look,' he said, 'you're obviously distraught. I suggest you go home and get some sleep. I could perhaps prescribe some suitable medication.'

'I want to see Jamie first,' I said.

'There's no point. She's heavily sedated, she won't even know you're there.'

'Just the same, I'd like to look in on her.' I fixed Latimer with a cold glare. 'Don't make me cause trouble for you,' I warned. 'I'm just in the mood for it.'

Latimer sighed, nodded. 'Very well. Five minutes, that's all.' He turned stiffly and led me across the corridor and through a doorway. Off to the left, there was a small room. By the entrance, a thick-set policeman was sitting on a metal-framed seat, reading a paperback novel. He glanced up, examined me for a moment then nodded curtly and resumed his reading.

'Five minutes,' Latimer reminded me. He turned and strode away.

I entered the room and stood for a long moment, looking at Jamie. She appeared to have grown visibly smaller, she looked frail and tiny in the hospital bed. She lay on her back, her eyes closed, her wax-white face turned up to the ceiling. I moved nearer and picked up one of her hands where it rested on the covers. It felt cold and unresponsive to my touch. She moaned softly in her sleep and her eyelids twitched as though she was plagued by bad dreams, but she did not waken. I bent and kissed her gently on the forehead, realising that Latimer had been right.

This was pointless, there was nothing I could do here till she woke. Still, I lingered by the bedside, searching for some sign of reassurance, hoping that by some miracle she would emerge from her nest of dreams long enough to grant me forgiveness. As I stood there, I turned the words over in my mind. 'Seth calls the tune. Chaos returns.' Where had I heard them before? *Where?* Why were they so maddeningly familiar and yet so beyond my grasp?

I swore beneath my breath and impulsively I leaned close to Jamie, whispering in her ear. 'He won't ever touch you again, my darling. I promise you that.' I reached out a hand to stroke her hair where it lay on the pillow, remembering how we had made love earlier that night, how I had left her sleeping in the warm sanctuary of our bedroom.

A brief surge of nausea ran through me. I turned away from the bed, made for the exit. Suddenly I couldn't stand to be there a moment longer. But neither could I stand to go back to the desecration of the empty house. I needed to purge myself in the best way I knew how, with noise and crowds and blinding lights. More importantly, I needed to drink till I had drowned the ache within me. I glanced automatically at my wristwatch. It was two-fifteen a.m. and there was only one place in Manchester where I would find what I was looking for.

Diary Extract

4th December
It's done. I've just got back and I'm shaking so much I can barely write. This time I let him guide me totally. The woman seemed nice, I can understand what Tom sees in her. But if He had wanted me to kill her, I would have done it. 'No trophies this time,' He told me. Instead the words. That was strange. I watched my hands working on the woman's legs and I didn't know what I was writing until I wiped the blood away and there they were, etched into skin. It doesn't have the permanence of stone, of course, and I was careful not to cut too deep. I didn't wish her any harm and I don't

think He does. After all, she's more than just a handmaiden. It was only when I read the words that I understood. Oh, He's a sly one and He's taking a risk but He doesn't seem to care. I think He wants Tom to recognise them. I think He wants to offer a sporting chance. He enjoys his little games.

This time there was no sexy feeling. I felt like a craftsman working for a patron. The feeling came later when I phoned Tom and He spoke through me and I felt the power we had over that poor man's life. I felt that I had him in my open hand and were I just to clench my fist, tightly, then I could have squeezed the very juices out of him. I think I might have masturbated then, but of course I had to leave quickly before they arrived. But now I'm home and I think this time we will have the needles, yes, a few more to quell the maddening itch where the old ones are beginning to rust. And I shall look in the mirror and as I come I shall see His great jaws thrown open in the heat of his passion, His long tongue lolling and with His sharp teeth I will taste a small morsel of the feast that awaits me, when Chaos returns.

Chapter Nine

The impassive bouncer, resplendent in black tuxedo and bow tie, nodded in recognition and stepped aside to let me enter. He gave me a little salute as I passed by – a jokey reference to my 'Captain' status. In so doing he glanced around, hoping that his little display of familiarity had been observed, believing that his own credibility was suitably enhanced by the fact that he knew me. Pathetic. I wouldn't have pissed down his throat if his lungs were on fire.

I went down the narrow stairs, presented my face at the desk and got a similar show of bonhomie from the idiot behind the glass. I walked on, without paying. One of the dubious perks of my profession was that I never had to put up money to gain access to a nightclub. I was what passed for a celebrity in this town and that meant that my presence was always appreciated. *Glitz* was currently the city's favourite late-night watering hole. The drinks were pricey but unadulterated and the place was licenced till four in the morning which, by my reckoning, gave me just enough time to get suitably legless.

I pushed open the swing door at the foot of the stairs and was struck in the face by a heady cocktail of music and body heat. I stood for a moment, surveying the territory. The place was packed with revellers in various stages of inebriation and the sunken dance-floor was choked tight with sweating bodies, jerking and bopping frenziedly beneath a blitz of strobe lights.

I pushed my way through the crowd and located a space at the bar, as far away from the dance-floor as possible. I was in pain and I needed a suitable anaesthetic. I slid on to a stool and waved a hand impatiently until I caught the attention of a young barman called Felix. I didn't much care for Felix either. He was a thin, prissy young gay with a seedy pencil moustache and his long hair tied in a pony tail. He had a high opinion of himself, but spent much of his time trying to climb up the backside of any available celebrity.

'Hey, it's the Captain!' he shrieked, over the music. 'Well, well, what are you doing in here tonight? I thought it was showtime.'

I shook my head. 'Finished early,' I yelled back. 'Give me a double tequila on the rocks.' I fished a fifty-pound note out of my wallet and slid it across the counter. 'Keep them coming,' I added.

Felix raised his eyebrows. 'Ooh, you must have a serious thirst!' He looked at me quizzically, but finding no humour in my eyes, he quickly changed the subject. 'Ray Wood was in earlier, he often drops by for a nightcap before he heads home. He's looking well knackered these days, isn't he?' He filled a large tumbler with tequila and lemonade and passed it across to me, together with a saucer of salt and sliced lemons. I lifted the glass, and cupped my hand over it. Then I brought it down sharply, slamming it on the counter top. The drink effervesced and I tilted it to my lips, draining it in one swallow, ignoring the salt and lemon. The tequila hit me like a clenched fist in the stomach. I gasped, smacked my lips. Then I slid the glass back to Felix and motioned for him to fill it up again. Felix frowned, examined his fingernails, but did as he was told. He watched dubiously as I repeated the exercise, totally misreading the pain in my eyes. 'Girl trouble, is it?' he asked. 'It's usually girl trouble.'

I shook my head. 'No, I'm just thirsty.'

Felix pouted. 'Well, perhaps I should leave the bottle here so you can help yourself,' he said sourly.

'Good idea,' I said and gave him my best 'Fuck off' expression. Felix raised his eyes to the ceiling and moved away to serve more accessible customers.

After the fourth glass, I felt the satisfying melting sensation at the back of my neck which told me that I was on the way to achieving my objective. I slowed the pace a little then, savouring the drink and taking it with salt and lemon, allowing the flavours to mix in my mouth before swallowing them. Behind me, the music switched abruptly to a different groove. Prince's '1999'. The familiar rhythm sent my thoughts spinning back to a night nearly a year ago. In remembering, I was trying to forget.

I'd been at a party at Des 'Weird-Beard' Connolly's place. As well as being the guy who'd got me my first introduction to *Metrosound*, Connolly was also my predecessor in the late-night slot. At one time he'd been *Metrosound*'s main man but his career had gone into a decline. When I joined, I became the new name at the station: a precocious young talent who initially was given nothing more than a series of fill-in spots on the daily review programme. Neither of us knew it at the time, but I was being groomed to take Connolly's place when his contract came up for renewal. I, meanwhile, was struggling through the last months of my relationship with Karen. She hadn't wanted to go to the party that evening, the two of us had rowed about it. So I'd gone alone, intent on having a good time. At first, it had proved difficult. The party was peopled mostly by media types intent on proving how cool they were. Connolly, aware of his failing social-standing had spent the evening moving from clique to clique, trying to ingratiate himself with various television producers and magazine editors. It was rather like watching a man drown in slow motion. I got pleasantly pissed and spent much of the evening insulting everyone I bumped into. For some reason I was able to get away with that kind of thing and I quickly discovered that the more I trashed people, the more they loved me for it. And then Jamie had come in, with a bunch of her friends and, suddenly, I had no other interest in the party.

I had liked the look of her, the way she prowled confidently around the room, fending off clumsy passes with a mocking glint in her eyes. She had a good laugh too, a deep-throated chuckle that rang out over the music, making heads turn. She clearly didn't give a damn what people thought. I steered myself in her direction and as soon as I had moved close enough, I weighed in with what I hoped was a confident introduction.

'Hi, I'm Tom Prince.'

She regarded me for a moment beneath half-lowered eyelashes. 'Lucky old you,' she said cuttingly. That put me in my place, but I went on with my pitch, just the same.

'Who are you with? Radio or TV?'

She laughed. 'Good God, you must be joking! I *work* for a living.'

I laughed too. 'Sorry. I thought everybody here was media.'

'No love, I've got a friend who does something at Granada.'

'Oh. What sort of thing?'

'God knows. She says she's in PR which probably means she makes the tea.'

'So what do you do?'

'Me? Oh, I'm in bed pans, hot baths and just occasionally, a warm soapy enema.'

'Ah, an angel!'

'With dirty wings,' she assured me. 'So . . .' She glanced scornfully around the room. 'Which particular circus are you a member of?'

'*Metrosound* Radio.'

'I see. I'm a Radio Four listener, myself.'

'Really. An insomniac are you? I understand that's the best cure.'

'Not at all. I find it riveting. *Gardeners' Question Time* has everything you could possibly ask in a radio programme. Drama, mystery, intrigue . . . greenfly . . . So, what do you do for *Metrosound*?'

'Oh news, views, reviews, interviews.'

'That's an awful lot of views.' She made it sound like the bullshit it undoubtedly was, but I wasn't going to give in so easily.

'Look, this party's a bit of a drag isn't it? I was thinking of cutting out and going somewhere more decadent.'

'Good for you. Hope you enjoy it.'

'What I meant was . . . would you like to come with me?'

She studied me for a moment. 'My, but you're a quick worker, aren't you? What would your wife say about it?'

'I'm not married,' I said, a little too quickly.

'All right then, what would the lady you live with say about it?'

'What makes you think I live with somebody?'

'It's a gift I have. I can smell an attached male at twenty paces.'

'And what about somebody who's looking to get unattached?'

'It's the same smell, only fainter.'

I shook my head. 'That's just my aftershave.'

She'd laughed again, her eyes flicking away, before returning to mine. I knew then that she was attracted to me, despite her stand-offishness. So I worked on her for the next half hour, gradually getting her to lower her defences. In the end, she agreed to go to the club with me, an uptown disco called '69'. It turned out well. We danced ourselves sober, then got drunk all over again. I liked the way Jamie insisted on getting her rounds in and how she insisted on going halves on the supper we had. Afterwards, we took a taxi back to her flat in Withington village. She invited me in for coffee. As she unlocked the door, she turned to look at me frankly.

'There's something we should get straight,' she said. 'You've probably got the impression that I'm the sort of girl who goes to bed on the first date.'

'Not at all,' I assured her.

She frowned. 'Then evidently I haven't been trying hard enough.'

We skipped coffee and went straight to the bedroom.

I have to admit that up to that point I hadn't had much experience of women. As a teenager there'd just been the occasional fumbling disaster in a car or the back row of the pictures. Karen was the first girl I ever laid and sex with her had always been a fairly one-sided experience. She tended to just lie there and think of England and, afterwards, I was always made to feel that I should be extremely grateful for her participation. This sounds cruel but I don't mean it to be. Looking back, I can see that we just weren't sexually compatible. Green as I was when I met her, I simply had no way of knowing how it could be.

Making love with Jamie was a revelation. I hadn't realised that a woman could be so aggressive in bed, so exciting. She fairly blew me away. I admit that at first it was mostly a sexual thing, but it wasn't just that. There was a warmth there, a sense of sharing that I'd never experienced with Karen. We laughed together a lot that night, we shared childish secrets, we lay awake for hours talking about crazy things and I knew, right from the word go, that I wanted Jamie, that I would not have a moment's rest until she was mine. Luckily for me, she felt the same way.

The very next day I set in motion the painful wheels of separation from Karen. I had never once regretted the decision.

'Hey! Hey, mate, I know you!'

I blinked violently, allowed my eyes to come back into focus. The bar was very crowded now and I'd lost count of the tequilas I had swallowed. I sat slumped on the bar stool, my elbows resting on the hard surface of the counter, though beneath my arms it felt somehow soft, rubbery, precarious. My head throbbed with a dizzy mingling of alcohol, cigarette smoke and noise as a hand pounded me relentlessly on the shoulder. I turned and saw a sweating face pushed up against mine, a mouth working as it shouted above the volume of the music. 'Hey, it is you, isn't it! Captain Tom! I thought I recognised you!'

I leaned back on my stool and studied the stranger, a solidly built young man with cropped hair, a sandy moustache and an accent that could only have originated in darkest Blackburn. He had one of the worst cases of terminal acne I've ever seen.

'Who the fuck are you?' I snapped.

The young man laughed uproariously as though I had cracked a joke.

'Yeah, you're the Captain all right! Nice one.' He grabbed my hand in his sticky fist and pumped it up and down vigorously. 'I can't believe this,' he yelled. 'I'm actually talkin' to Captain Tom! I'm Neil, I'm about your biggest fan in the world. Hey, let me get you a drink.' He jabbed his index finger at my glass. 'Wassat you're drinkin' Captain?'

'Piss and vinegar,' I told him.

He laughed again, clutching at his stomach and doubling over in an unconvincing pantomime of hilarity. 'Yeah, right on Captain. Jus' a minute.' Neil turned to the bar and gestured frantically at Felix. 'Give the Captain a drink. And give me four pints of bitter and a pint of lager!' He swung back and threw a meaty arm around my shoulder. 'Hey Captain, lissen, I'm here with some mates. What say you come over to our table and make out like we're old friends? They'd freak!'

I pushed the arm away irritably. 'I'm having a quiet drink,' I snapped.

'Oh, go on, it won't take a minute. I'm a big fan of yours, see. Never miss a programme when I'm workin'. I work nights as a driver, always have the radio tuned to *Nightboat*. It's the best bleedin' programme of all time! Hey! Hey, Captain, 'ow are you doin' with that sick fucker that keeps phoning you up? He's got some nerve 'asn't he? You any nearer to sortin' him out?'

I shook my head, reached for the drink that Felix had put in front of me and gulped it down. 'Leave me alone now, all right?' I said.

'Aww, come on. Look, my mates are just over here! All you gotta do, see, is come over to the table and say hello to 'em. It won't take a minute. Go on, I did buy you a drink.'

'You're a moron,' I told him.

He threw back his head and screamed with laughter, then snatched a pint from the bar and buried his face in it. When it emerged his moustache had a cloak of white froth on it. He shoved his ugly face up against mine. 'Here's how we'll do it,' he shouted. 'You help me take the glasses back to the table, see and then you just say hello to me mates and shake me by the hand. Whaddya say, it won't kill you will it?'

That did it. Something seemed to snap in my head and I felt a surge of hot anger flare up within me. I started up from the stool with a snarl and threw out an arm to jab Neil square in the chest, knocking him backwards a step and causing him to drop the pint of bitter he was holding. There was an abrupt scattering of the people around the bar.

Neil stood there staring at me in disbelief. 'What the fuck's wrong with you?' he yelled. 'I'm just trying to be friendly!'

'Well don't,' I said bitterly. 'Leave me alone, for Christ's sake.'

'Leave you alone? Who the fuck do you think you are?'

'You know who I am. But I don't know you and, frankly, I don't want to. Now do me a favour, get out of my face.'

Neil's eyes widened in anger and his cheeks reddened. He took a step forward. 'I never rated you anyway,' he snarled. 'Fuckin' record spinner, that's all you are. Anybody could do that. Think you're somethin' special because you're on the radio: you're nothin' pal! If it wasn't for that crazy twat that keeps ringing you up, you'd be . . .'

His sentence was interrupted by my fist as it smashed into his nose, crushing it flat. I realised then that this was something I'd been longing to do all night, only it was Latimer I'd wanted to hit. Neil had just happened along at the wrong time. He fell backwards against the people behind him, blood spurting from his nostrils. His face distorted with the realisation that he had been injured and he scrambled upright again, came lunging at me with his fists.

A remarkable thing happened. As if at some prearranged signal, several bouncers appeared from out of the crowd, wading into the fray with almost military precision. Neil was seized and propelled forcibly in the direction of the exit, protesting his innocence at the top of his voice. Behind him trailed the other members of his party, four similarly boozed-up youths who were not yet entirely aware of what was happening. One of them was attempting to staunch the flow of Neil's blood with a grubby white handkerchief, while the other three were arguing vehemently with the bouncers. The group disappeared into the crowd, their progress marked only by a jostling commotion as they passed. I was left, standing alone at the suddenly deserted bar, my fists still clenched. It was as though Neil and his friends had been beamed up by aliens. I knew full well that in normal circumstances both adversaries would have been escorted to the door. But I was a celebrity. I was Captain Tom and tonight the rules were bent in my favour. I realised with a shock that I had not wanted it to end there. I had wanted the strange comfort of violence, I had wanted to fight. More importantly, I had wanted to lose. I resumed my seat and beckoned to Felix.

"Nother drink,' I said.

Felix came forward with visible reluctance. 'I should say you've had enough for one night,' he observed testily.

'No, not quite. Just one more for the road.'

'For the road? Listen, I wouldn't go out there for an hour or so. Those arseholes will probably be waiting for you.'

I nodded. A powerful melancholy filled me. My eyes brimmed with tears. I could feel the old guilt gathering over me, the familiar fold of bruise-black cloud. In a moment, it would swamp me, choke me, smother me with its enormity; and when it hit, I wanted to be just that little bit drunker than I was at this moment. I watched blearily as Felix poured the tequila. Concentrating on the colourless fluid, I tried to put my own life into that glass, so that I could consume it, swallow it whole, obliterate it. I reached for the glass and for one terrible instant I was back there, running frantically into the bedroom where the policemen were gathered around the bleeding figure on the bed. I was looking into Jamie's staring eyes, seeing pain and madness flickering there in silent accusation, knowing that I was responsible.

'Please!' I gasped. 'Oh please.'

'Please what?' asked Felix, looking across the bar at me.

'No more.'

'What is it? Don't get sick in here, for God's sake, we've just decorated.' Felix leant forward to take the glass away, but I pushed his hand aside, grabbed the drink, downed it in one swift gulp. Felt the hot rush of the alcohol fill my chest, my head, my brain. I stood up, knocking the stool over.

'Don't go out there,' Felix warned me again. 'they'll use your head for a football.'

I said nothing. I turned and weaved my way unsteadily towards the door, pushing my way through the crowd, nodding to the bouncers who were still guarding the entrance. One of them tried to hold me back but I pushed him away. I went slowly up the staircase and out into the street. It was raining and the cold night air dashed over my face. Fresh adrenaline seemed to spurt through me. I moved onwards, through the straggle of people around the entrance and walked on to the road. I took a deep breath, moved on along the street. I could hear angry voices yelling somewhere off to my left. Instinctively I followed the sounds. I turned a corner and saw Neil and his friends waiting for me ahead. For the moment they were venting their rage on a telephone box, smashing out the panes of glass with their boots.

'Hey!' I yelled. 'Hey, arseholes!' I continued to walk towards them. They saw me coming and they left the phone box, moved to the middle of the road. They started beckoning to me, yelling taunts and obscenities. I laughed wildly, almost hysterically and raised my fists as I moved towards them.

'Come on then!' I said. 'Let's do it.' One of them ran to meet me and I lashed out with my hands, felt my knuckles crack reassuringly against a cheekbone. A fist crashed into my eye, knocking me backward a step. I shrugged, lumbered forward again, felt the sickening impact of a blow in my groin. I dropped to my knees, gashing my legs on the surface of the road and was unable to duck away from the flurry of feet that came lashing at me from every direction. A toe cap caught the side of my head, twisting me over on to my back and I curled up like a foetus on the surface of the road. They closed around me and my head filled with a redness and the sound of Jamie screaming. I closed my eyes and screamed with her, wanting to share the pain but my dulled senses and the adrenaline jolting through my limbs denied me that comfort.

'Jamie!' I whispered as I saw the blood soaking through the white sheet on her legs; heard the shrill wail of the ambulance; saw her white face staring up at the ceiling, her body still and small in the hospital bed.

The kicking stopped. I opened my eyes in surprise and saw that they were just standing there, gazing down at me. They seemed puzzled.

'Come on you bastards!' I yelled. 'Finish it! For God's sake, finish it!'

They drew back in disgust, whispering amongst themselves.

I lay there, my body shaking. I waved my clenched fists at them, spat saliva and blood at their retreating figures.

'Come back,' I screamed. 'Come back, fuck you!' I stared after them for a moment in complete indignation. There was no excuse for such behaviour. They had abandoned a job that was only half finished. Now they were drifting away along the road back into town.

I groaned. With difficulty, I got myself on to my hands and knees and felt nausea pulse through me. I retched violently and vomited on the rain-washed street. A blackness welled up from the base of my spine and filled my head. I fell back to the ground which was curiously soft and jelly-like. For a time I slept and there was no more pain. Only a disconcertingly familiar voice whispering in my ear, telling me that there was no rest for me, not even here.

Chapter Ten

The taxi driver kept shaking his head and tutting loudly. 'Bastards,' he said, with some feeling. 'I don't know what the world's coming to. It's got so you can't go out at night.' He was a good Samaritan this one, the only driver who had deigned to stop and pick up the bloody, staggering figure that had been trying to hail a cab from the side of the road.

I sat hunched in the back seat, shivering violently. My clothes were wet through and every part of my body hurt. My face felt like a swollen football and I kept probing my teeth with the tip of my tongue, expecting to find them loose in their sockets. Surprisingly, they seemed to be intact.

'I get all kinds of trouble myself,' continued the driver. He was a thick-set man with a stubbly, heavy-jowled face and a nose that looked like it had been broken several times across the years. He wore a grubby cloth cap that failed to hide his premature baldness. 'See this?' He fumbled in his glove compartment and brought out a large, snub-nosed revolver which he waved meaningfully at me. 'Haven't had to use it yet, but I've been close a couple of times, I can tell you.'

'Christ,' I muttered. 'Is it real?'

'Course it's fuckin' real. Got a licence for it and everything. You can't take any chances these days, not with the kind of scum I have to deal with.' He replaced the gun in the compartment and then glanced over his shoulder. 'You sure you don't want me to take you to Casualty? You look half dead.'

I shook my head. 'I'll be all right once I get inside,' I assured him. I had given the driver Karen's address. The thought of going home to my lonely house was more than I could bear. It was nearly five and I prayed that I'd be able to wake Karen without disturbing Daniel. I didn't want my son to see me like this.

'Well, you know best pal. Devonshire Court was it?'

'Yeah . . .' I peered through the rain-streaked windows as the taxi cruised along Karen's street. 'Just here will do fine.' I told him. I fumbled in my pockets for money and found a crumpled five-pound note. 'Keep the change,' I said.

'Thanks mate. You're bloody lucky they didn't rob you into the bargain. You'll be all right now?'

· 'Yes . . .' I got gingerly out of the car. My legs felt like they'd been modelled out of playdough and I hardly had the strength to stand upright. I slammed the car door.

'I'll hang on and make sure you get in OK,' said the driver.

'Thanks.' I limped across the pavement and rang Karen's intercom, supporting myself by hanging on to the door frame. I was obliged to ring several times before a sleepy voice crackled from the speaker.

'Who is it?'

'It's me . . . Tom.'

'Tom, for Christ's sake, have you any idea what time it is?'

'Sorry Karen . . . I've been in some trouble. Can I . . .?'

The buzzer sounded. I waved to the cabbie, pushed the door open and almost fell inside. I moved unsteadily into the hall and began the long, torturous climb up the staircase.

Karen met me at the door. She was wearing a dressing gown and her eyes had the heavy, gummed look that told me she had just been roused from a deep sleep. It didn't last long. The expression of shock that crossed her face told me that I must have looked as bad as I felt.

'Tom, for God's sake, what's happened to you?'

'A fight. Got into a fight. Look can I..?'

'Oh, Christ, you're probably concussed!' She held a hand out in front of me. 'How many fingers can you see?' she asked.

'What?' I was swaying on my feet. She moved forward and put her shoulder beneath my arm, helped me into the flat. I edged towards the sofa but she would have none of that. 'Straight into the bathroom,' she insisted. 'we'll have to get you cleaned up. Do you think I should phone for a doctor?'

I shook my head. 'No . . . be all right . . . in a minute.'

She got me into the bathroom and sat me down of the edge of the tub. 'My God, look at the state of you! Getting into fights at your age . . . will you ever grow up?'

I laughed grimly. 'I knew I could count on you for sympathy,' I said.

'Sympathy, my arse!' she snapped. She began to strip my clothes off, flinging them unceremoniously into the bathtub. 'These are all ruined,' she observed ruefully. She looked closely at my shirt and grimaced. 'Oh God, what's this? Vomit! You really are disgusting!' She went to the bathroom cabinet and took out a bottle of antiseptic. Then she switched on the hot tap and filled the wash basin. 'Some of these cuts might need stitches,' she warned me. 'What exactly happened?'

'I told you. I got into a fight.'

'With who?'

I shrugged. 'I dunno. I think they were Jehovah's Witnesses.'

'Skip the comedy routines. What happened?'

I sighed, realised that I would have to tell her everything. I began with what had happened to Jamie. She listened, her face impassive, while she soaked a flannel in the sink. 'She could have been killed,' she observed, when I had finished talking. There was almost a wistful quality in her voice as she said this and I stared at her for a moment, wondering exactly what was going on in her head. Is that what she wanted, I wondered? Jamie, conveniently out of the way and me running back for consolation? She squeezed out the flannel and moved back to me. 'This is going to sting,' she said.

I gritted my teeth while her capable hands worked methodically on all of my cuts and bruises. It hurt like hell and I yelped and protested like an injured kid. I had the distinct impression that she wasn't being half as gentle as she might have been. 'Stop making such a fuss,' she said irritably. 'Something bad was bound to happen. You should never have let it go on, like you did. I tried to tell you but you wouldn't listen.' She swabbed out a cut on my nose and it was all I could do to keep from screaming. 'It's not just you either. It affects Daniel and me. I've had colleagues say things to me and Daniel gets teased about it all the time at school. Maybe now you'll quit that damned radio station and find something worthwhile to do.'

'I already handed in my notice,' I told her. 'Only . . .'

'Only what?'

'Now it's personal,' I said quietly.

'Oh for God's sake, grow up,' she said. 'Who do you think you are, Clint bloody Eastwood?' She surveyed me critically for a moment. 'You know, this is just like you. Something happens and you can't deal with it. So you go out and get into a brawl, like some bloody sixteen-year-old. You never were any good at facing up to your responsibilities, were you? Maybe it's time you started.' She picked up a bathrobe and handed it to me. 'Here, put this on,' she said. She shook her head. 'Just my luck. I finally get you naked in my bathroom and you're no use to anyone. Come on, let's get you to bed. Sleep's probably the best medicine right now.' She seemed to soften a little. She bent forward and kissed me softly on the forehead. 'God, you're a worry,' she said.

'I'll take the spare bed,' I suggested.

'You will not. It's not made up and I'm buggered if I'm going to do it at . . .' She glanced at her watch. 'Six o'clock in the morning. You can climb in with me.' She raised a hand to still any protest. 'Don't worry, I won't take advantage of you. Your virtue will be perfectly safe. Christ, if I laid one hand on you you'd probably scream the house down.' She helped me to my feet.

'Karen,' I said quietly. 'Thanks. I'm sorry to call here like this I just didn't know where else to go.'

'Any port in a storm, eh? Come on, Rocky, let's hit the sack.'

She helped me in the direction of the bedroom and watched as I manoeuvred my battered body carefully beneath the duvet. 'What happens now?' she asked. 'With you and Jamie, I mean?'

I shook my head. 'Don't know. I haven't talked to her yet. Could be she'll never want to see me again.' I let my head drop back on the pillow, feeling a powerful weariness exerting a grip on me. 'She seemed . . . almost crazy at the house. Like she'd been driven to the edge, you know?' I closed my eyes. 'She said something about . . . about a black dog. Does that mean anything to you?'

'No, nothing.' She climbed into bed beside me and I was

vaguely aware of her hand, gently stroking my forehead, one of the few places that didn't hurt. 'Get some sleep,' she advised me. 'You look like death on two legs.'

'Yes . . . sleep. I'll go to the hospital tomorrow. Do you think . . . she'll be able . . . to talk then?'

Karen must have answered the question, because I was vaguely aware of the sound of her voice but the words seemed to break into shimmering fragments, I could make no sense of them. A powerful weight was dragging me down beneath the surface of the world and I succumbed to it gladly, letting myself go under, into the blackness below.

It was the smell of frying bacon that woke me, my empty belly lurching at the appetising aroma. I lay for a moment, staring up at the unfamiliar ceiling and for an instant I was calm, relaxed, without a care in the world. Then my memory bounced back abruptly, filling me with anxiety and I attempted to sit up. This set every nerve in my body jangling with pain and I fell back on to the pillows with a groan. I lay still, assessing the damage: face; neck; chest; back; arms, legs . . . I realised it would be quicker to count the parts of me that didn't hurt. After careful consideration, I decided that everything below my ankles felt fine. Well, at least I'd be able to walk.

My thoughts were interrupted by the sound of the bedroom door opening and Daniel came racing into the room. He clearly had every intention of flinging himself on top of me, but at the last instant he registered his old man's battered face and froze with a cry of alarm, his eyes fearful.

'Dad, what's happened to you?'

'It's all right Danny, don't be afraid. I've just been in some trouble, that's all.' I gritted my teeth and forced myself to sit upright. I did my level best to act naturally. Daniel approached the bed cautiously.

'Dad, you look horrible. Like a monster.'

I nodded. 'Thanks a lot,' I said.

Daniel climbed on the bed and settled himself beside me. He reached out a finger to trace a purple bruise on my cheek. 'Have you been fighting, Dad?'

119

'Er . . . yes.'

Daniel's brow furrowed. 'But when I got into a fight at school, you told me off.'

'I know I did, son. This was different, OK?'

'How?'

'Just different.' I put an arm around Daniel and tried not to wince as I pulled him close. 'Some bad things happened last night. I can't really tell you about them yet, but . . . well, the fight was all part of it.'

Daniel nodded. 'Was it something to do with John?' he asked.

I stared at him for a moment, trying to figure out what went on behind that innocent, wide-eyed mask. 'What do you know about John?' I asked.

'I know he's killed some people. Everyone at school talks about it. It was in all the papers. Mum wouldn't let me read any of it, but everyone at school has. They say . . .'

'They say what?'

Daniel shrugged. 'Things,' he said. 'About you. And about that man that phones your programme. I don't pay any attention to them.'

I reached out a hand to stroke Daniel's head. 'It's not over yet,' I said quietly. 'There may be some more bad things happening before it's over. I want you to know that whatever anybody says, I'm still your dad and I still love you. OK?'

Daniel nodded, smiled. 'Sure Dad, I know that.' He thought for a moment. 'Dad, how come you're back here, sleeping with Mum? Are you going to stay with us again?'

'No . . . I just needed somewhere to rest up last night. Your mum looked after me.'

Daniel frowned. 'Oh,' he said. 'Well, are you staying here today?'

'No. No, I have to go in a little while.'

Karen came into the room, carrying a breakfast tray. She stood looking at the pair of us uncertainly for a moment. 'Danny, I told you your dad wasn't very well,' she said. 'Inga's here, you'd better go and get ready for school now.'

'Awww, Mum!'

'*Now*, Daniel, please. Come on, you'll be late.'

Daniel sighed a deep sigh but clambered obediently off the

bed. 'See you then, Dad. You . . . you haven't forgotten about Santa Claus, have you?'

I shook my head. 'Of course not. We'll go soon. Come on, give your old man a kiss.'

Daniel planted a wet smack on my cheek which almost had me writhing in pain. Then he went out of the room, his hands in his pockets, gazing dejectedly at his feet. Karen brought the tray over and put it across my lap. I looked uncertainly at the full fried breakfast. 'I don't usually eat in the mornings,' I said.

She looked surprised. 'You used to love a full English breakfast,' she said. 'There was a time when you wouldn't start the day without one.'

'Well, I've been watching my weight.'

'Your weight! Honestly, Tom, you're like a skinned whippet! Eat it, it'll give you strength.'

It was easier to obey than to protest. I forked some bacon into my mouth and chewed it carefully. 'Even my teeth hurt,' I complained.

'Should have thought about that before you started throwing punches,' she said. She sat down beside me and studied me for a moment. 'You look dreadful. If you go to the hospital looking like that, you'll probably frighten Jamie to death.'

'Is it that bad?'

She nodded. 'If you want, I'll fetch you a mirror.'

'No, it's all right. I'll just imagine.' I prodded my fork half-heartedly into some scrambled eggs. Despite my empty stomach, I didn't have much of an appetite.

'Eat it up,' Karen urged me.

'Yes, Mum.' I did my best to comply.

'Your jeans are in the tumble-drier,' Karen told me. 'I managed to save them but the shirt was a total write-off. I found an old one of yours in the airing cupboard, you can wear that.'

I nodded. 'You've been very good, Karen. I don't know what I'd have done . . .'

'Skip it,' she said. 'You know you don't need any excuses to call here. I'm always glad to see you, but next time it would be nice if you arrived in a less dramatic condition.' She moved a little closer to me, lowered her voice as if confiding a secret. 'Listen,' she said. 'If things don't work out with you and Jamie,

I mean . . . I want you to know that I'm still here. I think we could give it another whirl, you know?'

I stared helplessly at my plate. 'Karen, I—'

'Sure, sure, I know how you feel about it. And I'm not much good at playing the faithful little woman, am I? But there's Daniel to consider and . . . well, whatever you might think about me, I do miss you.'

I nodded, pushed the tray aside. 'Can't eat any more,' I muttered. 'I should think about getting over to the hospital.'

Karen sighed. 'OK. For God's sake have a shave before you go, you might look a little less like an extra from *Night of the Living Dead*. There's one of Claude's razors in the bathroom. I'll go and see if your jeans are dry.'

She moved towards the door, then hesitated a moment, as though she had remembered something. 'Look, I know you think I hate Jamie's guts and everything, and I won't pretend she's my favourite person in the world, but I'm really sorry about what happened to her. I was thinking about what you told me last night. Those words on Jamie's legs. Didn't you say something about a Seth?'

'Yes. "Seth calls the tune." Why, does it mean something to you?'

Karen shrugged. 'Well, it's probably nothing.'

'Go on,' I urged her.

'You remember the series I worked on? *Lap of the Gods*? I did quite a bit of reading on Egyptian mythology before I composed the music for that.'

I nodded. 'What about it?'

'There's an ancient Egyptian God called Seth. He's sometimes called Set or Typhon. As far as I can figure it, he's their equivalent of the devil. And then, wasn't there something about chaos?'

I nodded. ' "Chaos returns." '

'Well, there's Nun: that's this great abyss that was supposed to have existed before the gods were born. It's usually perceived as a state of chaos.' She smiled, shrugged. 'Like I said, it probably means nothing.'

I shook my head. 'I'm not so sure,' I replied. 'John does talk about gods in the plural. It's something I've picked up on already, but the really weird thing is, I've heard those words somewhere

122

before – yet I can't place them, not for the life of me.'

Karen thought for a moment. 'Could they be lyrics?' she asked.

'Lyrics . . .' I stared at her. 'Yes, maybe they could. I'll look into that. Even if I can't place them there'll be somebody out there that can.'

'Out there?' Karen glared at me. 'You're not thinking about the radio show, surely? I thought you said you'd quit.'

'I thought I had. Now I don't know if I can afford to.'

Karen seemed to be on the point of saying something else. Then she sighed, shook her head. She turned back to the door. 'I'll get your clothes,' she concluded lamely.

I lay there, thinking about everything that had happened. I had blamed myself for Jamie's ordeal and the previous night had been a stupid attempt to atone for it. But now I saw, quite clearly, that I couldn't be held responsible. It would have happened anyway, maybe not to Jamie, but to somebody else. For his own reasons, John had chosen to involve me, had spent his time taunting me, using me. He could have killed Jamie but instead had chosen to terrorise her. It had been a warning, a show of power, a reminder that I was powerless in this game. So far, I had sat there and taken the punishment, had allowed myself to be humiliated, mocked, kicked around like a luckless human football. I'd had enough of that.

Now it was time to turn the tide. It was time to start fighting back. But first, I had to talk to Jamie.

Chapter Eleven

I limped through the hospital entrance and found my way to Jamie's ward. As I walked apprehensively through the doorway, I was dismayed to see Inspector Drayton waiting for me. He was sitting on a hardbacked chair studying some public-information posters on the wall. He glanced up uncertainly as I entered but once he had recognised me, beneath the layers of bruises, he could not conceal his delight. He got up from his chair and sauntered over, a smile of smug satisfaction on his thin face.

'Well, well, Mr Prince. Looks like you've been in the wars. I suppose this explains why I couldn't get in touch with you last night. What happened?'

I shrugged. 'I bumped into one of my fans,' I said.

Drayton snickered unpleasantly. 'If a fan did that to you, God help you if you ever bump into one of your enemies. Want to tell me exactly what happened?'

I shook my head. 'Not really. I came here to see Jamie.'

'Good. You'll be glad to know that she's conscious, has been for several hours. But she's refusing to talk to us until she's seen you.'

'Jamie always was a sensible girl.'

Drayton sucked his teeth. 'Sensible or not, she's going to have to talk sooner or later.'

'Look, give her a break can't you? Don't go pestering her for information, not yet. Hasn't she had enough to put up with?'

Drayton seemed to consider the question for a moment. 'Let's make a deal, why don't we?' he suggested.

I peered at him suspiciously. 'What deal?'

'You go in and talk to her. Afterwards, you report back everything she tells you. Then there's no need for me to go pestering her, is there?'

I sighed. 'I'll see what she thinks about it,' I said.

'You do that. You know, it's funny, isn't it?'

'What's funny?'

'The fact that John didn't kill her. He had every opportunity to do just what he did to those other women. Instead he chose simply to mark her. It's as though he was warning you, telling you that he can get to her any time he wants.'

I nodded. 'The thought occurred to me,' I said grimly.

'Well, we can talk about this later. You'd better get in there and see her. I've cleared it with the hospital, you can take as long as you like.' He stepped aside and indicated the doorway that led to Jamie's room. There was a look of amusement on his face, as though he sensed my discomfort. I took a deep breath and began to move forward. Then I hesitated. Now that the moment had come, I felt horribly apprehensive about facing her. I pictured her screaming abuse at me and I felt suddenly weak, had to support myself momentarily against the door frame.

'Something wrong Mr Prince?'

I was aware of Drayton's unsympathetic gaze. I shook my head and, steeling myself, I released my hold and moved into the corridor, placing one leaden foot in front of the other. Another uniformed policeman was sitting on a chair by the open doorway of Jamie's room. I took a halting step into the room and stood there for a moment, looking in at her. She was propped up in a sitting position, her body slumped back against the pillows. She was staring up at the ceiling and I noticed that her lips were moving, as though she was muttering something to herself. *Christ, she's gone mad*, I thought. In that instant a horrible scenario slipped through my mind: Jamie in some grim institution, dressed in a white gown, talking to herself in the corner of some godforsaken room. Me visiting her once a week, listening to her ravings and trying desperately to get through to her.

When she became aware of my presence, she turned her head in my direction and her eyes widened in shock. A look of terror crossed her face. At first, I didn't understand that look, I thought she was seeing John standing in my place. Then I remembered my battered features. I closed the door behind me and stepped forward quickly, raising a hand to reassure her.

'Jamie, it's all right. A fight. I got into a fight, that's all!'

She lay there, gazing at me and tears welled up in her eyes. 'Oh my God, Tom, I thought . . . I don't know what I thought.' She reached out a hand and I leaned forward, allowed her to trace her fingertips across my face. 'I've been so worried about you,' she whispered.

The enormity of what she had said struck me like a clenched fist. I realised then how much she must love me. I slumped down beside her and buried my face against her shoulder.

'You were worried about *me*? Oh Jamie, I'm sorry,' I whispered. 'I'm so sorry. I can hardly believe you're alive. I thought you were dead last night, when I got that call.' I couldn't find words, so I simply hugged her to me, marvelling at the warmth of her body, the familiar smell of her. She stroked my hair reassuringly.

'I'm all right. Scars, that's all. The doctors say that they'll go in time. They'll graft some skin. I knew that you'd be out there somewhere blaming yourself. When I woke up and you weren't here, I couldn't wait to see you.'

For some time neither of us spoke again. We lay there, touching each other, both of us weeping silent tears of relief. Finally, it was Jamie who spoke. 'There's been a policeman in here, asking all kinds of questions. But I wouldn't talk to him. I had to know you were all right first.'

I nodded, sat up, wiped my eyes on the sleeve of my jacket. 'He wants me to get you to talk about what happened,' I said. 'But if you don't want to, that's all right. And I won't let him pester you any more, I'll stand guard here myself if necessary.'

Jamie shook her head. 'I need to talk about it,' she assured me. 'Maybe it'll help to clarify it in my own mind. I really believed I was going to die back there. I just kept thinking, how awful to die and not be able to say goodbye to you. Never be able to talk to you, touch you. I thought of you finding me there, dead in our room and I . . .' Her voice dissolved into another flood of tears. I gripped her hand tightly, waiting for the storm to subside. After a few moments, she was able to go on.

'I was asleep, in bed. Something woke me. A sound, somebody coming into the room. At first, I thought it was morning, I thought it was you coming back from work. Somebody sat on the bed and I opened my eyes. It was dark in the room, I couldn't see anything. I said your name and there was no reply. And then I knew that something was wrong, I opened my mouth to scream. And then something was being held over my mouth, I could smell chloroform. Hate that smell. So familiar and yet, so . . .' She shook her head. 'When I came to, the lights were on and I was tied down. There was a gag in my mouth. I saw him, standing at the foot of the bed.' Her pupils dilated as though she were reliving the scene. I felt a violent shudder run through the length of her body.

'Jamie, this is important. Can you describe him?'

She shook her head and fresh tears spilled down her face. 'The mask,' she whispered. 'Black dog.'

'You kept saying that back at the house,' I whispered. 'I don't understand.'

She gasped for breath. 'He had on a mask. It was the face of a dog. A black dog, or maybe a wolf? Huge teeth coming down over the lips.' She gestured helplessly. 'I don't know. Hideous. He stood there and his head was, you know, moving to the music.'

'Music? What music?'

'I don't know what music. I could barely hear it, just the sound of the drums. He had on a Walkman, I could see the speakers against his ears. And he was singing along with the words, I think. Not singing, whispering. It wasn't a song I recognised and I was so frightened, Tom; I felt sure he would kill me and I couldn't think straight. Then he brought out this knife. I noticed he was wearing gloves, surgical gloves like they use in hospitals. He climbed on to the bed and he went to work on me. I felt a warm wetness on my legs and I thought I'd pissed myself but then it struck me that it was blood, my blood. I was screaming into the gag, but I couldn't make any sound through it and it seemed to go on for ever. I think I fainted a couple of times. I'd come back to my senses and he'd still be cutting into me, his head bobbing and that vile whispering. It was like . . . almost like he was praying as he cut me. Then suddenly, it was over. I think he went to use the phone. I heard him leaving the house.

I seemed to lie there for ages and then people were crowding into the room . . .'

She shook her head. 'That's it,' she said. 'That's all I remember. Not like the movies, is it? You're supposed to say that he had a distinctive scar, or a mole or a finger missing from his right hand. Christ, he could have had two heads and I'd have been too terrified to notice.'

I patted her shoulder reassuringly. 'You've done fine,' I told her. 'Better than anyone could be expected to.'

I got up from the bed and walked over to the window. Gazing out, I saw a scene of absolute normality, yet amidst the madness it looked strange, alien. A cold blustery December day. Raincoated visitors moving dejectedly towards the hospital entrance, clutching bunches of flowers and bags of grapes. An ambulance turning in off the main road, swinging wide to avoid a black van with a gold pyramid emblazoned on the side. I stiffened, stared at the van, but it was moving away along the main road now, was lost in the other traffic. The emblem had served to jog my memory. 'The music that was playing,' I said thoughtfully. 'Could it have been Egyptian?'

'It could have been anything. Why do you ask?'

'Oh, it's just this crazy idea Karen had – about the words on your legs.'

'Karen? When did you see her?'

'Last night.' I recognised, too late, the defensiveness in her voice. I turned back from the window, realising that it was useless to try and bluff my way out of it. 'I stayed at her place last night,' I said.

'Oh.' Her gaze flicked away from me but not before I had registered the look of betrayal in her eyes.

'Hey, it wasn't like that,' I assured her.

'Like what?'

'You know! It was because I was beaten up and I couldn't bear to go back to the house. She was great, she patched me up and gave me a bed for the night.'

'Oh, I bet she did.'

'Jamie!' I crossed back to the bed and sat down again. 'Look, don't read something into this that isn't there. Nothing happened between us, OK? Nothing ever will happen, that's a part of my life that's over now. But last night, I couldn't have been alone. I needed . . .' I left the sentence hanging. There was a long uncomfortable silence. I sat there studying my feet. I noticed that one shoelace had come undone. I bent to retie it but the effort sent a spasm of pain jolting through my back, so I abandoned the idea. I stared at Jamie for a moment. 'Have they given you any idea when you'll be out of here?' I asked.

'I can leave tomorrow,' she told me coldly. 'I thought maybe I'd go to my mum and dad for a while. They're coming up to visit this afternoon and I'm sure they'll want me to go back with them. I don't think I could stand to be in the house now, I wouldn't feel safe there.'

I nodded. 'It sounds like the best idea,' I agreed. I thought about Jamie's parents' place, a remote farmhouse in North Wales. Right now, it seemed like the safest spot in the world. 'I know this is difficult for you, but when do you suppose you'll be ready to come home?'

She gazed at me for a moment. 'Not while he's still out there, Tom. I don't know if I'll ever . . .' Another unfinished sentence. She stared at her hands for a moment. 'I'm confused right now. I need time to think about what's happened.' She looked at me frankly. 'It will give you time to think as well,' she said meaningfully. 'About us. About Karen and Danny.'

'Darling, there's nothing to think about,' I assured her. 'Please don't doubt me, if we're going to get through this, we have to stay strong.' I thought for a moment. 'Look, I'll drive over and visit you at the weekend. We can talk better then.'

'Why the weekend?' she asked fearfully.

'Well, because you'll need a little time on your own. And in the week, there's the show to do—'

Her eyes narrowed and suddenly there was an expression of sheer disbelief on her face. 'Tom, no, you can't be serious! Not now, not after what's happened. You were going to quit, remember?'

'I still have a month's notice to serve,' I said.

'But they won't hold you to that! Not even Radcliffe would—' She stared at me intently. 'Oh, but it isn't that, is it? You *want* to go on with it.'

'I have to go on with it, Jamie. Don't you see, because of what happened, I have to. I'm the only one who has a chance to reach John. It's not just you, this could happen to other women. If I just turn my back on it now . . .'

'Tom, listen to me!' Jamie was suddenly frantic, her face white with anger. 'You've done as much as anybody can expect. Nobody would blame you now if you called a halt. It's the only sane thing to do.'

I felt a surge of irrational rage pulse through me. 'Sane? Don't talk to me about what's sane, Jamie. That bastard has pushed me to the edge and so far I've let him do it. But no more, I swear, I'm going to get him, I'm going to start pushing back. Whatever it takes, I'm going to nail him.'

'You're talking crazy!'

'No, not crazy! I'm talking about something I have to do. Not just for me, but for everyone who's been terrorised by him.'

'Bullshit! Don't pretend this is for anyone but yourself! I'm not asking you to avenge me. I'm asking you . . . I'm begging you to give this up, now.'

I shook my head. I had already made up my mind earlier that morning. 'Don't ask me that, Jamie, please. Anything else in the world and by God, I'll do it willingly. But don't ask me that. Try to understand how I feel.'

'How *you* feel? My God, you're not the one who was attacked! You're not the one with those filthy words cut into your legs!'

That one really hurt; and she was absolutely right of course. But some tenacious intent deep inside me wouldn't let me give up on the idea.

'I have to do this, Jamie,' I told her. 'It's as simple as that.'

'And if it costs you more than you bargained for?' she whispered.

'Whatever it costs,' I said quietly. I put my arms around her and held her to me. 'He's trying to destroy everything that I care about,' I said. 'I'm not going to let that happen. Call it vengeance if you like. Right now, it doesn't seem an unreasonable word.'

'You'd better go,' she said coldly.

'Jamie, please.'

'You'd better go now.' Her voice was distant, toneless, as though she had simply switched off her emotions. I let go of her

131

and eased her back on to the pillows. I leaned forward and kissed her gently on the forehead, but she seemed barely aware of me. There were tears in her eyes again, but this time she made no sound.

'We'll talk at the weekend,' I said, my own voice hoarse with emotion. There was no reaction to this. 'I love you,' I told her helplessly. 'I always will.' I got up from the bed and stood there for a moment, awkwardly, wishing there was something else I could say, something that would make it all right. But I knew there was nothing. Jamie would have to consider my motives and make her own mind up about it. It would take time. I turned and walked quietly out of the room.

Drayton was sitting where I had left him. As I approached, he furtively slipped something into his pocket, a small black radio receiver. I froze in my tracks, staring at him in disbelief. He looked up at me and smiled coldly. 'So, you've decided to go on with the programme,' he observed, matter of factly. 'Good. I like the anger. Maybe we can use that.'

I stood there, shaking my head, realising that I had underestimated the depths to which Drayton could sink. 'You were listening in!' I cried. 'You had a bug in the room!'

Drayton spread his hands in an apologetic gesture. 'Small precaution,' he said. 'In case you forgot to mention something afterwards.'

Again anger exploded in my chest. It seemed to me that everybody I knew was giving me a good fucking-over. In three quick strides I was across the intervening space and I had Drayton pinned against the wall. 'You deceitful bastard!' I screamed. 'I ought to knock your teeth down your throat!'

'Now, now!' protested Drayton. 'Let's not add a case of assault on a police officer to your problems! I guarantee that won't help you in the slightest, Mr Prince.'

For a long moment, we glared mutual contempt at each other. Then somehow I got my temper under control and persuaded my hands to release their grip. Drayton sank back into his chair and quickly rearranged his clothing. I squatted down heavily beside him and buried my head in my hands. 'That had to be illegal,' I said grimly. 'That was a private conversation, I could have you hauled over the coals for that.'

'I doubt it,' Drayton retorted. He sighed, shook his head. 'Listen, there's something you should understand, Mr Prince. I'm not one of those coppers who goes by the book. I can't afford to, not with the kind of scum I'm dealing with. John clearly doesn't go by the book, he's writing his own. I want to catch him, just as much as you do. Maybe more. He's been making a laughing stock of me and my force for the last two months. We've spent a small fortune on this investigation. The forensic boys went over your place with a fine-tooth comb and do you know what they came up with? Nothing. The big 0. Sweet FA. We're getting desperate. I've got the chief constable on my back, asking for results; I've got a possible promotion that's swiftly going down the toilet. So I have to play dirty to catch him, I will; you can depend on that. I don't expect you to like my methods, I don't much like them myself. They've become necessary.'

'But I said things in there I'd never have said if I'd known . . .'

'Exactly, Mr Prince. Look, I'm not the least bit interested in your love life. I was listening for the facts and there were precious few of those on offer. Now, you said something about your ex-wife, some theory she came up with?'

'Go fuck yourself!' I snapped.

Drayton sighed, tutted loudly. 'Not very helpful,' he admonished. 'I can just as easily pull the lady in for questioning, if that suits you better.'

I thought about that for a moment and realised that I couldn't afford to hold out on this. He had me over a barrel and he knew it. 'All right' I said. 'It was about the words on Jamie's legs. Karen said that there's an ancient Egyptian god called Seth . . . and something about Chaos too, I don't exactly remember what she said about that. But you remember my theory, how John always talks about gods, plural. It seems to tie in, that's all.'

'Ancient Egypt?' said Drayton quietly. 'Wonderful. I can see it now. Police are looking for a ten-thousand-year-old man to help with their inquiries.'

Despite everything, I laughed at that. It surprised me, I thought I'd forgotten how to. Drayton sniggered too and in the sharing of the joke, I was amazed to feel several barriers crashing down between us. I shook my head. 'I don't understand it myself yet,' I admitted. 'But I think that the words might be from a song.'

Drayton perked up a little. 'What song?' he asked.

'Don't know yet. But I think I can find out. The *Nightboat* audience includes experts on any subject you care to name. Long-forgotten lyrics are one of their specialities. So on tonight's show . . .'

'You're going back on tonight?'

'I intend to, yes. But I'll need you to put pressure on Radcliffe on my behalf. I suspect that even he will draw the line after what's happened.'

Drayton nodded. 'I'll do my best. I have to admit, you've got guts going back so soon. It's strange isn't it. Not long ago, you were pleading with me to take you off that damned programme.'

'Things change,' I said.

'Well, it's time we admitted something. We both want the same thing. We'll do better if we work together on this.'

I frowned. 'I don't trust you,' I warned him. 'Everyone I've ever trusted has shit all over me.' I thought for a moment. 'Except Jamie,' I added.

'Trust doesn't come into it. I wouldn't leave you alone with my invalid grandmother, if it comes to that. Don't worry, Mr Prince, I'm not asking you to marry me. I'm not advocating the start of a beautiful friendship, either. We'll just make sure that we keep each other well informed of any new developments.' He got to his feet, nodded curtly. 'I'll listen to the programme tonight,' he said. Then he walked away in the direction of the exit, a thin awkward figure in an unfashionable raincoat. I watched until he turned a corner out of sight. It occurred to me once again, that I had no real friends, nobody who could help me with this. All I had was Drayton. He was a ruthless bastard but that was probably just the kind of ally I needed right now.

With a sigh, I eased my aching body upright. I had put off the inevitable long enough. Now it was time to go home and pick up the pieces.

Chapter Twelve

I unlocked the door and let myself into the hallway. A small act but I'd stood on the doorstep a long time working up the courage to do it. I stood there for several minutes, adjusting to the chilly, unfamiliar atmosphere in this once-familiar place. Turning, I closed the door gently behind me and saw the dark smudges of fingerprint powder all around the frame. I felt an instant of pure shock. My home had been violated and here was the evidence of rape, these grubby marks on the white paint.

I stooped and picked up a pile of mail lying on the doormat, placed it on the hall table without looking at it. I walked into the living room and gave it a cursory glance. Then I went into the kitchen and switched on the central heating. I kept stopping and listening intently. It was illogical but I was listening for the sounds of somebody else in the house. It was horribly silent and that was somehow infinitely worse. I went slowly up the staircase and stood by the bedroom door, steeling myself to go in. At last, I felt ready. I took several deep breaths, tried to get hold of myself. At last, I felt ready. I pushed the door open. The curtains were still drawn, it was dark in there and a strange smell exuded from the room, of sweat, mingled with fear. Involuntarily I relived the terror of the previous night and, irrationally, I half expected to see Jamie's blood-spattered body lying on the bed. When I switched on the light, the room seemed bigger than I remembered and it felt like years had elapsed since I was last there.

The police had really gone to town. Every item of furniture was blotched grey with fingerprint powder. Thankfully, they must have taken much of the soiled bedding and discarded clothing away for analysis but there was still a coagulated crimson spatter on the wall above the headboard. I pulled back the curtains and opened the windows. Then I went down to the kitchen, boiled the kettle and filled a bowl with hot water and disinfectant. I went back up to the room and did my best to clean up, mopping the blood from the wall and wiping the grey smudges from the furniture. I put all the remaining bedding into a plastic bag and threw it out in the dustbin. Blood had soaked into the mattress, so I dragged that downstairs and set light to it out in the garden. When it was burning well, I went back in, got the mattress from the spare bed and brought that into the room. I got clean sheets and duvet and made up the bed again. For some inexplicable reason, it was important to me that I should sleep there, rather than in the spare room or down on the sofa. It was the first move in my campaign to fight back against intimidation. Nobody – not even John, was going to turn me out of my bed. As a final measure, I lit several sticks of incense and set them up around the room.

I stepped back to survey my handiwork.

There now, you bastard. I washed you out. I swabbed you away like the filth you are.

I was sweating from the effort of cleaning up and I realised what I had been doing: claiming the room back from John, making it my own again. I took the bowl down to the kitchen and emptied the dirty water away. Then I boiled the kettle a second time and made myself a cup of coffee. I took it to my study, which I was glad to see was relatively untouched. Only the telephone had the characteristic grey blotches, the police must have thought that John had phoned from this extension. But he would have been wearing his gloves, he wasn't that stupid.

There were three calls logged on the answerphone and I played them back while I sat sipping my coffee. The first was from Simon Radcliffe.

'Er . . . hello, Tom? Look er . . . I've just been informed about what happened last night. Terrible business, I can't begin to tell you how sorry I am. Anyway, we'll talk about that when you feel ready. Obviously, it goes without saying I won't hold you to that contract now, you probably couldn't bear to come within a mile of the station after what happened. I'll sort out a temporary replacement to take over the show from tonight.' A long pause. 'I'm just thankful that Jamie is alive, she could so easily have . . . Jesus, it's difficult talking about this, I hate answerphones. I just never for a moment dreamed that anything like this would . . . look, we'll talk when you've had a chance to rest. I'm sorry Tom, I really am.'

I sipped at my coffee, totally unmoved by this show of crocodile tears. It was just as I had suspected. I'd have to fight to get back on the airwaves. Suddenly, it was all too real for Simon. Then, predictably, there was a call from Karen. Under the circumstances, her jolly tone sounded forced and inappropriate.

'Hey there champ, how ya doing? Hope everything went OK at the hospital. I've been thinking about you all day. I just wanted to say that it was really nice to have you home again, whatever the circumstances. Don't be a stranger to me, Tom; I still care about you an awful lot, you know? Ring me when you get a chance, let me know what's happening. And I know Danny would like to hear from you. He keeps going on about that visit to Santa Claus. You won't let him down on that, will you? Well take care, love. I'll see you soon.'

I frowned. I didn't like this new development with Karen. She seemed to be banking on some change of heart from me, but I knew that there was no going back, whatever happened between me and Jamie. That part of my life had been irrevocably laid to rest.

The third call hissed from the speaker and an electric jolt of fear rippled through me. I felt the hairs on the back of my neck stand up, one by one. I'd read about this kind of thing in books and had always believed it to be an invention of horror writers. Not so. It was happening.

'Hello, old son. Couldn't resist making a note of your number last night. Now I can phone you whenever I like. Quite a show I put on for you, wasn't it? Did you like my little message? Did it ring a few bells? It should have done. You commented on those words once before, didn't you? I wonder if you can remember when? Anyway, now you know I can get to you whenever I want. I won't lose your number, old son. She's pretty, your lady. I thought about changing her looks last night, but I decided against it. The thing is Tom, you're so vulnerable aren't you? There's all kinds of ways I can get to you. And it's not just Jamie.

There's your ex-wife. Karen, I think her name is. Oh yes, and that cute little kid of yours. Danny? Daniel. The little hawk. I've got their number, too. Think about that, Tom. I want you to lose sleep thinking about that. By the way, check your post. I left something for you to look at. All for now, I'll be in touch—'

The silence that followed the call was like a shrill scream of terror. I sat there, numbed. I was vaguely aware that I'd knocked over my cup of coffee, that the hot liquid was streaming across the top of the desk, soaking into letters and documents, staining the white paper a muddy brown. It was stupid of me, but somehow I'd never even considered Daniel as a potential target for John. I'd seen my former life as a watertight compartment, sealed off and out of harm's way.

I grabbed the phone and rang the number Drayton had given me, the incident room. The phone was answered by a minion, but the fear in my voice must have convinced him to go and find Drayton for me. After an interminable wait, Drayton's voice bled from the earpiece.

'Mr Prince. Problems?'

'You could say that. John left a message on my answerphone. He's talking about my ex-wife and son now. He says he knows where to find them. He's capable of hurting them both, we've got to—'

'All right, calm down. He made threats against them?'

'Indirectly. Look, you've got to give them some kind of protection. If I go back on the air and take him on, he'll go after them.'

'Right. Give me the address, I'll assign somebody to watch the house.'

'Twenty-four hours, round the clock. He's a devious bastard, if he gets an opportunity to slip through your guard, he'll . . . oh Christ, Danny will have to be escorted to school and back, John could follow him.'

'Yes, yes, I'll take care of that. You'd better phone your ex-wife and tell her what's happening. But listen, I want to keep this surveillance as low-key as possible. If there's a chance of drawing him out, we mustn't botch it by scaring him off. And give her this number. Tell her if she's going anywhere, even down to the corner shops, she's to phone and let us know her movements. We'll make sure there's somebody watching her at all times, don't worry yourself on that score.'

'That's easy for you to say.'

'I know it is, Mr Prince. But you're going to have to trust me on this one, aren't you? Now, did John say anything else out of interest?'

I forced myself to think rationally. It wasn't easy. I was spooked and my brain seemed like a badly rusted machine, clicking and grinding as I tried to make it function.

'He asked me if I got the message. By that I presume he meant those words on Jamie's legs. He also said that I had good cause to remember them, that I'd passed comment on them before.'

'Hmm. And you still don't recollect anything about them?'

'Nothing. I just have to hope that one of my listeners can come up with a connection.'

'I have bad news for you on that score. I phoned your Mr Radcliffe earlier and told him about your intentions. I also told him that I supported your wishes. But he was pretty adamant that he couldn't let you go back on the air.'

'Was he, now? Well, we'll see about that. As soon as I've talked to Karen, I'll head into the station. Get that surveillance sorted out straightaway, I won't rest till I know that they're safe.'

'I'll get on to it. Oh and Mr Prince?'

'Yes.'

'It might be a good idea if you could come up with a list of people who may bear you a grudge.'

'Christ, that could read like *War and Peace*!'

'Maybe. But just the same, I'd like you to think about it. Particularly people from before all this began. Anyway, keep me in touch of any new developments.'

'I will do.' I put the phone down and did my best to mop up the spilled coffee with a paper handkerchief. Then I dialled Karen's number. The phone rang and rang and I began to panic. Of course she could be out somewhere, I reasoned. Shopping, business appointment, recording studio. I was just about to put the phone down when somebody picked up the receiver at the other end of the line. There was a long silence and for a terrible moment, I expected to hear a familiar whispering voice answering the call. But then I heard Karen's voice, sounding rather put out. 'Hello, who is this?'

'Karen. It's Tom.'

'Tom, hello! Did you get my message? Sorry about the delay, I was in the shower.'

I tried not to let out a sigh of relief. 'Karen, I'm sorry to disturb you. Look, this is going to sound a bit dodgy but, well, I've asked the police to keep an eye on you and Danny.'

'The police? Why? Is something wrong? I mean . . . sorry, stupid question, of course there's something wrong. But is there any particular reason?'

'No, no, absolutely not!' I lied. Best to play it down, I told myself. No reason for panicking her unduly. 'It's just a precaution, that's all. So, if you should see any odd characters hanging around, chances are it'll be your friendly neighbourhood scuffers doing their good deed for the day. Tell Inga that there'll be somebody following her and Danny to school and back. And there's a number here to call if anything suspicious should happen.'

'Hang on, let me get a pen.' She took down the number. 'Christ, this is all a bit dramatic, isn't it? I mean, do you think there's any real reason to worry?'

'It's like I said. A precaution. If you're planning to go out at all, ring that number and talk to Detective Inspector Drayton. Let him know your movements, just to be on the safe side.'

'Drayton, OK, got that. I don't know if I like all this involvement with the Old Bill, though. How long does it have to go on?'

'Until it's over. Look, I'm sorry for involving you. Just humour me. OK?'

'OK. Is it all right if I get back under the shower now? Or should I phone the police and have them send somebody to stand in the cubicle with me?'

I laughed grimly. 'Listen, it might be a good idea if you could get one of your boyfriends to come and stay with you for a while. Lend a bit of moral support.'

'Boyfriends? What boyfriends? Bernard's off doing a provincial tour of *South Pacific* and Maurice is doing a documentary about the Camargue.'

'Hmm. What about the geezer with the beard and the biker's jacket? He looks like he can handle himself?'

'Who?'

'Oh, just somebody I saw coming out of your apartments a month or so back. I suppose I assumed—'

'Not guilty, pet! Besides, there are other flats in the building, you know. He could have been visiting the art student on the top floor. She has enough men in to make up a rugby team, though she runs more to yuppies with flash cars.'

'Hmm. Well—' I felt a shiver of apprehension run through me. I remembered how the man had smiled at me as he'd passed, a smug, knowing kind of smile. At the time I'd put it down to a look of recognition, or the self-satisfied expression of a man who was shagging my ex-wife. Now I wondered if there had been more to it than that. I shrugged off the notion. Like Karen said, he could have been visiting somebody else.

'One last thing,' I said. 'Your Egyptian documentary: does a black dog play any part in it?'

'A black dog . . . yes, you said something about that before.' A pause while she considered the question. 'A jackal, maybe?'

'A jackal. Yeah, could be. Which particular boogie man is that?'

'He's called Anubis. Body of a man, head of a jackal. But Tom, are you sure it's a dog you're talking about? Seth has an animal's head, you know.'

'What kind of animal?'

'Well, as I recall, it's a mixture of things, nothing recognisable. The Typhonian animal, they call it. A black creature with big teeth like maybe a wild boar or something. Do you think there's something in any of this?'

'I'm beginning to,' I admitted. 'You'd better get back in the shower, before you catch your . . . before you catch cold.'

She laughed at my discomfort. 'Very nearly a Freudian slip,' she observed. 'Keep in touch.'

'I will. See you.' I put down the phone and sat for a moment, considering this latest development. *Seth.* It kept coming back to Seth. I thought about what Jamie had told me. The mask that had looked like a black dog. I thought about the terror that must have inspired and I forced myself to put the image out of my mind. Then I remembered John's remark about the post and I hurried out to the hallway to examine the mail. The only thing that seemed out of the ordinary was a large brown envelope, lacking either a stamp or a postmark. Evidently it had been delivered by hand and the thought gave me an involuntary chill. I opened it carefully and withdrew a glossy promotional leaflet featuring an artist's impression of a large, pyramid-shaped office building. I recognised it immediately as one currently under construction on the outskirts of Manchester. We'd done a *Nightboat* phone-in on the building some months back. I remembered that the general concensus of opinion had been that it was highly inappropriate to its surroundings. Across the top of the brochure, somebody had written 'HOME SWEET HOME!' with a bold, felt-tip pen. I examined the rest of the document and saw that one sentence had been underscored: '—based on the dimensions of the famous Great Pyramids of Cheops, the Osiris Complex will provide thousands of square feet of workspace, together with conference facilities, health club and a fully equipped gymnasium.'

I frowned. More Egyptian mumbo jumbo. But what did it all mean? Where was the connection? I felt as though I was standing in a darkened room, seeing occasional flashes of light, but not knowing their source. It was evident that John was prompting me, perhaps mocking my inability to piece the puzzle together. I sighed, slipped the brochure back into its envelope. Something else to hand on to Drayton, I decided. I glanced at my watch: four p.m. Simon would only be at the station till five-thirty. I would have to get my ass into gear.

I went to the bathroom for a much needed shower and changed into clean clothes. I collected the envelope, picked out some records from my collection and then let myself out of the house and walked down the drive to where I had left my car two nights earlier. I stood there staring at it and, once again, I felt chilled to the bone, knowing that John had been back here during that time.

A hand had scratched four words deep into the paintwork of the bonnet.

'SETH CALLS THE TUNE' it read.

Chapter Thirteen

I drove into town. The Rolling Stones' 'Sympathy For The Devil' blasted from the radio and the clattering percussion and searing guitar suited my mood. I told myself that the damage to the car was relatively unimportant. After all, it was a mere possession, something that could be resprayed, put back to normal; but what had shaken me was John's sheer nerve, returning to the scene of the crime only hours after the place had been crawling with police. He must be a man with all the time in the world, I decided. Unemployed maybe? Or perhaps a man of independent means, a man who didn't have to go to work like the rest of us poor bastards.

Who are you, John? And what's your beef with me?

It was crazy but somehow I could sense him out there, planning his next move. I knew he wasn't finished with me yet and the knowledge knotted my guts with fear. But there was nothing I could do except carry on with my life and, meanwhile, try to find out whatever I could about him.

Eschewing my usual route, I took a detour past the Osiris Building. It had come on a lot since I had last seen it, the bare metal and concrete framework covered by walls of highly reflective glass. I parked for a while and sat staring up at its pinnacle which was silhouetted against the reddening sky. Around its base, in the mud and jumble of the construction site, an army of labourers moved to and fro performing their mysterious functions. Yellow JCBs resembled children's toys as they rumbled backwards and forwards beneath its massive shadow.

'Home sweet home,' I murmured. But how a home? A spiritual home, perhaps? Or could John actually have taken up residence somewhere beneath that glittering edifice? I frowned. Unlikely, I decided. Still, that was something for Drayton and company to look into.

I recalled Drayton's advice that I was to try and compile a list of potential grudge-bearers, but it was hard to know where to start. I'd made more than my fair share of enemies over the past few years. My outspoken critiques in *Scam* magazine had rubbed up many musicians and managers the wrong way and, more recently, *Nightboat* had given me the opportunity to insult, ridicule and generally humiliate a lot of powerful people – along with the more usual collection of bigots and headbangers. I envisaged a computer printout the length of the Bayeux Tapestry and promptly shrank from the idea. Maybe tonight's phone-in would yield some clues; provided, of course, I could talk Simon into allocating me my regular slot. It was ironic. The programme had never meant as much to me as it did now. I started up the car and continued on my way.

As I pulled into my usual space in the *Metrosound* car park, it struck me, for the first time, as a lonely threatening place, an ideal spot for somebody to attack me. I sat in the car for several minutes, looking apprehensively around the gloomy, concrete building and I thought seriously about arming myself in some way. I remembered the taxi driver who had proudly waved a pistol at me and I wondered how difficult it would be to get hold of such a weapon. It shocked and dismayed me that I should be obliged to consider this option, but these were exceptional times. John would have no qualms about carrying a gun, of that I was sure.

I got out of the car and started towards the *Metrosound* entrance, unnerved by the hollow clumping of my own footsteps in the semi-darkness; then I froze in my tracks as somebody stepped out of the shadows to my right. The terror must have shown on my face, because the small boy halted uncertainly, as though debating whether to run. Then he saw me relax and he moved hesitantly closer, one grubby hand held out in front of him.

'A pound to look after your car, mister?' he asked hopefully.

I examined the boy dubiously. He was perhaps a few years older than Daniel, dressed in a dirty, rumpled anorak and torn jeans. His black hair was almost plastered to his skull with grease and he looked as though he had been sleeping rough for weeks. Kids like this one often worked the city-centre car parks, but my late working-schedule meant that I rarely encountered them.

'I could have done with you last night,' I muttered.

'Mister?'

I pointed to the crude graffiti scratched onto the bonnet of my car. The boy stared at it for a moment, then shook his head, grinned. 'What's that supposed to mean?' he asked.

'I don't know, beats the hell out of me. What are you doing out by yourself so late?'

'It ain't late,' retorted the boy. 'Go on mister, a pound. I'll keep an eye on it for you.'

I frowned. I dug into my pocket, found a coin and flipped it to the boy, who caught it expertly in one hand. 'Thanks, mister.' He nodded towards the illuminated entrance of *Metrosound*. 'You goin' in there?' he asked.

I nodded.

'You a DJ? You famous or somethin'?'

I laughed bitterly. 'Something,' I replied. I turned away and started for the entrance, but the boy called after me. 'Gis yer autograph, mate! Go on, gis yer autograph!'

'Look after the car,' I said over my shoulder; then had an unpleasant vision of John, creeping into the car park to do some more damage. I stopped, turned back to look at the boy. 'On second thoughts, don't bother. Go home.'

The boy looked puzzled. 'Why?' he demanded.

'Never mind why. Look, if I give you another pound, will you go home?'

'Can't,' said the boy. 'Ain't got no home.'

'Well, will you go somewhere else, then?'

The boy considered this. 'Gis a fiver,' he said slyly. 'Then I'll go.' He noted my scowl and added defensively. 'I could easy make a few more quid. There's more jocks due in. Famous ones. They all pay me to watch their cars.'

I sighed, thought about telling the kid where to get off. But in another flash, I pictured his pathetic corpse lying beside the defaced car and I knew I couldn't handle the responsibility of it. It could be Daniel lying there, I thought. That really spooked

me. I took out my wallet, handed the boy a crumpled note.
'Here,' I said. 'But I'm serious about you going. If I come out
and find you still here, I'll kick your little arse the length of
Oxford Road.'

The boy shrugged, pushed the note into his pocket. 'You're
mental,' he said ungraciously. 'A head case.'

I took a threatening step towards him and the boy spun on his
heels and ran away, his footsteps thudding in the echoey silence
of the car park. I watched until he had vanished into the shadows,
reflecting that my current unease could turn out to be an expensive preoccupation. I shrugged, continued on towards
Metrosound.

There was a different girl on the desk and she hesitated a long
time before releasing the lock on the outer door. I remembered
that my face was still almost unrecognisable beneath the bruises
and I refrained from commenting on it. The girl, a slim blonde,
with scrubbed, antiseptic features, stared at me almost fearfully.
'Mr Prince. I'm sorry, I didn't . . . I wasn't expecting to see you
in tonight.'

I nodded. 'Any requests for me?' I asked.

'Umm, there's a few things here. But we thought . . . I
thought . . .'

I took the letters from her and slipped them into my pocket.
'Simon Radcliffe in?' I asked, matter of factly.

'Yes, he'll be in his office.'

'Good,' I made for the door to the inner sanctum. Once again,
she was very slow in releasing the lock. I glanced at her sharply.
'Something wrong?' I asked.

'No, no, of course not.' She was looking purposefully at the
intercom in front of her.

'Don't worry, you'll have time to warn him before I get there,'
I said and smiled venomously at her. The girl frowned, pressed
the door release. I pushed it open and strode down the corridor
beyond. I went past the studio entrance and turned left into
Simon's outer office. Peggy, Simon's diminutive secretary,
looked up from her typewriter and her eyes widened behind her
designer spectacles in a show of ill-concealed panic.

'Tom! I didn't expect—'

'Yeah, skip it. I'm going in to see His Majesty and we don't want to be disturbed, all right.'

'But wait, you can't just—'

I pushed open Simon's door and walked into the office. I was not surprised to see that Simon was on the phone. Dave Hibbert, was sitting in the chair opposite Simon's desk. He turned to look at me and his face fell.

Oh yes? I thought. *What are you up to, you slimy fucker?*

Simon put down the receiver and stared blankly at me for a moment. Then he remembered to give himself an expression. His features wrenched themselves into a look of deepest sympathy. It put me in mind of a look that might be worn by an undertaker at a funeral.

'Tom, this *is* a surprise. I wasn't expecting—'

'Listen, if one more person says that to me, I'll hit the fucking roof!' I snapped.

Simon swallowed loudly and his expression slipped momentarily to one of bafflement. He got to his feet. 'Well, come and sit down. Make yourself comfortable. My God, Tom, what happened to you? Your face!'

'Somebody offered to rearrange it for me. I was in no position to argue.' I pulled up a vacant chair and sat down opposite Dave, who seemed engrossed in a close scrutiny of his feet. I looked at him for a moment and then inquiringly at Simon. Something was evidently going on here. Hibbert was even less pleased to see me than Simon was. 'Sorry gentlemen. Was I interrupting something?'

Simon licked his lips nervously. 'You er . . . know Dave, of course. I was just briefing him about tonight, he's very kindly offered to step into your slot at short notice.'

'Has he now?' I smiled sweetly at Dave. 'Well, aren't you the all-round good egg, Dave? And of course, you've always wanted a crack at presenting your own show, haven't you?'

Dave spread his hands in a gesture of innocence. 'Hey, Tom, I'm just trying to help out, you know?'

'Of course you are!' I leaned forward and patted Dave none too gently on the shoulder. He winced beneath my touch. 'And all credit to you. But you see, there's no need to worry. I'm back now and I'm ready to carry on, so why don't you take yourself right back to the newsroom and prepare to stir the shit, as usual?'

There was an uncomfortable silence. Dave and Simon exchanged glances. Then Simon smiled pleasantly. 'Look Dave, why don't you give Tom and me a few moments to talk this over in private?'

Dave shrugged. 'Sure.' he said; but he shot me a look that spoke volumes. It was the look of a man who was close to clinching the deal of his life and who fervently wished that I had stepped under an articulated lorry on my way to work. He got awkwardly to his feet and trudged towards the door. He went out, closing it gently behind him. Simon and I were left staring at each other. He indicated his cocktail cabinet. 'How about a little drinkie-poo?' he offered.

'No thanks.'

'Well, I think I might just have a snifter. It's been a bit of a day.'

Simon got up and went over to the cabinet. He poured himself a generous measure of Scotch.

'I understand Drayton phoned you,' I said. I addressed the statement to his back.

'Uh huh.' Simon took his time pouring the drink. Then he recorked the bottle, came back to the desk and resumed his seat. 'He told me you were keen on going on with *Nightboat*. I told him—'

'I know what you told him, Simon. The question is, why?'

'Why?' Simon cocked his head to one side as though having difficulty understanding the question. 'Good Lord, Tom, I would have thought that was obvious. Surely you can see that it's all gone a bit too far. What happened last night, it . . . well, it puts an entirely different complexion on things. You're personally involved now. Thank God, all that you got was a bad scare, but it could so easily have been . . .' He left the sentence hanging and took a gulp at his drink. 'I feel it would be in the worst possible taste to allow it to continue further,' he concluded.

'Taste?' This was the best joke I'd heard all year. 'Since when have you been an authority on good taste? Jesus, Simon, this whole incident has been grotesque, don't try hitting me with that one. And besides, you were going to broadcast tonight, only you were going to put Hibbert at the controls.' I laughed scornfully. 'That's a good one! Have you heard Hibbert reading the news? The man's a complete balloon, you'd be able to market *Nightboat* as a cure for insomnia.'

Simon frowned. 'It was only a temporary move. Until we found somebody more . . . appropriate.'

'Yeah, but I bet you didn't tell him that, did you? Anyway, Simon, it's purely academic now. I'm going on tonight, it's as simple as that.'

'Not if I say otherwise,' retorted Simon forcefully. 'I'm still programme controller here.'

'Are you really? I thought you'd handed over to John. I thought he made all the decisions at *Metrosound* these days.'

Simon stared into his drink for a moment. 'I don't blame you for feeling bitter,' he said. 'In your position, I'd probably be just the same. But I hope you don't imagine that it's been easy for me, either.'

I rolled my eyes towards the ceiling. 'Spare me the sob story, please! Now, do I get to do my show, or what?'

'You're very persistent,' observed Simon.

'Oh, I can be when I want to be. And don't forget Simon, I'm still owed work till September. Here's something for you to think about. Supposing I was to sue *you* for breach of contract?'

Simon's eyes widened. 'Are you joking? You were just going to work out a month's notice.'

I shook my head. 'But I haven't signed anything yet, have I? You were going to draw up a contract, remember? I want to broadcast tonight. I want this very badly. I don't think you could begin to know how much I want it. The police want it, the general public want it. Oh, and one other thing. John wants it. And we can't upset him, now can we?' I took a cigarette from the box on the desk and lit it, then blew out a cloud of smoke. 'Think of the ratings, Simon.'

'Ratings aren't the be all and end all, you know!'

'Are they not? You surprise me, Simon. I thought you lived and breathed ratings. I thought they were what made your dick hard.'

Simon gave me a look of disgust. 'I'm getting a little tired of your attitude, Tom. You like to paint me as some kind of unscrupulous villain in this game, but at least I know where to draw the line between decency and exploitation. It's . . . it's out of control, Tom. It's gone too far. I can't allow it to continue.'

'Yes you can,' I assured him.

'For God's sake, will you be told? I'm sick of the whole business and I don't mind admitting that I'm beginning to be a little bit afraid.'

'Afraid?' I sneered. I could feel a sudden cold anger building inside me, an icy fist squeezing my guts in a vice-like grip. 'No, you're not afraid. You don't know what fear is, Simon. Not really. Would you like me to show you what's it's like to be afraid?'

Simon glared at me. 'What are you talking about?' he snapped.

'I'm talking about this.' I pulled the cigarette from my mouth and flicked it full into Simon's face.

He started involuntarily, spilling the contents of his drink into his lap. Sparks scattered down the front of his Armani suit. 'What the fuck? Have you gone—' His words were abruptly cut off as I lunged across the desk and grabbed him by the lapels of his jacket.

'*This* is afraid!' I yelled. And I hauled Simon towards me, scattering the contents of the desk top in all directions.

'Get your hands off me!' he screamed, outraged. I just laughed. I twisted Simon around on to his back and slammed him down hard on the desk. My blood was up now, there was a roaring sound in my head and I was deriving unutterable pleasure from this.

This is how John must feel, I thought. *Powerful. In control.* There was an ornamental letter-opener lying a few inches from Simon's shoulder. Impulsively I grabbed it and I jabbed the blade hard against his throat. I held it there, watching the white flesh redden under the pressure.

'For Christ's sake, Tom!' Simon's eyes bulged. He lay there unable to move a muscle as I leaned over him, relishing the new-found sense of power I had over my employer. For too long, this man had ruled my life. Now, suddenly, the tables were turned. He was at my mercy.

'Now you know how Jamie felt,' I told him. 'Lying there with that sick bastard holding a knife on her. Not knowing if he meant

152

to kill her.' I put a little more pressure on the knife. 'Or simply to terrorise her. Supposing my hand slipped now, Simon? Supposing I took this fancy little gadget of yours and pushed it right into your throat? By the time anybody got to you, you'd be so much dead meat. That's fear, Simon. That's what it's like. Not very nice is it?'

He whimpered, shook his head from side to side.

'Now, then.' I lowered my voice to a whisper. 'Do I get to do my show?'

Simon's mouth worked but all that emerged was a feeble squeak.

'Louder Simon, I can't quite hear you?'

'Yes! Yes, for God's sake, yes. Please just . . . let me up!'

'Not yet, Simon. It's not that easy. Listen to me. I want your promise that you won't do anything to interfere with my show. Not tonight. Not ever. Because if you cross me, I'll come looking for you and I swear I'll cut your balls off and make you eat them. Do you hear me?'

'Unable to nod his head, Simon blinked his eyes furiously.

'Then I have your word?'

'Yes. Yes. Please, just . . .'

Reluctantly I released my hold and let the knife fall from my hand. Abruptly the anger drained out of me and I turned and strolled over to the window, stood gazing down at the slow column of traffic on the darkened street below. It looked a long way down. Simon curled up into a foetal position on the desk top, his legs scattering a few last papers and executive toys on to the floor. He began to gasp violently as he fought to regain his breathing.

'I think we understand each other better now,' I said quietly. 'I'm going to go and prepare for my show.'

Simon sat up, massaging his throat. He tried to speak but all he could manage was a strangled choke.

I turned back to look at him impassively. 'Come again?' I said.

'Crazy,' gasped Simon. 'You're as fucking crazy as he is.'

'Yes. I think I'm beginning to be.' I said. I thought about that. *Crazy.* Crazy like John. Maybe it would drive me crazy before it was all over, but perhaps that was just what I needed to take on that sonofabitch and beat him at his own game. I moved towards the exit, then paused, indicated the litter on the floor. 'Terrible mess,' I said. 'Somebody ought to clear it up.' I went out, closing the door behind me.

Peggy and Hibbert were standing by the desk just outside the office. They'd clearly been alerted by the noise from within. Peggy had the phone in her hand and one finger poised over the dial. I smiled at her, took the handset gently but firmly from her grasp and put it back down on the cradle. 'Clumsy of me,' I said. 'Knocked a few things over. Perhaps you could . . .?'

She stared at me fearfully and then scuttled obediently into the office. Through the open door, there was a brief glimpse of Simon, still sitting on his desk, his face buried in his hands. His shoulders were moving up and down as though he was crying. Dave's mouth dropped open and he looked very uncomfortable. He began to sidle away but I slipped an arm tightly around his shoulders and walked him towards the exit. He was terrified of me now and that was just how I wanted him.

'Guess what, Dave! Simon decided your reports were just to good to miss, after all. What say we go into the newsroom and cook up some juicy items for tonight, just you and me? Hmm?'

Chapter Fourteen

'*Metrosound* Radio! The greatest sound around!' The jingle had never sounded more inane than it did now.

I ignored my usual theme-music and went straight into my first record, the Stones' 'Street Fighting Man'. The brash, martial feel of it was supposed to psyche me up for what was to follow, but I was still pretty vague about what I was actually going to say. I let the song settle into the chorus and then I faded down the music and came in with a voice-over.

'Ahoy shipmates! The Captain is back and he's pissed off! On tonight's programme, I'm declaring war on a certain person who's been making my life hell for the past two months. Last night he pushed me one step too far; so tonight, with your help, I'm going to start pushing back. Regular listeners to the show will know exactly who I'm talking about. If you're tuning in for the first time, let me tell you about John. He's a cowardly, sick maggot who thinks he's above retribution. But nobody is above retribution; so welcome to the great *Metrosound* witch-hunt!

I glanced up towards the glass screen ahead of me and saw Steve Acton freeze in the act of biting into a Mars Bar. His mouth hung open and he was staring vacantly back at me, no doubt wondering what in hell was going on. Beside him, the two CID men looked rather less baffled. I had briefed them beforehand and knew that they would be making a note of anything that came up during the course of the show. I went on with my introduction.

'You people out there must have suspicions. You must have theories about John and why he's doing what he's doing. Maybe you even know who he is, but you've been too frightened to tell anyone. So I'm inviting you to share those theories tonight, live

155

on the air. If you have anything to tell me, phone in now on 226 1234. If you want to remain anonymous, that's fine by me. I also have a puzzle for you. I have some words I want you to consider. I think they could be lyrics. Here's how they go. "Seth calls the tune. Chaos returns." If those words ring a bell, call me and tell me where you've heard them before. And for those of you who need incentives, I have prizes on offer, plucked hot from the *Metrosound* coffers. I have records and T-shirts, as usual; and I also have tickets for all the best gigs coming up in the next few weeks. I have videos, I have theatre seats, I even have a luxury holiday for two in Bermuda! You see, I've been plundering tonight. I've been into the lockers of all the day-time jocks and I've appropriated their prizes. It's going to be a thin day for competitions tomorrow, so if you want to win something you're going to have to talk to me. Because I want answers. And the most interesting answers will win the best prizes. So, get your brains into gear and phone the Captain. I'm waiting for your calls.' I faded the mike, cranked the music up to full volume and sat back in my chair. I took a cigarette from the pack beside me and lit it. Through the glass, I could see Steve frantically handling the switchboard, scribbling down names. A few moments later, he was hustling through with the first batch of callers.

'What the fuck are you playing at?' he demanded, throwing down the scraps of paper. 'You can't do this!'

'Can't I?' I sifted through the notes. 'Too late, I think. I've done it.'

'What's Radcliffe going to say when he hears about it?'

I shrugged. 'I'll handle Radcliffe,' I said, I indicated the exit. 'Let's get on with it.'

'I'm taking no responsibility,' Steve warned me, 'I'll tell everyone you made me do it.'

'That's the idea, Steve. Look after number one. After all, why change the habits of a lifetime?'

Steve scowled and hurried back to his post. The record was winding down and I directed my attention back to the microphone.

'All right landlubbers, it's time for the first round of Shop Thy Neighbour. First up, we have a gentleman called Roy. Roy, you're through to the Captain, what would you like to tell me?'

'Hello Tom. I've been thinking about this for some time now. There's that religious nut that phones your programme. William, I think his name is. He sounds like a classic headbanger, if you ask me.'

'Well, I did ask you Roy, but I can assure you that William has already been eliminated from the inquiries. However, since this is a night for dropping people in the shit, let me tell you about William. Good old god-fearing William, always ready with a quote from the bible and a few choice words about morality. William, it seems, has previous form for exposing himself to little children. There's nothing he likes so much as dropping his trousers and waving his willy at six-year-olds. So, next time you hear him preaching, you'll know to take it all with a pillar of salt.' I realised how vindictive I was being, but I was going for broke tonight and I didn't care who got hurt in the process. 'Well Roy, since you've started the ball rolling, I think you should have a T-shirt. Leave your address with our Mr Acton and we'll move on to . . . Beryl. Hello Beryl, what have you got to say for yourself?'

'Hello, Tom, can I just say that it's nice to be on your programme?'

'Skip the pleasantries Beryl, we're not being pleasant tonight.'

'Umm . . . yes . . . well, I think John could be my ex-husband.'

'What makes you say that?'

'He was always a very violent man and he swore he'd come back and get me one day. I think those other killings might have been done to draw people's attention away from me. I'm next on the list, I'm sure of it.'

'OK Beryl. And where is your husband now?'

'Well, I can't be sure. He died four years ago, you see, but I always knew he'd come back for me.'

I sighed. 'Beryl, you're evidently several coupons short of a toaster. See a psychiatrist.'

'Oh . . . well, can I have a T-shirt?'

'Not tonight, Beryl.' I punched the cut-off button and went to my next caller.

'OK, over to . . .' I glanced at my list. 'Mr X! Evidently some-body who wants to remain anonymous. Hey, Mr X, how ya doin?'

'Fine thanks. Look, it was a terrible thing that happened last night, Tom. I could hardly believe it. Your girlfriend. Is she . . . I mean, is she?'

'Dead? My goodness, some people are very squeamish about using that word, aren't they? But no, she's fine. John wanted to frighten me. He succeeded. Now I'd like to return the favour. Are you just phoning to offer your sympathy or do you have something to add?'

'Well, yeah . . .' A long pause.

'Come on Mr X, out with it or it's the cut-off button for you.'

'Well, I was trying to think about somebody who might want to see you punished. Then it occurred to me. Des Connolly.'

'Ah, the old Weird-Beard, eh? What made you think of him?'

'Well, he did host the late-night show before you came along, didn't he? You kind of took the programme off him. He works for Sundown Community Radio now, they have tiny listening figures. He's bound to feel resentful, he was a big radio-star once.'

'That's an interesting theory, Mr X. I think that deserves a couple of theatre tickets. Leave your address.' I wrote down the name Des Connolly on a scrap of paper and put a large question mark behind it.

As the show progressed I added more names to the list. There were rock stars and show-business celebrities, a couple of prominent members of the National Front, whom I'd once ridiculed on the show. There were a few people I'd never even heard of who, I was assured, hated my guts. It was strangely gratifying to learn how many people in the world disliked me.

Then somebody called 'Malcolm' came on the line. But he didn't want to point the finger of suspicion at anyone. 'I know where those lyrics come from,' he announced triumphantly. He had one of those irritating nasal voices that experts often seem to have.

'Do you now? Malcolm, you are indeed a man amongst men. Tell me more!'

Malcolm, however, was not immediately forthcoming.

'You said something about a prize.'

'Indeed, I did. How does a trip to Bermuda grab you?'

'Sounds great. All right then. The lyrics are from a Johnny Dark album called *Book of the Dead*.'

The instant I heard the name, I remembered. Johnny Dark! It should have occurred to me before but like so much stuff from my past, it had been buried beneath layers of falling dust. In the late seventies, Johnny had been a massive British pop phenomenon. He'd had three platinum albums, a string of Number One singles that had scored at home and in America. And then there'd been *Book of the Dead*, a horribly pretentious double concept-album based on Egyptian mythology, which had effectively finished his career overnight. Egyptian mythology! Jesus, this had to be the lead I'd been hoping for! Then something else occurred to me. I had good cause to remember the album. Many years ago, as a music reviewer, hadn't I done a cruel hatchet job on it in *Scam* magazine?'Yes, I was sure of it. It all added up beautifully but there was one big fat fly in the ointment. Johnny Dark was dead. He'd died of a drugs overdose, a few months after the album's release. A pity. It was the one factor that prevented him filling the slot of chief suspect. Still, there was something there, something that needed to be pursued.

'Malcolm, I don't suppose you have a copy of that record?'

'You're kidding. I used to have it. I think I played it once and that was enough. I swapped it for a Led Zeppelin album. A pity, because it's worth a fortune now as a collector's item. Johnny had an argument with the record company and all copies were withdrawn after about a week of going on sale. It's now about as rare as hens' teeth.'

'Do you remember anything else about the lyrics?'

A pause as Malcolm collected his thoughts.

'Not much. I know that "Seth calls the tune" was the opening line of the first track . . . which I think was the single. It was called "Talisman of Seth". The second bit, "Chaos Returns", I believe was the title of an instrumental on side four. I seem to recall that all the lyrics were printed on the inner sleeve.'

'Hmm. What about the cover?'

'The cover . . . yes, it was all black, with a tiny gold pyramid on it.'

That jogged my memory. Suddenly I was back, looking out of the window in Jamie's hospital room and seeing a black van with a gold pyramid emblazoned on the side cruising slowly past the entrance. A coincidence? Maybe. Maybe not. Now I felt sure that John had been driving that van, that he hadn't been able to resist coming to the hospital to gloat over his little trumph. Maybe he'd even followed me there. Well, the van was one more thing to check on. I smiled. I was getting closer now, I sensed it.

'Malcolm, you've been most helpful,' I said. 'More than you could know. And I have a terrible confession to make.'

'What's that?'

'I was lying to you. There is no holiday in Bermuda. You can have the top ten albums, how about that?'

'You f—'

I hit the cut-off button just in time and punched up a record. I patched myself through to Steve. 'Hold the fort, I'm just nipping into the record library.'

Steve glared at me through the screen and punched in his mike channel.

'You bastard, you can't offer non-existent prizes; you'll get us sued!'

I ignored him and hurried off to the library. This was a large room at the back of the studio, stacked high with racks and racks of LPs and singles, all of them filed in something approaching alphabetical order. I quickly located the Johnny Dark records. There were three of them, his earlier more popular stuff. But not surprisingly, no copy of *Book of the Dead*. As I recalled, it was not the kind of material designed to endear itself to FM Radio. I carried the albums back to the studio and sat there looking at the cover photograph of Johnny, a punky, blond-haired beefcake with a sneer affixed to his top lip. I examined the records carefully, hoping to glean further clues, but none presented themselves. They were just straight-ahead pop albums featuring catchy three-minute slabs of rock and roll, with titles like 'Born to Lose' and 'Speed Freak'. Still, there was a connection there, for sure. But what? A crazy fan emulating Johnny's lyrics? A relative who blamed Johnny's death on me?

Steve brought in a fresh batch of notes and dropped them on

to the mixing desk. He had a smug smile on his face. 'You've got a caller,' he announced. 'Wants to speak to you in private. I think you better had.'

I eyed him suspiciously. 'Why?' I demanded.

'Because it's Des Connolly and he sounds very pissed off.'

Well, well, I thought. *So old Des was listening in, was he? Well then* . . . 'Tell him I'll talk to him on the air or not at all,' I said.

Steve scowled. 'He isn't going to like that,' he observed.

'He doesn't have to like it. Tell him if he's got nothing to hide, he'll go on live.'

Steve shook his head. 'What kind of game are you playing?' he muttered. Receiving no answer, he trudged dutifully back to the phone.

The record reached the fade and I opened up my mike channel.

'All right people, I'm going to introduce a new element to the show. We're going to play Hunt the Van. Maybe some of you have seen a black van with a gold pyramid on the side. Maybe it's parked near your house. Why not get up, go to the window and have a look? If it's there, give me a ring. There'll be a prize for the first correct lead. If you can supply the registration number, so much the better.' I glanced at the glass screen and saw Steve give me the thumbs-up sign. 'Now, a little surprise for you. A fellow jock has phoned in to talk to the Captain. You may remember a certain Mr X was taking his name in vain earlier on. So, come in Des Connolly, you're through to the Captain.'

The familiar Dublin-accented voice in my headphones crackled with barely contained rage.

'Prince, what the . . . hell do you think you're playing at?'

'I'm hosting a radio show, Des. You may be out of touch these days, but surely you haven't forgotten how it's done? And I must say it's very reassuring to know that one of my rivals is also a fan.'

'Cut the crap, Prince! Where do you think you get off, libelling me on the air.'

'Libel? That's a very emotive word, Des. And I can assure you I haven't committed it. A certain Mr X suggested that you might have reason to dislike me, but . . .'

'Dislike you? I think you're a piece of shit, frankly, but if you believe for one minute that I'd be capable of *that* kind of thing.'

'Which particular kind of thing are we talking about, Des? Murder? Terrorism? I really couldn't say. After all, I don't know you very well, do I? And by the way, if calling me a piece of shit on the air doesn't constitute libel, I don't know what does.'

'You'll be hearing from my solicitors, Prince.'

I cued a record. Maybe it was time for a private *tête à tête*.

'Hey, hold hard there, don't hang up! We're off the air now; and we've never had much chance to talk have we? I mean, I still don't know how you felt about losing your seat on *Nightboat*.'

There was a long pause while Des mulled over the question. 'If you want to know the truth, I didn't much like the way it was done. Not after all the help I gave you at *Metrosound*.'

I had to admit I knew what he meant. I had used Des, a man for whom I had no particular liking, as a convenient springboard, a way into *Metrosound*. But I'd had no idea that one day I'd be replacing him.

'I owe you a lot, Des. I wouldn't deny that for one moment.'

'You owe me *everything*! When you first arrived at *Metrosound*, it was me who made sure you got listened to. It was me who invited you to parties and introduced you socially, and don't think it was easy for me. You weren't exactly Mr Sociable, were you? No social graces, no charm. A cold sarcastic sod with an acid tongue. It's no wonder you had no friends! Christ, you wouldn't even have met Jamie if it wasn't for me. And all the time, you were just waiting for your chance to stab me in the back.'

'Unfortunate turn of phrase, Des. All I know is, I was offered a job and I said yes. They weren't renewing your contract; if I hadn't taken it, somebody else would have.'

'Oh sure, so innocent! Listen, Tom, I'm not that naïve, I know there's no hearts and flowers in independent radio. Survival of the fittest, isn't that what they say? But there's a limit for Christ's sake! There's such a thing as professional integrity.' He was getting warmed up now, spilling out the resentment he must have kept bottled up for years. 'Anyway, I wasn't sorry to get out of that station. I'm working for community radio now, at least they still have a few values left. I mean, look what's happened to *Nightboat*! It used to be a few laughs, some good music. Now it's a free-for-all, a crude display of everything that's bad about

162

radio. And you encourage it Tom, you make a meal of it! After tonight's little number, I seriously doubt if you'll ever work in radio again.'

'You could be right, Des. But I feel duty-bound to ask you a question. If it's such a useless show, how come you were listening to it?'

There was a baffled silence at the end of the line.

'Let me suggest a reason, Des. Could it be that you're just like everybody else who tunes in to *Nightboat* these days? That you get a vicarious kick out of listening to my misfortunes?'

'That's ridiculous!'

'Is it? Well, there has to be some explanation. If I don't enjoy a programme, I give it a wide berth. We all of us have the power to use the off switch, don't we?'

'I don't usually listen to it! I couldn't sleep and I just happened to switch on the radio . . . listen, I don't see why I have to justify myself to you!'

'All right, you're clearly not enjoying this line of questioning. Let's talk about Johnny Dark instead, shall we?'

'What? What the hell's that got to do with anything?'

'I seem to remember you were a big fan of his.'

'I played his records, yes.'

'And didn't you devote a whole programme to him on the anniversary of his death?'

'I might have done. So what?'

'I don't suppose you own a copy of *Book of the Dead*?'

'No, I don't. What is all this stuff about Johnny Dark, anyway?'

'I don't know yet. Let's just say I'm looking for a connection.'

'If you want my opinion, I think you're cracking up, Prince. After what happened the other night, you've got no business to be on air. If I ever hear my name mentioned on your show again, I'll come down on you like a ton of bricks.'

'Are you threatening me, Des?'

'You can interpret that any way you like. Just lay off, OK?'

Des slammed down the phone. I faded the record and followed up without a pause. 'Well, there we have it folks, a rare glimpse of radio celebrities as they really are. Yes, underneath the tinsel and fake smiles, we're human beings. We sweat, we fart, we have to change our underwear daily, just like you unfortunate proles out there. Kinda gets to you, doesn't it? Now, moving right along the hard shoulder, here's an offer you don't get every day. You'll have gathered by now that I'd like to get hold of *Book of the Dead*. If you have that album festering away somewhere, send it to me here at *Metrosound* and I'll send you, by return, the ten chart albums of your choice. Is that an amazing deal, or what? If you don't think it's a good deal, write to me and name your price. If you don't want to part with the record, just send me a copy of the lyrics from the cover and you'll still be amply rewarded. Now, don't forget about the van with the gold pyramid. We'll take a record break. Back in a mo!'

Over the next hour, calls came in about the van. A lot of people claimed to have seen it driving about and most of the calls seemed to come from a leafy suburb of South Manchester. The two CID men had abandoned their tracing equipment and were kept busy relaying calls back to the incident room. An hour before the show came off the air, there was a breakthrough. A landlord phoned saying that a man was renting his premises in Chorlton; and that man drove a black van with a gold pyramid on the side.

When I finally left the studio I found Drayton waiting for me in reception. He was slumped on one of the sofas and he looked tired and far from happy.

'How did we do?' I asked.

Drayton sighed. 'Not as well as might have been hoped,' he admitted. 'We interviewed the owner of the van. He was quite irate at being dragged out of bed at three in the morning and I can't say I blame him. He works for a perfectly respectable company called Pyramid Insurance. They have a whole fleet of vans like the one you described. Needless to say, they were far from thrilled at being linked with something like this. They're demanding that you do a public apology on tomorrow night's show.'

'Oh.' I scowled and sat down beside Drayton. 'Shit, I felt sure I was on to something there.' I thought for a moment. 'Well, what about the Johnny Dark stuff? You're not telling me that's a coincidence.'

'At this stage of the game, I'm not telling you anything. I

suppose we'll have to talk to this character. Any idea where we can get hold of him?'

'You evidently weren't listening very carefully. Try Golders Green crematorium. I believe that's where they held the funeral.'

'Oh wonderful!' Drayton took off his hat and ran his fingers through his receding hair. 'Just for once, it would be nice to have something straightforward. How can the man be a suspect, if he's dead?'

'I didn't say he was a suspect. But everything fits. The Whisperer's lyrics are from that Johnny Dark album, a record that's about Egyptian mythology. I was just one of many reviewers who slagged the record when it came out but . . . I've got a feeling I was the first.'

Drayton frowned. 'Why do you say that?'

'Because *Scam* was the happening paper at the time, we generally got an exclusive review a week before the others. And as I recall, I really put the boot into it. It's probably true to say that I was instrumental in finishing his career.'

He shrugged. 'Yes, so that would have got up *his* nose . . . but who else's?'

I don't know. A rabid fan maybe? His record company, his management, a doting relative.' I handed Drayton the albums I was carrying. 'Start with the record company, Polygon. They're based in London. And he may still have some kind of fan club.'

'These people have fans *after* they die?'

'Sure they do! Most of them have more fans than they ever did when they were alive.'

He dutifully wrote down a few notes on a pad produced from his jacket. 'And this Des Connolly character. Does he qualify as a rabid fan?'

'Des?' I frowned. 'I don't know. The guy clearly dislikes me, but I don't think he dislikes me *that* much. Still, I guess you'll have to check him out. Oh, and while I'm unloading stuff, here's the list of suspects I drew up tonight. The names on the left are the people I know, these others are the ones I've never heard of.' Drayton examined the list and gave a low whistle. 'You must be pretty obnoxious,' he said. 'Hitler probably had less enemies than this.' He looked at me searchingly for a moment. 'Why do

I get the impression that if I asked you for a list of friends, it would probably fit on the back of a matchbox?'

I shifted uncomfortably beneath his gaze.

'Not much time for friendship in my line of work,' I muttered. 'Oh, one other thing. John left something in my post while I was away. Perhaps you'd like to pass this on to your forensic boffins?'

Drayton stared at me. 'He's been back?'

'Yes. He also spent a little time customising my car. This may seem like a silly question, but wasn't somebody assigned to watch the house?'

Drayton looked sheepish. 'It never occurred to me. People don't normally call back the night after a major violation.'

'I thought we'd established that John doesn't follow the usual pattern.'

Drayton was peering at the brochure, holding it carefully between thumb and forefinger. 'Home sweet home?' he muttered. 'What's that supposed to mean?'

'Your guess is as good as mine. Perhaps you'd better check the place out. It's out in City Road, big place, still under construction.'

We both got to our feet and moved towards the exit. Julie sat at her usual place in reception, engrossed in a paperback novel. She barely glanced up as we moved past. I opened the swing door and we stepped out into the semi-darkness of the car park, shivering in the chill of early morning. As we walked towards our respective vehicles, I noticed that a third car was parked alongside mine, a flashy red sports convertible. I recognised it instantly as Simon's and groaned inwardly, anticipating a slanging match. No doubt he had listened to the show tonight and hadn't much liked what he'd heard. Hardly surprising under the circumstances. As I moved nearer, I could see him sitting behind the wheel.

'I might need some back-up,' I warned Drayton. 'That's Radcliffe. He's probably come to chew my head off.'

'Nothing to do with me,' said Drayton unsympathetically. 'You handle it.' He unlocked his Ford Escort and climbed in.

'Thanks a lot.' I muttered. I moved around to Simon's door and bent to peer into the car. 'All right,' I said. 'I know what you're going to say. I fucked up. But if you'd just . . .'

I halted in mid-sentence, puzzled. Why, I wondered, was Simon wearing a pair of round black sunglasses at this unearthly hour? And why was he staring straight ahead into the darkness of the car park?

Drayton started his engine and turned on his headlights. In the sudden illuminating glow, I felt something lurch in the pit of my stomach. Simon wasn't wearing sunglasses. I found myself looking at two deep, empty sockets where his eyes used to be.

'Oh sweet Jesus.' I whipped around and threw up my hands to intercept Drayton, who was just beginning to drive away. Drayton hit the brakes and leaned over to wind down the window.

'What now?' he asked wearily. I opened my mouth to speak but a wave of nausea hit me, bubbling up from the depths of my stomach and flinging a surge of bitterness into my throat. I twisted aside and was violently sick down the side of Drayton's car. He cursed, threw open his door and clambered out again. He stood for a moment, looking at me in dismay and then he hurried around to Simon's car and bent to look in at the window. He took a sharp intake of breath, then sighed, shook his head.

'Well,' he said quietly, with a sense of resignation in his voice. 'Who needs sleep anyway?'

Diary Extract

6 December
I asked Him, 'Why this man?' After all, this is not a handmaiden. I could not see where he fitted into the scheme of things. He told me that this man had power over Tom. Taking a powerful man would display that nobody was safe from His wrath. He was going to let me handle this one all by myself. A test, He said. If I performed well, He would reward me. I packed some things He wanted me to take and I set out for Radcliffe's house. I knew where he lived, I knew his movements. I had been watching him for quite some time. There was a narrow walkway to his house.

It was dark and it was easy to conceal myself in the hedgerow. When he came strolling along I stepped out and used the chloroform. He was not a powerful man at all, little more than a boy.

I carried him upstairs and tied him to a chair. When he woke up, he began to cry and scream and I was forced to gag him, even though his house was well away from the others. I told him we were going to listen to Nightboat *together and that he should pray that Tom didn't say anything to upset Him. Radcliffe had noticed the big sheet of plastic I had put under the chair and he was very badly frightened.*

When the programme finally came on, Tom was very vindictive. Perhaps we've pushed him too far but there's no going back now. He has told me this. We listened for some ten minutes and then I started preparing the knives. Radcliffe watched me the whole time, his eyes nearly bursting out of his head. He had nice eyes, I thought, almost like a woman's. When I had the other equipment set up, I removed the gag. He pleaded with me, begged me to make some kind of deal. He said he would lead me to Tom if I would spare him. Then I knew he was without honour and that made me despise him a little. It was easier then to take out his eyes. I would have preferred to kill him first or even sedate him again, but of course in this case it was necessary to have him awake. He was securely tied so it wasn't much of a problem.

I've found there's quite a knack to doing it. The first time, I used the knife from the start and I scarred the eyes, which I thought spoiled their look somewhat. I have since found that it is easier to slip a finger over the top of the eyeball and pop it right out. I simply use a sharp knife to cut through the red stringy thing that anchors it in place. There's less mess this way and there were only a few splashes on the plastic when I'd finished. I'd remembered to bring the yoghurt carton, which saved me hunting through the man's rubbish.

He died shortly after the second eye came out. Shock, I suppose. Afterwards, I drove him back into town. He has a nice car, I must say. There was a mobile phone in it and I toyed with the idea of phoning Tom from there, but decided against it. Better to surprise him, I decided. I parked next to Tom's car and I noticed Drayton's car there, too, which appealed to me. I imagined them coming out together and finding Radcliffe and I was tempted to remain in

168

hiding so I could observe it. But He would have been angry if I'd endangered myself at this stage of the game. So I took a taxi back. I wrapped a scarf around my mouth and pretended I had laryngitis.

When I got home, He allowed me my reward. Three more needles. Afterwards, I made myself a light supper and settled down to watch some television. There was an American thriller film on, but the language was appalling and I was forced to switch off. Somebody should complain.

Chapter Fifteen

I had abandoned any hope of sleeping. I stood numbed in the chilly environs of the car park and watched as it was transformed into an inferno of sound and light. I had the powerful impression that I wasn't really present, that I was watching some third-rate cop show on the television. It was all there, the attendant paraphernalia of disaster. The car had been cordoned off with lengths of orange tape, and powerful arc lamps were erected which bathed the area in a flood of white neon. Forensic investigators examined the body carefully before it was put into a plastic bag and ferried over to Pathology. Then they went to work on the car, virtually dismantling it in their frantic search for clues. As usual, they appeared to be drawing a big, fat blank.

By now, the people working in *Metrosound* had got wind of what was happening outside and a small crowd of curious onlookers had gathered at the edges of the cordon. I noticed Steve Acton watching impassively as Simon's body was carried to the ambulance. From the blank expression on his face, he might just as well have been watching a television soap. Even Julie had forsaken her current paperback to come and observe the real world for a change. She was chewing gum, her red lips chomping rhythmically. She kept throwing glances in my direction, watching me with a detached curiosity, as though she expected me to break down in tears at any moment. I wasn't going to give her that satisfaction. Drayton seemed to be everywhere at once, issuing orders to uniformed men, chatting with the various experts who had turned up to case the scene.

Later, I went with him to Simon's house, a detached cottage that bordered an area of parkland in South Manchester. I had never been there before and I was struck by how twinky and

comfortably middle-class it was. The chintzy fabrics and Laura
Ashley wallpapers suggested the home of a middle-aged business-
woman. The place was already bustling with policemen and
forensic experts. Some were swabbing down surfaces with
fingerprint powder, one of them was photographing everything
in the house, capturing it for posterity on rolls of film. I noticed
a selection of hardcore gay magazines lying on a coffee table and
was momentarily taken aback. It made me realise how little I
had known Simon. I felt an irrational urge to put them away in
a cupboard, away from the merciless gaze of the camera. A
bearded detective came over and reported that they had found
the door ajar and everything inside neat and tidy. But in the
bedroom there was a wooden chair smeared with blood. Marks
around the arms of the chair suggested that somebody had been
tied into it and I listened, chilled, as an elderly pathologist, a
small, rumpled man with greying hair and wire-rimmed glasses,
told Drayton that Simon might well have been still alive when
his eyes were removed. I thought I had reached the stage where
nothing could shock me, but the thought of this was more than
I could stomach. If I'd had any food left in me I would probably
have thrown up all over again. I could not pretend to have liked
Simon, but I would not have wished him such a fate.

'Why?' I asked Drayton helplessly. 'Why Simon?'

Drayton shrugged. 'Just somebody else who had a connection
with you, I suppose.' He frowned, gestured at the chair. 'And
one more poor devil who can't tell us anything. What worries
me about this killing is it's another break in the pattern.'

'Pattern?'

Drayton nodded. 'The first three murders were similar. Young
women, killed at night. Serial killers usually fall into some kind
of discernible pattern and that's how you catch them, by predict-
ing their next move. But this man . . . he's so bloody unpredict-
able. Here we have a male victim, clearly tortured before he
died.' He paced restlessly for a moment, staring round the
crowded room as though searching for an answer. He turned
back to face me. 'And then, there's Jamie. He spared her when
he could so easily have killed her. Why? It doesn't make sense.'

'Oh, but it does,' I assured him. 'This whole thing is designed
to punish me. I don't know why, I don't know what I've ever

done to him, but that's his whole *raison d'être*. John probably knew that he could get more mileage out of it by simply driving Jamie away from me. I think he gets off on the misery he causes me. And besides, I think he wanted her to be able to talk. To describe that mask he was wearing. He's deliberately leaving clues for me to work out.'

Drayton sighed. 'Well, he's certainly left precious few of them here. But if you're right, that would suggest that he actually wants to be discovered.'

I nodded. 'Yes, I think so. But not by you, not by the police. He wants me to be the one to do it. Time and again I get the impression that he's throwing down some kind of challenge. He asks me, do I remember yet? Those lyrics. It's all tied up with them. And that bloody record. All I have to do is piece it together.' I ran a hand wearily through my hair. 'Look, is it OK if I go home now?'

'Yes, you may as well. I'll get somebody to drive you back to the radio station, so you can pick up your car. I'll hang on here and see if we can come up with anything else.'

I started for the door, then hesitated, 'If I were you, I'd be very careful,' I said. 'You're another connection.'

'The thought had occurred to me,' muttered Drayton bleakly. 'If you go on at this rate, you'll have less friends than Jonah.'

'I thought we'd already established that,' I said bitterly.

He said nothing, simply turned away to talk to a uniformed man. I left the house. It was good to get out in the fresh air.

I collected the car and drove home, slowly. The sun was well up by the time I got back but I was still far from sleep. I made myself a cup of coffee and took it into my study. There, I began to root through stacks of box files containing scrapbooks and clippings from my days as a rock journalist. I knew that what I was looking for was in there somewhere, but it was years since I'd written it and the piece would take some finding. I started on the first file, leafing through page after page of bands and musicians, some famous, some forgotten, some dead.

The phone rang and I picked it up automatically. 'Hello,' I said.

'Hello, Tom.' I winced at the familiar whispering voice and almost slammed the phone down again. But something prevented me from doing that. A terrible curiosity.

'What do you want, John?'

'To talk to you, of course.' The voice was somehow different. For the first time ever, he sounded confused, unsure of himself. 'I wanted to warn you. He's out now and I thought . . .'

'*Why*, John?' I could hardly prevent myself from screaming down the phone. 'Why Simon? Why kill him?'

A long pause as though he was considering his answer.

'He was close to you. I'm sorry, but I have to kill the ones who are close to you.'

'Have to? What do you mean? You can't just—'

'It's not *me*, Tom. You must understand that. It's Him. He makes me do these things . . .'

'Seth?' I finished.

Another pause, then a gasp, seemingly one of relief. 'You know about him? You understand?'

I glanced helplessly around the room, knowing that there was nothing I could do but talk to him.

'I know plenty.' I lied. 'I've found out about *Book of the Dead*. I know there's some connection with Johnny Dark. Were you . . . a fan of his?'

John laughed. 'Johnny's dead,' he cackled. 'And you killed him.'

'That's not true, John. You've got it all wrong.'

'I don't want to do these things, Tom. Really I don't. I like you. But Seth, He hates you, He says you have to be punished. He's stronger than me. He comes into my head and I feel his voice swelling under my tongue like a bubble. The bubble bursts and then His voice comes out of me, and He says you have to be punished.'

'Why John? Why does he hate me?'

'Because you killed Johnny.'

'No, that's nonsense! He died from a drugs overdose.'

'Oh, that's what they said. But you killed him, Tom. Don't you remember? You tore out his heart.'

'Who are you, John? Are you a relative of Johnny's? His brother?'

John giggled suddenly and slipped into a ghastly parody of James Cagney. 'You're the dirty rat that killed my brother!

You're the dirty rat that killed by brother! You're the—' He broke off abruptly and I could hear his tortured breathing at the other end of the line. 'He's coming back!' he hissed. 'He says I have to go now . . .'

'No, John, wait! I need to talk some more!'

'Can't. Wait. Tom. Speak to Him. If you must.'

There was a long silence. I waited, the handset clutched tight against my ear. There was the atmospheric crackle of static, the soughing of air, the sound a child hears in a seashell. Then, a long draw-out exhalation of air, culminating in a hideous croaking sound. The bubble bursting?

'John?' I cried. 'Are you there?'

'Yes, old son. I'm *here.*' The voice had inexplicably changed to its more familiar tone. It was mocking, cruel, fired with a wicked intelligence. It was hard to believe it was issuing from the same person I had just been speaking to. And then I understood. All this time I had been speaking with Seth.

'Trying to get to John, eh? Trying to get to him because you know he's weak. Well, he'll be punished for this, you can depend on that.'

'Why are you doing this? What have I ever done to you?'

'To me? Nothing. But to a friend of mine, and you can't imagine you'll be allowed to get away with something like that. Can you? We all have to pay for our transgressions, Tom. There's nothing personal in any of this. I love you. I love you like a brother, understand?'

'Then . . . then why don't you meet with me, face to face? We'll talk it through and—'

'—and you'll have your friends the police waiting for me! Don't worry, Tom, we will meet eventually. First though, I want to talk to that son of yours. Danny. Daniel? The little hawk. I want to tell him all about his father.'

Anger and terror welled up in me. It felt like iced water had been injected into my veins. 'If you go anywhere near him, I'll kill you, I swear it!'

'But I've already been near him, Tom. Near enough to touch. Near enough to kill.'

'No! *No*, you're lying!'

'Not at all. He's a sweet boy, your son. Such big blue eyes, just like his father. Trusting eyes. He has the universe in his eyes, do you know that? And I could have taken him, then and there, but I decided to wait. I wanted that to be the last act in this little passion play. I can get to him any time I want. Do you really think those pathetic bluebottles can protect him? Do you? They weren't much help to Simon, were they?'

'Listen to me!'

'No, you listen. I was with Simon last night. But you already know that, don't you? I waited for him outside his house. First, I made him sleep. Then, when he woke up, we talked about you.'

'Why did you kill him? Why any of them? If you've a grudge against me, then it's me you should wait for!'

'Funny. That's what Simon said! He begged me to let him go. Said he'd lead me right to you, if I did. But it's as I explained to him. Killing you is no fun. That's a very quick revenge. You want to take time over revenge. You want to enjoy the flavour. How do you feel, Tom? Do you feel guilty? I hope so.'

'Goddamn you! Why? Tell me, why?'

'Poor Simon. He wasn't very brave. He made a lot of noise when I took out his eyes.'

'*No.*'

'Yes, Tom. He called on his god, but I'll bet he wasn't a religious man. But why imagine it? I made something for you, Tom. A little memento.'

There was a pause, then a metallic click. Suddenly, horribly, a scream spilled from the earpiece, distorting the tiny speaker with its sheer power. It was the sound of an animal in pain, a cry of mingled agony and terror that was, at the same time, unmistakable. It was Simon's voice. The screaming went on and on, drilling into my head with its power and I wanted to slam down the receiver, but somehow it seemed to be glued to my ear and I sat there shaking with horror, my eyes filling with tears. I felt I was going mad myself, that I was a hair's breadth away from being as crazy as John. When he finally hit the stop button my whole body sagged with relief.

'Please,' I sobbed. 'Please.'

'Please, what? Are you begging me now? Are you pleading with me?'

'Yes. Just please stop this madness, stop it before . . .'

'Sorry, old son. There's more to do yet. I'll be in touch.'

The receiver was replaced. I sat looking blankly at the phone in my hand. Then something seemed to snap in my head. I flung the receiver aside and it struck the wall, bounced off, dragged the answerphone after it. The apparatus hit the floor with a satisfying crash. But that wasn't enough, not nearly enough. I stood up, gripped the edges of the desk and pulled with all my strength, tearing several fingernails in the process. It overturned, scattering its contents in all directions. As it fell, it struck my shin but I hardly felt the blow. I was crazy now, totally lost in the need for destruction. I rampaged around the study, systematically destroying everything I could get my hands on. I pulled prints from the wall, smashing glass and crushing them beneath my feet. I overturned bookcases, tore up the contents, kicked them savagely aside. I smashed pottery, wrenched the door off its hinges and, with little else left to wreck, I tore strips of patterned paper off the wall. As a final measure, I picked up a portable typewriter and threw it at the window. There was an almighty crash as the glass shattered and then another as the typewriter hit the pavement below. At last, exhausted, I sank down amidst the chaos and cried like a baby.

I don't know how long I lay there, but gradually sanity drifted back to me and I was able to function again. I sat up and surveyed my handiwork with a kind of dazed surprise. I crawled over to the telephone, pulled it out from beneath layers of scattered books and lifted the handset to my ear. Astonishly, there was still a dialling tone. I set it down on its cracked cradle and my repairs complete, I began to sift through the rubble, seeking out the box files I'd been searching through earlier. Clearing a space on the floor, I settled down to continue my search.

After an hour, I found what I was looking for. The review I had written of *Book of the Dead* over ten years ago. I read it through carefully.

'There comes a time in every popster's heart when he grows tired of making a living from three-minute, three-chord won-ders; a time when something deep within urges said popster to throw aside commercial considerations and weigh in with something serious, something meaningful, something *heavy*.

I AM extremely sorry to say that this is what's happened to Johnny Dark, formally a purveyor of first-rate thrash-pop. His previous albums have been unselfconscious invitations to the feet, knees and hips. Now he's aiming for the head (or more accurately, the grey cells contained therein) and the result is *Book of the Dead*, a double concept-album of such epic awfulness that mere words fail to do it justice. However, I will try. Johnny has discovered Egyptian mythology and (presumably after doing too many mind-expanding drugs) has reincarnated himself as some kind of minor demon with a personality defect. Seth, it seems, is dedicated to the destruction of Osiris. After listening to the album, my sympathies lie with OSIRIS, whom I ended up praying to in the hope that he'd come through and give SETH/Johnny the kind of kicking he so evidently deserves. A note on the inner sleeve babbles on about the age-old fight between Good and Evil and dedicates itself to "the return of chaos". What it boils down to is a slab of pretentious pomp-rock, lengthy synthesiser excursions tricked out with ponderous guitar solos, ethnic instruments and some really crass lyrics of the fourth-form poetry variety. The opening track, "Talisman of Seth", comes across like Black Sabbath on tranquilisers, while the fifteen-minute instrumental, "The Eyes of Ra", sounds like twenty ice-cream vans colliding with a grand piano under the dome of the Taj Mahal. What's particularly distressing about *Book of The Dead* is that it evidently cost a fortune to produce; but the whole project is spiritually and creatively constipated. There never was a more appropriate title. Mr Dark is clearly dead from the neck up and would be best advised to go back to the simple three-chord tricks which he previously employed to such enjoyable effect. Meanwhile, if anybody out there feels they MUST invest in two very expensive Frisbees, this is the one for you. On a technical note, I managed to get recorD one clear over the roof of my house, whIle record two, unfortunately, kept returning like a boomerang, no matter how many times I thrEw it.'

178

I pushed the scrapbook away and frowned. Well, it didn't tell me much, aside from the fact that the typesetter had evidently had a bad day. It was certainly an axe job, but then, I'd had a reputation for cruelty in those days; it had been one of the elements that made *Scam* such a crucial read. If a reviewer disliked a record, he was actively encouraged by the editorial staff to put the boot in. It was pretty much the party line. Set up the rock heroes, extoll their virtues for a while and then kick them down like ducks in a shooting gallery. In this particular case the ridicule was probably justified, but need I have been quite so facile? Frisbees, for Christ's sake! When Johnny Dark had died some months afterwards, I suppose I had felt vaguely uncomfortable about my treatment of the album, but I'd never for one moment considered that it might in any way have contributed to the singer's early demise. Now, I was not so sure. Was that it? I asked myself. A grudge? Somebody close to Johnny who blamed me for his death, who had let his anger boil and fester for all these years.

The shrill sound of the doorbell ringing almost made me jump out of my skin. I glanced quickly around the wrecked room, instinctively seeking some kind of weapon. Then I told myself not to be stupid. People were bound to call from time to time, I had to learn to take it in my stride. I got up, composed myself and went out to the hallway. I opened the door a fraction and peeped out cautiously. A man stood on the step, a big impassive fellow dressed in the black uniform and peaked cap of a chauffeur. I had never seen him before in my life and I began to wonder if looking for a weapon hadn't been such a bad idea.

'Yes?' I asked.

'Mr Prince? Mr Tom Prince?'

'That's me.' I opened the door a little wider and, looking over the man's broad shoulder, I saw that a black limousine was parked in the driveway.

'Just a moment, please. Gareth Parker would like a word with you.'

Fuck me! Gareth Parker. Now the shit really has hit the fan!

This was a revelation. I had never actually met the infamous Gareth Parker, though I knew of him by reputation as the self-

made millionaire businessman who owned *Metrosound*. I had
seen him on television commercials and in the business section
of the Sunday papers but he generally kept a very low profile as
far as the running of the station was concerned. The chauffeur
turned away and strolled back to the car. He nodded and opened
the rear door. Parker, a tall gangling man with a shock of prematurely grey hair, got out, followed by a small, bespectacled fellow
carrying an attaché case. The two men stood for a moment,
looking disdainfully around as though expecting some kind of an
ambush. Their eyes alighted on the wreckage of my portable
typewriter at the side of the house and they exchanged puzzled
glances. Then they followed the chauffeur back to the doorstep.
Parker smiled unconvincingly, displaying rows of crooked teeth.
His sharp features put me in mind of a fox and I took an instant
dislike to him.

'Do you mind if we come in for a moment?' he inquired.

I shrugged, stepped aside to let them enter. The chauffeur
came in first and stood looking around the narrow confines of
the hallway. He turned, nodded to the others and they followed
him in. I closed the door and pointed into the lounge. 'Shall we
go in there?' I asked.

The chauffeur moved through and, after a decent interval,
Parker and his diminutive companion followed suit. I trailed in
after them, wondering what in the world was going on. I felt as
though I was an extra in an absurd low-budget gangster movie.
Parker and the little man went across to the settee and took the
weight off their legs. The chauffeur remained standing, his arms
crossed as though defying the world to start any trouble with
him. He was built like the proverbial brick shithouse and I, for
one, wasn't going to argue with him. I stared at them for a
moment, baffled.

'Can I offer you gentlemen a drink?' I ventured half-heartedly.

Parker shook his head. 'No thank you, we won't be staying
long.' He motioned me to a vacant armchair, for all the world
like a monarch granting an audience. Then he indicated the little
man beside him. 'This is Giles Landon, my solicitor,' he said.
'He has something to give you.'

I didn't much like the sound of this. Landon opened his attaché case and withdrew a brown envelope, which he handed across to me.

I took it and glanced at it uncertainly. 'What is it?' I asked warily.

Landon gave me an oily smile. 'Open it, Mr Prince,' he suggested. 'I think you'll find it very acceptable.'

I scowled, but did as I was told. I was expecting some kind of threatening document couched in incomprehensible legal jargon, but I was pleasantly surprised. I pulled out a cheque, made payable to me. I glanced at the figures and gave a low whistle. 'Twenty thousand pounds,' I said tonelessly. I glanced up at Parker inquiringly. 'I don't understand.'

'It's quite simple,' Parker told me. 'I'm buying you out of your contract with *Metrosound*. The money's yours if you sign a simple release paper.' Parker fiddled with an ostentatious gold ring on the third finger of his left hand. 'I'm sure I don't have to tell you that the offer is totally unnecessary. After what happened last night, I could throw you out without giving you a penny. But that would be messy. Litigation, publicity . . . I think *Metrosound* has had enough bad publicity to last it a lifetime, don't you?' He pointed at the cheque in my hands. 'That will ensure that you go quietly, with a minimum of fuss. All things considered, it's a very generous offer.'

'Very,' I agreed. I glanced at my three visitors. 'And just supposing I was rash enough to turn it down?'

Landon shook his head. 'That would be very foolish, Mr Prince. There's a strong case to suggest that your handling of last night's show led directly to the murder of Mr Radcliffe. I also happen to know that you used physical intimidation in order to get on the air. We have two witnesses to the fact. Whatever happens, there's no way we'd let you go back. You're fortunate that Mr Parker is prepared to offer this alternative.'

I thought for a moment. 'The police may want me to go on with it,' I argued.

Parker smiled thinly and shook his head. 'The chief constable is a personal friend of mine,' he announced. 'We often play a round of golf. I can assure you that after having talked with him this morning, he's of the opinion that your relationship with the

181

killer is only exacerbating the situation. He's cautioned the officers dealing with the inquiry and instructed them to return to more conventional methods of detection. In short, Mr Prince, nobody will support you on this. So you either leave with nothing or you leave with that cheque in your pocket. The choice is yours.'

'It's not much of a choice,' I snapped sourly.

Parker sighed and brushed a small piece of fluff off the leg of his immaculate grey trousers. 'Let me spell it out for you,' he said. 'I'm not interested in radio. To me, the acquisition of *Metrosound* was purely an investment. I know or care nothing about popular music. But last night an employee of mine was brutally murdered and his body was found only yards away from the place where he worked. Now, I've been following this whole business since it started and I have to tell you that controversy makes me nervous, Mr Prince. No matter how appealing the financial rewards. I let the matter continue because I trusted in Simon Radcliffe's instincts. I appointed him to his position because I knew he was bloody good at what he did. On several occasions, I voiced my concern to him but in each case he managed to persuade me that he knew exactly what he was doing. Now it's plain that he misjudged the situation badly.' He lowered his voice to a whisper and I was strikingly reminded of John's voice, whispering its calm, precise logic. 'This whole episode is going to cause me grief. Grief on a personal level, since Simon and I were very close.'

I remembered the magazines on Simon's coffee table and reflected on his meteoric rise to power at *Metrosound*. Inevitably, I put two and two together and probably came up with the right answer.

'More importantly, it will cause me grief on a wider scale. There are enough people out there gunning for me, as it is. This debacle is going to make life very difficult for me. So, I'm taking steps to make a clean break.'

'What steps?' I asked.

'From today, I'm axing all talk shows from the channel. Apart from the news bulletins, *Metrosound* will become an FM music station and nothing more. Music, Mr Prince. Safe, bland, Top 40 music. There will be no place for shit-stirrers like you in the programming. I hope I make myself clear.

'Oh yes, very clear,' I said.

Parker nodded to Landon, who reached into his case and pulled out several sheets of paper which he handed to me.

'You will note,' said Parker calmly, 'that there are several conditions attached to this contract. You will not attempt to return to *Metrosound* under any circumstances. All effects that you have there will be sent to you. You will decline to talk to reporters about the subject and you will refrain from mentioning any connection with my station. It goes without saying that you will never attempt to work on radio again for any station in the Greater Manchester area. Those are the conditions, Mr Prince. Now, you will put your signature on that document. If you refuse to do so, I promise you I'll ensure that your personal reputation is on a par with a leper.'

I laughed bitterly. 'As things stand, that sounds suspiciously like promotion.'

Parker tilted back his head and chuckled. 'I'm glad to see that you still retain a sense of humour, Mr Prince. You're going to need that.' His smile vanished and was replaced by a hard mask. 'Hurry up and sign,' he said . 'I'm on my way to the airport. I'm going to my villa in Spain for a few months.'

'Until the heat dies down?' I asked.

'Precisely.'

I shrugged, realising that there was really very little else I could do. 'Anybody got a pen?' I asked brightly.

Landon took one from his top pocket and handed it to me. I uncapped it and scrawled my signature across the bottom of the document. It felt strange to do that. With one simple flourish, I was ending an entire chapter in my life. Sure, it was by now a rotten chapter, but I didn't have the first idea of how I would start the next one. And what about John? How the hell was I going to get to him now? I handed the papers back to Landon. 'Pleasure doing business with you,' I said.

Landon slipped the papers into his case and the two men got up from the settee looking well pleased with themselves. Parker nodded to the chauffeur who led the way back into the hall. I followed them and watched as the chauffeur opened the door. Parker paused in the doorway and glanced back at me.

'You know, Mr Prince, there's nothing personal in any of this. I'm actually a big fan of yours.'

I sneered at him. 'Yeah, well you've got my autograph now, haven't you?'

As he stared at me for another moment, I saw something in his expression that might have been genuine regret. But it was only for an instant. Once again, it was replaced by the mask. I thought about the mask that John wore and it struck me that his was the more honest disguise. Parker turned and indicated a couple of cars pulling up at the top of the driveway. Several figures were hurrying towards the house, carrying notebooks and cameras. 'Looks as though I got you just in time,' he observed. 'Remember our deal.' He nodded curtly and went out, slamming the door behind him. I stood there looking at the cheque in my hands. All things considered. it was a generous kiss-off. I told myself it could have been worse, Much worse. But I had lost my best chance of getting to John. Still, I reminded myself, he had my home number and he clearly had no reservations about using it.

I waited till I heard the purr of the limousine pulling out of the driveway. The doorbell rang. Best not to hang around here, I decided. Even if I was capable of sleep, the media vultures descending on the house would give me no rest and might get it into their heads to gain entry through the window I'd smashed. I'd be well advised to use my free time sensibly. I put the cheque into my pocket and grabbed my jacket, opened the door and stepped outside, almost colliding with the three journalists on the step. I turned back and locked the door behind me if only to keep up appearances.

'Mr Prince, would you like to comment on last night's murder?' somebody asked me. I shook my head.

Somebody else held a recorder under my nose. 'Mr Prince, is it true that you were the one who discovered the body?'

I pushed the machine aside. 'Get lost,' I suggested. 'I've got nothing to say to you.'

'Wasn't that Gareth Parker who just left the house?'

'Never heard of him,' I said and, jostling my way past them, walked towards my car. They all followed, persistently asking questions. One of them was blocking my way to the car and I shoved him aside unceremoniously. I could feel the anger building within me but I wasn't about to fight with them. I had enough on my plate. I unlocked the door and climbed in. A skinny individual with receding hair and a bad case of acne, pushed his face into the opening. 'You'll have to talk to us sooner or later,' he announced.

'Don't count on it.' I said, slamming the door shut and obliging him to jump back out of harm's way. I gunned the engine and accelerated up the drive. As I pulled out on to the road, I noticed that more cars were arriving. I drove away and one of them started following me until I pushed the accelerator pedal to the floor, leaving the company way behind.

I drove downtown and parked outside the central library. I went up the steps and took the lift to the second floor.

'Can I help you?' asked the bespectacled girl on the counter.

'Yes,' I said. 'I want to see everything you've got on Egyptian mythology.'

She nodded. 'Well, let me see now, the best-known source is *The Book of the Dead*. You might like to start with that.'

I nodded. 'Sounds perfect,' I said. 'Where do I find it?'

Chapter Sixteen

I moved slowly beneath the shadow of the pyramid, looking for a way in. The great glittering peak towered above me, blotting out the moon, and darkness settled around me, dense, impenetrable; but from within I could hear the sounds of music, shrill piping flutes, gongs and skin drums thudding rhythmically in time with the beating of my own heart. I groped my way along the wall like a blind man, fingertips exploring the mirrored surfaces, seeking an opening. It was stiflingly hot, my body was sticky with sweat and I didn't know exactly what had brought me here.

'Home sweet home.' I kept repeating the phrase over and over, the words falling like alien sounds from my dry lips. Someone had said those very words to me and, now, they seemed important. At last, my fingertips found an opening in the glass, a place where the hard unyielding surface became wet and jelly-like. My hands sank up to the wrists and I followed them, pushing my body into the enveloping softness. It filled my mouth and eyes and I was obliged to hold my breath for a moment. Then I was through, into the spacious interior of the pyramid. I found myself in a vast, empty chamber, the floor flagged with alternating black and white tiles. Far away on the other side of the room, there was a reception desk. Behind it, a uniformed man was sitting, reading a newspaper.

I approached the desk but the floor, too, was jelly; I kept sinking up to my ankles, making slow painful progress as I traversed the floor. Every time I glanced up at the desk, but it seemed to be no nearer. So I tried to run, my feet making vile sucking sounds as I wrenched them free of the clinging, mud-like surface, and at last I neared my goal. The man in the uniform was still engrossed in his paper, his face hidden behind it. I could see his peaked cap moving from side to side as he read. There was a familiar headline on the front page. PRINCE OF DARKNESS. Below it my own photograph stared back at me with a sickly smile. I reached the desk, which now seemed massive, some twenty feet wide. There was a brass bell standing on it. I raised a hand and brought it down slowly to depress the button. The sound it made was like a huge gong being beaten and the noise swelled in my head to a long, dinning roar. I felt as though my head would burst. The man at the desk continued to read. I stretched out a hand to take the newspaper reaching slowly across the intervening space. My arm seemed to melt like warm rubber, growing from the shoulder joint, elongating, allowing my fingers to close around the paper and pull it aside.

Beneath the peaked cap there was the face of a beast, a black dog-like face with small slitty eyes and huge yellow teeth protruding down from the curled lips. When the beast gave a guttural snarl of warning, I yelled triumphantly and lunged for the throat, but the man flapped his arms and shot upwards into the air like a great black bird. I turned and ran towards a staircase which spiralled crazily upwards into darkness. I reached the first flight of steps and began to climb frantically, my feet slipping and stumbling on the crumbling stone. I could see nothing ahead of me but I could hear the flapping of wings above my head and I continued to climb, going up the stairs three at a time, breath bursting from my chest in a series of shallow gasps. I knew the beast was waiting for me, somewhere up on the top floor.

I woke and lay still for some time, familiarising myself with the oddly unfamiliar room. I was covered in a thick, cold sweat and the sheets were clinging to me like wet paper. There were tears in my eyes. The dream had terrified me and even now, in the relative security of wakefulness, I was still frightened. I turned my head and glanced at the clock. A little after midday. Exhaustion had finally claimed me around seven o'clock the previous night and I had slept fitfully since then, my mind haunted by images gleaned from the reference books I had been reading. Feeling muggy and disorientated, I threw back the duvet, put on my dressing gown and stumbled across to the window.

I opened the curtains to a grey, windswept day and a driveway still full of reporters. One of them caught sight of me and shouted to the others. I pulled back from the window with a curse. I felt like a prisoner in my own house. An instant later, the doorbell rang. I realised that it had been ringing all morning, translated in my dreams as the sound of a gong being struck. I went out of the bedroom and down the stairs congratulating myself upon having somehow found the energy to board up my broken downstairs window before I'd collapsed in a heap early last night. The bell continued to ring but I ignored it, I picked up the morning mail from the doormat and carried it to the dining-room table where I had left the items of research I had collected the previous day. They were spread out on the table's surface in various piles. I sat down blearily and stared at them listlessly. On the first pile was a photocopy of a mask of Seth, taken from a photograph of a nineteenth-Dynasty bronze statue. The long dog-like snout and the huge curved canine teeth were the features I had seen in my dream. I was fairly certain that this would prove to be the same mask that had terrorised Jamie. I thought now that I was beginning to understand the twisted logic of John's campaign. In his mind, he had become the protagonist of the Johnny Dark album: Seth, the storm God, the thunderer, the deity that most resembled the Christian concept of the devil. More significantly perhaps, I had deduced that in this particular story, John had identified me with the rôle of Osiris, Seth's brother. I thought I now understood the wording written on the brochure for the Osiris complex. It was not John's spiritual home at all. It was mine.

I had realised something else. The review I had written of the *Book of the Dead* was more influential than I might initially have supposed. On returning from the library, I had re-examined it carefully. The typesetting mistakes seemed to imbue certain words and letters with extra importance. Incredibly, when removed from the review and set down in chronological order, they appeared to contain a message. I AM OSIRIS SETH MUST D I E.

It was a coincidence, a million-to-one shot; but to somebody as unstable as John, it must have appeared as a declaration of intent. The question was, why had he waited so long to respond?

I had also gleaned pages of photocopied text relating the long battle between Seth and Osiris, explaining how Seth had murdered Osiris and cut his body into fourteen pieces, scattering them throughout Egypt. But Isis, Osiris' wife had found the various parts and had reunited them by sorcery, bringing him back to life. After that, Seth had become the adversary of Osiris' son, the hawk-god Horus. I remembered how John had twice referred to Daniel as 'the little hawk'. This was the element that frightened me most. For Seth was pledged to destroy Horus. In various accounts of the legend, Seth had sodomised the young god and had torn out his eyes, which symbolised the sun and moon. In the ancient myths, Horus had eventually vanquished Seth; but what chance did a young boy have against such a force of evil? At all costs, Daniel had to be protected.

I turned my attention to the post and in particular to a small jiffy-bag. I tore it open and pulled out a brown cardboard box. There was a handwritten note taped to the lid. 'Something to see you through the week', it read. I frowned, cut through the seal with my thumbnail and opened the box. I stared at the contents and the contents stared back at me. For an instant I failed to register exactly what I was looking at. Then I dropped the box with an exclamation of disgust, scattering the eyes across the surface of the table. They made soft splatty noises as they hit the wood and I became aware of an unpleasant smell. They were all there, four pairs of them, in assorted colours. I sat where I was, trembling, feeling my gorge rise. I would have been sick if I'd eaten anything in the last twenty-four hours. All I could do was retch loudly. I stumbled from my seat, knocking the chair over in my haste to put distance between myself and the table.

I hurried to the phone and managed to dial Drayton's number.

I watched in horrified fascination as the young, bespectacled man from Forensic went about the unenviable task of collecting the eyes with a pair of tweezers. A couple of them had rolled off the table on to the floor and he was obliged to get down on his hands and knees and hunt for them.

'They're in excellent condition,' he observed gleefully. 'Some of these are what . . . two, three months old? He must have kept them in the ice-box or something.'

190

Drayton laughed grimly. 'Remind me not to go to any cocktail parties at *his* place,' he said. 'God knows what you'd find floating in a gin and tonic.'

I snapped at him angrily, 'I'm glad you find this all so amusing.'

Drayton shrugged. 'We have to use something to deal with incidents like this,' he explained. 'It usually comes out as a sick sense of humour.' He indicated the note on the table. 'Seems our John is a bit of an amateur comedian, as well. Something to see you through the week, indeed.'

'Frankly. I've heard funnier jokes,' I said.

'I'll bet you have.' Drayton turned to look at his colleague. 'Have you got them all now?'

The young man stood up and jiggled a transparent plastic box full of horror. 'Aye aye, Captain!' he said and gave me a mock naval salute. He shrugged apologetically. 'Sorry. Couldn't resist it.' He moved to the table and carefully put the cardboard box, the note and the jiffy bag into another container. 'What about all this stuff?' he asked, indicating my research.

'That's mine,' I assured him.

'You've made a bit of a mess of it,' he observed, indicating several vivid pink splotches on the photocopied sheets.

'All right. George.' said Drayton. 'Get that stuff over to the lab and see if you can come up with anything. I'll catch you later.'

'Right you are, guv.' George moved towards the door.

'Don't let those reporters see what you're carrying,' Drayton warned him. George nodded and slipped his grisly trophies under his jacket. He went out of the room. A moment later, I heard the front door open. There was the sound of a scuffle on the step and a barrage of questions which went unheeded. The door slammed.

'Bastards,' I said quietly. I lit a cigarette with shaking hands. Drayton studied me for a moment.

'I bet you could use a coffee,' he observed. 'Come on, I'll make you one.'

I followed Drayton through into the kitchen and watched as he filled the kettle.

'So, the programme's off the air,' said Drayton.

'Yeah.' I blew out smoke. 'They've buried it.'

'I'm sorry about that.'

'Don't be. I got a pretty healthy payoff.'

Drayton grinned. 'I'm evidently in the wrong line of work. All I got was a chewing over by the chief constable. I even thought he was going to take me off the case.' He plugged in the kettle, switched it on. 'No such luck,' he added.

'You'd like to be taken off it?' I asked.

'I wouldn't lose sleep over it.' He smiled, realising the irony of what he had just said. '*Sleep*. That's a good one! You manage to grab any since I last saw you? You look awful.'

'Thanks. I feel bloody awful.'

Drayton spooned coffee into a cup. 'All that Egyptian stuff on the table,' he said. 'Made any sense of it?'

I nodded. 'Yes, I have. I understand a lot more about John now. He thinks he's a god. He thinks I'm another god. His brother as a matter of fact. These two have some kind of cosmic grudge. If he gets his way, he's going to cut me into fourteen pieces and scatter the bits to the four winds.'

'Charming.' Drayton shook his head. 'You'll have to excuse me. I'm just a simple copper. All this Tutankhamun nonsense is a bit out of my league. And this business with the eyes.'

'Oh, that makes a twisted kind of sense, as well. The Eyes of Ra.'

'Pardon?'

'There's a track on the Johnny Dark album called "The Eyes of Ra". I did a little reading on the subject. Ra was the Egyptian Sun-god. His eyes were detachable. He used to send them to destroy men. Sending eyes came to be seen as a kind of death curse.'

Drayton pondered this for a moment. 'Well, as he sent you four pairs of them, he clearly isn't leaving anything to chance. So, you think he's going to make a play for you?'

'Eventually. But first he'll try for Daniel.'

'Your son? How can you be so sure?'

'Because he told me. He phoned me again.'

Drayton frowned. 'We really ought to get a tap on that phone,' he said.

'No,' I said firmly. 'I need some bloody privacy, for Christ's sake. I won't have you lot taping all my conversations, do you hear?'

'All right, all right, calm down! It's up to you, of course. What else did he say?'

That Daniel's a god, too. He has the universe in his eyes.'

Drayton looked at me sharply, as though wondering if all this had unhinged me. I couldn't blame him for his thoughts. Right now, I felt pretty close to the edge. I sensed it not far away, a yawning chasm just itching to claim me. What was it Karen had called it? *Nun*. A state of perpetual chaos. It would have been oddly comforting to let myself go down into that blackness, to join John in his demented world. Easier somehow than clinging on to the last vestiges of my sanity.

Drayton frowned. 'Well, we're still keeping a close watch on your ex-wife's place. There's not much chance of John getting past us.'

I laughed hollowly. 'Excuse me, no offence, but that doesn't exactly reassure me. John told me he's already been close to Daniel. Close enough to touch him.'

Drayton shook his head. 'Not possible. He's winding you up.'

'Maybe. But he's never lied to me before.'

'Well, he's lying now. Nobody can get in or out of that place without us seeing him. Unless he can make himself invisible or something.'

'I'm beginning to think he could do anything,' I muttered. 'He . . . he played me a tape.'

'What kind of tape?'

'He made a recording. Of Simon. The sounds he was making when John was . . .' I broke off. The strength seemed to have temporarily left my body and I had to lean back against the wall. Drayton hurried to me, a look of genuine concern on his face. 'Are you all right?' he asked. 'You've gone white.'

I nodded. 'I'll be OK,' I muttered.

'Here, let's get you to a chair.' He helped me back into the dining room and sat me at the table. 'Have you any brandy in the house? I think you could do with something stronger than coffee.'

I shook my head. I found myself staring at the research material and its pale, purply-pink stains. 'Did you check out the Johnny Dark angle?' I asked.

Drayton frowned. 'I made some inquiries with the record

company, but as usual they led me nowhere. This Dark character has no surviving relatives. The only name I came up with was his ex-manager, one Micky Hart. He's dropped out of the business now, become a bit of a recluse by all accounts. I had some colleagues in the smoke check him over but they don't think there's anything to be gleaned from that direction. Apparently he never leaves his house these days.'

'Did they by any chance get a copy of the album?'

Drayton shook his head. 'I didn't think it was important . . .'

'Of course it's bloody important!' I snapped. 'Don't you listen to anything I tell you? The whole thing is linked to those lyrics, don't you see? If we had them, we might be able to plot John's next move.'

The kettle began to boil, making a fierce bubbling hiss. Drayton walked back into the kitchen, switched it off and poured water into the cup. He went to the fridge and took out a bottle of milk. 'Do you want my advice?' he asked calmly.

I shrugged. 'No,' I said. He gave it to me anyway.

'You're getting too involved in all this. If I were you, I'd put some distance between yourself and here. Leave the worrying to us. Milk?'

I nodded, sighed. I felt as tense as a tightly wound clockspring. 'Well, I was planning to go to Wales to visit Jamie. That's if she'll see me.'

'Sounds like a good idea. You could go crazy sitting here, waiting for the next thing to happen.' He came back and handed me the cup. 'This Egyptian stuff is becoming an obsession with you. But I think you could be barking up the wrong tree.'

'Oh for Christ's sake! How can you..?'

He held up a hand to silence me. 'Oh yes, I know it all seems to fit but that's because you *want* it to. I still think it's best if we pursue more established lines of inquiry. At least I know where I am with that approach. I know you think we're doing very little to sort all this out, but believe me, we've got a very thorough investigation going on. John's getting too big for his boots. Eventually he's going to make a mistake and, when he does, we'll be down on him like a ton of bricks. But it's going to take time. So, take my advice. Get away for a while. Stay up there in Wales for a few weeks.'

'Can't do that. Can't leave Daniel unprotected.'

'He's not unprotected! Tom, you're going to have to trust me on this. I can't order you to stay away from here, but I think it's for the best. I mean, look at you, you're a bag of nerves as it is. A few more tricks like the last one and you'll be in line for a breakdown.' Drayton glanced at his watch. 'I have to get my skates on,' he announced. 'On the way out, I'll make a short statement to those vultures on the doorstep. With luck, it should get rid of them for a while. It would be an idea if you gave me Jamie's address and phone number in Wales, just in case I need to contact you.'

I nodded. There was a pen and paper with my research material and I wrote down the information. My hands were shaking so badly I could scarcely write. I handed the note to Drayton.

'Thanks. When do you suppose you'll go up there?'

'This afternoon. I can be there in an hour or so. You . . . you promise me you'll watch out for Danny?'

'He's being covered twenty-four hours a day,' Drayton assured me.

I nodded. 'OK. I guess that's as much as anyone can ask. One more thing. This Micky Hart character . . . Johnny's ex-manager. You got a phone number on him?'

Drayton frowned. 'I thought I just said you were getting too involved.'

'I know. But you surely wouldn't mind me giving him a ring, some time, asking him a few questions? We need to know more about this Johnny Dark stuff. You don't seem to be putting yourself out over it, so . . .'

Drayton held out a hand in capitulation. 'All right, all right, I'll get it for you. But I don't want you pushing him too hard and causing any trouble. Promise me you'll keep it low key.'

'I'll be the soul of discretion,' I assured him. 'I just want to ask a few questions, that's all.'

'OK. I'll be in touch.' Drayton turned and headed out of the room. A moment later, the front door opened and I heard his voice calling to the reporters. 'Right gentlemen, if you'd like to gather here for a moment, I've just a few words to say to you.' The door slammed shut.

195

I sighed, ran my hands through my hair. I went into the study. It was still in a mess and darker than usual because of the boarded-up window. I picked up the phone and dialled Jamie's number. Her mother answered, her voice cold and hostile, but she said she would see if Jamie would speak to me. After a short interval, Jamie's voice spilled from the earphone. She sounded anxious. 'Hello, Tom? Is everything all right?'

'Yes love, everything's fine. I was thinking about coming up to see you. This afternoon, if that's OK?'

There was a brief pause before she answered. 'Yes, Tom, please come up. I need to talk to you. I've just heard about Simon, it's in all the papers. I've been going out of my mind with worry. I was going to ring you as soon as I could get five minutes away from Mother.'

'I'll be there in a couple of hours,' I promised her. There was another pause, this one long and awkward. I couldn't think of much else to say, so I concluded with, 'See you soon.' I put down the receiver then dialled Karen's number.

I made an effort to sound light-hearted. Karen was in the firing line and I didn't want to spook her. 'Hi Karen. How's tricks?'

'Terrible. I've got two baboons in a car trailing me everywhere I go and they park right outside the flat every night. They're supposed to be inconspicuous but even Danny keeps asking me who they are.' A pause. 'I heard about Radcliffe. I must say it couldn't have happened to a nicer person.'

'Karen!' I was shocked by her callousness.

'Oh come on, he was a right bastard and you know it. Finally got his comeuppance for too much pushing people around. Listen, what are you doing tonight? Fancy coming up and keeping me and Danny company?'

'I can't. I've arranged to go over and see Jamie.'

'Oh well, I suppose true love always comes first. A pity, I was planning to make my special spaghetti. Perhaps I'll invite the two gorillas in for a bite. I could always do a banana split for dessert.'

'Maybe I'll see you when I get back. I seem to have plenty of spare time on my hands now. I got the boot from *Metrosound*.'

'You shouldn't have given them the satisfaction. I hope they made a decent settlement.'

'Yes, they did. Look, I'm going to give you Jamie's address and phone number, just in case you need to contact me.'

'Thanks awfully! I'm sure she'd love to have me ringing her while the two of you are canoodling.'

I ignored the taunt. I gave Karen the information and she said she'd made a note of it, but I wasn't sure if she was just fobbing me off.

'I mean it Karen, if you need to call me, don't think twice. Jamie will understand.'

'Yeah, she's such a paragon, isn't she? Well, give her my love.' She put the phone down.

I shook my head. Just for once, I could have done without the old guilt trip. I went upstairs, shaved, showered and changed into fresh clothes. Suddenly, the idea of getting away from the house seemed very agreeable. I packed a small bag with a couple of spare shirts, a towel and some toiletries. As an afterthought, I collected my Egyptian research and put that into the bag. I moved around the house, locking up doors and windows. When I finally let myself out of the front door, I was relieved to find the driveway empty. Whatever Drayton had said to the news-hounds, it had worked.

I got into the car, pulled on to the road and headed in the direction of the motorway. I reached automatically for the switch on the radio, but checked myself at the last moment and put on a cassette instead. I wasn't in the mood for radio just now. I turned left on to the slip road that branched on to the M56 and accelerated up to speed. The grey skies had temporarily broken up and a pale watery sunlight was drying the rain off the surface of the road. I reflected that I was leaving John somewhere back there in the grey huddle of the city and I felt an oppressive weight slipping from my shoulders. Maybe Drayton had been right. Distance would put the whole thing in perspective.

But my mind refused to relax. It fixed on the tape that John had played me over the phone and my spirit sagged. It didn't matter how many miles I clocked up, the sound of that message was still in my head. I turned up the cassette player to full volume in a vain attempt to drown out the screams.

Chapter Seventeen

I eased the car down into the long declivity of the Llanarmon valley. Bare trees reared up on either side of me, filtering the pale winter sunlight through a web of stark limbs. The range of hills away to my left were capped with white but the fields that swept away from their base were surprisingly lush and green. Sheep browsed contentedly on the slopes and only the absence of lambs signalled the fact that this was not spring, but early December. I felt a long-absent sense of wellbeing spreading through me and I found myself toying with the idea of moving to the country, using my payoff from Gareth Parker to set myself up as a freelance writer. Almost immediately, I dismissed the idea. I was a townie at heart and wide open spaces had always disconcerted me. In order to function properly, I needed to be near clubs and cinemas, fast-food takeaways and art galleries. While the valley seemed welcoming today, I knew that soon the narrow roads would be choked with deep snow and the winds rushing down from the hills would be cold enough to cut to the bone. Cooped up in some remote cottage, I also knew only too well that I'd go round the twist in no time.

As I headed up the winding lane that led to my destination, I began to feel apprehensive again. I knew that Jamie's parents had never been particularly keen on me. They both worked in education and considered my chosen vocation as something rather facile, *lowering*. On my previous visits they had tolerated me with a patronising good humour; after what had happened to Jamie, I could hardly expect to be greeted with open arms.

I turned in at the wide gateway and motored slowly up the gravel drive to the converted farmhouse. I pulled the car to a halt and sat for a moment, gazing at the building, steeling myself

199

for my grand entrance. But then the front door opened and Jamie came out, she must have been watching for me. Bessie, the family's cocker spaniel, stood beside her, gazing uncertainly towards the car. Jamie was dressed in jeans and a heavy sheepskin jacket. She wore no make-up and her long hair was hanging free over her shoulders. Though still a little pale, she looked much more herself, I thought; indeed, she had never seemed more lovely to me than she did at that moment. I opened the door and got out. I stood there a moment, aware of the short distance between us which felt somehow like a vacuum. It was very quiet. I cast around in my mind for a suitable greeting, but nothing came. I could only shrug helplessly, hoping against hope that she would make the first move.

She smiled warmly and walked towards me. 'Hello, stranger,' she said.

'Hi. You look great.'

'So do you, I'm glad you came.'

Reassured, I went forward to meet her and a moment later she was in my arms, her head resting on my chest as she hugged me to her. Bessie trotted over to join us, snuffling curiously at my feet, I glanced down.

'I don't think she recognises me,' I observed.

'Of course she does. It hasn't been that long.' Jamie pulled away a little and gazed inquiringly at me. 'Are you all right?' she asked.

I nodded. 'I'm fine. It's finished now.'

'Finished?' Her face brightened. 'You mean, they've caught him?'

'No, I wish to God they had. I mean . . . with the station. They've paid me off. I'm out of there.'

She studied me for a moment. 'Well, I won't pretend I'm sorry,' she said. She stepped back a little, stood there gazing at her feet. 'I didn't understand, back at the hospital. But I've had time to consider it and I think I know why you felt you had to go back. Now, it seems it's out of your hands and I'm thankful for that.' She glanced apprehensively towards the house. I noticed the twitch of the curtains where somebody, presumably Jamie's mother, was peeking out. 'Let's not go in just yet. We've time for a walk. We'll go down to the copse.'

I nodded. 'Sure, why not?'

She linked arms with me and steered me back towards the gate. The copse was a favourite place of hers, a stretch of deciduous woodland where she'd walked since she was a little girl and the two of us had spent many happy hours there when we'd first started going out together. Maybe Jamie thought that visiting it would help to heal the breach between us. Bessie stared after us, her tail wagging hopefully. Jamie laughed and gave the dog an encouraging whistle. Bessie trotted forward and fell into step.

'How are you?' I asked warily. 'I mean, your . . . your injuries . . .'

'A lot better. They give me the occasional twinge but they're fading fast. You can barely make out the words now.'

I shuddered. She sounded so matter of fact about it, it was hard to accept that she was talking about her own body. Thinking about it brought a surge of hot anger into my veins. 'I want to kill him,' I said quietly. 'For what he did to you. I'd like to tear him to pieces with my bare hands.' I gazed at my hands for a moment, surprised I think, by my own vehemence. It was the first time I had given voice to my true feelings. 'I never thought I'd be capable of such hatred for another human being. Or such guilt.'

She stroked my back reassuringly. 'There's no cause for guilt,' she told me. 'Listen, this is important. I don't blame you for what happened. You have to understand that.'

I stared at her for a moment. 'I *don't* understand,' I admitted. 'How you can be so forgiving.'

'There's nothing to forgive,' she assured me. 'I've had a lot of time to think about this. I came to the conclusion that you've just been very unlucky. You're the real victim, Tom, not me. Everything that's happened has been designed to punish you. He must hate you an awful lot. And you see, he wants you to feel guilty. He wants you to feel responsible for everything. But you can't help any of it. You must get that straight in your mind.'

I laughed bitterly and nodded back towards the house. 'I bet they don't see it quite like that.'

'It doesn't matter how they see it. I love you, Tom, nothing's going to change that. If he wants to stop me from loving you, he'll have to kill me.'

'Jamie, don't talk like that!' I squeezed her hand gently. 'This man is an animal, a killing machine. And he's so bloody devious. Sometimes I think he's not even human. If you'd seen what happened to Simon . . .' I shook my head, not wanting to pursue that train of though. 'I want him dead,' I concluded. 'I won't rest until he is.'

We passed through the gateway and moved out into the lane. Bessie, guessing our destination, trotted eagerly ahead.

'Try to put Simon out of your mind,' Jamie advised me. 'We need to start thinking about the future.'

'The future . . . yes.' I shrugged. 'I keep thinking, what future? What future can there be, as long as he's out there?'

'Listen. We could move away. We could leave Manchester, start over in a new town, somewhere he wouldn't find us.'

I scowled. 'Where's that?' I asked bitterly. 'Baghdad? Rio de Janeiro? He knows all about me, Jamie, what's to say he won't just follow us and pick up where he —'

I broke off with a start as a car accelerated around the bend from behind us. Instinctively I threw an arm around Jamie and pulled her to the grass verge. The car, a battered grey saloon, raced past us and disappeared round the curve of the road.

'Mad bastards!' I snapped. 'Why must they drive like they're at Brands fucking Hatch?' I was shaking, my frayed nerves stretched to breaking point by the sudden intrusion.

Jamie paused and took me in her arms again. 'Calm down,' she whispered. 'You see how this thing's affecting you? You're jumping at shadows.'

I sighed, nodded. 'It's getting so I'm afraid to wake up in the mornings,' I told her. 'I keep wondering what the next disaster will be.' I glanced at her apologetically. 'Christ, you're handling this better than I am. You're the one who should be freaked.' I slipped an arm around her shoulder and we walked on. Around the curve of the road, there was a long declivity. On the right-hand side of it, the copse stretched away, a lair of dark shadows. Bessie paused at the verge for a moment, glancing back to make sure we were following. Then she trotted away into the trees, knowing from experience the route we would take.

'Maybe we *should* move out,' I mused. 'I won't get work in Manchester again, that's for sure. By the way, I got a handsome payoff from *Metrosound*. Twenty thousand.'

Jamie glanced at me in surprise. 'Well, that's not bad,' she observed. 'Enough to tide you over till you find something. How about Bristol. Didn't you know a couple of people at the BBC?'

'South?' I gave an exclamation of disgust. Jamie smiled at my reaction.

'You say it like it's a dirty word,' she observed. 'The trouble with you is, you always see it as selling out. You've become a professional northerner, do you know that? I wonder you don't go around in a cloth cap with a couple of whippets at your side. What's so bad about Bristol anyway?'

'Oh, it's all right, I suppose. I could always buy some red spectacles and a dickie bow.'

She shook her head. 'OK, maybe not Bristol. How about Newcastle? Is that macho enough for you?'

I didn't answer. We had reached the entrance to the copse, but I had stopped in my tracks, staring apprehensively into the trees. In the grip of winter, they looked stark and dead and the track was piled high with rotted leaves. The sun was too low to filter through the canopy of criss-crossed branches and a few steps from the road it was chill, clinging twilight. I took an experimental step forward and a couple of wood pigeons launched themselves from some overhead branches, their wings drumming with unnatural volume in the stillness. I felt a prickle of foreboding clawing at the base of my spine and I turned back to Jamie.

'Let's not go in,' I said tonelessly. 'It's too dark.'

'Nonsense! We've walked that track a hundred times.' She looked at me inquiringly. 'Look, if you're worried about me, don't be. I feel safer in there than anywhere else. I've always thought of it as a welcoming place. Sort of womb-like.'

'It's not that. It's just . . . something doesn't feel right.' I couldn't really articulate what I was feeling. My skin was crawling and I had a heightened sense of apprehension. I indicated a remnant of stone wall. 'Let's just sit here for a moment while I have a smoke, OK?'

She nodded. She sat beside me on the wall and watched as I fumbled for my cigarettes, noting the clumsiness of my hands as I struck a match.

'Are you cold?' she asked me. 'We should have got you a warmer jacket before we left.'

'I'm all right,' I assured her; but I wasn't, I was shaking like a leaf. I inhaled on the cigarette, blew out smoke. 'I feel nervous, that's all.'

Jamie stared at her feet for a moment. 'Have you sorted yourself out with Karen?' she asked.

I shook my head. 'I told you at the hospital. There was nothing to sort out. I went there that night because I needed help and I couldn't think of anywhere else to go. That's all there was to it.'

Jamie nodded. 'I guess I was a bit irrational. I had it at the back of my mind that you were running back to her, after what had happened. And I thought, you know, Danny means so much to you and you must be worried about him. About what could happen, I mean. So . . .' She shrugged, spread her hands.

I looked at her. 'How are you?' I asked her.

'I told you. The scars are . . .'

'That's not what I mean. How are you in yourself? How do you feel after what happened?'

She shrugged, seemed reluctant to speak. 'OK, I guess. I thought I'd be too frightened ever to leave the house again, but it hasn't happened like that. I still have a lot of bad dreams. That mask. I see the mask and . . . and sometimes I dream that I'm dead. I dream that he killed me back there and I see people at my funeral, stuff like that. I don't know what any of it means. I think the hospital's lining up a shrink for me, I'm sure he'll be fascinated by it all. I'm also not too keen on being alone, but I suppose that's only natural. I'll rest easier once he's been caught. Do you think they'll get him soon?'

'Sorry?'

'I said, do you think they'll catch him soon?'

I was glancing about nervously. There had come into me the distinct conviction that we were being watched. Off in the copse somewhere, I heard Bessie yapping excitedly. 'What's that?' I asked fearfully.

'She's probably seen a rabbit.'

'Sure, a rabbit. Lot's of them in there. People go in with guns and hunt them, don't they? It can't be much fun being a rabbit.

I think I know how they feel.' I paused, closed my eyes for a moment. I could feel the sensation of dread mounting within me, rising steadily like the mercury in a thermometer. My skin was itching now and I was aware of the sledgehammer thud of my heart crashing away beneath my ribcage.

He's here. The thought flashed across my mind like a shaft of cold steel. *No,* I told myself. *You're just spooked, that's all. You've got to get hold of yourself.*

'Perhaps we should go back to the house,' suggested Jamie.

'Yes . . . yes, I think maybe . . .' I broke off, opened my eyes and raised them to meet hers. It was no good. Now it was more than just a sense of foreboding. Now, somehow, I just knew. 'Jamie,' I said quietly. 'He's here. He's somewhere nearby.'

'Who?'

'John.' The word sounded strange on my own lips. It might have been the name of an old friend.

'No!' Jamie shook her head, not wanting to entertain the idea. 'How could he be? You're just jumpy, that's all. He doesn't know this place, he couldn't . . .'

'He might have followed me,' I said. 'That car. The one that passed us. I think he might have gone into the copse to wait for us.'

'Tom, no, it's not possible! You've got to get a hold of yourself.'

'I'm trying, but—' Bessie barked again, louder this time. I turned my head in that direction, craning my neck to try and get a glimpse through the screen of intervening trees. 'I just feel that he's here, I can't explain it. It's like—' Bessie's barking terminated abruptly in a terrible high-pitched yelp. My blood ran cold in my veins. I jumped to my feet, dropping the cigarette. 'Oh Jesus,' I said. 'He's in there! I know it!'

Jamie, too had got to her feet and had started instinctively along the track into the woods after her dog, but I ran to her and grabbed her arm, pulled her back.

'Keep to the road,' I urged her. 'Don't go in there.'

'But Bessie!'

'Do what I tell you, Goddamnit!'

We began to move along the verge, trying to see into the depths of the forest but we couldn't make out much. Jamie called the dog's name several times, her voice seeming to echo in the silence. Bessie usually came when she was called but there was no sign of her.

'We should go and look for her,' pleaded Jamie. 'She might have fallen into a trap or something.'

I nodded. 'That's what I'm afraid of,' I said. I kept a tight grip on Jamie's arm and walked on for ten minutes perhaps, though it seemed longer. The light was failing and the silence from within the forest seemed to scream at us. I kept thinking about the tape John had played me and I knew that I dared not go in to the chill embrace of those trees, not for anything.

Then I stopped in my tracks as I heard the sudden roar of an engine ahead. The grey saloon appeared around another curve in the road, heading back towards us at speed. I stood rooted to the spot, staring at the oncoming vehicle. As it drew closer, I could see the driver quite clearly, a bearded man wearing a black leather jacket. He was smiling as he drove straight at me, just as he had smiled that first time, when I had seen him coming out of Karen's apartment building. I was vaguely aware of Jamie's hands tugging furiously at my arm, pulling me into the safety of the trees by the roadside. The driver gave me a cheery, mocking wave and raced by.

'It was him,' I whispered. 'It was John.'

Jamie swore beneath her breath and raced off into the copse, still calling the dog's name. I remained where I was, watching the rear of the car as it drove away. My gaze went instinctively to the licence plate and I saw that it was obscured by a sheet of black plastic. Then, to my surprise, I noticed that the car was slowing down. There was a long silence, broken only by the unexpected sound of a blackbird singing, a bright, sibilant tone. I could hardly control the trembling in my body. I took a step towards the car, expecting it to move away, but it remained where it was. I began to walk towards it, hesitantly at first, then with growing purposefulness. I broke into a run. I put my head down, lengthened my stride, closing the gap between myself and the car in a matter of moments. But as I neared it, I heard the revs rise and the car pulled away, moving off at a tantalisingly slow speed and keeping just out of my reach. Then it accelerated and I was left behind. I slowed to a halt, mouthing a string of obscenities, the air wheezing in my lungs. I bent over, hands on hips, trying to catch my breath and then, glancing up, I saw that the car had stopped a second time.

It stood there in the road, fifty yards away, mocking me, challenging me, daring me to try again. 'Goddamn you,' I whispered. 'Goddamn you to hell.' I spat emphatically on the road. A cold, calm anger washed over me. I snatched a breath, put my head down and began to run again, digging my toes into the tarmac and pumping my arms like a sprinter. As I drew nearer I heard the engine stall, then a brief splutter as the driver tried in vain to start it again. I felt a sense of elation fill me and I was no longer aware of my own exhaustion. My stride lengthened. John had made a mistake! His luck had finally deserted him! I narrowed the gap, heard the ignition fail a second time as I flung myself across the last twenty feet. I could see the driver, hunched in his seat, desperately trying to start the car. His head was down and his long black hair hung over his face. The ignition coughed a third time, spluttered, then caught feebly, the revs building.

'*No!*' I screamed. I cleared the back of the vehicle and threw myself at the door handle on the driver's side, just as the car began to move away. My hands closed on steel and I found a grip, but then I was jerked off my feet as the driver hit the accelerator. My shoes grazed the road and my arms were nearly wrenched from their sockets. I clung on grimly as the car dragged me down the road, picking up speed. John turned to look through the glass. He was grinning at me. He moved his head mockingly from side to side. Inevitably one hand slipped free and then I lost my grip altogether, went sprawling and tumbling on the road, grazing my knees and elbows. Before I had even stopped rolling, I had spotted a large stone by the verge. I scrambled to my feet, raced over to it, picked it up, hefted it like a shot-putter and flung it with all my strength. I heard the satisfying crash as the car's rear windscreen shattered. The vehicle weaved crazily from side to side and its left tyre slammed a sod of earth out of the grass verge. For a moment it looked as though it might grind to a halt, but then the engine roared and it was accelerating away out of reach. I watched it swing recklessly around the bend in the road and I slumped down exhausted on the verge, burying my face in the cold grass.

Close, I thought. *So fucking close. But the bastard has the luck of the devil.*

Jamie's shrill scream echoed through the copse, snatching me back to life. I reeled to my feet and ran to the track she had disappeared down. I headed into the trees, blundering through bushes and overhanging branches. Jamie screamed again and I followed the sound of her voice, veering to the left and pounding along the track, my feet slipping and stumbling in the morass of dead leaves and broken branches. I didn't have far to run. I found her kneeling in a small clearing. From a low branch in front of her hung Bessie. Her back legs had been tied with a short length of rope and blood was still spattering from a gash in her throat, staining the surrounding bushes with crimson. Her body was twitching convulsively as though some life remained in her but the eyes were glazed over in death and her tongue lolled obscenely from her open mouth.

Jamie kept screaming, close to hysteria. I grabbed her by the shoulders and shook her roughly, until the noise subsided. Then I held her against me, stroking her hair, rocking her in my arms like a child. Despite everything, a sense of elation remained with me. I had seen John's face. For the first time since it all began, I knew who I was looking for.

I tried to draw comfort from the fact as I helped Jamie to her feet and guided her back through the trees in the direction of home.

Chapter Eighteen

I stared intently at the computer screen as the face began to take shape. The eyes were right now, I decided, small deeply set on either side of a thin, straight nose; and the hair looked OK, long, unkempt, centre-parted. It was just the beard that needed work. It looked too tidy, too well groomed.

'Can you give him a fuller beard?' I asked the operator. 'More ragged than that?' The man nodded, punched some keys. The beard began to fill out around the edges, growing magically upwards to cover more of the cheekbones.

'How's that?' I was asked by the chubby, chain-smoker in his early twenties whom Drayton had introduced as a 'computer wizard'. They'd brought him up from London to do the identikit.

I nodded. 'Yes. I think that's it. If you could just make him smile. He's always been smiling when I've seen him.'

He shrugged, spread his hands in a gesture of helplessness. 'Identikits don't smile, I'm afraid. It's not in their nature.'

Drayton chuckled and patted the operator on the shoulder. 'Give us a couple of print-outs, Frank,' he said. 'That didn't take too long, did it?' He turned to look at me. 'Technology,' he said. 'Makes you wonder how we used to manage before the silicone chip.'

I nodded. 'I have another identikit to give you,' I said. I pulled a folded sheet of paper from my pocket and handed it to Drayton.

'Looks a bit like my mother-in-law,' he quipped after he'd opened it. 'What is this?'

'It's a mask of the Egyptian god, Seth. I showed it to Jamie before I left. She identified it as the same mask that John was wearing the night he attacked her.'

'Did she now?' Drayton frowned. 'How is she bearing up, by the way?'

'Very well considering what she's been through.'

'This business must be putting an awful strain on your relationship.'

I laughed bitterly. 'That's the understatement of the fucking year! All things considered I'm amazed she still wants to have anything to do with me. Jesus, she was safe and secure out there in Wales and I led that maniac right to her. Now there has to be round-the-clock surveillance on her parents' house. Needless to say, they hate my guts, they couldn't wait to see the back of me.' I thought back to the moment when Jamie and I had returned to the house, me carrying the bloody corpse of the dog. I'd wanted to leave it where it was but Jamie wouldn't allow it. Her parents had come running out to meet us, wild with panic and then all hell had broken loose. Jamie's father, a feisty war-veteran had burst into tears, blubbering like a child. The mother had just stared at me in undisguised hatred and her eyes had flashed an unmistakeable message. 'It should have been you.' After that, it had been the local constabulary, asking questions in that annoying Welsh accent and me having to run through the whole story once again.

I nodded at the image on the screen. 'The one positive thing to come out of it was that I saw him. We'll surely be able to get him now. Somebody will recognise the picture, won't they?'

Drayton didn't answer the question. Instead, he indicated the interior of the incident room. I glanced around at the thirty or so detectives in the untidy office, all of them seated before computer terminals, or answering telephones or running frantically backwards and forwards with sheets of printed paper.

'We've had this lot up and running for over two months,' Drayton told me. 'Two months without a single lead. This is the biggest thing that's happened yet, but it's something he's *chosen* to give to us. From what you say, he deliberately let you see his face. I don't think he'd have done that unless he was pretty confident of staying one step ahead. I still have the impression that he's very much in control.'

I scowled. This was not what I wanted to hear. 'To hear

you talk, you'd think this sighting was absolutely worthless!' I complained.

'No, not worthless. But I'm trying to be realistic. I'm convinced that John is somebody without any previous form, somebody who's suddenly flipped.' He pulled a completed identikit from the printer and studied the face for a moment. 'Oh, we'll shove this out everywhere we can. Television, newspapers, you name it. And you can be sure we'll get plenty of phone calls, ninety-nine per cent of which we'll eliminate very quickly. Whenever something like this happens, half the population becomes convinced that the picture is their next-door neighbour. We just have to hope that one of those one-per-cent tip-offs will be what we're looking for.'

His train of thought was interrupted by the arrival of a bulky detective sergeant. He handed Drayton a faxed report. 'From Clwyd CID, sir,' he announced. 'They've found the car . . . or what's left of it.'

Drayton perused the report for a moment, then raised his eyebrows. 'He torched it,' he told me. 'Took the licence plates with him. There's not much of it left for the Forensic boys.' He smiled, dismissed the sergeant with a curt nod. 'Probably shat on the seat when that stone hit his window,' he observed. He thought for a moment. 'Tell me . . . who else, besides me, knew that you were going down to Wales?'

I frowned. 'Only Karen. I rang her just before I left.'

'Hmm. Strange that, wouldn't you say? Particularly in light of the fact you once saw this same man coming out of her apartment building. You sure she doesn't know him?'

I stared at Drayton, shocked by the suggestion. 'She denied all knowledge of him when I asked her about it. But look, he could have just followed me, couldn't he?'

Drayton looked doubtful. 'That suggests that he's keeping you under surveillance twenty-four hours a day. Personally, I find that very hard to swallow. I suppose it's just possible that he could have been watching you when you drove away, but . . . I think it's much more likely that somebody tipped him off.'

I stared at Drayton. 'What are you suggesting?' I asked.

'I'm suggesting that we go round and have a nice long chat with your ex-wife.'

Karen studied the identikit in silence while we sat waiting for her reaction. I felt distinctly awkward about the whole thing. It's not every day you call on your ex-wife to ask if she's an accomplice to murder. I found myself studying her expression, half expecting to see traces of guilt in her face and terrified that I might, because then I wouldn't know what to think. But she just looked blank.

'No,' she said at last. 'Sorry, I don't know him.' She handed the picture back to Drayton.

'He was here,' I assured her. 'The day after the first killing. I saw him coming out of the front entrance. Christ, he even held the door open for me! And he smiled at me, like he knew who I was. I got the feeling then that he'd been visiting you. I mentioned it to you on the phone yesterday.'

Karen shrugged. 'What can I tell you? I don't know him and frankly I resent the insinuation that I do. Do you honestly think I'd be involved with something like this?'

'Nobody's suggesting that,' Drayton assured her. 'But if he was here, he must have been here for a reason. Try to think back. Was there anything suspicious that happened that day? Anything out of the ordinary?'

'I'm not even sure what day we're talking about,' protested Karen. 'It was what . . . two, three months ago? Christ, who can remember that far back?'

'Try, Karen!' I urged her. 'It was the day I called round to see you about Danny. He'd been in a fight at school.'

'Oh, yes, that's right. He painted that weird picture.' She thought for a moment. 'Well OK, I remember that but I don't . . .' Karen halted in mid-conversation. The look on her face suggested that despite her protestations, she'd recalled something. 'Just a minute,' she said. 'Let me see that picture again.'

'What is it?' I asked her.

'There *was* a man that day. He . . . yes, I think . . . my God, you mean, this is him? He was here, in the flat?' Her face drained of colour. 'Jesus. I invited him in. He could have—'

Suddenly, everything was going too fast for me to take in. 'What are you talking about?' I cried. 'I thought you said—'

'Yes, yes, but I'd forgotten. He was the telephone man. The deaf-mute.'

I stared at her, bewildered. 'Karen, what are you talking about?'

Karen's face was still pale. 'I think, yes, I was working on some music for a TV show. He came to the door. He had one of those little printed cards with him. It said he was deaf and dumb and he was working for charity. He was cleaning telephones and putting these things into the mouthpiece.

Drayton stiffened. 'Things? What things?'

'Air fresheners. You know, they make the mouthpiece smell nice or something. I suppose I felt sorry for him. He cleaned the phone while I carried on working. Now I think of it, he seemed really interested in the photographs on the mantel.'

I glanced up, saw the large, framed school photograph of Danny gazing back at me and remembered what John had said to me on the phone.

Such big blue eyes, just like his father. This, then, was as close as he'd been to my son. But it was close enough, close enough to make me shudder, to make the sweat trickle from every pore.

I groaned, shook my head, thinking of what John could have done if he'd taken it into his head. I turned back to face Karen. 'And you invited him in here? A complete stranger!'

'For God's sake, I didn't think anything of it! And I hadn't even heard about what had happened at the station.'

'And it never occurred to you afterwards that this guy was suspicious?'

She gave me an indignant look. 'Well, I'd hardly suspect a deaf-mute of phoning you up, now would I?'

Drayton shook his head. The expression on his face was suspiciously like one of admiration. 'Oh, he's a clever bastard, isn't he? He knew his voice would be a dead giveaway. So he becomes a deaf-mute.' He glanced around the room and spotted the telephone on the coffee table. 'That was the phone he worked on?' he asked.

Karen nodded. Drayton went over to it, took a handkerchief from his pocket and lifted up the receiver. Using the handker-

213

chief, he carefully unscrewed the mouthpiece. He let out a low whistle. 'Well, Tom, that explains how he knew where to find you yesterday,' he said. 'You told him yourself, He's bugged the phone. He's probably recorded every word you've said over the last three months.'

I got up and went over to have a look. There was a small, cylindrical metal gadget fixed into the mouthpiece.

'Very sophisticated,' observed Drayton. 'Radio controlled, I think. Must be linked to a recorder somewhere.' He looked thoughtful for a moment. Then he smiled, carefully replaced the mouthpiece and set the phone down on its cradle.

'Well, aren't you going to remove it?' asked Karen.

'No, I'm not. Since he's evidently listening in to every conversation you make, I suggest that we give him something he wants to hear. I think we should set a little trap for our friend. Something he won't be able to resist.' He turned to look at me. 'If what you told me the other day is correct, we know what he wants more than anything else, don't we?'

'Do we?' I gazed at him blankly. 'And what's that?'

'Your son, Mr Prince. Danny.'

My heart lurched when he said that. I could see what was coming and, frankly, it scared the shit out of me. 'Now, just a minute—'

'No, think about it! If all this Egyptian twaddle is the key to it, then we need to use it in our favour. John knows that Danny is under constant surveillance, right? If we let him think that the two of you are out on your own, he won't be able to resist. I want you to go home and phone Karen. I want you to arrange to take Danny out somewhere. We'll be following you. The instant that John shows his face, we'll close in.'

'No,' I said. 'It's too risky. You're asking me to use Danny as some kind of bait.'

'Yes, that's exactly what I'm asking.' Drayton stepped closer to me and fixed me with a searching look. 'Think about it, Tom. He's already killed four people. I've no reason to think that he'll leave it at that. This is our opportunity to trap him.'

I licked my lips nervously. 'I don't like it. Supposing something goes wrong? Couldn't you try and trace back from his bugging device? To where the recorder is?'

Drayton shook his head. 'Look at the success we've had with tracing so far. That's a very sophisticated device he's fitted. It's bound to have some kind of fail-safe in the system. He's not stupid, Tom, if we try meddling, the chances are it'll just cut out, and we'll be back to Square One. I'm not going to jeopardise our chances like that. Best if we let him go on thinking he's got one over on us. Confidence makes a man reckless.' He moved back to the sofa and sat down. 'Now, we need to think of a place where we can set this up, somewhere that won't seem suspicious. We'll let him think that you've taken Danny out without informing us. When you phone Karen up, you'll need to discuss it. You'll feed him a line . . . say you're sick of having us breathing down your neck all the time. Karen, you'll argue back. You'll say you don't like the idea of the two of them going out without surveillance. Tom, you'll be adamant that you aren't going to let us know your movements. And you could add some kind of goad to it. You could say that John wouldn't dare try anything in a public place, that there's no way he could find out about this. The man's all ego, it will be like throwing down a challenge to him. If you pull it off, John will be convinced that you're out there without help.' He was warming to his theme now, becoming quite excited about it. It occurred to me that he had already forgotten that it was my son he was talking about. 'Yes, a public place would be best, somewhere my men can just mingle with a crowd. It's the easiest way of concealing people. Is there anywhere that you regularly take Danny? A football match perhaps, something like that?'

I shook my head. 'I don't see that much of him,' I mumbled. 'I was . . . I was planning to take him to see Santa Claus. There's a department store in town that's got a grotto. We've talked about it a few times.'

'On the telephone?'

I looked at my hands, not wanting to answer the question, but Drayton persisted.

'On the telephone, Tom?'

I nodded glumly.

'That's perfect,' said Drayton. 'He must already be expecting you to arrange that. Well, this time we'll be one step ahead of him. We'll set up the bait and—'

'For Christ's sake, this is my son you're talking about!' I snapped. 'Don't forget that. If anything happens to Danny . . .'

'Relax,' Drayton assured me. 'I'm not about to let anything happen to him. We'll have more coppers in that place than you can shake a stick at. Your son's safety will be our first priority.'

'I wish I had your confidence in the police force,' I snarled. 'So far, they've done very little to reassure me.' I glanced at Karen. 'What do you think?' I asked her.

She shook her head. 'I hate the idea,' she said. 'Supposing this maniac goes in there with a gun. He could kill Danny before anybody had a chance to get to him.'

Drayton shook his head. 'Guns aren't his style. He's always worked close up.'

I laughed bitterly. 'Oh so suddenly, you know all about him, do you? Face it Drayton, you know nothing about John. All you see here is a chance to get back on line for your promotion.'

'That's not true!' protested Drayton. He sighed. 'Look, I know this is a difficult decision for you both, but you've got to accept that it's our one good chance of nailing this bastard before he does more damage. Now, I wish to God there was some other way of doing it, but frankly I don't see it. If you refuse this and somebody else is killed . . . well, you'll have to live with the knowledge that you could have stopped him.'

'Oh, thank you,' I said. 'Thank you very much.' I glanced at Karen. 'You decide,' I told her.

She shook her head. 'Don't ask me to accept that responsibility,' she said. 'Danny's your son as much as he is mine. And I've told you before that it's time you stopped running away from the fact.'

I nodded. 'So it's down to me again,' I observed. 'Funny how it always comes back to me, isn't it?' I sat looking at my hands for a moment. 'There's no other way?' I asked quietly.

'None,' Drayton told me. 'Listen Tom, think about those women that he's killed. Think about Simon. Think about the things he's done to Jamie. Get angry. Use the anger. Tell yourself, *it stops here*! There's one place for a sick animal like John and together we can put him there. But we've got to be prepared to take risks on this. Nothing comes easy, nothing comes on a plate. You want assurances? I can't give them to you. All I can say is that the moment he puts his nose into that store, he's trapped. And I'll see to it that he never hurts anybody again.'

I thought about it. I thought about it long and hard, my mind desperately searching for an alternative. 'Couldn't we just use me as bait?' I reasoned. 'If I said I was going someplace with Danny to lure him out, but turned up alone.'

Drayton shook his head. 'For a start that'd make him suspicious. And anyway he's had plenty of opportunities to get at you. Think about how he works. He wants to inflict pain on you, not kill you. My God, he's already said as much to you. If you're dead, that's his fun over with, right? But your son, now. Think how attractive a proposition that must be . . .'

I stared at Drayton and suddenly all my old hatred of him came flooding back. He knew how desperate I was. This all had to end and he knew that he could talk me into putting anything on the line, even my son's life. if it meant that it could finally be over.

'All right,' I said wearily. 'When do we do it?'

Drayton brightened. 'Saturday will be perfect. The store will be crowded with shoppers and I'll have time to organise a good team.' Drayton thought for a moment. 'Now listen, both of you. The phone call is very important. You've got to sound natural, matter of fact. If there's an edge to your voices, he'll notice it and he won't come within a mile of that store. We'll go over what I want you to say beforehand, but it mustn't sound rehearsed. Think you can handle it?'

'We can only try,' I said. 'Oh and one more thing.'

'Yes?'

'If it goes wrong. If anything happens to Danny, it won't just be John you have to worry about. Do you understand?'

We stared at each other for a moment. Then Drayton nodded.

'I understand,' he said. It was a long time before either of us spoke again.

Back at home, Drayton and I went into my wrecked study to make the phone call to Karen. He glanced around at the debris and shot me a quizzical look.

'I had a party,' I told him offhandedly.

He inspected the phone first, to ensure that John hadn't left one of his bugs there on his last visit. It checked out clean. I poured a couple of gin and tonics and we drank them in silence. When I felt I was sufficiently loosened up, I sat down and made the call, while Drayton paced around restlessly in the background.

I tried hard to keep my voice natural, to sound as though I was actually looking forward to the trip, but I couldn't tell how successful the deception was. At the other end of the line, Karen sounded distinctly forced and I told myself that John wouldn't be fooled for an instant. He'd read us like books, spot the jaws of the trap we were trying to set and keep well away. Maybe he would surprise everybody, would simply snatch Danny in the street or from school. I didn't want to think about the possibilities. I arranged a time to pick Danny up and signed off as quickly as I could. I replaced the phone receiver and sat staring at it for a moment. Then I turned to look at Drayton.

'How did I sound?' I asked.

'Pretty good. I think he'll go for that.'

'I'm not so sure,' I said. 'I think I sounded like a phoney.'

Drayton shook his head. 'I've got a good feeling about this,' he said. 'It smells right.'

I drained my glass. 'It stinks,' I corrected him.

'Only the sweet smell of success.'

I stared at him. 'That's odd,' I said. 'Simon said the same thing about something else. It turned out badly.'

'Was he a close friend of yours?'

I shook my head. 'I barely knew him. I can't say I liked him much.'

'You're an odd one,' he observed. 'I mean, you worked with him for some time, didn't you?'

'Well, there was nothing in the contract about liking him.'

Drayton laughed, shook his head. He finished his own drink and set the glass down on the desk. 'I'd better head into the station and get things organised,' he said. 'I'll contact you later with full details.' He glanced at the phone. 'I'll call round,' he added. 'I'm beginning to distrust those things. What are you going to do for the next two days?'

I shrugged. 'Hadn't thought about it.'

'Listen, if you'd like to go for a drink or something, we've a decent social club – the beer's cheap and there're some interest-ing blokes get in there.'

'Oh, I'll be fine,' I said quickly. I realised he was just trying to be friendly, but I was too wound up to respond to it. Maybe when all this was over, I'd be ready to drink with him. For now I was painfully aware that he was pushing me into places I didn't particularly want to go. He wished me good night and let himself out. I sat there at the desk, listening to the silence in the house. I had the impression of sinking slowly into warm treacle. I had nothing to occupy myself and a lot of time to kill. I pulled a scrap of paper out of my back pocket and stared at it for a moment. There was a phone number written on it, the one that I'd finally managed to wheedle out of Drayton earlier that day.

It was the number of Johnny Dark's former manager, Micky Hart.

I had decided that I needed to dig deeper into this connection. I was frankly not satisfied that Drayton's contacts had looked into the matter closely enough. It was time to do a little fishing on my own account.

I picked up the handset and dialled the number. It rang for ages and I was just on the point of giving up, when somebody finally answered.

'Hello Hector? I'd just about given you up, man. Where've you been?' The voice had an American twang and it sounded sleepy, irritable.

'Excuse me?' I said.

There was a long pause. 'Oh sorry, I was expecting somebody . . . hey, who is this?' The voice had a slow, rambling quality that any former rock-journalist would have been familiar with, the sound of somebody who habitually did drugs.

'Is that Micky Hart?'

'The same. Look man, I don't mean to be rude or anything . . .' Another pause. 'Who is this?'

'Mr Hart, you don't know me. My name's Tom Prince.'

'Prince? Prince, I know that name.'

I frowned. My current notoriety was bound to have brought me to the attention of a lot of people who hadn't actually met me.

'You er, you may have heard of me. I'm the guy who—'

'Sure! Tom Prince. You write for *Scam* magazine!'

This was a surprise, literally the last thing I would have expected. I wondered if Micky Hart had been living in a time capsule for the past decade.

'I *used* to write for them. They folded years ago.'

'You don't say! Hey, I thought I hadn't seen it on the news-stands for a while. I guess that's the appropriate thing for any-thing that's made of paper. To fold, I mean.' A strange nervous giggle. 'I'm kind of out of touch these days. Fact is, I don't read any more. I don't even watch television. I got sick of all the bad news, I guess. So, Tom. Who you writing for now?'

I hesitated, sensing an opportunity. I had intended to ask straightforward questions about Johnny Dark, but maybe there was a better way of doing it. I began to improvise. 'I'm, er . . . I'm freelance these days. Yeah, I do a lot of stuff for *Rolling Stone*, *NME*. Maybe you saw the piece I did on Clapton in the *Guardian*?'

'Uh . . . no, I didn't.'

'Well, thing is, Micky, I'm putting together a book at the moment. Yeah, it's called . . .' I groped mentally for a convin-cing title. 'It's called *Live Fast, Die Young*. Well, that's just a working title. I'd very much like to devote a chapter to Johnny Dark.'

I paused, waited for a reaction. When it came, it was encouraging.

'Hey, right, man, nice one. It's about time somebody did that. I've been saying for years, Johnny deserves a book all to himself. That guy was one special dude, I don't mind tellin' ya. Just a chapter, you say? Who's in the other chapters?'

Time for more improvising. 'Oh, the usual. Jim Morrison, Brian Jones, Hendrix. I thought it would be interesting to er . . . compare all those so called sixties legends with their counterparts in the seventies. People like Johnny who er, I think was incred-ibly underrated. Now, you knew him better than anyone. I thought maybe an interview?'

Another long pause. 'I wouldn't be opposed to that. I'd get paid for my contribution, I take it?'

'Yes, of course. I'll have to iron out a fee with my publishers. But the thing is Micky, I'm working to a tight deadline here and

220

to be honest they aren't as keen on including this chapter as I am. So I'd need to get something from you as soon as possible. I thought maybe I could drive down to see you, some time next week.'

'Drive down?'

'Yeah, I'm based in Manchester at the moment.'

'Manchester? Shit! What are you doing up there, man? Researching a novel or something?'

'No, I live here. It's not so bad these days.'

'Manchester. Christ!'

I sensed I was somehow losing credibility and that Micky hadn't caught up with the Manchester sound. 'Well, it's only temporary. I'm up here for a couple of months, doing a series about Indie rock bands. There's a whole scene happening here you know.'

'Yeah?' Micky sounded distinctly unconvinced. 'Well, I wouldn't know about that. Like I said, I'm a little out of touch. So, you figure this book is a hot cookie, huh?'

'It's going to be big, Micky. Naturally you'd get an acknow-ledgement.'

'The hell you say! Well, lemme see now, when would be a good time?' Again that high-pitched giggle. 'Shit, fact is, any time is OK for me, long as it's not too early. I'm retired now, I do zilch but sit around and get stoned . . . and I'm kinda allergic to daylight. I'm tied up over the weekend. Come over Monday evening, why don'tcha? Say around, six o clock. I should be up and functioning by then. We'll chew the fat.'

'Great. If you could give me a note of your address?'

'Sure. I'm kind of out in the sticks. Essex. You know Essex at all?'

I took down the address. 'I'll find it,' I said.

'Just look for the most desirable fuckin' residence, you ever saw,' Micky advised me. 'I did pretty well out of Johnny. That's why I don't have to work any more.'

'OK, thanks Micky. I'll see you Monday.'

'Right. Take it easy.'

The line went dead. I replaced the handset and pencilled the appointment into my desk diary, reflecting that if things went well on Saturday it was an appointment I wouldn't have to keep.

Maybe I'd go anyway. I had no idea what I was looking for from Micky Hart. Answers, I supposed. The trouble was, I didn't quite know what the questions were. One more thing I'd have to improvise.

I glanced at my watch. It was three-fifteen p.m. and I had two more days to fill before the weekend. I wondered how I was going to pass the time. The last thing I wanted to do was to sit around working up a sweat over what might happen on Saturday. With a sigh, I got up from my desk and went into the living room. In the drinks cabinet, I found a full bottle of gin. I poured myself a generous measure, then settled down in front of the television set. There was a dumb game-show on that involved lots of people running down staircases and squealing like stuck pigs. I drank myself steadily into a stupor. When I woke up, it was late and Boris Karloff, swathed in bandages, was chasing a luckless young woman around the interior of a pyramid.

'Home, sweet home,' I muttered; and reaching for the gin bottle, I drank myself to sleep again.

Diary Extract

8th December
'It's a trap,' I told Him.
　'Yes,' He said; and He grinned. I don't think He cares any more.
　I advised caution. I told Him that I could read their voices. They were like bad actors trying out for a rôle that was beyond their limited abilities. He just yawned with His great jaws and said that He'd always wanted to see Santa Claus. And since it was nearly Christmas, perhaps it was time I went shopping for a few things. He's into rewards in a big way. So I went out and I let Him guide me to the shops and then I began to understand what He had in mind. I used the old deaf-and-dumb trick again. It always works, people become embarrassed and sympathetic and then they forget to use their heads. I got some odd looks from shop assistants but that was only because of what I was buying. I just smiled and let them think what they liked.

The grotto is lovely, all tricked out for Christmas, lots of shining baubles and seasonal music. It almost makes you want to be a child again. I came back and showed Him the things I had bought. He said nothing but I knew He approved. He asked what I had bought for myself and I showed Him the large gold earring. I asked if I could wear it now but He said I must be patient.

'When?' I asked Him.

'Soon,' He said. 'First, we must see what Santa brings us.'

And He threw back His great head and howled with laughter. I understood. He doesn't believe in Santa Claus.

Chapter Nineteen

The taxi drew to a halt outside the department store and Daniel scrambled out excitedly. I leaned over to grab his arm, not wanting to let him out of my sight for a moment.

'Come on, Dad! Hurry up!'

'Slow down, there's plenty of time.' I turned back to pay the taxi driver, nervously aware of the bustle of shoppers around the entrance to the store. I'd decided to leave my car at home, aware of the problems of parking in town. I hadn't wanted to risk the isolation of a multi-storey car park, the memory of finding Simon's body was still too fresh in my mind. Somewhere in the crowd, I knew, there were several police officers in plain clothes but Drayton had warned me not to try looking out for them. 'Just go about your business as normal,' he'd said. An impossible order.

The taxi pulled away into the high-street traffic and I turned back to Danny, keeping a tight grip on his hand. My palms were clammy and I was aware of an uncomfortable prickle of sweat under my armpits, despite the chill of the weather. I still felt muggy after a two-day binge and I desperately wanted this to be over but knew only too well that it was only just beginning. I hadn't told Danny about any of it and, not for the first time, I wondered at the morality of such a thing. But what was the alternative? 'Excuse me son, but there may be a homicidal maniac following us around the shops today.' No, how could you make a seven-year-old kid understand something like that? His concept of monsters went little further than the colourful illus-trations of Maurice Sendak and Raymond Briggs, goofy creations with paper fangs and spawny eyes. He would grow up in a world where monsters were an everyday occurrence and I wanted to delay that part of his education as long as possible.

'Come on Dad, he's in here.' Danny was dragging me through the crowds towards the glass doors of the department store. I watched in dismay as I saw how close people were to my son, shouldering past him on the jammed pavement. How close were the police, I wondered? And how long would it take them to move in if there was trouble?

The glass doors swished back automatically and we stepped into the stale, warm air of the interior. Perfume counters stretched away in every direction, gaudy with tinsel and holly. White-coated females wearing too much make-up extolled the virtues of expensive fragrances and skin preparations. Seasonal Muzak spilled from unseen speakers, accompanied by the reassuring clang of cash registers. The annual Christmas orgy was underway once more and as always the message was spend, spend, spend!

A few steps into the store, I spotted Drayton pretending to peruse the goods displayed on one of the counters. Illogically, I almost burst out laughing. He looked so out of place there, I thought it would make the whole store suspicious. He was dressed in a quilted parka and a pair of shapeless blue jeans. It was the first time I'd seen him without a hat and the effect was somehow comical. And pretending to be interested in perfume for Christ's sake! He was the sort of bloke who always bought practical gifts for his wife.

I found myself wondering about that. I'd never asked Drayton if he was married. I didn't recall seeing a wedding ring. I'd have to ask him about that sometime. As I moved past him our eyes met fleetingly. A young female assistant asked if she could help him with something and he looked momentarily startled. Then he shook his head, muttered something about 'Just browsing'.

I moved past. I glanced surreptitiously over my shoulder and noticed that Drayton was following a few yards behind us. I felt vaguely reassured by this.

'Come on, Dad, hurry up!' Danny was alive with the excitement of Christmas, intent on wasting as little time as possible. I wondered if the kid really believed in Santa Claus. He'd made a point of telling me, several times, exactly what he was going to ask for – as though he was hedging his bets, just in case the whole thing did turn out to be a con. A *Time Blasters* back pack with a realistic laser gun that emitted three different-coloured lights for opening up doorways to other dimensions. Whatever happened to cowboy outfits, I wondered? Or was the back pack just another six-shooter decked out in the season's new colours? I would have to find time to get into town alone and buy him one. But not today. Today I was too concerned with keeping him alive.

My thoughts were rudely interrupted when I caught sight of a bearded man in a leather jacket, standing at a counter just ahead of us. His hand was reaching into the inside pocket of his jacket. Instinctively, I grabbed Danny and pressed him in close against me, but then the hand came out clutching a wallet and I could see that it was a much older man, hair greying at the temples, beard immaculately trimmed. He was pointing to something on the shelves behind the counter, an assistant was reaching it down for him.

'Dad, you're squashing me!' Danny wriggled indignantly against me and I temporarily released my hold. Glancing back, I saw that Drayton was still with us. He had seen what had happened and his eyes flashed a message. 'Don't get rattled,' they said, 'I'm right here.' He then turned aside and pretended to study a display of electrical goods.

I took a deep breath, reasserting a firm hold on Danny as he strained to move ahead. 'For Christ's sake, will you stop pulling me!' I snapped.

Danny glanced up at me in surprise, his eyes registering dismay.

'Sorry,' I said. 'Didn't mean to snap. Just take your time, OK?'

'Dad, is something wrong?'

'No! No, of course not.' I laughed nervously, made a miserable attempt at jollity. 'Where's the . . . where's the grotto then?'

'Next floor. Shall we go in the lift or the moving stairs?'

'The escalator,' I replied. The thought of being trapped in a lift with John was too horrible to comprehend.

There was a crowd milling around the foot of the escalator, parents with kids, just like myself. We joined the tail of the queue and gradually moved forward through the crowd, until our feet connected with the metal steps. We began to glide upwards. Ahead of us, a huge sign read, 'Welcome to Santa's Grotto.' I allowed myself another glance back and saw to my dismay that Drayton had got snarled up in the queue down below. He was shouldering his way roughly past people to try and gain access to the escalator, looking for all the world like a superannuated bovver boy in his parka.

'Great,' I thought, remembering his reassurances. *Saturday will be perfect. The store will be crowded with shoppers.* Still, I reasoned, there must be lots of other police waiting around the area of the grotto. The trouble was, I wouldn't know who they were.

We reached the next floor and pushed our way through the crowd. The designers had really excelled themselves here, the place was piled high with displays of toys and dolls, guns and models. In a large open pit to the left, a harrassed-looking young woman was demonstrating radio-controlled cars, while kids jostled around her, anxious to try one out for themselves. Danny paused to watch and I took the opportunity to scan the floor. I didn't much like what I saw. Every aisle was crowded with shoppers, most of them with noisy, unruly kids in tow. Up against the far wall I could see the entrance to the grotto, a gharish construction of plaster and polystyrene, made to resemble some kind of building hued out of solid rock. A couple of young women dressed as elves were doing their level best to control a queue of kids waiting to take their turn. The women were dressed in bright green hoods and tights. They had fake plastic ears, cotton-wool beards and pointed shoes, but the costumes did nothing to hide the shapely mounds of their breasts. No kid worth his salt would be fooled for one second. I turned to say something to Danny and saw to my horror that he was no longer standing beside me. I glanced frantically around, then spotted his distinctive red jacket. He was making a beeline for the grotto. I ran to catch up with him, almost colliding with a middle-aged woman burdened with presents.

'Watch where you're going!' she snarled in a distinctly unseasonal tone.

'Sorry,' I called over my shoulder. I caught up with Danny

228

and grabbed his arm. 'Hey you, will you stop wandering off by yourself?'

'Sorry, Dad.' Danny gazed up at me, confused. 'You're in a funny mood today.'

'Yeah, I know.' I found it difficult to look him in the eye. 'It's just . . . well, it's just so crowded here, you could get lost.' I took Danny's hand again and we joined the tail of the queue.

'We'll be *ages!*' complained Danny.

'No, we won't. Look, they're moving in quite quickly.' This was true. Kids were stepping into the entrance with only a couple of minutes between them. Evidently Santa was too busy to spare them more than the briefest of audiences. I noted with a hint of alarm that no parents were accompanying the children inside. They were adjourning to an exit over on the right to wait for their offspring to come out again. As we got nearer to the entrance, I saw a little sign over the doorway. 'Children only,' it said. This was something I hadn't bargained for. I glanced down at Danny, wondering what to do. I'd just have to try to argue it out, I supposed.

'Dad, look at that!' I looked down. Danny was pointing to a little boy in the queue behind us, who was wearing a brace around his neck. 'What's wrong with him, Dad? Why's he wearing that thing?'

I was aware that the boy's parents were staring at me with interest, as though wondering what I would say. I winced, quickly changed the subject.

'I er . . . I see Santa Claus has bought a couple of elves with him to help out.'

Danny sneered. 'Huh, they're not real elves. You can see their tits!'

'Yes . . .' Well, I reflected, he couldn't be anybody else's son, that was for sure.

After what seemed no time at all, we reached the entrance. One of the elf-women stepped up to Danny and shook his hand. 'Hello,' she said. 'Welcome to Toyland! Santa is waiting inside to meet you.' She drew Danny towards the door then glanced up in surprise as I moved with him. She pointed to the waiting area across the way. 'You go over there,' she told me.

229

'If it's all the same to you, I'd like to go in with him,' I said. 'He gets a bit nervous on his own.'

'No I don't!' retorted Danny indignantly.

'Yes you do,' I assured him.

The elf-woman indicated the sign over the doorway. 'Can you read?' she asked sarcastically.

'Yes, of course I can read. But nevertheless, I'd like to—'

The woman held up a hand to silence me. I noticed she had long fingernails painted a bright shade of red, something no self-respecting elf would be seen dead in. 'Look, give me a break will you? The sign says "Children Only", and that's what it means. Your son will be out of there in two minutes and you can be sure Santa Claus will take the best possible care of him.'

'Yes, but you don't understand, my son—'

'I'm all right, Dad!' protested Danny. He was glancing about, embarrassed by the incident.

The elf-woman gave a long sigh. She stepped closer as if to confide a secret. 'Look,' she said quietly, 'I've been standing here for four hours solid without a break. My legs are killing me, my uniform is a size too small and I'd like to visit the ladies' loo, but I can't until my replacement arrives. Now, nobody else in the store seems to have a problem with this, but if you can't trust us to look after your son for two minutes, perhaps you'd better go somewhere else.'

I stared at her for a moment and saw the simple, unyielding face of authority peering back at me through layers of badly applied cotton-wool. I could argue till I was blue in the face but it would get me nowhere. I shrugged, reluctantly letting go of Danny's arm. 'I'll be right over there,' I said. I watched as Danny entered the grotto, then turned back to the elf-woman. 'I hope a reindeer shits in your dinner,' I said and moved across to the waiting area.

'Thank you, sir. Have a nice day!' she called after me through gritted teeth.

As I took up my position, I pulled my cigarettes from my pocket, extracted one and put it into my mouth.

'No smoking!' snapped a voice. I turned and saw another elf-woman, a tubby malevolent-looking creature standing by the exit. Her arms were folded across her ample breasts and the expression on her face invited me just to try lighting up.

I sighed, put the cigarettes away and turned to look at the exit. The kids were emerging one by one, clutching brightly wrapped little presents against their chests. They all looked very happy and I told myself that there was surely nothing to worry about. Then my mind went into overdrive. I pictured a suspiciously thin Santa Claus inviting Danny to climb up on his knee. 'What would you like for Christmas, son?' he was whispering, as he gazed into Danny's big blue eye. I shook my head, dispelled the vision. Even John couldn't talk his way into a job like that. I knew for a fact that this store had had the same Santa year after year.

I spotted a vacant space on a wooden bench and slipped into it. Then I saw Drayton wandering across to me. He paused beside the bench and bent down as though to tie his shoelace. I noticed he was wearing Doc Marten's boots and again I felt the urge to laugh.

'What was the fuss about?' he asked quietly, addressing the question to his footwear.

'I didn't like him going in there on his own, that's all.'

'Oh, he'll be all right,' said a young woman, sitting beside me.

I turned to her in surprise, then realised that she had assumed the comment was addressed to her. I glanced sideways, but Drayton had already moved over to a display counter a short distance away. Ironically, he was looking at boxes of Cluedo. I frowned. This James Bond stuff was beginning to wear me down. I smiled at the woman.

'Well, you know how it is,' I said. 'When you're a parent, you worry.'

'Kids grow up fast these days,' she assured me. She was a good-looking brunette in her mid-twenties, dressed in an expensive cashmere coat. 'They're so independent. You take my Monica for instance . . .' Before I had a chance to take her Monica, a bespectacled little girl emerged from the exit, holding out a bright package for her mother's inspection. The woman smiled, nodded to me and went to collect her daughter. The two of them moved away into the crowd.

I frowned, glanced at my watch. Then I gazed around the store again and I had a bad feeling. It seemed to me, all of a sudden, that everybody in the goddamned place looked suspicious. There was a thin man standing a short distance away from the grotto's exit. He was wearing an imitation leather cap with woolly ear muffs and his angular frame was draped by a shapeless, grubby raincoat. He was watching the children come out of the grotto with a strange, faraway expression on his face. I noticed a trickle of saliva dribbling down his chin and a jolt of revulsion went through me. A short distance away from him, a spotty youth in a torn leather jacket was carefully perusing a display of Barbie Dolls. The youth had a Mohican hairstyle and a collection of tattoos on his face and neck in which the words 'Anarchy' and 'Chaos' featured prominently. I could scarcely credit it but there was a large clasp knife hanging from his belt. By the same display, a dumpy, middle-aged woman was pushing a pram that appeared to contain nothing more than a jumble of carrier bags and old newspapers. As I watched, she took a small doll from the display and slipped it under her coat.

The bad feeling was growing. I thought back to standing near the woods when I had gone to visit Jamie. It was a similar sensation, a cold sickness spreading through my guts. I was beginning to sweat profusely.

The Muzak was abruptly interrupted by the nasal tones of a young woman announcing that, for today only, there was a special reduction on First Strike – the tactical game of nuclear warfare. She added, almost as an afterthought, that if Mr and Mrs Morton would like to report to the information desk, they would find their daughter waiting for them.

I shook my head, turned my attention back to the grotto. The little boy wearing the neck brace was emerging from the exit, clutching his present.

I stiffened, got up out of my seat. That boy had been behind Danny in the queue, I remembered. I continued to stare at the exit. Another child came out, then another. But not Danny. Not Danny! A cold feeling settled in my stomach and I ran the tip of my tongue over my lips, which were suddenly very dry. The boy with the neck brace was being collected by his parents and I hurried over to them.

'Excuse me,' I asked the little boy. 'Did you see my son in there? The boy with blond hair. He was just ahead of you.'

The boy frowned, did his best to shake his head. His parents stared at me suspiciously, as though they doubted I even had a son.

'But you must have seen him! He was before you in the queue. He . . .'

I abandoned the idea. I was wasting valuable time. I turned quickly and hurried over to the grotto's entrance, beckoning to Drayton as I did so. Drayton looked baffled for an instant, but then, realising something was wrong, he dropped all pretence and ran to catch up with me. 'What is it?' he asked.

'Danny hasn't come out,' I said. I shouldered my way past the head of the queue. The elf-woman stepped up to bar my way.

'Now, just a minute!' she protested. 'I've already told you, you can't—'

I had no time to argue. I gave her an uncermonious shove in the chest and she went sprawling over a barrel of presents, her skinny legs sticking up in the air. I ducked my head and entered the grotto. Drayton followed. We moved along a dimly lit corridor and then emerged into an opening designed to look like the interior of a cave. There were mechanical reindeer standing about the place and a few strategically placed snowmen. By a huge Christmas tree, I could see a burly Father Christmas sitting on a decorative throne. He had a little boy on his knee and he was deep in conversation with the child, one arm around his shoulder. The pose looked somehow sinister, compromising. Santa looked up in surprise as we approached him.

'Now, just a minute,' he, too, boomed. 'You can't come in here!'

Drayton flashed his ID. 'We're looking for the boy who was in here a moment ago,' he said.

'Little boy?' echoed Santa, mystified. It must have been a bit like asking to see a particular piece of corn in a haystack.

'Seven years old,' I added, trying not to panic. 'Blond hair. He'd have asked for a *Time Blasters* back pack.'

'Oh him. He left ten minutes ago.'

'He didn't come out,' I assured him.

'He must have. There's only one exit.' He pointed to an illuminated sign over the entrance to a tunnel and I hurried towards it, with Drayton close behind me. Santa put his child on one side and trailed after us. In the corridor leading out, I spotted a disguised doorway that had been left slightly ajar. 'Where does this lead?' I demanded.

'My changing room,' said Santa indignantly. 'But look here, nobody's allowed in there but me!'

I threw open the door to reveal a spartan little cubicle, littered with clothes, carrier bags and several empty beer bottles. 'Those aren't mine,' said Santa, pointing to the latter. 'They were left here, I don't know who put them there.'

But I had already moved across to the other side of the room and thrown open a second door, revealing a flight of concrete steps leading down. 'Where do these go?' I yelled, my terror mounting.

'To the ground floor,' said Santa. 'But look, I don't—'

I didn't wait to hear the rest of the sentence. I headed for the stairs, with Drayton in hot pursuit. He whipped out a radio receiver and yelled instructions into it as we went down the stairs two at a time.

'This is Fox 1 to all units!' he shouted. 'Seal the coop. Possible abduction of Chicken!'

I didn't have time to consider the unfortunate wording of the message. I was down the stairs in an instant and through a set of swing doors which led into the ground-floor Food Hall. I stood for a moment, frantically scanning the crowded interior. There were high, supermarket-style aisles and it was impossible to get a clear view of the area. I was finding it hard to catch my breath. 'Goddamn it, Drayton,' I snarled. 'He's got Danny! He could be out of here by now.'

'He won't have had time,' protested Drayton. 'He must be here somewhere.'

'He'd better be!' I snarled. I checked the first aisle then ran along to look down the next one. Not there. Drayton moved off in another direction, jabbering something into his radio. I noted that he looked less confident than he sounded and I felt a wave of nausea ripple through me. I ran frantically from aisle to aisle, my apprehension mounting by the second. Shoppers, noting my agitation, stopped to stare at me in surprise. The last aisle yielded no results. I swore and moved out of the aisles into the delicatessen. Glass display cases of cheese and meat were obscured by the hundreds of shoppers jostling around them. A jaunty Christmas Carol was playing: 'God rest ye Merry Gentlemen.' I walked quickly, fighting the fear rising within me, my gaze sweeping frantically left and right, searching for a familiar face, a distinctive red jacket.

Please God, let him be all right, let him be here.

And then I saw Danny, standing ahead of me, by a food counter. He was eating an ice-cream cone and he had his present tucked under one arm. He looked perfectly safe and happy.

'Danny!' I ran to him, went down on my knees to grab him, feeling relief flood over me. I almost laughed out loud. 'Danny, for God's sake, where've you been?'

Danny eyed me. 'Down here,' he said. He looked startled, wondering no doubt why I was hugging him to me.

'But . . . how did you get down here?'

'The lady brought me.'

'Lady? What lady?'

He pulled away from me. 'She was waiting for me in the grotto. She said you'd told her to bring me down here. She bought me an ice-cream.'

'She . . .' My eyes focused on the ice cream as Danny's tongue licked a big chunk out of it. I saw the scattering of pale blue crystals on the soft white surface and reacted instinctively, lifting a hand to strike the cone out of Danny's grasp. It went skittering across the floor, trailing a long white smear on the tiles. Danny's mouth dropped open and his bottom lip began to tremble. 'Dad, why did you do that?'

I took Danny by the shoulders, fresh panic speaking through me. 'How much of it did you eat?' I cried.

'It's just an ice cream.'

'How much, Danny? Tell me!'

'Just a bit. Dad, I don't understand . . .'

'Tom!' Drayton came running over to me, relief etched into every line of his face. But then he saw my grim expression and he slowed to a halt. 'What's going on?' he asked cautiously.

I got up and moved closer to Drayton, grabbed him by the lapels of his parka. I kept my voice low, not wanting to panic Danny. 'I think he's been poisoned,' I whispered.

'What?' Drayton stared at me for a moment. I saw a look

come into his eyes, a look of helpless bafflement as he realised that his carefully laid plans had badly misfired. 'What are you talking about?'

I indicated the remains of the ice cream. 'Somebody took him out of the grotto. A woman. She bought him an ice cream. We've got to get him to a hospital . . .'

Drayton seemed to jolt himself awake. He moved across to the ice-cream cone and knelt beside it. He scooped up a little of it on his finger and sniffed at it gingerly. Then he put it to his tongue and quickly spat it out again. Shoppers looked at him as though he was mad. I saw his eyes narrow and then widen, seemingly in recognition. He got quickly to his feet and turned to face me. 'My car's right outside,' he said. 'Come on.'

'What is it?' I gasped fearfully.

He ignored the question. 'Come on, we've no time to lose!' He hurried towards the nearest exit.

As I grabbed Danny up in my arms, he dropped the present he'd been carrying and began to protest loudly. I stooped, snatched up the present and followed Drayton. He was yelling into the radio again. 'Fox 1 to all units. Clear the coop, I'm making a run.'

As we neared the exit, I saw to my dismay, that a big crowd was jammed up around it. Disgruntled shoppers were arguing with several men who were guarding the doors, and who were holding up their ID cards to prove their authority. I noted with a dull sense of surprise that one of them was the youth with the tattoos and the Mohican haircut.

'Make room!' bellowed Drayton. 'This is an emergency!' The crowd parted abruptly and Drayton, a latter-day Moses, shouldered a path through a sea of humanity. 'Get those doors open!' he yelled. His men were well trained. They hurried to obey the order. The crowd spilled out and we moved with them, out on to the jammed pavements.

'She'll get away,' complained Drayton helplessly.

'Never mind about that!' I snapped. 'Where's your car?'

Drayton led the way around the side of the store where his grey Escort was parked in a narrow alleyway. He ran to the car, flung the doors open and got behind the wheel. I eased Danny into the back seat and climbed in beside him. I noticed his face was unnaturally pale.

'You OK?' I asked.

Danny shook his head. 'I feel sick,' he said.

Oh God, I thought, *No, no, no, this can't be happening*. I glanced at Drayton. 'Get us the fuck out of here,' I snapped.

Drayton picked up a light from the floor and reached through the open window to clip it to the roof. He hit the siren and accelerated out of the alley without bothering to wait for a convenient space. He turned sharp left and there was a screech of brakes as a car behind narrowly avoided a collision; then a crunch as a third car slammed into the back of it.

Drayton swore under his breath but kept his foot down and started overhauling slower cars on the street, blasting his horn at them in order to get them to pull over. But then we were approaching the congestion on Piccadilly, rows of cars waiting at the lights. He slowed for a moment, scanning the way ahead.

'We'll have to wait here at least until the lights change,' he yelled.

I studied my son's face, which was now wax white and covered with beads of sweat.

'He can't wait,' I yelled back.

Drayton swore again. He studied the way ahead for a moment then seemed to come to a decision. He stamped down on the accelerator and wrenched the wheel to the left. The car lurched as it hit the curb and swung up on to the pavement. Pedestrians leapt frantically out of the way as the vehicle bumped and shuddered across the uneven flagstones. Drayton pounded his horn, adding the sound to the wailing shriek of the siren. We travelled several hundred yards like that until we got up to the traffic lights. Then Drayton wrenched the wheel back, got the car on to the road and steamed full speed across the face of the oncoming traffic at the crossroads. Horns blared and there was the shriek of rubber as one car took drastic evasive action. But then we were through and picking up speed as we entered the trunk road out of town. 'Christ,' gasped Drayton. 'I wouldn't like to have to do that too often . . .'

Danny groaned and clutched his stomach. Suddenly he twisted

sideways and was violently sick on to the back seat. I pulled out a handkerchief and mopped his mouth, cradling him in my arms as I did so.

'It's OK,' I said. 'You're going to be all right, Danny, you hear me? You're going to be all right.'

'I'll call the hospital,' said Drayton. 'Have them standing by.' He reached for the radio, began to speak into it, precisely, calmly. I envied him his composure, but then told myself it was understandable. After all, it wasn't his kid choking his life away in the back of the car. He began muttering something into the mouthpiece, keeping his voice low so I couldn't catch the words. Then he replaced the handset. 'We'll be there in ten minutes,' he announced.

'Make it five,' I said. 'He's in a bad way.'

Danny was gazing up at me through eyes that were circled with black. His whole body was shuddering and he seemed barely able to draw breath. Desperate now, I put my fingers into his throat and Danny retched again, vomiting down the front of my coat. I paid no heed to it, simply cradled him tighter in my arms. 'Hang on,' I whispered. 'Don't give up, we're nearly there.' I could feel the tears burning my eyes and I told myself that I must will Danny to go on breathing, that I must somehow keep him alive until we reached the hospital. If we could just get to the doctors, then it would be all right. They would take care of Danny, they would know what to do . . .

And then I heard Drayton swear softly. The car began to slow down. I glanced up in alarm. We'd forgotten about the football match. City playing at home. The roads were jammed with traffic, the sidewalks filled with supporters draped in rosettes and football scarfs. A few harassed policemen were vainly trying to make some sense of it all. There was no way a car could force its way through that. No way at all.

Drayton turned to gaze at me in dismay.

'Tom,' he said. 'I—'

But I didn't stop to listen. I threw open the door, scooped Danny up in my arms and shouldered my way on to the pavement. Sobbing, half blinded by tears, I began to run.

Chapter Twenty

Exactly seventeen and a half minutes later, I staggered into the entrance to Casualty. I'll never know where I got the strength to run that distance. My breath was wheezing in my chest, my legs were jolting columns of fire. A thick, acrid sweat glued my shirt to my chest. I had discarded my jacket some distance back and I was reeling under Danny's dead weight, barely aware of where I was going.

Two white-coated porters were waiting for me. They lifted Danny out of my arms and lowered him gently on to a stretcher. His face was now chalk white and his lips were blue. 'He'll be . . . all right. Won't he?' I gasped, but nobody answered me. I heard the pounding of feet and, glancing back, I saw Drayton coming in at the gate, running in an awkward, loping style. He was carrying my jacket and he looked ready to drop. I was momentarily astonished that he'd managed to run the distance with me. I thought he'd stayed back at the car. He came to a halt a short distance away, gasping for breath, unable to speak for the moment. He handed me my jacket and we exchanged a look. I saw guilt in his eyes, and terror, and a quiet pleading desperation. I can't say what he saw in mine.

The porters pushed Danny quickly up the ramp into the interior of the hospital. We stumbled after the trolley in silence and watched as a young houseman took charge, he was feeling for Danny's pulse and holding a stethoscope against his chest. In the silence our tortured breathing seemed loud and intrusive. The houseman lifted his head and looked at us. 'Do we know what the poison was?' he asked tonelessly.

'Warfarin,' gasped Drayton. 'I'm sure of it.' I glanced at him sharply.

The doctor nodded. 'How old is the boy?'

'Seven,' I said.

He nodded. 'We daren't use the stomach pump on him.' He turned to a young nurse who was standing beside him. 'Prepare five mills of ipecacuanha,' he said. 'Better have a Vitamin K injection as well. There could be internal bleeding.' The nurse nodded, hurried off through a doorway. 'How long ago did he swallow the poison?'

I glanced at my watch. 'Thirty, maybe thirty-five minutes. I made him vomit in the car.'

'Good. You did the right thing.' He appraised me for a moment, noting the way I was swaying on my feet. 'You'd better sit down here and get your breath back. This won't be pleasant.' Instead I made as if to follow but Drayton put a hand on my shoulder and restrained me. I watched helplessly as the trolley was pushed through a set of swing doors into the corridor beyond. It occurred to me then that this might be the last time I would see my son alive. The realisation gripped me like a fist and squeezed the last shreds of strength out of me. I stumbled and nearly fell.

'We'll wait here,' Drayton said. He drew me across to a bench and got me to sit down beside him. It took me a good five minutes to get my breathing back to normal. Then I fumbled instinctively for the cigarettes in my jacket pocket, ignoring the 'No Smoking' signs. I managed to get one alight and sat there inhaling deeply, reminding myself that this was the second time I'd found myself sitting in Casualty during John's reign of terror, helpless and afraid. My mind flashed through a succession of images: Danny, just born, howling in Karen's arms, his impossibly tiny body still wet with placenta; Danny, aged two, smiling at the video camera as he blew out the candles on his birthday cake; then Danny as he had looked in the car, his eyes ringed with black, his lips rapidly turning blue.

'I think he'll be OK,' Drayton told me. 'I don't think the poison was meant to kill him.'

I snapped out of my thoughts and glared at him scornfully. 'I've about had it with your theories,' I said. 'What's this about warfarin?'

'I know the smell. Rat poison. But there couldn't have been

a big dose on that ice cream. It's an anti-coagulant. It kills by causing internal bleeding and I don't think it's had time to do much damage.'

'Why didn't you tell me this before?'

'I didn't see the point in worrying you unduly.'

'Worrying me?' I almost laughed. 'You have a gift for under-statement, do you know that?'

Drayton nodded. 'So I've been told. Anyway, if I'm right and it's a small dose, then it looks worse than it is. It won't kill Danny, just make him very sick. I think John's doing what he loves to do, namely, make you suffer.'

'Oh, he's the best at that! But these days he gets plenty of help from you.' I ran my fingers through my hair. I was angry, frustrated. I wanted to rant at somebody and Drayton was the only available target. 'Jesus, I can hardly believe that I let you talk me into this mess. I must have been crazy.'

'No, not crazy,' Drayton corrected me. 'Just desperate.'

I shook my head. 'I fail to see the difference,' I said. 'God, why did I listen to you? *Nothing can go wrong*, you said. *The minute he shows his face, we'll get him*. But he didn't show his face, did he? We never even saw him. As usual, he was one step ahead of you all the way.'

Drayton looked sheepish. 'How could I have known he'd use an accomplice? He's always worked on his own before.'

'As far as you know, he had. Face it, Drayton, you know nothing about John, despite everything that's happened. I mean, you've even got a visual image of him, what more do you need?'

'A break,' said Drayton quietly. 'I need just one lucky break.'

There was a long silence which was suddenly broken by the distant sound of violent retching. I instinctively got to my feet but once again Drayton clapped a hand on my shoulder, pulled me back down to the bench.

'That's just the ipecacuanha taking effect,' he told me. 'It's an emetic, it will bring up whatever's left in his stomach. Believe me, you don't want to see that. Just sit tight.'

I ground my cigarette out beneath my foot. I felt sick myself with worry.

'How long before they tell us something?' I asked.

'Not long. Just hang on.' Drayton patted my hand comfortingly and I noticed, for the first time, the slim gold band on his third finger.

'So you are married,' I said.

'Hmm?' Drayton looked at his hand absent-mindedly as though he'd forgotten that the ring was there. 'Oh, yes, I'm still married. Separated though.' He smiled sadly, shrugged his shoulders. 'It's difficult to keep a relationship in my line of work. Dorothy lives in Cheshire now. She's . . . a good woman. But she couldn't take the anxiety. In the end I didn't blame her for moving out on me. It was almost a relief.'

I nodded. 'Any kids?' I asked. I wanted to occupy my mind, to keep it from concentrating on what might be happening in the room down the corridor.

'Two.' Drayton seemed to brighten a little. He reached into his coat and took out a wallet. He extracted a crumpled colour photograph and handed it to me. A plump woman with a warm smile was flanked by two teenagers, a lanky dark-haired boy and a younger girl with severely short hair that was dyed a flamboyant shade of red.

'Johnathan's eighteen now, he's at police training college. Tricia's a year younger. She works at an alternative book store in town. She er . . . prefers the company of other girls, if you know what I mean.'

I raised my eyebrows, imagining the shock that must have caused to somebody as straight-laced as Drayton.

He shrugged. 'I'm learning to live with it. They're good kids. I have no regrets.'

I frowned, felt the resentment creeping back. 'And how would you feel about using one of them as bait?' I asked caustically.

Drayton stared at me for a moment. 'I'd do it,' he said frankly. 'If it was necessary.'

'Well, I hope to God you never have to make that decision,' I told him. I looked at my watch. 'I'd better go and phone Karen. I'll have to tell her something.'

'Tell her the truth,' Drayton suggested. 'Tell her I cocked it up. Tell her it's all my fault.' He glanced towards the swing doors leading into the ward. 'And tell her Danny will be OK.'

'We don't know that yet.'

'Tell her anyway.'

I nodded. I got to my feet and went to look for a payphone. As soon as it rang at the other end it was picked up. 'Hello? Hello, Tom, where've you been? I was expecting you to ring half an hour ago.' Karen's voice was hoarse with apprehension.

'Karen listen. I'm at the hospital.'

'Oh God, Tom, no, no!'

'Karen, listen to me.' I outlined what had happened with a calmness that surprised me. I didn't feel calm inside. There was a storm raging there and I felt ready to scream.

There was a stunned silence before Karen spoke again. 'I'll be there in ten minutes,' she told me, and replaced the receiver.

I walked slowly back to the bench and saw Drayton deep in conversation with the young doctor. Their faces were grave and Drayton was shaking his head.

Ah, he's dead then. The thought was almost a reassurance. For an instant I felt a strange peacefulness settle within me. Then something hit me in the pit of the stomach, driving the breath out of me. My aching legs seemed to turn to jelly and I had to lean against the wall to support myself. I waited there, trembling, convinced that Danny hadn't made it; but then Drayton glanced up and noticed me. He gave me an encouraging smile. 'He's all right, Tom, there's nothing to worry about. They just want to keep him in for a couple of days, until he's fully recovered.'

I remembered to breathe, snatching a mouthful of air like a diver resurfacing. I moved unsteadily back to the bench and sank into it with a sigh of relief.

'He's been very sick,' the doctor explained. 'He brought up a little blood but not enough for serious concern. It's a particularly nasty experience for anyone to go through, especially a young-ster. But a couple of days rest should see him right.' He stared searchingly at me. 'Perhaps you'd like to tell me how a kid of that age managed to get his hands on a tin of poison?'

Drayton glanced at me, then took the doctor's arm. 'This wasn't an accident, Doctor,' he said quietly. 'Frankly, the less you know about it, the better.' He turned back to me. 'I'll pop to the phone and make arrangements for surveillance. We'll make damn sure that nobody has a chance to get to him while he's in here.'

I nodded dumbly and watched Drayton stride away down the corridor.

'Can I see my son now?' I asked the doctor.

'Give us a few minutes to get him cleaned up and into a bed. I think we've a private room going spare at the moment.' The doctor paused and looked thoughtfully at me. 'You're the radio chappie aren't you? The one who gets those calls?'

'Yes, that's me,' I snarled irritably. 'What's the matter, do you want a fucking autograph or something?'

The doctor took a step back, clearly surprised by the vitriol in my voice. Then he shrugged, moved back to the swing doors. 'I'll go and make sure your son's comfortable,' he muttered.

'Oh look, wait, I'm sorry . . .' But the doors closed with a dull thud behind him, leaving me to kick my heels again. I slumped back on the bench and took out my cigarettes.

A few minutes later, I heard the furious clacking of high heels approaching along the corridor and knew it was Karen, even before she came into view. She was dressed in a belted trenchcoat and for some reason had put on a pair of dark glasses, as though she was afraid that she might be recognised. Behind the frames, her face was pale and drawn. She stopped a short distance away and glowered at me.

I got to my feet. 'He's all right, Karen, there's no need to—'

'Where is he?' she demanded and her voice was brittle with anger.

'They're just getting him into bed. He—'

'My God, I could kill you for this!' She took a step nearer and I actually shrank from her, dropping back down on the bench. 'I should have known he wasn't safe with you. I should have known better than to let you talk me into this lunacy.'

I stared at her. 'Excuse me, but I think you've got that wrong,' I protested. 'I didn't talk you into anything. When Drayton asked for permission, I tried to put the ball over into your court. I said it was you that should decide, but you—'

'Oh, of course! Isn't that entirely typical? Duck the responsibility, push it on to somebody else! Well, I wasn't prepared to handle it. For once, I wanted you to make the decision and naturally you made the wrong one!'

'That isn't fair, Karen! I gave you every opportunity to object, but you said nothing. I didn't like the idea from the start, you know I didn't. But Drayton assured me Danny would be safe and I . . .'

'Drayton! Haven't you learned by now, Tom? It's no good depending on them for anything. They're amateurs, they haven't a clue what to do about any of this. You let that maniac get to our son and I'll never forgive you for that. *Never!*'

'But he's all right, Karen, the doctor says . . .'

Her anger suddenly seemed to boil over. '*The doctor says, the doctor says*! Christ, you make me sick! Did you ever once, Tom, come to a decision all by yourself without having some yes man to back you up? Blame it on the police, blame it on the doctors! You're responsible for this. *You!* Tom bloody Prince. Well thank God I'm out of it now. Thank God I don't have the responsibility of dragging you from one day to the next.'

I sat there stunned and considered her words. I recognised in them the anger of long years of frustration, for which this latest incident had just been the catharsis. I nodded. 'You're absolutely right, Karen,' I said quietly. 'It's all my fault. It's my fault John called me up, it's my fault he murdered those people, it's my fault that Danny got poisoned. There. Feel better now I've confessed?'

There was a long silence while we stared at each other. Then Karen let out a long breath and slumped down on the seat beside me. She took off the shades and buried her face in her hands. I could see why she'd worn the glasses. Her eyes were red from weeping and, even now, they were filling up with fresh tears.

'I'm sorry,' she gasped. 'I didn't mean that. I was just so frightened. I thought . . .' She shook her head, unable to say what she thought.

I slipped an arm around her shoulders. 'Take it easy,' I said. 'I won't make the mistake of putting Danny on the line again. I just didn't know what else I could do.'

She nodded, dashed at her eyes with the sleeve of her coat. 'Got a cigarette?' she asked me.

'You don't smoke,' I said; but I got the packet out and handed her one anyway. I lit it for her and she took a couple of amateurish drags before the coughing began.

'Filthy things,' she spluttered. 'Don't know how you can use them.'

I shrugged. 'You get used to it,' I said.

'I didn't have time to bring anything for Danny. He doesn't even have any pyjamas . . .' She gestured helplessly, inhaled on the cigarette again. 'Will he be able to come home with me?'

'I doubt it. Doctor said a couple of days. They had to give him an emetic.'

'Oh God, how awful!' She gazed at me for a moment. 'I don't understand,' she said. 'How he got to Danny. I thought you were being protected.'

I nodded. 'Something we hadn't allowed for. Danny had to go into the grotto by himself. There was another way in, something we didn't know about. John knew though, he must have been there and checked it out beforehand. But he didn't come himself. There was a woman, she led Danny away, bought him an ice cream. The poison was in that.'

'A woman? You mean . . . somebody's *helping* him?'

'It seems so. We didn't even catch a glimpse of her. Until we can talk to Danny, we won't even know what she looked like.'

'But what woman would do a thing like that? To a child. She'd . . . she'd have to be as mad as him.'

I nodded grimly. 'The thought of two of them out there!' I shrugged, spreading my hands. I did not want to pursue that line of thought any further.

Karen looked at the cigarette in her hand, watching the plume of smoke that coiled upwards towards the ceiling. 'Maybe you should think about going away, Tom. Leaving Manchester. Perhaps if you went, he'd stop doing these terrible things.'

I glanced at her. 'Maybe,' I admitted. 'But I'm not convinced by that. I think he'd keep going after Danny, I think that's his ultimate goal.'

She stared at me, not wanting to believe this. 'But why?' she cried. 'He's just a little boy. What possible reason could there be?'

'You remember the Egyptian stuff we talked about? I've started to figure out what's behind it. As I understand it, John thinks he's been possessed by Seth. I'm Osiris, Danny is Horus. I did some reading on mythology: Seth set out to destroy Osiris first, and then when Osiris was reborn, Seth transferred his hatred to Horus, did everything he could to destroy him. In one story he ripped out one of Horus's eyes, and in another he sexually abused him.'

'Yes, I know the stories,' said Karen irritably. 'Frankly, I'd rather not be reminded of them just now.'

I frowned. 'I'm sorry, it's just that I'm convinced that those stories are the key to all this. That and the Johnny Dark record. I'm going down to Essex in a couple of days to talk to Johnny's manager, see if I can dig up some kind of real connection there.'

'And meanwhile, what do I do? Sit in that bloody flat while the police watch my every move?'

'Couldn't you take Danny away for a while? Go on holiday or something?'

Karen shook her head. 'It's impossible. I've got too much work on. I'm in the middle of composing a soundtrack, though God knows how I'm supposed to concentrate on it with all this going on.'

I glared at her. 'Stuff the soundtrack! It's Danny's safety we're talking about. Yours, too, if it comes to that. And you can compose music anywhere, take one of your portable keyboards with you. I'd feel a damn sight happier if you and Danny were miles away from here right now.'

Karen sighed. 'I'll see what I can come up with,' she said.

Footsteps approached along the corridor: Drayton coming back from the phone, his hands in the pockets of his parka. He looked tired, rumpled, downtrodden. He hesitated when he saw Karen there, then gave her a polite nod.

'God help us,' muttered Karen. 'It's Fabian of the fucking Yard.'

Drayton winced. 'I'm sorry about what happened,' he said. 'I'm afraid he caught us napping.'

'Spare me the excuses!' snapped Karen. 'Just be thankful Danny's all right. I swear if he'd been injured in any way, I'd have . . .'

'I don't blame you for being angry,' Drayton assured her. 'But you have to understand, I was just doing what I thought was best for this investigation. That's all any of us can do. John is too clever by half, he always seems to keep one step ahead of us.'

'A quadriplegic could keep one step ahead of you,' observed Karen. 'Listen Inspector, keep away from Danny in future. If you have any more dick-brained schemes about using him as bait, don't even think of mentioning them.'

Drayton nodded dumbly. He stood there looking extremely awkward, one hand playing with the loose change in his pocket. Despite everything, I felt sorry for him. It was not pleasant being on the receiving end of Karen's scorn. I ought to know, I'd had nearly ten years of it.

The door opened and the young doctor popped his head out. 'You can see your son for a moment,' he announced. 'He's very groggy, so try not to pester him too much.'

'Can he talk?' asked Drayton hopefully.

'Not to you,' Karen assured him. 'Stay out of there.' She got off the bench and hurried through the swing door. I went to follow her but Drayton barred my way for a moment.

'We have to ask him about the woman,' he said. 'It's important. Will you..?'

I nodded. 'I'll see what I can do,' I said. I pushed through the door and followed Karen and the doctor along the corridor.

Danny was propped up in bed, looking frail in a pair of over-sized hospital pyjamas. His face was waxen and there were bluish rings under his eyes, but he looked a hundred times better than when I had last seen him. He succumbed to a frantic hug from Karen but his eyes stared inquiringly at me all the time, as though he suspected me of being responsible for what had happened. I found it hard to meet his gaze, but I moved to the other side of the bed and took a seat.

'They say I was poisoned,' said Daniel at last. His voice was slow and rather slurred, as though he'd been indulging in some underage drinking.

I took his hand and squeezed it. 'That's right, Danny. It was the ice cream you had. Somebody played a nasty trick on you.'

'But why, Dad? Was it . . . was it something to do with John?'

'Don't talk about it now,' Karen urged him. 'You have to rest.'

Daniel shook his head. 'That woman. Was she trying to kill me?'

'No,' I assured him. 'Just make you very sick. Danny, I need to ask you about the woman.'

'Leave him alone,' snapped Karen. 'Hasn't he been through enough?'

Daniel glanced at her. 'It's all right, Mum. What did you want to know?'

'Just what she looked like.'

Daniel thought for a moment. 'Just an ordinary woman,' he said.

'What about her hair? Was it dark or light?'

'Light. Sort of like her that's in those old movies . . . the one you like. Maryanne?'

'Marilyn, you mean? Marilyn Monroe? So she was a blonde?'

'Yeah.'

'What about her eyes?'

Danny shrugged. 'Can't remember.'

'All right. Was she young or old.'

'Old.'

'What, old like your gran?'

'No, old like you and Mum.' Danny paused and grimaced for a moment. 'I feel awful,' he said. 'My stomach.'

'I think he's answered enough questions for now,' said Karen testily.

'Just a few more,' I insisted. 'Danny, what was she wearing?'

Danny frowned. 'A coat . . . like, you know, with all hair on it.'

'A fur coat?'

'Yeah, and white gloves. And she had those shoes like Mum wears sometimes, with like high heels on them.' He thought for a moment. 'She smelled nice.'

'Perfume?'

Danny nodded, closed his eyes for a moment. 'I feel sleepy,' he said.

'OK Danny, you can sleep in just a moment. 'Was there anything else about her? Anything strange, anything funny? Something maybe we could recognise if we saw her again?'

'Will you let him alone?' said Karen. 'Can't you see he's exhausted?'

Daniel's head had flopped back on to the pillow but his eyelids flickered, as though he had recalled something.

'Her voice,' he murmured sleepily.

'Her voice? What about her voice, Danny?'

'It . . . it was . . . funny.'

'Funny in what way?'

'You could hardly hear it. I had to listen real close to what she was saying.'

I looked at Danny intently. 'Do you mean, Danny, do you mean that she was whispering?'

A brief nod of the head, before the eyes closed and the breathing became rhythmic.

Jesus H. Christ. It was John! It was John all along.

I wondered why I was so surprised. I should have been beyond being surprised by now.

I glanced at Karen. 'Back in a moment,' I said. I got up from the chair and hurried out of the room. I found Drayton waiting out in reception.

'There was no accomplice,' I told him.

He didn't understand. 'What are you talking about?'

'The woman. Danny says she was whispering.'

Drayton considered the implications for a few moments, then he let out a long breath. 'Jesus,' he said quietly. 'It's perfect. He must have known we were in there looking for a bearded man. So he shaved the beard and put on a frock.' He laughed and once again I sensed his admiration. It worried me that he was beginning to admire somebody like John. It was like admiring a King Cobra shortly before it buried its fangs in your neck. 'Christ, he might just as well have been invisible.'

'He probably walked right past us and we never knew it. A blonde woman, late twenties, fur coat, white gloves, high-heeled shoes. That's all Danny could give me.'

'It's not bad for starters.' Drayton thought for a moment. 'Maybe he didn't need to shave. Could be he wears a false beard.'

I nodded. 'It's possible. With him anything's possible. One other thing. He's somebody who can pass for a woman. That's not easy. If you or I put a dress on and walked downtown, we'd stand out like sore thumbs. Could be he's a known transvestite or a drag artiste, something like that.'

'It's worth checking out.' Drayton got to his feet. 'I'll get on to it now. We'll also need to get our identikit sorted out. We'll put out one of him without the beard. Maybe I can get one of our whizz kids to produce a print of him as a woman.' He checked his watch. 'There'll be a couple of my men along in a few minutes to keep an eye on Danny. Thornton and Devane. For Christ's sake ask them for their ID before you let them anywhere near the kid.'

'I will.'

'You know, it's a relief,' he said. 'The thought of two psychos out there, instead of just one.' He shook his head. 'One I can live with,' he concluded. He nodded and set off along the corridor. Then he paused, glanced back at me. 'That was quite a run we made back there,' he said.

'Yes!' I said. 'Wasn't it just?'

He flashed me a grin, then walked on with fresh spring in his step. I gazed after him thoughtfully and considered my next move. Essex. Micky Hart. I didn't know what I expected to find down there. Maybe nothing. I just knew I had to try. Meanwhile, there were other things to attend to.

I went back to Danny's room and found the boy fast asleep in his mother's arms.

Diary Extract

11th December

It worked like a dream. I followed His instructions to the letter and, as always, He was right about every detail. For a moment back there, I thought there was going to be a problem. They had me trapped in the store, along with hundreds of others. But He had guessed they would make the little hawk the priority and He was correct. They opened the doors and I was able to walk free. I had been very careful measuring out the poison. Just enough, He had said. Just enough.

When I got back, He was waiting for me. He looked on me with approval. I was still dressed from the store and I enjoyed Him seeing me like this. When I wear a handmaiden's clothes, I move differently. I am a different person. He watched me for some time as I moved about the room and I knew He was thinking about what would happen next. We are entering the most important phase. Now the incantations begin. Now we usher in the great change, the time of Chaos. But first, there was my reward.

He told me to remove my clothes, slowly. I did so, in front of the mirror and then I prostrated myself in front of Him. His great head nodded. He understood that I was ready. He told me to fetch the gold earring and the other equipment I needed. I lit the gas fire and I placed a long darning needle into the flames to heat up. I fetched a low stool and placed it near the fire and I placed a wooden board on top of it. I put the ring nearby. Then I waited until the needle was glowing red.

He watched me the whole time, interested to see if I would weaken. But I knew I wouldn't hesitate. What is a little pain, when the reward is so great? To become a god. How many men are given so much in their lifetime?

When the needle was ready, I picked it up in a pair of pliers and I laid my manhood across the board. My hands were steady as I positioned the needle. I positioned the point of it just behind the head and I said a prayer that He would guide my hand. Then I pushed down with all my strength. I smelled burning before I felt the pain; and I heard the sizzling of my own blood. Then the fire danced through my loins and, for an instant, I thought I would faint. But I did not cry out. When the tip of the needle had sunk into the wood, I paused for a moment, for I knew that withdrawing it would hurt me more than putting it in. Then I felt His spirit filling me and the pain became insubstantial. I took a firm grip on the pliers and pulled the needle out. The blood jetted out in a thin stream, spraying across the floor. Now all that was left to do was to fit the ring.

I shall always wear it for Him. It is a visible sign of my devotion. When we become as One, it will be there to remind me of a time when I was mortal. There will be constant pain from now on, but that doesn't matter. Now begin the incantations, the prayers, the summoning of Chaos. It is already close, I sense it humming at the back of my eyes, like white noise. Just two short days and the cycle will be complete. He and I will be One. This is my destiny. This is why I was summoned into the world. When Chaos is come again, none of this will matter.

Chapter Twenty-One

I woke from a fitful sleep to the unfamiliar sound of wind bluster-
ing against the curtained windows. I remembered that it was
Monday, the day I'd fixed up an appointment with Micky Hart.
I glanced at the bedside clock and saw that it was already well
past midday. I'd sat up deep into the small hours, planning out
my 'interview'. I shook myself awake, climbed out of bed and
went to pull back the curtains. Blinking down into the garden, I
saw that the weather had changed dramatically. The slender trees
at the bottom of the drive were swaying to and fro in the wind
and pockets of drizzle were cutting down at a forty-five degree
angle, bouncing off every surface in a misty spray. I frowned.
Just the day for a drive down south, I reflected. Stifling a yawn,
I went to the bathroom to shower and shave.

I examined my reflection ruefully in the full-length mirror. I'd
lost a lot of weight over the last couple of months and what I
saw put me in mind of an elegantly wasted skeleton. I could
count every rib in my chest and my face had the sunken look
associated with a heroin addict. Not a pretty picture. I sighed,
strolled back to the bedroom, dressed myself and went down to
the kitchen to prepare breakfast. I wasn't particularly hungry but
I forced myself to eat a bacon sandwich with the usual cup of
coffee. I chewed methodically, not tasting the food. *Where are
you now?* I asked myself. *What are you doing? Do you eat
breakfast like other people or do you only come out at night and
feed on the misery you've caused?* It occurred to me that I was
increasingly thinking of John, not as a man, but as something
supernatural; a dark, lithe creature with the head of an unnamed
beast. But no, I argued. He was just a man. And like a man,

he could be beaten. It was just a question of finding the right ammunition.

When I had finished, I dug out an old briefcase and packed a few things that I hoped would make me look more like a journalist. I put in a notebook, a dictaphone and a road atlas. As an afterthought, I added a half bottle of whisky. I hadn't met a journalist yet who didn't drink and luckily I already smoked like a chimney. Then I went into the study, picked up the phone and dialled Karen's number. Drayton had already told me he was going to have the bug on her line removed. She had taken Danny home from hospital the previous evening and I felt I should check on her before I left. Especially as I knew Inga was away on a week's leave.

She answered, sounding brusque and irritable. 'Hello, Cell Block H. Prisoner 116 here.'

I smiled. 'Hello Karen, it's Tom.'

'Oh, good of you to call. How's things out in the free world?'

'So so. How's Danny?'

'He's OK, but I've decided to keep him off school for a couple of days. The two of us are going crazy cooped up here. He keeps pestering me to take him to the zoo, but the weather's so shitty this morning and if we went we'd have Drayton's trained gorillas following us every step of the way. You still going down south?'

'That's the plan. I'll call in tonight on my way back.'

'Big of you. I'll open a tin of salmon.'

I sighed. She hadn't forgiven me for the debacle at the department store and now she seemed to be holding me personally responsible for her current incarceration in the flat.

'Cops still watching you?' I asked.

'Worse than that. I've got Inspector Drayton himself camped out on my doorstep. He must be feeling guilty about what happened. Every time I look out of the window I see his mournful face staring up at me.' She gave an exclamation of disgust. 'I had a team of so-called experts checking out the bug in my phone this morning. Naturally, it was dead. No way they could trace it back, they said. He must have taken care of it straight after the department-store cock-up.'

'He's a clever boy, isn't he?'

'Too fucking clever. There's no way the likes of Drayton can

254

get near him. I keep asking myself, is this the way it's going to be for the rest of my life? God, what a prospect!' She sighed. 'Take care on the roads, they're forecasting gales later this afternoon.'

'I didn't think you cared what happened to me any more.'

'I'm thinking about the car,' she assured me. 'Anyway, it's all right for some of us, isn't it? Some of us can go swanning off down south when we feel like it. I have to inform the police if I want to use the lavatory.'

'I'm sorry about that Karen, but you must see it's for the best.'

'I suppose so. Anyway, Danny and I are about to curl up with a video. *Return of the Swamp Thing*. It's got an 18 certificate so it should keep him happy. See you later.'

She hung up and I dialled Jamie's number. It occurred to me that I always seemed to dial these numbers one after the other and that I invariably called Karen first. I felt vaguely guilty about that. I was relieved when Jamie answered in person. The frosty reception I always got from her parents was increasingly difficult to take.

'Hello,' I said. 'How you doing?'

'I'm all right. Thanks for ringing.' It was hard to hear her voice over the crackling of static on the line. The weather, I supposed.

'What's happening over there in Wales?'

'Not much. Tom, I've been thinking about coming home.'

'Really? That's great news.' This wasn't exactly the truth. With things as they were I figured she would be a lot safer staying as far away from me as possible. But, I reasoned, it would be a relief not to have to face up to things alone. 'Do you . . . I mean, do you feel up to it, yet?'

'Yes. And to be honest, I'm going nuts out here. I think Mum and Dad are feeling the strain too, they don't say anything, they try so hard to be pleasant but there's a terrible atmosphere all the time. How's Danny?'

'He seems fine. He's back with Karen now.'

'It must have been an ordeal for you. I wish you'd told me about it earlier, I'd have talked you out of it.'

'I figured you had enough on your plate. Look, I'll ring you when I get back from Essex. I'll come up and collect you.'

'There's no need, I can always get a train.'

'No way. I'm not letting you out of my sight for an instant. Not till all this is over. I'm going to stick to you like glue.'

'Sounds great.' A pause. 'This Essex trip . . . What are you hoping to do down there?'

'I don't know exactly. I just feel it's something that the police haven't followed up properly. And anything's better than just sitting here, twiddling my thumbs.'

'Be careful on the roads, Tom. The weather . . .'

'Yes, I heard about that. I'll be fine. Look, I'm really glad you've decided to come back.'

'Me too. I wish I'd made the decision sooner. I let him intimidate me for too long, that's all. But I'm not afraid of him now.'

'You're not? That's funny, he scares the shit out of me!'

'Tom, be careful. Down south I mean. He might follow you again.'

I had no answer for that. 'I'll talk to you later,' I said. 'Love you.'

'Love you back. Take care.' I hung up. Then I moved around the house, locking the doors and windows. I was just on my way back downstairs when the phone rang. I went over to it cautiously, hesitating a long time before I picked up the handset. Part of me was expecting to hear John phoning in to crow about his latest filthy trick but I was surprised to hear my father's voice. He hardly ever called me, he usually delegated the task to my mother.

'Aaah . . . hello, Thomas?' The clipped, precise tones which spoke of a lifetime of military service.

'Hello, Dad, how's tricks? You just caught me, I'm on my way down to Essex.'

'Oh, really? You're a busy man these days, Thomas. Very busy. I just phoned to tell you about your mother.'

I felt a rush of concern. 'Mother? Is she all right? I mean, there's nothing wrong is there?'

My Father sighed. He sounded a long way away.

'All this business has taken its toll on her,' he said. 'To be honest with you, she's not herself lately. Too many damned worries.'

I thanked God that she hadn't heard the latest news. Drayton had kept the lid down tight on Danny's poisoning and miracu-

lously none of the papers had picked up on it. My parents doted
on Danny and the thought of somebody trying to harm him
would have been too much for them.

'Has she seen the doctor?' I asked.

'Several times, but there's nothing he can do other than prescribe valium. She's worried half to death, Thomas. So am I, for
that matter. The best thing in the world would be a visit from
you, yet you can't seem to find the time to get over here.'

'It's difficult, Dad. There are things here in Manchester that
have to be taken care of, you know? I'll try and pop in as soon
as I'm able.'

There was a long silence. I could hear my father's stentorian
breathing at the other end of the line. Like me, he found it hard
to articulate his feelings.

'Are they no nearer catching that lunatic?' he asked at last.

'I think maybe they're beginning to get a handle on him,' I
lied. 'I was talking with the police the other day. They say it's
just a matter of time.'

'Well, I hope they get some results soon. For your mother's
sake. Her nerves are shot, Thomas, I don't think she's had a
decent night's sleep in months. We keep praying that it will all
end.' Another pause. 'Essex, you say? Are you going after a
job? Something else in radio?'

'Yes . . . a chat with somebody in the business.'

My father had taken the news of my expulsion from *Metrosound* hard. To him there was no greater shame than being out
of work, whatever the reasons for it.

'Well, good luck with that. It's time you had a little luck,
Thomas. When I think about what happened to you, the sheer
chance of that maniac latching on to you.'

I considered that. Not chance at all, I thought. But how could
I explain to him the logic of it? How could I talk to him about
Egyptian gods and ancient legends, record reviews and old
grudges. He'd never understand it. Sometimes I wondered if I
did.

'You know, Thomas, your mother and I were talking last
night . . . about . . . about what's wrong between you and us.'

I fidgeted awkwardly with the phone cable.

'Wrong, Dad? I don't . . .'

'It's hard to talk about, I know, but it's something I bitterly regret. I don't really know how it came about. Something to do with you going off to boarding school, I think. We used to be so close when you were a little lad. I don't know if you remember, but we used to—'

'Listen, Dad, I've got to be going now,' I said. 'I'll be late for my appointment.

'Hmm? Appointment. Oh, yes. Well . . .'

'We'll talk about this again. When I come over.'

'Yes. Try to make it soon, Thomas. Your mother. It really would be the best medicine.'

'Sure. OK Dad, got to go now. Bye.'

'Goodbye son.'

I put the phone down with a sigh of relief. *Running away again*, I thought sadly. I couldn't handle it when the old man had got too near to the truth. It had panicked me, somehow, made my defence mechanisms spring to attention. But I'd have to make time to visit them soon. Dad always played things down, so it was for certain that Mum was probably a good deal worse than he was admitting to.

I collected my briefcase and went out to the car. The wind tore at my clothes, snatching my breath away. I climbed in behind the wheel, started up and drove in the direction of the motorway.

Once on the open road, I put my foot down and gave the car its head. There wasn't much traffic and I surmised that many people had heeded the storm warnings that were being transmitted on the radio at fifteen-minute intervals. I tuned in to *Metrosound* and found that even there, the regular FM programming was subject to the same warnings.

'. . . winds gale-force eight, gusting up to a hundred miles per hour, with the probability of structural damage to houses. The meteorological office is warning people to stay indoors and to keep off the roads. We'll be giving you regular updates on the situation throughout the day.'

A pause, then the familiar jingle. '*Metrosound* Radio! The greatest sound around!' A pounding rock intro followed and was immediately replaced by an unmistakeable deadpan voiceover.

'Hi, David Wilson here, welcoming you to the afternoon rockshow. Whew, sure is freaky weather we're having today, isn't it?

If you're going out, break out the sou'westers and gumboots! Meanwhile, here's U2 to raise the temperature a little!'

I grinned. So, Owen Parker's bland new programming schedule had finally given Dave Hibbert his chance. He had changed his name but there was very little he could do about his voice. He was hosting his own show with the same spectacularly lacklustre qualities he had brought to newsreading. I listened for ten minutes or so, marvelling at my former colleague's ineptness, his total inability to say words like 'freaky' and 'rock n' roll' without sounding as if he was reading them off a prompt sheet. When it became too much to bear, I switched to Radio One, where the DJs all sounded alike: slick, professional and totally insincere. One day, I reflected, all radio would sound like that. But it no longer had any bearing on my own career. I was finished with that. Today, I was a journalist; and I was en route to my first interview in a long, long time. I hoped to God that it would provide me with the answers I was looking for.

I glanced up at the sky and saw massive folds of black cloud broiling in over the western horizon. Rain hammered against the windscreen. It was going to get a lot worse before it got any better.

Chapter Twenty-Two

Micky Hart had been right. It was easy to find his place. Tucked away on a remote country road south of Epping, it was a massive three-storey Georgian mansion set in extensive grounds and half hidden behind high stone walls topped with barbed wire and broken glass. It was the kind of home one might more readily associate with a politician or a famous rock star; and it was apparent at a glance that Micky had indeed done very well out of Johnny Dark.

By the time I pulled up outside the huge ornamental iron gates, the weather had worsened. Due to the chaos on the motorway, I was an hour later than planned and it was already dark. The sky was piled high with angry black clouds and the wind was hitting the car like a terrier shaking a rat. I peered through the rain-streaked windscreen and spotted an intercom mounted in the wall to the side of the gate. I scuttled out of the car and stood cowering by the wall. I pressed the button repeatedly, until I heard a sleepy voice crackling from the speaker.

'Who is it?'

I leaned in close to the speaker. 'Tom Prince, Mr Hart! We made an appointment for this evening.'

'Oh yeah, Tom, how you doin'? I figured you wouldn't be coming down in this lousy weather. OK, I'll open the gates. Drive down to the front of the house, but stay in your car.'

There was a mechanical click and the gates began to glide open. I ran back to the car and drove through into the well-tended gardens. As I accelerated along the wide driveway, I glanced in the rear-view mirror and saw that the gates were swinging shut behind me. I passed by all the trappings of wealth; a glass-domed swimming pool, a deserted tennis court, an exten-

261

sive patio where massive plant pots had been overturned by the wind. I moved the car around a bend and approached the marble porch that framed the front door. There appeared to be nobody about though there were lights on inside. I parked and sat waiting impatiently for somebody to appear but the house remained closed and there was no sign of life within. After ten minutes, I decided to walk up to the front door and ring the bell.

I reached out and began to open the door of my car. With heart-stopping suddenness, a face appeared at the window: the snarling, malignant face of a black dog, teeth bared, eyes blazing feral rage. For an instant, I was lost in nightmare, believing that John had finally caught up with me; but then, above the roaring of the wind, I heard the guttural snarl that emitted from the dog's open jaws and realised that this was a more tangible horror, a guard dog that had been trained to kill. I swore and pulled the door shut again, watching in mute shock as the Rottweiler clashed its teeth against the glass and left strings of foam on the window. I remembered to breathe and pressed the horn, hoping that the noise would scare the beast off, but it merely served to infuriate it even more. It renewed its efforts to get inside and I could hear its claws scraping against the paintwork on the wing. I was just considering backing the car away from the house, when the front door opened and a man stepped out on to the porch, his face illuminated in the light from the hallway.

He was a thin, grizzled-looking individual, bearded and dressed unseasonally in a loud Bermuda shirt and a pair of knee-length khaki shorts. He said something to the dog which immediately seemed to pacify it. It dropped down into a sitting position beside the car and when its master whistled, it trotted obediently over to join him, sat down obediently at his feet. The man beckoned impatiently to me to get out of the car and I did so gingerly, holding myself ready to dive back inside if the dog showed any signs of reverting to its former self. I stood beside the car, looking uncertain.

'Mr Hart?' I inquired, having to shout over the tumult of the wind.

'Damn right. I told you to stay in the car.' He grinned, showing a collection of badly decaying teeth. 'You're late. Hurry on in here, I'm freezing my ass off!'

Reassured, I slammed the car door, hurried over to the porch and shook hands with Micky Hart. Close up, he looked much older. The face beneath the beard was gaunt and pale and the eyes had the vacant, staring look of a man who habitually did too many drugs for his own good. Micky stared up at the broiling sky. 'Fucking hell, looks like you brought some of your Manchester weather down with you,' he observed. 'Good trip?'

I shrugged. 'Dreadful.' I glanced cautiously at the dog. 'Is he safe now?' I asked.

Micky laughed. 'Don't worry about ol' Seth. He's only a killer when I want him to be.'

I glanced at Micky. 'Seth?' I inquired.

'Yeah. Stupid name. He was Johnny's dog, he named him. Come on, let's get inside out of this shit.' He turned and led the way through the entrance. I followed, noting that Seth trotted obediently alongside me, as though he had orders to keep me under surveillance. The door slammed shut behind us. We were standing in an opulent hallway. A cut-glass chandelier glittered overhead and a curved marble staircase led upwards past a procession of large-scale oil paintings.

'I guess we'll be most comfortable in the den,' announced Micky. He led on, through a doorway to his right. We passed through an enormous dining room, where a long mahogany table looked capable of seating upwards of twenty people. The room seemed designed solely to tell you that the owner had a lot of wedge but not much taste. Through another door we entered a smaller room that was clearly Micky's favourite hang-out. There was a state-of-the-art hi-fi, racks of records, tapes and CD's and a couple of expensive but tacky sofas covered in what looked like zebra hide. A set of French windows gave on to the wind-blown garden. The walls were adorned with framed gold and silver discs, and photographs of Johnny Dark. Over the marble fireplace, where a convincing flame-effect fire was blazing, hung a huge David Oxtoby oil painting of Johnny. He was pictured on stage, singing into a microphone and wielding a flying V guitar that was decorated with Egyptian hieroglyphics. Behind him, a huge pyramid towered, backlit by a gaudy sunburst. I moved closer to examine the picture.

'Pretty impressive, huh?' observed Micky. 'Johnny had that

commissioned just before his last tour.'

I nodded. 'All this Egyptian stuff. Very interesting.'

'Yeah. Bit of an obsession with Johnny. Strange kid.' He motioned me to one sofa and sank into the other. Seth curled up on the mat in front of the fire, but he kept his gaze fixed firmly on me as I crossed the room and sat down. Micky reached forward to an onyx coffee table in front of him and opened a large wooden box. I wasn't surprised to see him taking out the paraphernalia of coke sniffing. A small golden spoon, a silver razor-blade and an ornate onyx inhaler. He spooned a generous amount of white powder on to the table top and started arranging it into lines with the blade.

'Care for a toot?' he asked casually.

'No thanks. I want to keep a clear head.'

Micky raised his eyebrows. 'They keep you clean up in the North,' he observed.

'Not that clean.' I opened my briefcase and took out the whisky. I set it down in front of me.

'You want a glass for that? They're around here someplace.' Micky gestured helplessly. 'Max usually takes care of all that stuff, but he phoned to say he couldn't make it this morning. Said a tree had come down across his driveway, or some shit. You tell me, how come you can travel halfway across the country, yet my fucking butler can't even manage a six-mile trip. I've a good mind to sack his ass!' He shook his head despairingly.

'It's all right, I'll manage without.' I opened the bottle and took a swig. Micky snorted a line of coke, then sat back with a sigh of deep pleasure.

'Man, that is the stuff,' he said. 'Top-grade Columbian. Lot of shit around these days, you need a good supplier. My man's the best.'

I raised the bottle again. 'Cheers,' I said.

Micky studied me for a moment as though sussing me out. 'So, you wanna talk about Johnny, huh? Funny thing, some guy phoned me about him about a week back. Police. Made me nervous, I don't like talking to the cops at the best of times.'

I feigned surprise. 'Odd. What did they want to talk about?'

'Oh some shit about could I give them the names of any of

Johnny's surviving relatives? And did he have a fan club? I said to them, listen, Johnny was an orphan, didn't have anybody but me. And as for a fan club, I said, ordinary stars have fan clubs. Johnny had a *following*. Johnny had disciples, know what I mean? Ain't no fan club as such, just a lot of people who keep his memory alive in their hearts. It's true man, that guy was worshipped, like a god, you know? Fan clubs are for Bolan and Glitter and shit like that.' He laughed. 'Anyhow, they seemed happy enough to leave it at that. I figure they were probably checking up on some dumb claim or other.'

'Claim?'

'Sure. You'd be surprised how many assholes tried to pass themselves off as his true father or mother or long-lost brother, once he hit platinum. Weird man. When he was nobody, there wasn't a single person wanted to lay claim to him. Then people get them ol' dollar-bill signs up in their heads and suddenly he's related to everybody. I chased those fuckers off, though. Took 'em into court and proved they were talking through their asses. Schmucks!' He laughed again, as though he had cracked some unbelievably funny joke. I laughed with him, keeping him sweet. I reached into my bag and took out the notebook and the dictaphone. Micky eyed the latter suspiciously.

'You can put that right back in your bag,' he said. 'I don't trust recorders. I'll tell you some things and you can write 'em down. Then I'll say which ones are for publication.'

I shrugged. 'OK,' I said. 'Look, before we start,' I indicated Seth, who was still staring at me balefully. 'Dogs make me nervous. Do you think . . . ?'

Micky chuckled. 'Sure, sure. Ol' Seth's just staring you down, is all, but if it makes you jumpy . . .' He clicked his fingers and pointed to the open door. Seth got obediently to his feet and slunk out of the room.

'Well trained,' I observed.

'Oh, that he is. Damned dog would do anything for me. If I told him to jump up on his hind legs and tear your face off, he'd do it in a flash.' Micky smiled dangerously. 'So, you'd better make sure you stay on the right side of me,' he said.

I laughed nervously. 'I'll do my best,' I said. 'Right . . .' I picked up my notebook and uncapped a pen. 'Let's go right back to the beginning shall we? How did you first become involved with Johnny?'

Micky thought for a moment. 'Lemme see now, it would have been way back in 1973. I'd been managing a progressive rock band called Brix. Remember them?'

I didn't but I nodded anyway.

'Well, the band fell apart that year. The usual excuse. Musical differences. Which can be translated as the bass guitarist is screwing the lead guitarist's wife. I was left out in the cold. I started scratching around for something to earn a crust and I got roped into being a judge on this talent contest for kids from Doctor Barnardo's. You know them, the orphanage people? Right. Well, most of it was amateur shit, you know, but there was this one kid on the bill. Eighteen years old, brassy, full of confidence.'

'Johnny.'

'Sure. Or Michael Webb as he was called in those days. Mind you, not that you'd have recognised him then. His act was about a million miles away from rock n' roll.' He laughed strangely.

I was intrigued. 'So what was the act?'

'He was a drag queen. A female impersonator.'

I stared at Micky, thinking of the 'woman' who had abducted Danny. Hell of a coincidence. And it couldn't be anything more than that under the circumstances. I forced myself to scribble down notes on the pad. 'A drag queen! Well, that's incredible!'

'He was, too! He'd created this classy dumb-blonde character, Babs. And you know, he looked fantastic. You would have fucked him and not realised!' He leaned close to me and waggled his eyebrows like Groucho Marx. 'Anyhow, I'd been toying with this idea for a new pop persona. Young kid, straight-ahead rock, somebody who sounded good, but looked even better. Johnny had that quality. So I adopted him.'

'What, literally? I mean, officially?'

He nodded. 'Wasn't easy, but I managed to do it. Took him out of the home and into mine. Then I spent a couple of years uh . . . grooming him, you know?' He gave me a sly wink. The effect was highly unpleasant. 'I came up with the name 'Johnny Dark'. Simple but effective. Blond hair, Aryan look, but with that name. Dark. A real contradiction, right? We wrote the songs, I put together a band of session musicians, made him rehearse every day for six months before I felt he was ready to gig.'

'So you created Johnny? You were his Svengali.'

Micky shrugged, nodded, helped himself to another line of coke. 'Sure, why not say it? Johnny would tell you the same thing if he was here now. I was like a father to that kid . . . no, more like a mother, you wanna know the truth. I gave him every opportunity, I set him up for stardom. When it all came together, he was understandably very grateful.' Micky gestured around the opulent room. 'When he died, naturally I inherited. I don't feel guilty about that. I spent my last red cent on that kid because I believed he could do it. I hocked my home, my car, I borrowed money from the bank to set up his first tour. Gamble paid off. Kid had what it took, but it costs dough to put the talent on show.'

I nodded, scribbled down more notes. I was already champing at the bit to get to Johnny's final album but I restrained myself, telling myself that that would look suspicious. I followed Johnny's career through chronologically, as any journalist would have done. Micky seemed happy to talk, mostly about himself and I was careful to bolster the man's ego at every opportunity. Johnny's story seemed to follow the established pattern. A series of tours in Britain to establish the name. A sleeper hit single. A second single, a successful first album, a tour of America . . . It was tedious working through the story but I knew it was necessary to do this if I was going to convince Micky that the interview was on the level.

The best part of two hours had passed before I was able to broach the subject that was uppermost in my mind. I tried to keep my voice casual.

'That brings us on to *Book of the Dead*,' I observed.

Micky scowled. 'I'm afraid it does,' he said. 'If I had my way, I'd go back and erase that album from Johnny's history.'

'Why do you say that? I know the record was unpopular . . .'

'Unpopular? Shit, that's gotta be the understatement of all time. Goddamn thing was about as popular as a dead mouse in a loaf of bread. I begged Johnny not to do it. I told him, Johnny, the kids don't want this esoteric stuff, they want music to dance to, music to fuck to. What they don't want is a friggin' education. But he wouldn't listen to reason. He was obsessed with this Egyptian shit.' He pointed to the painting over the fireplace. 'He figured he was creating a work of genius and that when other people heard it, they'd see the same things in it that he saw. When the critics got hold of it, they mauled it. I've never seen reviews like that, not for anything. The bubonic plague probably got better press.' He looked pointedly at me. 'Of course, I don't have to tell you about that. You were one of them.'

I frowned. 'Well, in my defence, Micky, I was only saying what I thought.'

Micky waved a hand dismissively. 'Hell, I don't blame ya! You were right, it was a piece of shit. A very expensive piece of shit. It hit Johnny hard though, 'specially your review.'

'Why especially mine?'

''Cos the kid idolised you.'

This was a shock. 'He did?'

'Sure. He was a *Scam* reader and he thought you were the best there was. The earlier reviews you did, when you liked his stuff? He had them framed, man, I'm not kidding you! I still got them stored away some place. Used to show them to everybody. He used to say that getting the thumbs-up from you was the only thing that mattered.' Micky scratched his beard thoughtfully. 'Thing you've got to understand about Johnny, he was an orphan, he had no father-figure to look up to. I played that rôle to some degree but he was always looking for approval, you know? He was just a kid in many ways. Getting that bad review from you, well . . . it floored him. And like a kid, he took it out on the record company. Claimed they'd mastered the record all wrong, threatened to litigate them, all kinds of stupid shit. So they withdrew the album a week after its release. Johnny bought back the master tapes, claimed he was going to re-record it all. But of course, he didn't live to do it. So, there ain't many copies of the record around these days. No great loss to the world, I suppose.'

'Do you have a copy of the album?'

'Sure do. Right over there on that rack.'

'May I look at it?'

'Yeah. But take it easy, it's worth a bit of dough. Something I'm keeping for my old age.'

I got up and walked over to the record racks. I found the distinctive black album with the embossed gold pyramid and carried it back to the sofa to examine it. There was a gatefold sleeve and, inside, the lyrics were printed in gold calligraphy. I found the track called 'The Talisman of Seth'. The words told a chilling story.

> Seth calls the tune, the puppets dance,
> unable now to break the trance,
> Osiris, he has many wives, but Seth breaks in and steals their
>   eyes,
> then carves his name on a bitch's thighs,
> for none can see past his disguise.
> At midnight on the 13th day,
> then Chaos will again hold sway.
> When Chaos comes, the heavens break,
> and Seth will make the planet shake,
> Osiris' son, will feel Seth's power, and perish in that timely
>   hour,
> when strong winds blow and fling down rain,
> beneath the pyramid of pain,
> the hawk-lord's death will then portend,
> the time when darkness shall descend.
> No stars, no sun, no shining moon,
> just Chaos, when Seth calls the tune.
> The young hawk's scream, his dying breath,
> shall forge the Talisman of Seth.

'Any chance of me borrowing the record?' I asked tonelessly.

'I don't know, man. Like I said, it's worth some dough.'

'OK then, I'll just copy down some of these lyrics. I'd like to refer to them in the book.'

Micky shrugged. 'Suit yourself. Christ knows what they're about. Me, I like lyrics about sex, drugs and rock n' roll.' He grinned crookedly. 'Not necessarily in that order.

'So tell me,' I said, as I copied down the verse. 'How did

Johnny become so obsessed with Egyptology?'

'Well, that was my fault. After the world tour in '78, Johnny was pretty much exhausted. So I figured we'd take a holiday, give him a chance to wind down a little. He'd been doing an awful lot of drugs, speed mostly, to get him through the tour; and he'd been messing about with all kinds of other stuff. Qualudes, acid, coke . . . you name it. Kid had become a walking cocktail.' He glanced at me. 'This stuff isn't for publication, by the way. Anyway, schmuck here decides that Egypt would be a good place to spend a little time. So we go and, of course, Johnny falls in love with the place. We spend some time in Giza, you know, the big pyramid? We go inside it and Johnny freaks. Tells me he can hear voices talking to him in there and all this weird shit. At first I figured it was just the drugs talkin' but then I realise there's more to it than that. He keeps going back to the place. Comes time for the end of the holiday and he doesn't want to go home. We stay on there, two, maybe three months, I dunno. Back home there are commitments piling up, I have to pull the plug on a European tour and postpone recording sessions. Johnny is literally driving me up the wall. He's reading all these books about Egyptology, buying weird statues and stuff. He's also found himself a local dope connection and he's doing all kinds of stuff looking for a high.' Micky shook his head, leaned forward and helped himself to another line of coke. When he sat up again, there were white smudges around his nose and his eyes had a glazed look.

'Kid just went ape-shit,' he said. 'I finally persuaded him to come back home and that's when he lays this whole Seth trip on me.'

'Seth?' I played dumb. 'You mean ... . the dog?'

Micky laughed. 'The dog was just part of it. The kid believed, actually believed, that he was possessed by this god, Seth. I mean, OK, it seems funny looking back on it, right, but at the time he was deadly serious. And he tells me about this record he's planning to do. And can I talk him out of it? No way! I mean, see the kid's a multi-millionaire by this time – he wants to do something, he's gonna do it, no matter how crazy.' He giggled, a high-pitched stoned giggle. 'Tell you something else he was planning. He was gonna build a pyramid, right here in the grounds, he was gonna found some kind of religious order devoted to this Seth character. All kinds of crazy stuff. It may sound uncharitable, but if he hadn't OD'd when he did, I don't know what else might have happened. Still, like I say, I think we should play all this down, in the book. Kid's won't like it if they read that their hero was as nutty as a fruitcake.'

'Quite.' I slipped the notebook into my pocket, got up and went to the rack to replace the record. As I turned back, a framed photograph on the wall caught my eye. I stopped and studied it for a moment, then felt a coldness rising through me. The picture showed Micky Hart, some ten years earlier and considerably plumper than he was now. He was standing in front of a pyramid, grinning into the camera and his arm was around the shoulders of another man, a dark-haired, bearded guy who was staring into the camera lens and smiling enigmatically. Just as he had smiled when I'd bumped into him in Karen's doorway. Just as he'd smiled as he'd driven past me after killing Jamie's dog.

'Who is this?' I asked calmly.

Micky glanced up in surprise. 'It's me,' he said. 'I've lost a little weight since then, but—'

'No,' I interrupted him. 'Who's this with you?'

Micky sniggered. 'Who do you think it is? Franklin D. Roosevelt? It's Johnny, of course. That picture was taken in Egypt, just before he started going weird on me.'

I turned and stared at Micky. 'But this man has dark hair.'

'Sure. Johnny wasn't a natural blond. He used peroxide. On holiday his hair grew out and he left it that way. Stopped him from being recognised all the time. I remember when . . .' He stopped in mid-conversation, aware of the sudden change in my demeanour. 'Hey! Are you OK?'

I walked slowly back to face Micky, numbed by this latest revelation. Something I had never even considered. 'He's not dead, is he?' I said. 'I don't know how you fixed it, but Johnny Dark is still alive. Where is he? Where's Johnny now?'

Micky stared at me. 'What the fuck are you talking about?' he demanded.

'You know what I'm saying. Oh, you know perfectly well. There's been some kind of conspiracy. You must have helped to arrange it.'

'Now listen . . .'

'No, you listen! Do you know what he's doing now? Do you know what your Johnny is up to? Christ, you must know! How did you fix it? How did you set it up? You're going to tell me if I have to beat it out of you!'

Micky's expression changed dramatically. I saw fear there, but also guilt. He was involved, right up to his glazed eyeballs. He seemed to be thinking hard, then suddenly, he snapped his head sideways and yelled. 'Seth! Kill!'

I heard the deep-throated growl from the next room and acted instinctively. I ran to the heavy oak door of the room and grabbed the edge of it just as I registered the lithe, black shape loping towards me with open jaws. I swung the door shut with all my strength, just as the Rottweiler neared the threshold. There was a dull thud and an agonised howl from the other side of the door. I slid the bolt shut. There was an instant of silence and I thought perhaps I'd knocked the brute unconscious. Then the door shook violently as something was launched against it. The bolt held but I could hear a savage snarling from the other side, the sound of claws scrabbling frantically against bare wood. Unsure how long the door could withstand the assault, I crossed the room back to Micky and grabbed him by the lapels of his expensive Bermuda shirt.

'Right, you bastard,' I snapped. 'Spill the beans. I want to know how you did it. I want to know everything.'

'You're crazy!' protested Micky. 'I don't know what you're talking about. Johnny is dead, I'll take you to his fucking grave if you don't believe me.'

'Oh, somebody is dead right enough. But not Johnny. He's out there murdering people. He's killed four, he's attacked my girlfriend and he very nearly killed my son. I want to know how the fuck a dead man manages to do all that.'

Micky's jaw dropped in astonishment. 'No,' he whispered. 'Johnny wouldn't do that. He wouldn't hurt anybody. Sure, he's confused but . . .'

Micky's use of the present tense was the final confirmation of his protégé's existence.

'So, we're agreed. He's alive. And are you trying to tell me you don't know anything about this? For Christ's sake man, you must! Don't you read the news?'

Micky shook his head frantically. 'Mister, you've got to believe me! I don't even take a newspaper, I don't own a television. I never leave the house. But you've got to be wrong about Johnny. He wouldn't do something like that!'

'He is doing it, believe me. And he's going to keep on doing it.' I let go my hold and pushed Micky back against the sofa. I glanced back at the door which was beginning to buckle on its hinges. 'Call the dog off,' I said with a calmness that surprised me. 'Call it off or so help me, I'll break every bone in your body.'

Micky nodded, licked his dry lips. 'Seth, hold!' he shouted. It went suddenly quiet on the other side of the door. I pictured the dog waiting, ready for another command. I sat down opposite Micky and stared at him for a moment.

'Now talk,' I suggested.

Micky reached out instinctively for his wooden box but I grabbed it and slid it to my side of the table. 'Talk first,' I said. 'Then you get this.'

Micky leaned back again. He looked pale now and unsure of himself.

'You've got to understand,' he said. 'It wasn't my idea, none of it. It was what Johnny wanted. I just went along with it.'

'Talk,' I said.

Micky nodded. He closed his eyes for a moment, took a deep breath. Then he began to explain.

Chapter Twenty-Three

'Johnny was very depressed after *Book of the Dead*. "Depressed" isn't the right word, he became near suicidal. In fact at one point, he did try to kill himself. Drank a bottle of bleach. I managed to get to him in time, but he ruined his voice. Could barely manage more than a whisper after that.'

I nodded. 'I've heard him,' I said.

Micky looked at me blankly and I realised that to some degree he had been telling the truth. He didn't know about the killings.

'We had a tame doctor on the payroll. Doctor Robert, I used to call him, like in the Beatles song, you know? We managed to keep the whole thing quiet, but it was plain that Johnny's singing career was finished. Either he was going to do instrumentals for the rest of his life or we were going to have to hire a session singer to masquerade as him. Johnny didn't seem to care any more. He told me he wanted out of the whole business. Of course, by this time, there was no need for him to work again. He was as rich as anybody could expect to be in one lifetime and he'd made some pretty shrewd business investments.' Micky shook his head. 'Question was, what was the kid going to do? He became totally apathetic, sank himself into doing alcohol and drugs. Put on a lot of weight, he was barely recognisable as Johnny Dark. It got so he could walk down the street and nobody would bat an eyelid.' Micky paused for a moment, as though reluctant to continue. He glanced at the wooden box I was guarding and that seemed to prompt him.

'One day I got a call from Johnny at the office. He sounded pretty frantic, asked me to get back to the house as quick as I could. When I got there, I found a real mess. Johnny was smashed out of his mind and there was a young kid lying dead in the bedroom.'

'A kid?'

'Some down-and-out he'd picked up on the street. He'd taken to bringing all kinds of people home with him, fans, vagrants, people he got talking to at some club or other. This kid had come back with him and they'd mainlined heroin. The kid must have taken more than he could handle, he was cold meat by the time I got there. Hell of a mess. Thing was, the kid looked a lot like Johnny – or at least how Johnny *used* to look. Cropped blond hair, leather jacket. He'd obviously styled himself on the Johnny Dark image – if you'd stood the two of them side by side and asked which one's the pop star, there'd be no contest. That's what gave me the idea. I suggested it to Johnny and he went wild for it. It was what he wanted, man, to get out of the business, to just disappear. All we had to do was talk over the financial side.'

I sneered. 'That's how you managed to take early retirement, right?'

Micky glanced at his feet, nodded. 'If you think about it, I was only getting what I'd have got if Johnny *had* died. I was his sole beneficiary, it would have all come down to me. We worked out that we'd create a new identity for Johnny. Every six months I'd pay a certain amount of money into his account and he'd just melt into the shadows. He loved the idea, talked about going back to Egypt.' Micky frowned. 'There wasn't much time to arrange things, but I was a manager right, I'd had a lot of practice in cutting corners. I called in ol' Doctor Robert and asked him for a death certificate. At first he didn't much like the idea, but then we talked money and it was surprising how quick he came round to it. From there on it was pretty easy. We got Johnny out of the way and I called an ambulance. I went to the morgue to officially identify the body. I arranged a quick service at Golders Green Crematorium and Johnny Dark was laid to rest once and for all. Neatest job I ever did.

'Whoever the dead kid really was, his folks didn't come knocking on our door. Must've been a loser.'

He glanced at me defiantly as if daring me to suggest there was anything wrong with what he had done. But I wasn't ready to pass comment yet. I wanted to hear the rest of it.

'Later I got some friends to forge up a birth certificate and a passport in the name of John McNeil. Johnny took off for Egypt, just like he said he would. From time to time, I'd get postcards from him, from one weird place or another. I carried on making the payments, had a direct debit made to his account.'

I nodded. 'When did you last get a card from him?' I asked.

Micky shrugged. 'Ain't heard anything from him in over six months. Last card I got I couldn't make head nor tail of. Just a bunch of lyrics from the last album.'

I scowled. 'Seth calls the tune, Chaos returns,' I said.

Micky stared at me in surprise. 'Yeah. But how did you . . .?'

'I've had the same message,' I said. 'But not on a postcard.'

Micky thought for a moment. 'Look man, everything I've told you here. It's in confidence, right? I mean, there's no reason why any of this needs to go further.'

'You've got to be joking! Maybe I didn't explain myself clearly to you. Johnny's a murderer. Worse than that, he's a sadist. Do you know what he does to people? He cuts out their eyes.'

Micky stared at me. 'Say what? Jesus!'

'So you see, there's really no choice. He has to be stopped.'

'All right, all right, I take your point. But there's no reason to involve me, right? I mean, we can work something out.'

I looked at Micky in disgust. 'What did you have in mind?' I asked.

Micky grinned confidently, displaying his rotten teeth. 'I mean, what's your price? Don't tell me there isn't one, everybody has a price.'

I thought about it for all of five seconds. Then I shook my head. 'There are some things even you can't buy,' I said coldly.

'Aww, man, I don't think you appreciate the figures we're talking. You name it, you can have cash or cheque. C'mon, don't be shy about it. How much?'

'How about a million?'

'A million!' Micky laughed unpleasantly. 'Boy, you don't believe in half measures do you? A million . . .' He considered for a moment. 'OK, it's not out of the question. Where do you want me to deposit the money?'

277

I smiled at him. 'I want you to shove it up your arse, note by note,' I said. I enjoyed saying it.

Micky glared at me for a moment. Clearly he wasn't used to being turned down. Then he sneered. 'Oh, I get it. Mr Self-Righteous, huh? Look man, I thought I was helping Johnny. I was just looking after his interests, that's all.' He ran one hand through his hair in exasperation, then pointed to the wooden box that I had in front of me. 'At least give me my stash back,' he said, 'I could use a hit right now. I can't think straight.'

I felt anger rising within me in a cold, steady stream. I picked up the box. 'You want this? You want it? How much will you give me for it?'

'Hey man, chill out! Just give me the fuckin' box, OK?'

'Here.' I held it out to Micky and then as he reached for it, I turned aside and flung the box into the open fire.

'You sonofabitch!' Micky leapt from his seat and scrambled across the floor on his hands and knees, tried to snatch the box out of the flames. But it was too late. The dry wood had caught in an instant and it went up with a rush of air. Micky turned back and stared at me with dull hatred. 'You shouldn't have done that,' he said. 'Now you've really pissed me off.' He reached out and grabbed a brass poker which was hanging beside the fire. 'So, you're gonna bust my ass, are you? We'll see about that.' He began to advance towards me, then seemed to think better of it. Instead he moved towards the bolted door.

Realising his intentions, I ran at him. He swung at me with the poker but I managed to duck the blow and I hit him with a good, solid jab in the mouth. He went down in a sprawl, blood pulsing from his lips. He stared up at me stupidly for a moment, then grinned. He turned to glance at the door. 'Seth!' he yelled. 'Kill!'

There was an almighty crash as the dog recommenced his assault on the door, its bark rising to a gut-wrenching volume; then came a splintering sound as the hinges began to buckle. I glanced round frantically, realising that burning the coke had not been the most intelligent move I had ever made. It was time to make an exit. I crossed the room to the French windows and fumbled for the bolt. My fingers didn't seem to be working properly but I managed to fling the doors open and I ran out onto the night.

The wind and rain struck me like a clenched fist, snatching my breath away. Behind me, I heard the prone Micky yelling something and there was a crash as the door was finally smashed open.

'Jesus Christ!' I said. I'm not a religious person but it seemed very appropriate at the time. I ran around the side of the house towards my car, groping in my pocket for the keys. Out of the corner of my eye, I was horribly aware of a huge black shape lunging through the illuminated oblong of the French windows.

I reached the car and stabbed the key at the lock. Panic made me clumsy and it took several attempts to get the key located correctly. Behind me, I heard a deep-throated growl that turned my legs to jelly. I turned the key, flung the door open and jumped into the seat. I attempted to slam the door behind me but it was intercepted by a snarling, brutish head, the slavering jaws inches away from my right arm. I swore, pulled the door as tight as possible and tried to get the key into the ignition, but in my haste I dropped it on the floor. Teeth snagged in the fabric of my leather jacket, tearing, rending. My flesh shrank as if anticipating the same impact. I pulled harder on the door, keeping the dog's head pinioned, while I fumbled for the key with my free hand. This brought my face inches away from the beast's jaws and I could smell its raw-meat breath gusting on to my face like slow death. In the interior of the car, the canine roar was deafening.

I got hold of the key, brought it up, jammed it into the ignition. I turned it and the engine started first time. The muscles of my right arm ached with straining to hold the door shut and slackened for a second as I put the car in gear with my left hand. The dog pushed in closer and locked its jaws around my right arm, the teeth sinking through leather and deep into flesh. It was like shards of broken glass tearing into me. I screamed, jammed my foot down on the accelerator and let out the clutch. The car lurched forward but the dog would not relinquish it's grip. I felt the grinding of teeth against bone and pain blazed like fire along the length of my arm. I gritted my teeth and pushed my foot

279

harder on the pedal. As the car took off along the drive at full speed, I snatched an instant to release my hold on the wheel and desperately I jammed the fingers of my left hand into the dog's eyes. I was rewarded by a howl and the teeth slightly relaxed their grip. Ahead of me, through a screen of rain, I saw the wrought-iron gates, resolutely shut against my approach. I had no option but to push my foot down to the floorboards, knowing that if I didn't break through at the first attempt, the Rottweiler would tear me to pieces.

The roar of the engine mingled with the scream of the dog and then there was an impact which jarred every bone in my body. I would have gone forward into the windscreen but, ironically, the dog's pressure had anchored me in my seat. The gates collapsed and fell away beneath me with a grinding crash. The car bumped and lurched over them and suddenly my arm was free. The dog's head had slipped back out of my doorway and the car was heading for the road beyond the fallen gates. Glancing in my mirror, I saw a body twitching and thrashing amongst the debris of the gate. A stray iron shaft had pierced Seth's chest like a spear.

I glanced down at my arm. Blood was pulsing through one of the rents in my jacket and I felt dizzy with pain, but I managed to keep the car hammering along in a straight line. I remembered to flick on the windscreen wipers and dropped back to a safer speed. When I was a mile away from Micky's house, I pulled over and climbed out into the rain, letting the cold shock of it revive me. I gently took off my jacket, tore the sleeve off my shirt and bound it tightly around my arm, a makeshift bandage. Then I managed to get the jacket back on again, a tighter fit this time. The weather was worsening by the minute, the sky flinging down rods of icy water. I got back into the car, started the engine up. It spluttered a few times before catching, almost certainly damaged by the impact with the gates. The windscreen wipers had to work overtime to channel away the deluge that was striking the glass. Suddenly, the lyrics from the album cover came back to me. 'At midnight on the 13th Day, then Chaos will again hold sway . . .'

I was looking at the lead-crystal display on my dashboard. It was a little after eight o'clock on the thirteenth of December. A coldness settled in my guts. I fumbled in my pocket for my notebook and scanned the rest of the lyrics I had written down. 'Osiris' son, will feel Seth's power, and perish in that timely hour, when strong winds blow and fling down rain, beneath the pyramid of pain.'

Suddenly, an image came looming out of the curtain of rain in front of me: Danny's face, his eyes shut, his mouth open to scream. I knew then that he was in terrible danger. There was no time to stop and consider. I had to get home as soon as possible. I threw the car into gear, let out the clutch and accelerated away from the verge, heading for the motorway with all the speed I could coax from the car's failing engine.

Diary Extract

13th December
Tom left early this morning, just as He said he would. I know because I watched him drive away. He went right by me and didn't even notice me standing there. I believe I was invisible at that moment. I can do it sometimes, I can walk through the midst of the biggest crowd and nobody sees me, I am like a ghost. As I come closer to the point of transformation, I get flashes of true power, a taste of what it will be like when tonight's ceremony is over.

I know where Tom has gone – to talk with Micky. It was always going to happen, but this way, the timing is perfect because I don't want to exclude Tom totally from the transformation. On the contrary, I want him to see everything, to stand in awe of his brother's metamorphosis. But I do want him out of the way for at least a while. So he will go down to Essex and he will talk to Micky and, eventually, Micky will tell everything he knows. Micky is weak, degenerate, he has always been a threat to me and there have been times when I have considered putting a stop to his weakness once and for all, but He has always stayed my hand. He has always said that, one day, Micky will be of some use to us. Now I understand what He meant. Micky will send Tom back to me; and by then I shall be ready to greet him. By then, I shall have taken his son, Daniel. Horus. The little hawk.

It's going to be easy. They are up there in that flat, the two of them, quite alone. I've already proved to my own satisfaction how ridiculously easy it is to gain access to the place. Oh, that pathetic police inspector is hanging around, but he won't even see me. I'll be invisible. I'll slip in that doorway like a shadow and nobody will even notice.

The boy is beautiful. He has his father's eyes. I remember him in the department store, staring up at me with those big, trusting eyes as I prepared his ice cream. Though of course, then I was my other self, totally in touch with the woman who lives beneath my skin. I like her but sometimes, I distrust her. She is the kind of woman who lies with many men, she has vast hungers, insatiable appetites. She is more devious than I am and when I put on her clothing, allow her to blossom through my skin, I am in danger of losing myself. It's as though I want to remain with her forever, forget my real identity . . . but that, too, will be purged in the change. When I am a god, I must put aside all human weakness.

The pain helps – the exquisite fire in my genitals that reminds me at every step that I am still no more than a man. But only for a few more hours. The change comes soon and I can taste it on my tongue. It tastes hot and sweet, like blood.

Chapter Twenty-Four

Visibility was down to a few yards now and the car was lurching left and right as the wind gusted around it. I had been driving for about an hour and the engine was making a horrible grinding roar. Up ahead of me, I could make out the blurry red smudges that were the tail lights of an articulated lorry. It was swerving dangerously from side to side, the driver fighting to keep control of the vehicle. I had the radio on, but through a maelstrom of atmospherics I could only make out the occasional phrase.

'. . . high winds . . . bringing chaos to the North-west . . . gusts in excess of one hundred . . . trees down in . . . roof torn off school building . . . reports coming in . . .'

Chaos returns. I scowled. Was the mad bastard controlling the weather now? I shook my head grimly. Coincidence. Had to be. And maybe it was the weather that had me spooked but my skin was crawling with apprehension and I kept getting that same vision of Danny's terrified face looming out of the rain-spattered darkness. I glanced at the lead crystal display on the dashboard. Nine forty-five and there was still a long way to go. I had to hurry, I had to overtake the lorry. I got my foot down and moved into the outside lane. The back spray from the juggernaut coated the windscreen with filthy water and I was fighting with the steering wheel every inch of the way, aware of the wind attempting to fling me into the lorry's massive wheels as I drew nearer.

It happened suddenly. I saw the tail lights lift to an impossible 45-degree angle, heard the protesting roar of the lorry's engine as the wind overturned it. Then there were brilliant white sparks as its chassis made contact with the road and it went sliding along like a beached whale, the cab jack-knifing in front of me. I wrenched the wheel desperately to the right and headed for the

283

narrowing gap between the cab and the crash bars in the centre of the motorway, keeping my foot down hard, knowing that if I braked I would smash headlong into the vehicle. The lorry's headlights blazed at my windows, momentarily dazzling me, and I braced myself for the impact of metal against metal; but my luck held by a rotten thread. I shot through the gap with inches to spare and the interior of my car lit up as the cab smashed into the crash bar and burst into flames, fire blossoming beneath the falling rain. I left the blaze behind me, counting the seconds as I raced onwards, rating my son's life above that of a stranger's in the night.

Diary Extract

13th December
The weather reports are proof that my power is emerging. The many nights spent in meditation, attuning myself with the spirit of Nun, the realm of Chaos, was time well spent. Now my labours have at last come to fruition. Hours of self-inflicted pain, blood sacrifices and chanted rituals. People would laugh if I told them that I had the power to control the wind and rain, they would make foolish sounds and dismiss me as a madman, because such an idea would terrify them. I, in turn, could tell them that this is nothing – let them experience the full brunt of my powers when I am a god! How I will rack their puny bodies then! How I will smite them with cancers and sickness and, sweetest of all, with pain; simple, unadulterated pain! Let them experience the pain I felt when they turned their faces from me, when in ignorance they dismissed my attempts to elevate them to a higher plane. There was a conspiracy, they were all in it and thus, are all equally guilty. I should have realised they were not ready, that confronted by my genius they would only smile foolishly, shake their heads and make their pathetic, sarcastic remarks. How they will tremble before me when the Day of Judgement comes! How they will crawl and fawn, and beg for my mercy!

Even Tom became one of them. Tom, my brother, my Osiris

here on earth, forsook his own powers to join them in denouncing me. I weep for him because he doesn't know what he could be with just a little commitment, a little personal pain. I have tried to teach him about pain and perhaps I have made him stronger. His ultimate test comes soon. I am prepared for it. I wonder if he is?

Indeed, everything is prepared now. I go to collect my sacrifice. Seth is watching me. At last I feel worthy enough to write his name. He watches and, for the first time, I detect a glow of pride within Him. He is ready to accept me into His heart, His soul, His blood. In a few hours, I will no longer exist. He and I shall be as One.

When a sign for a service area came up to my left, a great distance later I decided to risk stopping off for a few minutes. The engine was badly overheating and I was getting low on fuel. The last thing I needed was a breakdown on the motorway, just a few miles from my destination.

I nursed the car on to the slip road and motored slowly up to the forecourt. The lights were on in the main building but the place looked somehow beleaguered, deserted, a grey concrete building against a background of ugly black cloud. I brought the car to a halt and got out. The wind almost swept me off my feet. I noticed a row of public telephones off to my right, beneath the restless shadows of a row of oak trees that were swaying and shuddering alarmingly in the wind's onslaught. I put a hand in my pocket and fumbled out some coins. Walking, almost bent double against the rush of air, I moved to the nearest booth and swung back the door. Its telephone had been vandalised, the handset smashed and hanging by its cord. I moved to the next booth. A cardphone. Fuck it! I made for the next booth in the line, then froze in my tracks as the tree directly overhead made a slow creaking sound. I eyed it nervously but it was a mature tree that must have withstood many a gale in its time. I opened the door, assured myself the phone was in working order, stepped inside and fed the paybox with coins. I dialled Karen's number and waited in nervous silence for what seemed an age.

It rang and rang; and I felt fear settle like a chill liquid in my guts.

'Come on,' I whispered. 'Pick it up, please!'

And then there was an answer. It was Karen.

'Hello?'

'Karen, it's Tom! Listen to me, you—'

'Hello?'

'Karen, it's Tom. Can't you hear me?'

'Hello, who is this?'

'Listen, Karen, you're in danger! Phone the police, phone them now, he's coming for Daniel. Karen, for God's sake, can you hear me? Please say you can hear me!'

'Hello? Look if somebody doesn't say something soon I'm putting the phone down.'

'Who is it, Mum?' Danny's voice, off to one side but as clear as a bell.

'I don't know, love. Must be a bad connection or something. All I can hear is static.'

'Let me try.' A clumping noise. Then Danny's voice, louder. 'H'lo? Who's there?'

'Danny, it's me, your dad. Can you hear what I'm saying?'

'Dad, is that you?'

I nearly screamed with delight.

'Danny, put your mum on, I have to talk to her urgently.'

'Dad? Oh, he's gone again! It was Dad, I heard him, just for a moment!'

'Are you sure? I don't think there's anyone there, Danny. Put the phone down, they might try again.'

'No!' I screamed. 'No, Danny, listen to me, please, you've got to listen!' Danny, I love you. I should have said this before and I hope I will again, but right now I'm afraid something bad is going to happen. I'll try to get to you, I promise. I'm coming straight home now. Just please, hang on there for me. Don't—'

The line went dead. I slammed down the receiver with a sound of exasperation. I considered giving it another try but I was out of coins and out of time. Maybe the operator? Maybe 999? I was standing there, thinking about that, when a noise cut into my thoughts; a long, drawn-out squeal, like an animal in pain. I turned in astonishment and glanced up through the glass of the booth. One of the trees was coming down on top of me. As simple, as terrible as that. I stood there, open-mouthed, frozen

286

in terror and wonder as the tree's roots tore themselves out from the earth accompanied by a grinding, thunderous roar. Then some last instinct of self-preservation snapped into action. I threw open the door of the booth and made my run, horribly aware of a dark shadow spreading around me like a shroud. And as I ran, I was thinking, *He's done this, somehow, I don't know how, he's influencing the weather, the trees, the fucker's not human.*

And then the booth was crumpling like a cardboard carton, the glass exploding out of the collapsing frames, peppering my retreating back like shotgun blasts. The earth shuddered beneath my feet as the oak connected with the ground in a mighty splintering of wood and foliage. A thick branch scythed the air inches from my shoulder and debris was hurled like rifle pellets by the wind.

When I had reached a safe distance, I turned and looked back at the telephones. The booth I had so recently occupied no longer existed. The tree's massive branches had effectively destroyed it and all of its companions. Nobody would be making a call from there for quite some time.

I was shaking now, convinced that this was more than coincidence and that Danny and Karen were in mortal danger. I headed for my car, which was parked just beyond the fallen oak's reach. I realised that I daren't waste any more time. The engine and petrol would just *have* to last out. Maybe if I had faith, they would. Maybe if I prayed.

'Wait for me,' I said grimly. 'I'm coming.'

At the time, I didn't know whom exactly I was talking to. It was only later that I understood. I slammed the car into gear and took off at speed, heading back to the motorway.

Diary Extract

13th December
Hear the wind as it howls and roars! It proclaims the coming of a New Age. Down on the streets, everything is deserted. People cower in their homes, terrified as the gods vent their wrath in the

heavens. To me it is a sound of exultation. They are preparing a place for me in their world and they are celebrating my imminent arrival. The time is at hand. This is my last entry in this journal; my last written words as a mere man.

Chapter Twenty-Five

Pulling into Karen's street, I reflected how odd it all looked. It seemed totally devoid of life like some weird ghost-town. It was nearly eleven-thirty. Fear, or maybe the following wind, had lent me wings and I'd made a record speed despite the driving conditions and a throbbing right arm. I'd bypassed several jams on the way back and I'd seen more accidents than I could count. There was thunder now, and the occasional flicker of lightning away to the West picked out the towering, broiling landscape of nimbus in the sky. There was a light on in Karen's bedroom and I prayed that she was up there with Danny. I did spot one reassuring sight: Drayton's grey Escort parked a short distance from Karen's entrance. I pulled up behind it and got out, having to push hard to open my door against the rush of wind. I ran to the Escort, my head lowered against the sting of the rain. I could just make out Drayton's hunched figure in the interior. I hammered on the window but there was no response. I felt my mouth go dry. Asleep, perhaps? The desperate hope died the moment I opened the door.

Drayton looked peaceful, his gaze still fixed on the illuminated square of Karen's window. His jugular had been neatly cut and the front of his shirt was sodden with blood. When I put a hand on his shoulder, he slumped sideways and his head hinged backwards, the gap in his throat grinning at me like a second mouth. His hands still gripped the steering wheel, as though it had happened suddenly, no time to put up a fight.

'No!' The cry wrenched itself from my throat and I brought one fist down on the roof of the car, hard, the pain dispelling the need to scream. In that instant I had no pity for what had happened to Drayton. I hated him for being so careless, for allowing John to creep up on him like that, when he was supposed to be looking after my son. Then the anger passed and I felt an overpowering sadness course through me. I had grown to like the man. I had begun to think of him as a friend. I tried not to look at him as I leaned into the car and fumbled for the radio receiver. It came away in my hand, the cable neatly severed. I swore, flung it aside, threw a desperate glance towards the entrance door, saw that it was swinging open in the wind.

Oh God, he's in there! He's in there now with Danny and Karen!

Frantically I began to go through Drayton's pockets, looking for a weapon, something I could use to defend myself. Nothing. Not so much as a Swiss army knife. I remembered the taxi driver I had ridden with the night I had been beaten up, and I reached across Drayton to flip open the glove compartment. The handle of a pistol offered itself to me like a dark blessing. I grabbed it and was momentarily surprised by the weight of it. It was a chunk of sleek black lead in my hand. I stepped back from the car and ran across the street to the entrance, pushed the door open with my foot and stepped inside. I reached instinctively for the staircase light switch and then thought better of it. Why make myself an easy target?

I stood in the darkness listening intently. I could hear the sounds of a television in one of the downstairs flats, a droning voice interspersed with bouts of canned laughter. I thought about asking for help at one of the flats but realised that I daren't wait around any longer. And I recalled that most of the ground-floor residents were elderly folk. I moved up the staircase, peering ahead through the gloom. I halted at Karen's door and saw that it, too, was slightly ajar. I took a deep breath, cupping the gun in both hands, as I had seen them do in movies. I felt faintly ridiculous, knowing that I had never fired a gun in my life, not even sure if the damned thing was loaded. I told myself that I should take more time to prepare, but knew that there probably wasn't any time left. I put the toe of one shoe against the door and pushed it open slowly. Silently it swung back on to blackness. Gritting my teeth and trying to control my breathing, I stepped inside and hesitated, gazing around the darkened room. A flash of lightning lit up the interior for an instant and the scene remained fixed in my mind. It seemed empty but there were several places where a man might hide. Behind the curtains there, or down at the back of the sofa.

No time to think. I began to inch forward, heading now for the bedroom where I could see a slit of light beneath the closed door. I tried to steel myself for what I might find there. A succession of horrific images ran through my mind and I tried in vain to banish them.

I reached the door, took one hand from the pistol and cupped it around the door handle which I turned gently. I waited for a moment, but nothing happened. I leaned my thigh on the door, resumed my double grip on the gun and took a deep breath. I counted to three, then kicked the door open and stepped into the room, the gun levelled in front of me. I froze, stunned.

Karen was sitting in a chair in the centre of the room. She was bound and gagged and her eyes bulged as she saw the gun levelled at her chest. The door swung back behind me and I whipped around, expecting to see somebody standing there. Nobody. I remembered to breathe and ran over to Karen, untied the gag. She began to talk even before the cloth was out of her mouth, the words falling over themselves as they fell from her dry tongue.

'Dannyhe'sgotDannyhetookhimhe . . .'

'Slow down!' I warned her. I moved behind her and began to untie the ropes. 'What happened?' I asked, trying to keep my voice calm and matter of fact, though inside I wanted to scream in panic. I could smell the sweet odour of chloroform on Karen's breath.

She shook her head, forced herself to speak more slowly. Her body was trembling uncontrollably. 'Knock at the door. Answered . . . it. Thought Drayton . . . would have checked on anybody . . . calling. Mask. He had on a mask.'

I nodded. 'Go on,' I urged her.

'Pad . . . on my mouth. Woke up in chair. Tom, he had Danny! He . . . was carrying him. Unconscious I think. Said . . . he wouldn't hurt me. Said I was . . . Isis?' She stared up at me in confusion.

'And Danny?' I asked fearfully.

'Told me he was taking Danny.' She hesitated, shook the muzziness from her head.

I prompted her. 'Taking him where, Karen? *Where*?'

'He said he was taking him home.'

I nodded. Yes, that much figured. I had a good idea where home was. Home sweet home. I grabbed Karen, pulled her close. 'Listen to me! How long ago did he leave?'

'Fifteen . . . maybe twenty minutes.'

'OK. Phone the police. Tell them Drayton's dead. Tell them to follow me up to the Osiris Building.'

'Where?'

'The pyramid. You know the place, on City Road? The Osiris Building! He'll take him there, I know it. Just call them, Karen. I can't explain. No time.'

She got up from the chair and nearly fell. I caught her, helped her across to the bed. Then I picked up the phone from the bedside cabinet and handed it to her. She lifted the receiver with unsteady hands and held it to her ear. She shook her head helplessly at me. 'It's dead,' she wailed. 'He must have cut the line.'

'Try a neighbour. Or find a call box. I can't stay, Karen, I've got to hurry.'

I ran out of the room and through the one beyond. I hit the lights on the landing and went down the stairs three at a time, almost tripping and falling in my haste. A door to one of the downstairs flats opened and a grey-haired woman popped her head out. Her eyes widened as she took in my dishevelled appearance and the gun in my hand.

'Woman upstairs!' I yelled. 'Needs to use your phone. Please, can you—'

I broke off with a curse as the woman ducked back inside, slamming the door behind her. I shook my head. *Perfect! Just fucking perfect.*

I raced back out to the street, yanked open the door of my car, shoved the gun into my jacket pocket and clambered into the driver's seat. When I turned the ignition key, the engine spluttered dismally. I swore, tried it again. A rasping cough. 'Come on, come on, come on!' I snarled. On the sixth attempt, the engine turned over. I swung the wheel and lurched away from the pavement, grazing Drayton's Escort in my haste to get away. In the glare of the headlights I saw his slumped figure lurch in his seat. He was still staring up at the window. It struck me that my one useful ally was dead. Drayton should have been riding with me, he'd know what to do.

Then I was clear and racing down the street, knowing it would take a good fifteen minutes to reach the pyramid. But I was sure of one thing. That's where John would be waiting for me. That's where we would finish it once and for all.

Please God! let me be in time.

The speedometer was up around ninety as I clattered through the deserted streets, oblivious to my own safety. At that moment Danny was about all I had in the world and I would only sell the boy's life dearly. I glanced at the clock on the dashboard. Eleven-forty. I remembered the days when I had raced to work for my own pleasure, but now there was a more urgent reason to get to my destination. I coaxed the car up faster. Maybe, I reflected, cops would see me speeding, would follow me to the pyramid and provide the kind of professional back-up I needed. But there were no police cars in sight, just the rain and the worsening storm, and the barrage of wind that kept threatening to wrest the controls of the car from my hands.

Easy now, watch the bend.

I screeched around a corner, burning rubber, skidding side-ways on the wet tarmac. I almost lost control, but corrected the swerve, the left front-wheel bouncing off the kerb with a bone-shaking jolt. I straightened the car, raced on up the street.

Got to keep my head. Can't afford a crash. Got to get there for Danny.

Shopfronts flew past me in an oily blur. To my left, a concrete streetlight had succumbed to the wind and lay twisted and broken in the road. I swerved to avoid it and accelerated towards the traffic lights at the top of the street. They showed red but I didn't check my speed, shot through them and turned on to City Road.

Not far now. I'm coming Danny. Hold on.

After a few minutes, the Osiris Building came into sight: a sleek, smooth pinnacle against a backdrop of poisonous sky. Lightning flashed, forked like a snake's tongue and the glass sides momentarily reflected it's glare, shining with a spectral brilliance that seemed to sear itself into my vision.

Turn now. Kill the lights, he might be watching for me.

I turned off the street and headed for the main gates, bumping and jolting over the uneven ground. I slewed the car to a halt and was out of the door and running almost before it had stopped moving. The main entrance towered in front of me, huge wooden gates, topped with barbed wire. But there was no need to climb them. A cursory glance showed me that the massive padlock that secured them had been broken open and the gates swung to and fro in the wind. They pushed inward at my touch and I stepped through into the construction site.

Night watchman. Surely, there ought to be . . .

I spotted the prefab building away to my left and ran to it, having to bend myself almost double in order to make progress with the wind in my face. There was a light on inside the hut, but no sign of any life. The door opened at my touch and the wind gusted in behind me, scattering sheets of paper around the interior. A uniformed man was slumped over a desk, head resting on folded arms. His peaked hat had fallen on to the desk top and most of his brains were inside it, a viscous red stew already beginning to congeal. I felt a wave of nausea, but I forced myself to move nearer. There was a telephone a short distance away from the man's right hand and I could see that the cable had been neatly cut through. The bastard wasn't taking any chances. There was a clock on the wall above the man's desk. It was now eleven-fifty.

All right then. Just you and me, sunshine. The thought was strangely comforting. It came to me that this was how it was always meant to be.

I let myself out and stood staring across the yard at the pyramid. Then I noticed that there was a faint glow of light, high up beneath the apex of the building. This galvanised me into movement. I ran across the yard, picking my way through the rubble and the machinery. As I neared the glass doors of the main entrance, I saw that one pane had been smashed clean through. If anybody had heard it on a night like this, they would have paid it no heed. I stepped through the frame and my shoes crunched on the shards of glass littering the floor.

The interior of the building was yet to be finished. In the gloom I could make out bare concrete walls and flooring and, further back in the shadows, a litter of tools and equipment stacked up on every side. Set in one wall was an elevator and I ran across to this, tried pushing the button to summon the lift. Nothing happened. Not working yet. I searched around and then, suddenly, I knew where I would find the staircase. The same place it had been in my dream. There wasn't time to ponder the strangeness of it. I directed myself forward and found the steps waiting for me, leading upwards into blackness.

I began to climb, one hand clutching the temporary safety rail. Outside, the wind moaned and wailed in exultation as I moved deeper into the heart of the pyramid. I reached the first floor, which was much like the ground floor and cast about for the next flight of stairs. They switched back in the opposite direction and I quickened my pace, terrified of what might be going on above me. As I started up them, a new sound came to me, the distant booming of rock music. I didn't have to concentrate to identify the tune. 'The Eyes of Ra.' He was playing our song.

As I climbed the subsequent flights, the music got louder, an eerie cacophony that seemed to blend with the shriek of the wind howling around the glass building. Johnny's favourite music. His own. The music he liked to kill to . . . I quickened my pace, sprinting up flights of stairs until my legs ached and the breath exploded in my chest. How far now? I'd lost count of how many floors I'd climbed. I paused a moment to wipe the sweat from my face with the sleeve of my jacket. My watch informed me that it was four minutes to midnight. I went on my way, gasping for breath, stumbling and tripping in the uncertain light.

I seemed to climb for ever, the only indication that I was getting nearer to my goal was the rising volume of the music. Amplified by the great empty shell of the pyramid, it seemed to fill my head, blocking out my ability to think. I ran now like an automaton, a dry ache in my chest, my legs powering me up the stairs until I rounded a corner and saw a faint glow of light filtering down from above. At the top of one more short flight of steps, a square hatchway led into what must be the apex of the pyramid. I snatched a few seconds to regulate my breathing and realised that my body was trembling with apprehension. It occurred to me how much easier it would be to walk away now, to go back down and wait for the professionals.

Not this time, I told myself. This time there would be no running away.

I pulled the pistol from my pocket and began to climb slowly upwards, into the light.

Chapter Twenty-Six

I reached a trapdoor-like opening and cautiously lifted my head to peer out of it.

The top floor was as bare as all the others but, lit by the glow of a workman's lamp, it seemed bigger than any of them. The first thing I spotted was a portable stereo in one corner, the source of the music. I turned my head to the side. In the very centre of the room stood a large wooden packing case. Danny was lying on it, naked, his eyes closed, apparently still unconscious. John was standing over him. He, too, was naked – save for the mask he was wearing. His squat and muscular body glistened with a covering of sweat.

He held a long curved knife in his right hand and, with this, he was tracing intricate designs over my son's chest. I could hear a muffled sound coming from behind the mask, as though he was chanting along with the music. I considered my options. I had never fired a gun before and I realised I couldn't risk a shot even from this distance. I would most likely miss completely or, worse still, hit Danny. No, I would have to get closer. I dropped my right hand to my side and tucked the gun into my back trouser pocket. Then, moving slowly, I began to climb out into the room.

John became aware of me and he froze for an instant, the tip of the knife inches away from Danny's chest. He waited and I sensed the expression of triumph behind the mask. 'Hello, old son,' said his muffled voice. 'You made it then. I was beginning to think we'd have to start without you.'

I moved closer. 'Let the boy go,' I said, my voice hoarse with anxiety. 'This is between you and me.'

The mask shook from side to side and there was an amused chuckle. 'No, it's not, Tom. It's between me and *him*. It always

297

has been.' The music hit a climactic chord and finished abruptly. In the ensuing silence, the noise of the wind seemed even louder. John lifted a naked arm to point to the sloping glass wall behind him. 'What do you think of the little show I've laid on?' he asked.

'What show?'

'The weather, of course. I made that happen.'

'Did you?' I kept my voice calm, inquisitive. Had to keep him occupied until I was close enough. 'And how did you do that?' I asked.

'The right prayers, the right sacrifices. The world is ready for the transformation now. And so am I.' He pointed to Daniel. 'When this is finished, I'm going to change for ever.'

I kept walking nearer. My clammy hand was itching to reach behind me for the handle of the gun. 'Into what?' I asked. 'A fucking white rabbit?'

He laughed shrilly. An unpleasant sound. 'No, Tom. No cheap conjuring tricks. I'm going to become a god, of course. Haven't you figured it out yet?'

'No, tell me about it.'

'That's as near as you come,' warned John. He pressed the tip of the blade down on Daniel's chest and I stopped in my tracks. I was pretty close now. Close enough to see the gold ring through the head of Johnny Dark's erect penis and further back, around the dark wrinkled sac of his scrotum, something glittering obscenely. I realised with horror that they were the heads of pins that had been pushed deep into his testicles. There were dozens of them, some of them rusted with age.

'Oh sweet Jesus,' I whispered. I hadn't meant to say it aloud, it just came out. John giggled. He made a feint with the knife up around Danny's throat.

'Please, don't do that,' I said desperately. 'You don't have to hurt him.'

'Oh, but I do, old son. You have to understand. You have to know what he is. He's—'

'Horus,' I said.

There was a brief silence. I could see John's eyes glittering malignantly through the slits in the mask. 'So, you do understand,' he said.

I nodded. 'I understand that this is what you *believe*,' I said. 'But you're wrong. He's just a little boy. And I'm just a record-spinner.'

John chuckled behind the mask. 'People often aren't aware of their own powers,' he said. 'For years I didn't even know about my own. It was you who made me aware of them, Tom.'

'Me?' I risked taking another step forward, but halted when I saw the tip of the knive cut into Daniel's flesh. A scarlet trickle spilled across his breast.

'Yes, you. The review you wrote, all those years ago. At first, it threw me. I thought it was just a put-down. I thought you'd betrayed me. But I knew you would never do that to me. So I looked for the message *behind* the words. The hidden message.'

'There was no hidden message, John.'

'Oh, yes there was! Even if you weren't aware of it. Do you know what it said?'

I shook my head. 'Tell me.'

'*I am Osiris. Seth must die.*'

'You're crazy,' I told him. 'I sussed that so-called message out for myself, but you know what it was, John? A random printing error! You hear me? A simple, mechanical error. I had nothing to do with it.'

He ignored me. 'When I saw that, I realised that you knew about me. That you knew what I would one day become. I knew that we were brothers, Tom. And I knew that when your son was born, he'd have special powers. That he would be there to destroy me. So I began to prepare myself for the fight. It takes years to prepare. I had to wait till the kid was seven years old. The magic age. Then I began making sacrifices. Tonight we take the last step in the ritual. Tonight, I'm going to kill your son.'

'And what about me, John. You going to kill me too? You going to cut me up into fourteen pieces?'

John laughed gleefully. 'You see! You *are* Osiris. You do understand how it all works. But maybe I won't kill you, Tom. Maybe I'll just leave you to consider everything you've lost . . .'

'Listen to me, John. You're wrong about all this. Danny's nothing special, he's just a kid.'

'No Tom, not just a kid. *Your* kid. The son of Osiris. He is special. Have you seen his eyes, Tom? Course you have, you've looked into them lots of times.' John's hand moved and the knife traced a slow course across Daniel's chest and throat up to his face. The blade made a slow circle around one eye. 'This eye is the sun, Tom.' The blade moved an inch to the right. 'This eye is the moon. When I remove them, I remove all light from the world. Then it becomes my territory. That's how I shall forge the talisman. And you, Tom, you get to watch me do it. That's a real privilege. A front-row seat for the end of the world.'

I shuddered. I couldn't afford to delay any longer. I reached back for the gun and pointed it at John. 'Put the knife down, you sick fucker, or I'll blow you out of your socks,' I said.

John gazed at me a moment and then giggled. 'Not wearing any socks,' he observed. 'And *where* would you like me to put the knife, Tom. In his throat? In his eye?'

'It won't be any consolation to you if you're dead, now will it?' I said quietly.

'And what makes you think you can kill a god with a gun?' sneered John.

'You're not a god yet,' I reminded him.

'And you're not a marksman either. Have you ever fired a gun before, Tom? I doubt it very much. Why, I bet you don't even know if the safety catch is on or not.'

I tried not to let the dismay show in my face. 'I've used a gun lots of times,' I said. 'At this range I could spread your head all over the ceiling, no problem.'

'Then why don't you do it?'

I licked my dry lips. 'Just stand back from my son and I might let you live.'

John tilted back his head and laughed. 'Well, I'm hardly going to do that, now am I? Because you and I know, that you could just as easily hit him. So why don't you—'

The music surprised both of us. There must have been an automatic rewind on the machine. When the power chords introducing 'Talisman of Seth' blasted out, John half turned and the knife lifted a few inches clear of Daniel's face. I reacted instinctively, knowing it was the only chance I was going to get. I squeezed the trigger and the gun jolted in my hand, kicking high to the right. The bullet struck one of the ears of John's mask, breaking it off and flying on to punch a hole in the window behind him; but the impact threw him backwards, on to the floor, away from the packing case. I yelled triumphantly and dashed forward, placing myself between Daniel and John. I was aware of a rending splintering sound above us and I saw that great cracks were appearing in the glass, radiating out from the bullet hole. John was on his knees, clawing at the broken mask with one hand, but the other still held the knife. I moved in close, levelled the gun at John's chest and squeezed the trigger a second time. There was only a metallic click.

'Oops!' said John. He brought his right hand up suddenly, driving the knife deep into my stomach. I felt the impact first and then acid seemed to splash through my guts. I screamed and grabbed John by the throat with one hand, while I smashed at the remains of the mask with the barrel of the gun. The mask shattered, fragments burying themselves in the flesh beneath, revealing John's clean-shaven features. His face was white and sickly, his head also clean shaven, the teeth gritted, the dark eyes bulging grotesquely. I saw him for just an instant before he was masked once more, this time by trickles of his own blood. His other hand came up, clawing at my eyes, and then, suddenly, he was on his feet; the two of us were swaying and grappling in the centre of the room. The gun dropped from my fingers and went skittering away across the concrete floor. John's right hand tugged at the knife he'd already implanted within me and it began to slide free from its fleshy sheath, sending fresh pain rippling through me. Screaming, I brought one knee up hard into John's testicles. I felt the sting of the pin heads grazing my own flesh and John's bloody face contorted, the breath jolting out of him. But then he did pull the knife free. In my agony I saw that it was swinging up in an arc, it was poised to strike. Desperately, I released my hold and threw up my hands to grab the upraised wrist. I caught it in time but my already damaged arm was incapable of matching his strength. He began to force me back, the blade inching closer and closer to my face. John grinned triumphantly. His free hand closed around my throat and began to throttle the life out of me. I felt the remaining strength ebbing from my body and I dropped to my knees, my arms shuddering as they strove to hold back the blade.

It was like an explosion: the sound of the cracked glass disintegrating as it came raining in at us, driven by the wind. Simultaneously, the strength went out of John's arms and he lost his hold with a thin scream of surprise and a harsh exhalation of breath. He twisted away from me, dropping the knife as he tried to reach over his own shoulders to claw at his back. Through my own dizzy fog of pain, I could see the large shards of jagged glass sticking out of John's naked shoulders. He thrashed away from me, his bare feet crunching over the layers of glass that covered the floor. Then, out of control, he turned back, reeling and writhing in front of the destroyed window. I sensed an opportunity and marshalling my very last reserves, I launched myself head-first at John, striking him hard in the chest, knocking him backwards. But he held on to me as he fell and then the two of us were scrabbling at the very edge of the shattered window. I could feel the force of the wind claiming us, wanting to drag us both out into the night. My left shoulder thudded against an upright frame and I flung my good arm around it. At the same time, the wind caught John, lifted him clear of the ground for an instant. He was left with his bare legs dangling over the edge of the sheer drop, but his hands were clutched tight around my neck and would not relinquish their purchase. He hung there, half in, half out of his precious pyramid, his face inches away from mine. I could feel the metal window-frame beginning to buckle beneath our combined weight. He began to laugh hysterically.

'Well, old son!' he hissed, above the noise of the storm. 'We're in a bit of a fix, aren't we?'

I groaned. Life seemed to be ebbing out of the wound in my stomach like water going down a drain. And while John's arms were still locked like a vice around my neck, the arm I had flung around the metal upright was beginning to go numb.

John was trying to pull himself back in. He got one leg on to the edge of the frame and attempted to heave himself upwards. But the pull of the wind was too much for him. He shook his head, stopped struggling. His eyes glittered into my own. 'Together then,' he gasped. 'We'll fly together, shall we?'

'Go to hell,' I said; and he laughed again. I felt a giddiness ripple through me. The front of my shirt was sodden with blood. I tried to raise my damaged arm to punch at him, but it was trapped between my body and his. I could do nothing. The window frame made an ominous cracking sound beneath my left shoulder. The wind screamed.

'Say your prayers, brother!' said John calmly. His face seemed to swell like a great white moon, filling my vision with his smile of triumph. 'Time to go!'

I concentrated on that face for a moment, the face that had mocked me for so long. I focused every ounce of my hatred on it. 'I don't think so,' I said. And closing my eyes, I lunged forward with my head and bit into his nose. I felt, rather than heard, his scream as my teeth locked deep into his flesh. My mouth filled with warm blood and gristle. His hands opened convulsively and lost their precarious grip on life once and for all. I wrenched back hard, taking most of the nose with me. I opened my eyes and watched as John's naked body began to slide down the side of the pyramid, moving faster as it picked up speed. He seemed to be staring back at me in surprise, a large bloody rent in the centre of his face. And he was laughing, laughing in sheer disbelief. I spat the remains of his nose after him and his hysterical laughter came echoing up to me. Some thirty yards down, a gust of wind caught him and lifted him clear of the glass surface. I watched the white body twisting and turning on the air like a mannequin. Then the wind dropped and he fell straight down to the ground below. His body struck the concrete and shattered on impact into glistening red fragments that spilled steam out into the cold air.

I closed my eyes, took a deep breath. A new sound came whirling up from below, the sound of a police car siren. Blurry red lights advanced on the edge of my vision as vehicles pulled in through the open gates. The Seventh Cavalry arriving, as ever, too late. Aware of the wind tearing at my own body, I began to drag myself back to safety, crawling over layers of broken glass, unmindful of the sharp edges that cut into my flesh. I had been close for a while. Too close. A layer of shock must have cushioned the effects of my stab wound because I managed to reel back over to the packing case where I dropped to my knees and cradled my son in my arms.

'It's all right now, Danny,' I whispered. 'He's gone. Gone for good.'

An iron hand seemed to claw at my torn guts. I groaned, gathered Daniel tight against me and gave in to the weight that was pulling at the back of my eyes. We slept together, while the rock music pounded on, an unlikely lullaby.

Chapter Twenty-Seven

I stood in the drive and watched as the removal van pulled away, it was taking all my belongings to a new home. I waited till it was out of sight down the street, then turned back and began to walk towards the house. I had to rest for a moment, leaning my weight on the 'Sold' sign by the door. I still got cramps in the stomach, even months after the event.

Jamie appeared in the doorway, holding the last suitcase. 'I think that's everything,' she said. She looked at me, concern flickering in her eyes. 'Are you OK?'

I nodded. 'No problem. Why don't you put that in the car while I lock up?'

'All right.' She went to walk past me then paused. 'You know, we don't have to go straight away, not if you don't want to. There's over a week before the new people move in, you might like to . . .'

'What?' I asked her sharply. 'Relive old memories?'

She smiled sadly, shook her head. 'I'll wait in the car,' she said.

I reached out a hand, squeezed her arm gently. I was all too aware that things had been wrong between us since she came back. I wasn't sure what she needed right now, I only knew that I intended to try. If nothing else, I owed her that much. I had thought that John's death would guarantee my security but all I felt now was a vacuum, a numbness, an inability to come to terms with my own life. The past months in hospital were a blur to me. I had lain in the narrow bed, waiting patiently for a sense of rebirth that hadn't come. I still felt as though I was waiting. I watched as Jamie carried the case to the car, then I turned and walked back into the house.

The place seemed more alien than ever, empty and echoing with bad dreams. I went upstairs and walked into the bedroom that no longer belonged to me. It was strange, but I couldn't remember ever being happy in this room. I drew the curtains and left it in darkness. I went back down the stairs, having to pause halfway to catch my breath. It would take time to heal properly, they had told me. *And a lifetime to forget*, I told myself.

A movement at the door caught my attention. Karen and Danny come to say goodbye. I looked into my son's eyes and was grateful that he remembered nothing of the night of his abduction. He was blanking it out, the doctors said. Some day he would recall it and then he'd need to talk to me. I'd have to be ready for that, ready to supply the answers he needed. He was looking up at me now, trying to understand why his father was going away, but taking it in his stride because it was, after all, nothing new.

'When will we see you again, Dad?'

I reached out a hand and tousled his hair. 'Soon. Don't worry, Wales isn't so far away, I'll visit you as often as I used to.'

Danny and Karen exchanged knowing glances. *Not very often*, their eyes said.

'And you'll have to come out and visit me and Jamie. It's an old farmhouse. There's a stream and stables, we'll even have some chickens.'

'Chickens! Wow!' Daniel seemed impressed.

'It gets cold out there in the winter,' said Karen. ' Take plenty of warm clothes.'

I laughed. 'Still worried about me, then?'

She shrugged. 'I just want to make sure that you write that book.' She softened, smiled. 'I'm glad you finally decided to take my advice.'

I shrugged. I still didn't know if I could pull it off. 'Just set it down as it happened,' the publishers had told me. 'If there are some rough edges, we can always hire somebody to tidy it up for you.' The advance had been too good to ignore. Funny, I'd thought about fiction. Maybe I'd try that next.

'I heard something about a diary,' said Karen.

I nodded. 'Yeah, they found one at his flat. It's weird stuff. I managed to get photocopies of it and I'm trying to obtain permission to use extracts.'

She grimaced. 'You sure that's a good idea?'

'No. I'm not sure of anything any more. But the publishers want the real story, so . . .' I shrugged. 'If it doesn't work out, I'll just have to go back to radio.'

Karen grimaced. 'No, don't do that. Life's too short.' She frowned, seemed temporarily at a loss for something to say. 'Well, we'd best get going. I'm finally taking Danny to the zoo. We're going to see the monkeys, aren't we Danny?'

'Yeah, and the tigers,' said Danny, grinning.

I frowned. For some reason I couldn't exactly identify, I wasn't keen on him seeing the tigers.

'Don't get too close to the bars,' I warned him.

Karen laughed. 'Don't be silly. They do have railings.' She glanced at me, then at Danny, then at me again.

'Well, say goodbye to your dad,' she suggested.

'Bye Dad!' The arms, tight around me, making me wince. The blue eyes staring up into mine, trusting, vulnerable. Breath like milk and cornflakes. I thought about how close I'd come to losing him and some of the pain in me seemed to recede. I hugged back for a moment, then let Danny go. I watched as he ran over to the car to speak to Jamie. The three of them seemed to have grown a lot closer while I was in hospital. The two women had even exchanged the odd civil word and, of course, my parents had been there to act as mediators. I'd promised to visit them soon and this time it was a promise I intended to keep.

'See you, slugger.' Karen pecked me politely on the cheek, aware that Jamie was watching from the car. I returned the favour and she glanced self-consciously at her feet. 'Hey, don't miss out on your mail!' she exclaimed. Then she was bending, picking up an envelope from the carpet. She handed it to me. I gazed at it, puzzled. I didn't remember it being there a moment ago.

Karen and Daniel moved off up the path, waving. I waved back automatically, gazing at the letter. I turned it over. No stamp. No postmark. Delivered by hand. Just my name, printed in black letters with a bold felt-tip pen. I felt a weight settle on my shoulders, a chill inside me that was nothing to do with the weather. I reached a finger under the flap, tore the letter open. Inside, one sheet of paper. I unfolded it, read the contents.

Don't think it's over. John.

I stared at it blankly for a moment, my mind racing. Not possible, I assured myself. I had seen him die. I had seen him fragment. Nothing and nobody could have reassembled the pieces of torn flesh and viscera they had scraped off the concrete. Who then? Somebody with an unfortunate sense of humour? Somebody else with a grudge? Or maybe . . . maybe he *had* become a god. Maybe he was immortal.

I shook my head, dismissed it, not wanting to inquire too deeply. I crumpled the paper into a ball and shoved it deep into my trouser pocket. Later, I knew, I would unfold it carefully, would sit for hours reading and re-reading its brief message. And only then would I notice how familiar the writing was. How very like my own.

But for now there was the urgency of putting miles between myself and my former home. I pulled the door shut behind me and posted the keys back through the letter box. Then I walked slowly to the car and climbed into the driver's seat. Jamie looked at me inquiringly as I turned the ignition.

'Letter?' she asked.

I nodded.

'Bad news?'

I shook my head.

'Who was it from?'

'An old friend,' I said.

I put the car into gear, let out the clutch and drove away.